A White Picket Fence

Laura Branchflower

For Joanne

Prologue

"Lina!" Phil Hunter sat up in his bed, looking frantically around the darkened room, his seventeen-year-old body drenched in sweat. "Lina!"

He scrambled from the bed to his desk, his hands feeling around blindly in the dark for his car keys. He grabbed for the small chain to turn on the lamp but pulled too hard, and the light fell onto its side. He quickly righted it and turned it on with shaky fingers before his eyes searched wildly for his keys.

Yanking his jacket off the back of the desk chair, he dug his hands into the pockets, swirling them around in vain before throwing the jacket angrily to the floor. "Where are my keys?" he shouted to the empty room.

His bedroom door banged open. "Phil?" His father's face was etched with concern. "What—"

"Where are my keys? Did you take my keys?" Pushing past him, Phil stepped out into the hall.

"What's going on?" His older brother, Mike, his eyes puffy from sleep, came out of the bedroom across the hall.

"I need your keys." Phil shouldered his brother out of the way and stormed into his room.

"Is he okay?" His mother joined the others in the hallway.

"I think he's sleepwalking," his father said.

They watched in stunned silence as Phil reappeared, sprinting towards the stairs with Mike's keys gripped in his hand. "Phil! Stop!" his father shouted. "Stop!" He bounded after him down the stairs, catching him at the front door as Phil frantically undid the locks. "Stop!" He pushed his body against the door as Phil attempted to pull it open.

"Get out of my way!" Phil gripped his father's arm and roughly pushed him aside.

His father lost his balance, falling hard on his side. "Mike, stop him!" he yelled as he struggled to his feet.

Phil wrenched open the door, but was engulfed in his brother's powerful arms before he made it outside. "Calm down!" Mike, who outweighed Phil by thirty pounds, dragged him backwards.

"Let me go!" Phil elbowed him hard in the stomach, causing Mike to fall back against the stairs, and then he was lunging for the door and his escape.

He was halfway out when his father grabbed him by the collar of his shirt and he was again dragged backwards. Before he could fight his way free, Mike was lifting him by his legs and dropping him to the floor, then following, trapping Phil's flailing body beneath his own.

"Get the fuck off me! Get off! Lina needs me! I need to go to Lina!"

"Phil, wake up!" His father was kneeling beside his head, holding down his shoulders as Mike struggled to keep the rest of his body pinned. "Son, you're dreaming."

"I'm not fucking dreaming! Lina is in trouble." His face was bright red.

"It's one o'clock in the morning. Lina's home in bed."

"No—God! Let me go!" Phil fought to free himself, managing to roll onto his side, but he was no match for the combined weight of his brother and father and was quickly subdued, his face pushed hard against the floor.

"Honey, what's her phone number?" his mother asked, rushing up with a cordless phone. She quickly dialed the number Phil recited. "No answer," she said after several seconds. "Did you talk to her on the phone? Did she call you?"

"No, Mom, please." Phil was crying. "I need to go to Lina. Lina needs me. I know she needs me. Mom, please," he cried. "Please."

"Take him," his mother said. "Take him, Bruce."

— ~

"Faster!" Phil yelled less than a minute later. "There's something wrong." He stared out the window, unfocused, clenching and unclenching his hands as he endured the longest five minutes of his life.

As soon as their car turned up Lina's lane, Phil's eyes focused on a white van in her driveway, and his heart began to pound. He was out of the car and running towards her front door before his father had the car in park, Mike on his heels.

Mr. Hunter slammed the driver's door and was jogging towards the house when he heard Phil's heart-wrenching scream. "Lina!" And then, seconds later, his older son's, "Call 911!"

1

Lina Hunter heard the sound of the shower running when she entered her bedroom. It was Phil. She'd seen his car in the garage when she arrived home from the grocery store moments earlier. She crossed to the garment bag splayed out on their bed and began unpacking his clothes, hanging his suits in the wardrobe and tossing his dirty shirts and underwear into a hamper. She frowned when she saw a pink tie looped around a hanger with one of his suits. He didn't wear pink. She recalled the time early in their marriage when he refused to wear a salmon-colored shirt she bought him, claiming real men didn't wear pink and yet, as she studied a small stain marring the silk material, it was obvious he had worn it. Where had it come from? She knew it wasn't in his bag when he left for his business trip four days earlier because she had packed for him.

A buzzing sound caught her attention as she left the wardrobe. She crossed to Phil's cell phone, which was lying on his dresser beside his wallet.

Any chance you can get away for a few hours tomorrow? Monday's too far away.

Lina's hand shook slightly as she reread the text. It was from someone named Kim. She wracked her brains but couldn't recall him ever mentioning a Kim. She typed in his passcode to see if there were any other messages from the woman, but the phone vibrated and displayed a message indicating the code she attempted was incorrect. She carefully typed it again with the same results. He'd changed his passcode. There were only three passcodes they used: The anniversaries of the day and month they met, the day and month they bought their first house, and the day and month he was promoted to partner at his law firm. She attempted each without success.

She replaced the phone before lowering herself onto the edge of the mattress, staring unfocused out the window as she contemplated the significance of both the text and the fact that her husband had changed his passcode without telling her. She couldn't shake the unease in her stomach. The wording of the text seemed off for work, but what else could it be? He wouldn't be having an affair. He would never do that to her, not after twenty-five years, not after everything they'd been through together. But who was Kim, and why was she texting him?

The opening of the bathroom door had her shifting her gaze as Phil emerged naked, a towel hanging loosely around his neck, his dark hair tousled. Her eyes traveled over his chest and perfectly toned stomach. He looked as good—no, better—than he had on the day they met. The kids, in particular their oldest daughter, Megan, often complained that his triathlon training kept him out of the house too much, but there was no denying the benefit to his physique. At forty-one, he was in the best shape of his life.

"I thought you weren't going to be home until late." She was surprised how normal her voice sounded when her heart was jumping so hard she could hear the beat in her head.

"Things wrapped up earlier than I expected." He met her lips for a brief kiss before crossing to his bureau. "Where are the kids?"

"Where did this come from?"

He glanced back over his shoulder at the pink tie she was holding. "I spilled a drink on my tie yesterday and one of the paralegals ran out and got me that one."

"It's from Neiman Marcus," she said, fingering the label on the underside of the tie. "I don't recall a Neiman Marcus in New York City."

"I have no idea where she got it." He stepped into a pair of boxer briefs. "She could have taken it from another attorney. Why do you care?"

"It just isn't your normal style."

"That's probably because you didn't pick it out." He lifted his phone, his eyes scanning the display, and then he was darkening the screen and setting it back down. "What time is Logan's game tomorrow?"

"Ten." She watched him cross to his wardrobe, trying to recall the last time they had sex. Too long ago, she decided when she couldn't immediately recall. "We have dinner at Wayne and Diane's tomorrow night," she said when he reappeared in khaki shorts and a faded Georgetown Law School T-shirt.

"I wish you wouldn't do that," he said, frowning.

"What?"

"Make plans without consulting me."

"When have I ever consulted you before making plans with Wayne and Diane?" His annoyance surprised her.

"Exactly, but I'd like you to start. I was looking forward to a work-free weekend, but that's clearly not going to happen now."

"Phil?" She followed him back to his wardrobe, watching as he began to slip on a pair of running shoes. "What's going on?" Wayne was one of the senior partners at his law firm, but also his best friend.

"Nothing. It's been a long week and I wanted to stay in and relax, not socialize." He walked back out into the bedroom, his arm brushing hers as he passed by.

"I could cancel."

"No." He slipped his cell phone into his pocket before heading towards the door. "You've already made the plans."

She stared after him, a tingling of anxiety in the pit of her stomach.

Hours later, Lina glanced at the clock on her nightstand. It was after midnight, and Phil still hadn't come to bed. When she left him an hour and a half earlier watching television with Logan, she assumed he would follow, but that clearly wasn't the case. She was considering going back downstairs when the bedroom door opened.

"I expected you to be asleep," he said after closing the door.

"I was just reading." She closed her magazine and set it on the nightstand. Another five minutes passed before he emerged from the bathroom and then the mattress was shifting as he stretched out beside her. "I'm tired," he sighed as he lay back against his pillows.

Lina rolled onto her side to face him, stroking her hand over his bare chest. "Did you know it's been three weeks?"

He turned his head slightly, meeting her eyes. "No."

"I miss you." She leaned in and kissed the corner of his lips.

"Do you?" He pulled his head back so he could meet her eyes.

"Yes." She saw the doubt in his eyes. "I was waiting for you to come to bed."

"Yeah?" He trailed his fingers down her cheek.

"Yes." She covered the back of his hand with her own, holding it against her face. "I love you."

He met her lips for a deep kiss. "I love you too, baby," he said before kissing her again.

When Lina awoke the following morning, after her first full night's sleep in five days, Phil was still asleep beside her, sprawled out on his back with one arm over his head and the other resting on his stomach, the sheet barely covering the lower portion of his body. The distance she'd felt when he returned from his trip was gone. When he'd looked into her eyes while his body moved within hers and told her he loved her, she'd felt the invisible force pulsating between them, a force that had been missing lately, as if it had taken a hiatus, but it was back last night and, in the light of day, she could still feel it like a warm blanket.

As if sensing her attention, his eyes opened. He pushed his arms against the headboard for an intense stretch. "Good morning."

"I didn't mean to wake you." She was lying on her side, propped up on her elbow, facing him.

"It's okay. I want to get in a run before I leave for the game."

"You're not running with your group this weekend?" He'd joined a running group in Baltimore a few months earlier and usually ran with them on Saturday or Sunday.

"No."

"What's your plan for the day? Besides the game and Wayne and Diane's, I mean." Her thoughts were on the text from the previous evening.

"I told your mom I'd put in a new garbage disposal. Hers is leaking. I'll swing by with Logan after the game."

"There's nothing else you have to do?"

"Not that I know of. Why? Do you need me for something?"

"I was hoping you could fix the frame around Katie's door," she said, relieved he wasn't planning to see Kim. "She asked again the other day. You said you would."

"I said I would when I was sure it wouldn't happen again. Do you think it's safe to do that?"

"Yes, I really do." The Katie who slammed her door hard enough to break the wooden frame was thankfully a distant memory. "She watched television with us on Thursday night. Did I tell you that?"

"No."

"Dr. Drayton said—."

"No." He shook his head as he covered her lips with his fingertips. "I'll fix her door, but in return, I'd like to go a day without discussing Katie or Dr. Drayton."

Lina stared at the picture of Kim Ryan on her computer screen. Of the seventy-five associates at Phil's law firm there was only one named Kim. She'd almost convinced herself the text was innocent, but one look at the blonde who looked more like a model than an attorney ramped the apprehension she'd felt the evening before to new heights. She combed her fingers back through her hair, staring at the woman she was sure had authored the text to her husband. According to her bio, she'd graduated from law school five years prior, which meant if she'd gone straight from college to law school she was about thirty—ten years younger than Lina. She'd come to the firm six months earlier. Lina tried to recall her face at the holiday party without success. She closed her laptop and pushed it away from her as if trying to create distance between herself and the other woman.

This was crazy. She was finding Phil guilty of having an affair because he'd received a text from an attractive associate. Lina conjured up an image of him the night before, his body over hers as he looked into her eyes and told her he loved her. She was being crazy. He wasn't having an affair.

Wayne Hurte, eight years Phil's senior, was one of three founding partners at Hurte, Dunlop and Smith and a man Phil highly respected. Three inches shorter than Phil's six-foot-three height, he was noticeably fit and despite his receding hairline and fifty-one years, still gave off a youthful energy. He'd hired Phil out of law school, served as his mentor, and promoted him to full partner before his thirtieth birthday, making him the youngest associate to ever obtain the status. His wife, Diane, was one of Lina's closest friends, and the couples often socialized together.

"Love the dress," Diane said after greeting them in the foyer. "I can't believe you're old enough to have a daughter graduating from high school."

"Me either," Lina laughed. At five foot six, Lina and Diane were the same height, but there the similarities ended. Diane was blonde and blue-eyed with a curvy figure prone to put on weight if she wasn't careful, while Lina had dark, wavy hair and deep brown eyes, with a slight figure that looked even smaller next to her broad husband.

Over the course of the next thirty minutes, Lina noted that Phil and Wayne barely interacted, conversing with the other couples in attendance—two other partners and their wives—but not with each other, so when they disappeared into Wayne's study before dinner, Lina asked Diane what was going on.

"I didn't notice anything," Diane said. "Are you sure you're not imagining it?"

"I don't think so," Lina answered. They were alone in the kitchen and although she hadn't planned to, she blurted out the suspicions she had been harboring since the night before, telling Diane about the tie, the text and the sudden drop in their sex life.

Diane's eyes widened as she faced Lina, her hands on her hips. "You can't be serious."

Lina lowered her chin to her chest, sighing. "I'm being ridiculous, aren't I?"

"Yes." Diane gave an exaggerated nod. "You're being ridiculous. This is probably your reaction to Megan turning eighteen. It's your version of a midlife crisis."

"So Wayne hasn't mentioned anything about a Kim?"

"Lina!"

"Sorry." She held up her hands. "I just—I had a bad feeling when I saw the tie and then all these things kept coming to my mind."

"The man loves you. I promise you, he isn't cheating."

"You're right." Lina nodded. "I'm being silly."

When the last of the dinner dishes were cleared away, the group moved to the patio to enjoy the cool May evening, sitting around a fire pit as music flowed through outdoor speakers. Whatever chill Lina had thought she witnessed between Phil and Wayne earlier was no longer evident, and she decided Diane was probably right. She'd been imagining it.

"Did you see the pitcher the Orioles pulled up? He almost had a no-hitter last night," Wayne said.

"No." Diane waved her hand. "We are going to go one evening without the conversation digressing to sports."

"Seven innings isn't bad," Phil said. "If he—"

"Did you hear Diane?" Lina said, squeezing Phil's thigh. "No sports talk."

"Let us just finish this conversation," Wayne said.

"It will never end," Diane said.

"I just want to make this one point," Phil began. "If—"

"No," Lina interrupted, coming to her feet. "Dance with me." She held out her hand.

As Phil pressed his body to the length of hers, leading her around the patio, their bodies swaying to the beat of the music, Lina forgot where they were, so when the song ended and there was light applause and whistling from the other couples she was momentarily surprised. And when Phil dipped her backwards and kissed her until her knees were weak she was even more surprised. "We're in public," she said breathlessly when he finally lifted his head.

"I don't know how you do it," Gina Smith said to Lina after the men disappeared to the other side of the deck to enjoy cigars. "After all these years, you still act like you're in love."

"We are in love." Lina's gaze traveled to Phil, who was laughing at something one of the other men had said.

"We are too," Diane insisted. "But with you and Phil it's out there on display. You just have to look at the two of you to know."

"If Bob looked like Phil, I might still be in love too," Gina said, eliciting laughter from the other wives.

"I just wish he wasn't working so many long hours. And the travel—it feels like he's gone more than he's home lately." Lina looked around at the other women when no one seconded her complaint. "Is Phil the only partner traveling?" When they all nodded, Lina's eyes again traveled to Phil, her unease returning.

2

"I'll try to keep an open mind," Dr. Drayton was saying to Katie as they stepped out of his office and into the waiting area a few days later, "but if it's anything like the music my son listens to, I probably won't like it."

"It won't be," Katie promised. "And you'll get him—everyone doesn't. He's pretty deep. But I know you will."

"Well, I hope I don't disappoint you."

Lina observed their light exchange, feeling the same mixture of awe and envy she always felt when she witnessed the easy rapport Katie shared with her psychiatrist. She wished she and Phil could experience this happier version of their daughter instead of the hostile, argumentative one they dealt with most of the time.

Lina's eyes shifted to the man responsible for breaking through to Katie. *Baltimore* magazine referred to him as a leading authority on the adolescent mind and one of the premier child psychiatrists in the country. When Lina had initially called his office eight months earlier she'd been told he wasn't taking new patients and was offered the name of one of his colleagues. Over the next eight weeks, Lina watched helplessly as the other psychiatrist failed to reach Katie and she slipped further into what he was diagnosing as adolescent depression.

Lina again called Dr. Drayton's office, this time pleading for an appointment but was again told he wasn't taking new patients. At that point, Lina did what any desperate mother would do. She drove to Dr. Drayton's main office at Johns Hopkins Hospital and told the receptionist she wasn't leaving until she spoke to him. It took three hours. He came out into the waiting area after his last morning appointment.

"Mrs. Hunter, I'm Nicholas Drayton," he'd announced. "What can I do for you?"

She'd been momentarily surprised by both his sudden arrival and his appearance. She'd expected him to be older, but he looked close to her own age and, with a head of unruly sandy-colored hair falling to his collar, a golden tan, and green eyes that seemed to radiate warmth, he looked more like one of her mother's hippie friends than a doctor.

"I read that you've never met a patient you couldn't reach. I need you to reach my Katie," she'd told him.

He'd considered her for a long moment and then he was glancing down at his watch. "If you don't mind sharing me with a chicken panini, I'm all yours for the next hour."

She wasn't sure whether it was his quiet confidence that day, or his focused attention, but as she left his office with an appointment scheduled two days later, she knew if anyone could get through to Katie, it was him.

"Mrs. Hunter?"

Lina brought her mind back to the present, realizing Katie had taken the seat beside hers and Dr. Drayton was speaking to her. "Sorry." She smiled. "I was a million miles away."

"Shall we?" He held his hand towards his office.

"I really wish you would call me Lina. Is there some type of ethical rule against you using first names?"

"Something like that." He watched her walk across his office and then slowly followed, lowering himself into a chair opposite her spot on the couch.

"I won't tell anyone," she teased. "Your reputation will remain above reproach."

"I'll take it under advisement." A smile played at the corners of his lips. "I was pleased with our session today. I'm lowering her Prozac again."

"So soon?"

"The goal is to have her medication free by the end of the summer."

"I know. It's just—what if she reverts back or—"

"She won't." He leaned forward and held out a slip of paper. "That's the new dosage."

Lina took the paper, glancing down at his barely legible handwriting. "You write like a doctor." She laughed. "I mean, I know you're a doctor. It's just strange the way your handwriting fits the stereotype when the rest of you doesn't."

He leaned back in his chair, crossing one leg casually over the other. "No? I don't fit your vision of a doctor?"

"Not exactly," she answered, looking up from the paper. "You don't look conservative enough."

"That's probably because I'm not conservative, but I can assure you we come in all types."

"I'm sorry," she said, embarrassed she'd shared her thoughts aloud. "I shouldn't generalize."

"You can generalize all you like. No offense taken." He smiled then, and she thought, not for the first time, how handsome he was. "Tell me about Katie's week. Is she continuing to interact more with you and your husband?"

"If arguing is interacting, then yes." She sighed. "She's definitely interacting more."

He laughed. "That's actually positive. Katie is in the process of deciding who she wants to be. Part of that process will be rejecting beliefs she determines have been imposed by her parents. Expect more of that in the coming weeks. I think you could benefit from a book one of my colleagues just wrote." He paused as he scribbled down the name of a book on his prescription pad. "Hopefully you can decipher my handwriting." He winked at her as he held out another slip of paper. "This book offers methods for handling argumentative teenagers. It's important to have a dialogue with her, to listen to her demands and if you don't agree, logically explain why. No 'because I said so' or 'this is the way it's done in this house.' She's intelligent. Treat her that way."

"Great." She hated the idea of more conflict.

"Be patient. We're in the home stretch. I don't think I need to remind you of where we were six months ago."

"No." She shook her head, not wanting to rehash even for a moment the dark period in Katie's life. "Definitely no."

"Okay, I just want you to see how well she's doing. She's ready to start socializing with her peers again outside of school, and I'd like you to encourage it."

"She said that?" Her eyes swung to his. "She wants to go out?" It had been ten months since Katie had gone out socially with friends.

"Yes."

"That's great, isn't it?"

"It is. We'll take it slow at first. No sleepovers away from home. And hold her to her curfew. Pay close attention to the friends she's spending time with. But it's time for her to get back out there."

"Okay." Lina dropped her eyes to her hands, her thoughts turning to Phil and his reaction to Katie leaving the house.

"Is there a problem?"

"I was just thinking about my husband. I'm not sure he's going to agree. I think if it were up to him, he'd keep her from going out until she was eighteen," she said, only half joking.

"Would it help if I spoke to him?"

"No, I'll talk to him." They'd been closer since Friday night, and she hated the thought of fighting with him about Katie.

"Are you sure? You don't look very convincing."

"I'm sorry. It's just been a tough week."

"Is there something I should know?" The gentle timbre of his voice rolled over her.

"My husband cheated on me," she burst out before quickly covering her mouth. "I'm so sorry. I don't know what compelled me to share that with you."

His eyes widened, and there was no mistaking his surprise.

"I'm sorry," she said again, coming to her feet. "I'm just going to leave and we can pretend I never said that."

"Please sit down." His eyes were full of concern. "Lina?"

She drew in a deep breath in an attempt to settle her nerves and slowly sat back down. "You used my first name." She tried unsuccessfully to smile.

"Tell me what makes you think your husband was unfaithful to you."

She looked into his eyes—eyes she'd looked into so many times over the past months—and began to talk, telling him of the long hours, the travel Phil was suddenly taking for work, the tie, the text message, the cell phone she could no longer access and Diane's opinion. "All of the stress with Katie—it pushed us apart. I neglected our relationship."

"So if he indeed cheated, it was your fault?"

"In part I think, but everything has been better since Friday. I shouldn't have even mentioned it."

"And yet you did."

"I feel comfortable with you," she admitted. "It just came out."

"What changed on Friday?"

"I made a conscious effort to put him first. And I've started instigating, you know..." She trailed off.

"Sex."

"Yes." She blushed. "Phil has a high sex drive, and if I had been paying a little attention, I would have noticed the sudden drop in our sex life."

Dr. Drayton shifted in his chair. "Communication is the key to a healthy relationship. If you're truly concerned there is someone else, talk to him."

"I'm not. I mean I think there may have been, but there couldn't be now. He's been too..." she paused, searching for the right words, "attentive to me all week."

Dr. Drayton gripped the arms of his chair. "Anything else you'd like to discuss?"

Lina sensed he was ready for their session to be over. "No, I think I've shared enough for one week."

Moments later, he was following her out into the waiting area. "Five minutes, Scottie," he said to a boy of about thirteen who was waiting with his mother and then, after a quick goodbye to Lina and Katie, he was stepping back into his office.

He closed the door, leaning his forehead against it. "Fuck."

3

"He's amazing," Lina told her sister, Adele, as they stood in the living room of a house about to go on the market a couple of days later. "He brought her back to life. I just feel so grateful to him, I could kiss him."

"Really?" Adele's eyes opened wider. "Is he good-looking?"

Lina laughed. "Actually, he is good-looking. Here, take the other end," she said, pausing as she gripped the end of a couch. "We're going to slide this beside the window and then move the two chairs here." Moments later, Lina stood back, inspecting the change to the room. "Perfect."

"Oh my God, it opened up the whole room. You're like a decorating savant. Are you sure you don't want to make money doing this?" What had started as a favor to Adele, looking at a few homes she was preparing for resale and suggesting ways to best showcase them, had resulted in an almost-weekly job offer from the owner of the real estate firm where Adele worked.

"Maybe after Logan starts high school in the fall. Help me move this," Lina said, taking the end of a coffee table.

"So back to this good-looking doctor," Adele said several minutes later as they walked towards their cars. "Is he single?"

"No more Dan? I liked Dan." Unlike most of Adele's recent boyfriends, Dan had lasted long enough to warrant an introduction to the family.

"Dan was too blah, too predictable. Seven months was three too many with him." Adele went through men like shoes, constantly finding a new favorite. At forty-two, she was twice divorced but still determined to find Mr. Right, a feat Lina saw as nearly impossible considering Adele seemed to lose interest after the infatuation stage of a relationship. "Why are you avoiding my question? Is the doctor single?"

"I think he's married, and even if he wasn't I would never let you near him. He's done too much for me to pay him back with a broken heart."

"You could be standing in the way of true love. Speaking of which—is Phil still working an insane amount?"

"Not so much," Lina said, avoiding her eyes. "The trial in New York ended, and he's been working less."

"That's a relief. Do you still have to take sleeping pills when he isn't with you?"

"Yep."

—◦ ◦—

"You beat me home," Lina said after finding Phil in the kitchen. "Why are you so early? It's barely five."

"Are you complaining?" He returned her kiss.

"No, definitely not." She kissed him again, running her hands up the lapels of his suit jacket as she leaned into him.

The sound of the door opening preceded the entrance of eighteen-year-old Megan, and Lina reluctantly dropped her hands as Phil turned away to greet their oldest child.

"There's the graduate." He smiled as he gave her a hug.

"Guess what?" Megan's gaze swung between her parents. "The class elected me to give the keynote speech at graduation!"

"That's fantastic!" Phil pulled her back into his arms, kissing her on the side of her head. "I couldn't be more proud of you."

"Congratulations." Lina forced a smile, trying to muster enthusiasm for Megan, who seemed to have a new accolade to share daily. "That's great."

"Will you help me write it?" Megan asked Phil.

"You don't need my help, but I'll read it over after you have a draft."

"You're the best." She gave him another hug. "I just ran into Kelly Donnelly and Mike Stevens," Megan said. "He's the one who asked me to prom but I turned down," she added when she saw the confusion on Phil's face. "Anyway, he's taking Kelly, but everyone knows I was his first choice, so it was really awkward." She scrunched up her face. "I felt sorry for her. I could feel him staring at me. We were at the deli near school, so everyone was there."

"Watch the ego, Megan," Lina said.

"What? I'm just telling you what happened."

The door leading in from the deck opened, and Logan, at fourteen the youngest of the Hunter children, stepped into the kitchen. "Hey, Dad!"

"Logan, you're wet," Lina said after seeing the trail of water between the door and the refrigerator. "How many times do I have to tell you to dry off before you leave the pool area?"

"Sorry. I'm thirsty." He lifted up a water bottle, and gave her a grin that rarely failed to dissipate her anger. Standing a smidgen over six feet and still growing, he was her gentle giant with dark, wavy hair that he was constantly pushing out of his eyes and a smile that seemed to always light up his face.

"You want to play catch?" He was looking at his father as he tossed the water bottle from one hand to the other.

"After dinner," Phil said.

"Megan," Lina said, eyeing a bag of chips she'd pulled from the pantry, "we are going to eat soon."

"I'm not." Megan slipped onto one of the high-backed leather chairs at the kitchen island. "I just came home to change. I'm presenting at the middle school awards ceremony. I'll get something on the road."

"Do you ever stop?" Lina asked. "Everyone needs downtime." Between school, her active social life and volunteer work, Megan was always moving.

Phil stopped beside Logan. "When are you going to get a haircut?" He pushed the hair back from his son's eyes. "How can you even see?"

"I can see." Logan pushed his hair back down onto his forehead. "And it's cool."

"It won't be cool when you run into a wall. How much did you practice on your own this week?"

"I had three tests and—"

"I'll take that as none."

"He's been busy, Phil." Lina couldn't keep from defending him when she saw the downtrodden expression on Logan's face. "School comes before lacrosse."

"I bet you found time to swim and play video games."

"Phil—"

"He asked me how to make varsity as a freshman," he interrupted, his gaze remaining on Logan. "Were those just words?"

"No. I want to make it."

"Wanting isn't enough. It's the actions you take." He patted Logan's arm as he stepped around him. "Clean up the water you tracked in and then see if your mom needs any help. I'm going to change."

"I barely swam," Logan insisted to Lina as soon as his father was out of earshot.

"I know." Lina ran her hand down his back and kissed his cheek. "You have all summer to practice."

Phil was halfway up the staircase when Katie, wearing frayed jean shorts and a black T-shirt with the words "religion kills" emblazoned on it, appeared at the top of the stairs. At five foot two and barely one hundred pounds, she was missing the tall, athletic gene Phil had passed on to both Megan and Logan. She hesitated, as if debating whether she could escape without being seen, and then she lowered her head, causing her dark, shoulder-length hair to fall forward and began to descend the stairs.

When she attempted to step around Phil, he moved with her, his body blocking her passage. "How about a hello?"

"Hello." She avoided his eyes as she attempted unsuccessfully to pass him.

"How was your day?"

"Good. Will you move?"

He tilted his head slightly. "I'm trying to have a conversation with you, Katie."

She looked up then, her expression blank as she stared into blue eyes the exact same shade as her own. "Why?"

"Because I'm your father and I care." His gaze widened when it dropped to her T-shirt. "Where did that come from?"

"New to You."

"New to You," he repeated. "Is that a used clothing store? Mom took you to a used clothing store?"

"Grandma."

"Of course. Well, the shirt's offensive. Take it off."

She frowned up at him. "Have you heard of the First Amendment?"

"My laws supersede the Constitution in this house, and that shirt is blasphemous. I don't want to see it again."

"Dr. Drayton said I should be able to express myself."

"I. Don't. Care. This is not Dr. Drayton's house. Get rid of the shirt."

She glared at him before turning and stomping back up the stairs.

"Katie," he called after her, "if you slam the door, I'll remove it permanently."

— ~

Lina tried to show no visible reaction to Katie's announcement that she was going out. Katie was still wearing the jean shorts from earlier but had changed from her T-shirt to a tank top and highlighted her delicate features with a touch of makeup. If it weren't for the dour expression on her face, Lina knew she'd look cute. "Where are you going and when will you be back?"

"Dr. Drayton said you aren't supposed to nag me."

"I don't recall him ever using that word, but in any case, this isn't nagging. This is parenting. You can't go out without telling me where you're going and when you'll be back."

"I'm going to Emma's to see her brother Ryan's band play. I'll be home by midnight."

"Emma?" Lina repeated. Emma was a friend of several years who disappeared from their lives during Katie's brief experimentation with drugs.

A soft knock on the mudroom door preceded the appearance of the most welcome visitor Lina could remember. "Hi, Ms. Lina."

"Emma." Lina hugged her tightly. "It's so good to see you." Looking at Emma reminded her of the old Katie, the Katie who laughed and sang and made silly faces at Logan, who always wanted to join Lina on trips to the grocery store so she could pick out her favorite desserts, and who spent hours following Lina around the back yard telling her funny stories while Lina tended to her garden. "You look wonderful." With red hair, freckles and a shy smile, Emma looked like she belonged on a poster for Ireland tourism. "Did your mom drive you, or—"

"I drove. I have my license."

"Right." Lina nodded. "You're all grown up. How are—"

"Mom," Katie interrupted. "We're already late."

Phil tossed the lacrosse ball to Logan before jogging up towards the driveway "What's going on?" His eyes were on Katie, who was walking towards Emma's car.

"Phil, it's fine." Lina was beside him. "She's already cleared it with me. She's just going to Emma's."

"I want to talk to her."

Lina laid a hand on his chest. "I already handled it. Just let her go."

"Lina—"

"Please. Just trust me."

He watched in silence, the side of his jaw clenching and unclenching, as Emma's car slowly disappeared down the driveway.

"Thank—"

"That decision," he bit out, his eyes intense, "was counter to every instinct I have as a father." He crossed to the edge of the driveway, staring unfocused into the woods flanking one side of their yard as he continued to talk. "It's the first time, Lina—the first time she's going out in close to a year, and you don't discuss it with me?"

"I didn't know until Emma showed up."

"You didn't know?" His eyes swung to her. "She," he began, pointing in the direction of the departing car, "shouldn't be making plans without consulting us first."

"She isn't grounded. It was her choice not to go out before now." Lina fought to keep her emotions in check, not wanting their conversation to escalate into an argument as it so often did when they were discussing Katie.

"This is insanity. It's just going to start all over again."

"No, it's not. Why are you being so negative? She's better. Why can't you see that? We have to trust her."

He exploded. "Trust her! We don't even know her. She doesn't talk!"

"That's not true. She talked during dinner."

"What's going on with Katie?" Logan asked as he approached.

"Nothing you need to worry about," Phil said. "Go inside and get out that math problem you need help with. I'll be in in a minute." He waited until Logan was out of earshot before continuing. "If something happens to her tonight—"

"It won't. Dr. Drayton—"

"No! No more Dr. Drayton! Can we go one fucking evening without his name coming out of your mouth?"

— ~

"What's up with your dad? He looked angry," Emma said as soon as she turned onto the main road.

"He's completely out of touch," Katie answered. "That's what's up with him."

"Did he really ground you for six months?"

"It was more like forever."

"What did you do? I mean, you don't have to tell me if you don't want to."

And just like that, the make-it-or-break-it moment in their fragile relationship arrived. Katie knew this instant would come, she just didn't expect to reach it in the first two minutes of the evening.

There was a litany of offenses she could share, including the time she was caught sneaking back into the house after a night of drinking, the time she poured half of her father's favorite scotch into a thermos and replaced it with water and a touch of orange food coloring, which, in her defense, he could never prove definitively she did, or the time her father saw her with a marijuana joint hanging from her lips, courtesy of a narc named Megan who texted him and told him Katie had skipped school and gone to a friend's to celebrate National Weed Day. But she wasn't going to share any of that with Emma, not yet.

She would confess to her most serious transgression, the reason she became a prisoner in her own house, and Emma's reaction would tell Katie if there was any possibility for the friendship to go forward. As much as she didn't plan to do drugs again, Katie wasn't hanging out with a nerd.

"I did shrooms in my bedroom."

"Oh my God, Katie. You didn't! You must have unconsciously wanted to be caught."

Emma sounded like Dr. Drayton and although Katie suspected he didn't believe her when she assured him it wasn't a play for attention, he was wrong. Doing shrooms at home was a mistake, a momentary lapse in judgment which, because of her uptight, irrational father, cost Katie sophomore year. But she did it with good intentions.

She'd just finished writing a comparative analysis on the seventeenth-century English philosophers Hobbes and Locke and was lying on her bed contemplating truth when she recalled a quote from a William Blake poem she'd read in English class days earlier. *If the doors of perception were cleansed everything would appear to man as it is, infinite.*

The shrooms she'd been handed at a party weeks before seemed like a logical way to cleanse her perceptions. There wouldn't even be Apple computers or iPhones if Steve Jobs hadn't tripped on LSD, she'd reasoned. "I was planning to stay in my room," she told Emma. "I was going to lie on my bed and experience whatever happened, but then everything looked like it was on fire, so I had to escape—I mean, you have no other choice when you think your bedroom is on fire. I don't remember a lot after that except thinking my dad was the devil. It was so real. He had horns and a tail and red skin and—" She looked at Emma. "Are you laughing?"

"I'm sorry," Emma said but continued to laugh. "I'm sorry. I know it's not funny. I know I shouldn't be laughing."

"No, it's funny." Katie laughed too. "I mean the last year wasn't, but remembering what my dad looked like is." She continued to smile as she looked out the window.

The band was good, really good, but that wasn't what kept Katie rooted to her spot on the blanket about twenty yards from the makeshift stage in Emma's backyard. No, the lead guitarist, the boy with the serious eyes and full-sleeve tattoo was why she hadn't moved in the past hour.

He was nothing like the preppy boys Katie was used to seeing at parties in the ritzy section of Howard County where large houses and country club memberships were the norm. He looked like someone more likely to step off a motorcycle than out of a BMW, and his dark spiked-up hair, jeans and tight black T-shirt stood out in the sea of collared polos and pastel shorts.

Emma's brother, Ryan, wasn't preppy either, nor any of the other band members, with their dark clothes and longish hair, but they looked like boys trying to *look* like rockers as opposed to their guitarist, who looked like the real thing.

Katie's stomach did a little jump when their eyes met. Until tonight she'd never experienced what it felt like to be drawn to a boy. She'd had boyfriends but none that gave her butterflies.

"That's Matt." Emma yelled to be heard over the band. "He moved here from New York last summer. He's kind of quiet, but he's cool. You want to walk around and see who's here?"

Katie didn't, but she reluctantly came to her feet, not prepared to share that all she wanted to do was stare at Matt, so moments later she was following Emma into the crowd of kids who had gathered to hear the band.

The band played until about 11:00 p.m. As soon as they left the stage, Katie watched a blonde in a short skirt and tight tank top approach Matt. Katie was hoping she was a groupie, but when he started kissing her it was obvious that wasn't the case, and she turned her back to them, unable to stomach her new crush making out with another girl.

"Katie Hunter!" Katie heard Ryan's voice before a pair of sweaty arms wrapped around her from behind. "I haven't seen you in forever."

"The band's awesome." Katie turned and returned his hug. She'd always liked Emma's older brother, who looked more like a boy scout than a band member with his red hair and freckles, but there was no denying his talent as a drummer.

"Water?" He lifted his eyebrows after peering into her cup. "Are we out of beer?" It had been a recurring inquiry all evening, other kids questioning why Katie wasn't drinking, as if her lack of alcohol was somehow impinging on their ability to have a good time.

"I can't afford to get in trouble," she admitted. And she couldn't. Tonight reminded her of what it felt like to be free, and she wasn't about to do something to lose it.

"Could you spend the night?" Emma asked, joining them. Her eyes had the glassy look that came from consuming too much alcohol.

"My parents aren't going to let me," Katie said. "Don't worry, I'll find a ride." She began to look around, hoping to see someone who lived close to her.

"Matt can take you," Ryan said. "Hey, bro," he called to someone behind Katie. "Are you headed out?"

"Yeah."

Katie's heart jumped at the sound of the unfamiliar voice because even before she turned around she knew exactly which Matt he was talking to. He was still with the blonde, his arm draped around her shoulders, and he was looking right at Katie. Katie felt her mouth go dry as she looked into his dark eyes, eyes that looked way too serious for a boy.

"Do you mind giving her a ride? You pass right by her neighborhood."

Katie was about to say he didn't have to take her, that she'd find another ride, but when he took her cup, the words dried up in her throat. He smelled it—she assumed to make sure it wasn't alcohol—and then brought it to his mouth and took several long swallows.

"I'll take her." He wiped the back of his hand across his mouth as he handed her back her now almost-empty cup. "You ready?"

He led her to an older-model black Mustang that fit the image she had of him almost as well as the motorcycle she'd pictured him on earlier, and opened the passenger door. "You can wait here," he said.

She sunk down in the worn leather seat, watching as he led the blonde to a car several yards away. When he pushed her up against the car and began kissing her, Katie dropped her eyes to her hands, not looking up until his door was opening. He smelled like sweat, like someone who'd just finished exercising, but not in a bad way like he hadn't used deodorant. More in a pure male way that had her stomach tingling in response to him.

He turned the key in the ignition, bringing the engine to life. "What's your name?"

"Katie."

"Matt."

The fifteen-minute drive was mostly in silence, but it was a comfortable silence intermixed with enough conversation for him to learn Katie's last name, that she liked music and went to private school, and for her to learn his last name was Hudson, he was eighteen, about to graduate from high school and lived with his grandmother.

"So you moved here right before your senior year? Why would you do that? You can just pull over here," she said as they approached her house. "Don't go in the driveway unless you want to meet my dad." She had no doubt her father would be out of the house the moment he saw the unfamiliar car.

Matt pulled his car to the side of the road past her mailbox, staring at her sprawling house in the distance. "You're rich." It sounded like an accusation.

"It's not my fucking fault."

He looked at her then, and her heart leapt when she saw a flash of respect in his eyes. "You're right, Hunter."

"You didn't answer my question." Her shyness was overshadowed by her curiosity about him. "Why did you move here before you finished high school?"

"My mom died," he answered.

4

"How was she?" Lina asked when Phil returned to the bedroom after leaving briefly to check on Katie, who had just arrived home.

"Fine." He shrugged out of his T-shirt as he crossed to the bed and then he was stretching out on the mattress beside her. He'd been angry after their earlier interchange, but over the course of the evening as they watched a funny movie, Lina nestled on the couch between him and Logan, Phil slowly relaxed, laughing aloud several times, and, by time the credits rolled up the screen, his arm had made its way around Lina's shoulders, and she was snuggled into his side.

"Did she say anything?"

"Only that her curfew should be twelve thirty instead of twelve."

"What did you—" The sound of his cell phone vibrating had her pausing midsentence as she watched him get up and move to his bureau. "Who is it?"

"No one." He silenced the phone and then turned it off altogether before returning to bed.

"It had to be someone."

"It was a wrong number."

"How could you possibly know that when you didn't answer it?"

"I didn't recognize the number." As he turned off his bedside lamp, the home phone on the nightstand began to ring. Phil answered it before it rang a second time. "Yes, hello? You have the wrong number, don't call it again." He replaced the receiver.

Lina stared at his profile, a sick feeling gripping her stomach. "Was it the same person who called your cell phone?"

"It was a wrong number."

"So in less than a minute, your cell phone and our home phone received calls by mistake? Why don't you look at the caller ID and see if it was the same number?"

"Because I don't care. It was a wrong number."

"Doesn't that seem a little odd to you?"

"I don't know. I suppose, but why does it matter?" He was lying back against his pillow, his head turned in her direction.

"It's just strange."

"It was just a wrong number, Lina. It's late. Let's go to sleep."

When Lina entered the kitchen the following morning, Megan was at the table eating yogurt and looking down at her cell phone. "I took the last yogurt. Would you make sure you get more?"

"Would you make pancakes?" Logan asked as he came in from the family room, his dark hair tousled and his eyes puffy from sleep.

"Sure." Lina combed her fingers back through his hair as she kissed his cheek. "Don't forget the paper. Your dad's on his way down." It was Logan's responsibility to bring in the paper that was left at the end of the driveway.

"Good morning." Phil, dressed in his running clothes, entered the kitchen and joined Megan at the table.

Lina set a container of creamer and sugar on the table before him. "Coffee will be ready in a minute and Logan's getting the paper. What would you like for breakfast? Pancakes? Egg-white omelet?" She rubbed his shoulder.

"I'll have an omelet."

"Are you going to Baltimore to run?" Megan asked.

"No."

"If I had known I wouldn't have made plans with Amanda. I'd rather run with you."

"We can go after church tomorrow," Phil said.

"Do you want more to eat?" Lina asked Megan.

"No, I'm going shopping with Amanda. I have to buy a dress for the after-prom party. I have to leave in a minute."

"A dress for the after-prom party? You just spent a ridiculous amount on a prom dress. I'm sure you have a dress in your closet you could wear," Lina said.

"No! Everyone gets a new dress. This is my senior prom."

"You don't need a new dress."

"Dad?" Megan turned to Phil. "Talk to her. She's being ridiculous. I only have one senior prom!"

"Lina, it is her senior prom."

"We bought her a dress for her senior prom. If it's so important for her to have a dress for the after party, she can spend her own money."

"That's not fair. This is like a school event. I shouldn't have to spend my own money."

Phil pressed his index finger over his lips, raising his eyebrows at Megan before coming to his feet. Seconds later he led Lina into the dining room. "What's the big deal?"

"She probably has twenty dresses."

"So she'll have twenty-one."

"You're spoiling her."

"She deserves it. Her scholarship alone is going to save us eighty thousand over the course of her four years in college."

"Fine," she sighed.

"Don't say that unless you mean it."

"It's fine." She patted his chest before going back into the kitchen. This was an argument she knew she wouldn't win. Even if Megan had to use her own money, Phil would figure out a way to reimburse her. Last time Lina insisted Megan purchase her own concert tickets, Phil had paid her a hundred dollars to wash his car.

Katie arrived a few minutes later with earbuds in place and, after pouring herself a bowl of cereal, dropped down at the table across from Phil and beside Logan, who had returned with the paper.

"Take out the earbuds and join the conversation," Phil said to Katie. When she didn't respond he reached out, tapping the table in front of her and then motioning for her to remove her earbuds.

"What?" She scowled as she pulled them from her ears.

"Be part of the family. No music at the table."

"I read that listening to music just thirty minutes a day through earbuds could reduce your hearing by twenty percent by the time you're forty," Megan said. "You shouldn't be using them at all."

Katie's gaze shifted to Megan. "Did you know that some people consider unsolicited advice an act of hostility?"

"Fine." Megan shrugged as she pushed back her chair. "Go deaf."

"I want to get my license," Katie announced moments after Megan left. "And I don't want to drive any of the ostentatious cars in the driveway."

"Ostentatious, huh?" Phil raised his eyebrows, and Lina could tell he was fighting hard not to smile. "What do you suggest?"

"A used car. Something older that didn't cost a lot when it was new."

"And who is going to pay for this *used* car?" When she didn't reply immediately, he continued. "You expect me to spend money on a used car because you don't want to drive any of the cars we currently own? That sounds profligate."

"I don't know that word," she said.

"Wasteful, decadent, reckless," he said. "You have a thirty-minute commute to school. You're going to drive a safe, reliable car. A car I choose, unless you have some money I don't know about."

"That's not fair," Katie complained. "You're punishing me for not being pretentious like the rest of you. I shouldn't be punished for being different."

This time he did laugh out loud. "I assure you I can afford everything I own, so there's nothing pretentious about me. Now if you feel strongly about this and feel unauthentic driving one of the cars your mother and I so generously provide, you can take the school bus. How does that sound? Nothing pretentious about that."

"Except for the name of my twenty-five-thousand-dollar-a-year school displayed on the side of the bus."

Lina went about the task of preparing breakfast, keenly aware that Phil and Katie were having an actual conversation. Katie continued to throw out insults about what she perceived as his materialism, and he defended himself as masterfully as any lawyer, mostly by turning her words back on her, but Lina knew he was trying to connect with her, and for some reason, maybe because Megan wasn't around monopolizing the conversation or because Katie was in a good mood from her night out, she appeared to be cooperating.

Logan eventually switched the conversation to gossip about one of the neighbor kids, but Katie continued to participate, and as Lina stirred pancake batter and cut up vegetables for the omelet, she believed for the first time in a very long time that Katie was going to be okay.

"You're not going to hurt it," Alice Rayburn said as she approached Lina, who was carefully pruning an azalea bush. "Your technique is fine. You can go twice as fast."

"Is it already noon?" Lina turned from the bush, wiping her hands on her shorts as she faced her mother.

"No. I'm a few minutes early."

"Where are you taking her?" For the past several months her mother had been taking Katie out for lunch on Saturdays. Even during Katie's darkest period, when she went days without speaking to Lina and Phil, she never shut out her grandmother.

"I don't know. It's her turn to choose." Tall and thin, with long, dark hair sprinkled with strands of gray, piercing hazel eyes her daughters and grandchildren often believed could see right into their souls and a tan complexion earned from hours in the sun tending to her vegetable garden, Alice looked like a throwback from the sixties. "She wants to spend the night."

"You know that can't happen," Lina said.

"Why can't it happen? It's been over twenty years, for heaven's sake."

"Don't." Lina shook her head. "Just drop it, please. Phil's coming over to your place after Logan's game to fix your faucet, so he can bring her home."

To Lina's surprise, Alice didn't belabor the point, instead launching into a discourse on the astrological compatibility of Adele and her ex-boyfriend. "They had three trines and two sextiles. If she really wanted a relationship it could have worked. She may regret letting him go."

Lina began pruning again, only half listening as her mother used her forty-five years of astrological experience to theorize on Adele's inability to stay committed to a man, pointing out specific aspects in her chart that would have to be overcome if she were interested in having a long-term relationship.

"Wait—could you repeat that?" Lina asked several minutes later when she realized Alice was no longer talking about Adele.

"I said your chart shows a heightened risk of infidelity for the next year, so you need to keep your guard up."

"Heightened risk of infidelity for who?" The phone calls from the previous night flashed through her mind. "Were you looking at me or Phil?" She didn't normally give any weight to astrology, but every now and then her mother's rambling struck a chord, and she hated the part of her that still believed.

"You. I'm not saying you're going to act on it, but your chart shows a new love interest. Your moon is in Jupiter, and there's opposition in your seventh house, which is you and Phil, so be on guard."

Lina rolled her eyes. "Okay, I'll be on guard."

"Just because something is in your chart doesn't mean you'll act on it. It just shows you'll have the opportunity."

"I'm not cheating on Phil, Mom!"

"You don't have to get defensive."

"Well, it's ridiculous."

"I'm just telling you what I see."

"Can we talk about something else, please? I don't want to waste another second on something that's never going to happen."

"Oh, I've been meaning to ask you. Did you remember to invite your father to Megan's graduation?"

"Of course not. Why would I do that?"

"Well she is his oldest grandchild."

Lina raised her eyebrows at the sheer ludicrousness of her mother's comment. "You know he's never met her, right? And that I haven't spoken to him in over twenty years?"

"Well then all the more reason to invite him."

"No. It would never have crossed my mind to invite him."

Lina was still gardening when Phil and Logan returned home from the lacrosse game. "How was the game?" she called out.

"Good," Logan answered before disappearing into the house.

"Torture," Phil answered after greeting her with a kiss. "Next time you can take him."

"Okay." He always threatened not to go when he didn't feel Logan played well.

"I don't get him—he backs off when he should be going forward. And when he gets the ball, he acts like it's a grenade. He just wants to get rid of it."

"You're expecting too much of him. He's only fourteen."

"When I was fourteen, I was being recruited by colleges."

"He isn't you, Phil," Lina said, not for the first time. "I hope you weren't hard on him."

"No, I wasn't hard on your precious boy."

"He is precious and sensitive, unlike you, so you have to be careful with him."

"I'm trying to raise him to be a man, Lina, not a woman."

— —

"Religion is a decisive force in this world," Katie fumed the following morning from the back seat, glaring at the back of Phil's head as they drove to church. "I shouldn't have to be a Catholic just because you are."

"I think the word you're looking for is 'divisive,'" Phil said. "Not 'decisive.'"

"Whatever."

They had been going back and forth since Katie announced at breakfast she didn't want to go to church anymore. Lina stared out the window only half listening, her head aching from too little sleep, her thoughts, like they had been most of the night, still preoccupied with Friday night's phone calls.

"I'll tell you what," Phil said. "When you're supporting yourself and living on your own, you can choose whatever religion you want, but until then you're a Catholic."

"Just like that? I have no say in it?"

"That's correct. Whether you like it or not, you're a member of this family, and this family is Catholic."

Katie folded her arms over her chest, staring out the window. "You can make me go to church, but you can't make me listen to what they're saying."

The sanctity of marriage and family was the subject of the homily, and as the priest espoused the importance of fidelity, Lina stole a sideways glance at Phil, searching without success for a discernible reaction to the words. Halfway through, he reached for her hand, bringing it to rest on his thigh, his thumb moving in a circular motion over the sensitive skin along the inside of her wrist. As she focused on their hands, an image of his hand touching the skin of another woman flashed in her mind.

5

*L*ina looked up from her magazine as Phil closed the parenting book, tossing it along with his reading glasses onto the bedside stand several nights later. "You're not done, are you? Not even you read that fast." She'd been bugging him to read the book for two days, and he'd picked it up less than thirty minutes earlier. "It took me four hours."

"I've read enough." He turned out his light. "That book is exactly what's wrong with the kids of this generation. Parents aren't parenting anymore. Apparently our only role is to provide food and shelter—it's insanity."

"The book isn't saying we shouldn't guide them. It's saying we shouldn't control them to the point where they lose their own inner direction."

"You want her to follow her own inner direction? Isn't that what got us here in the first place? Do you know why you like this book so much? It strikes a nostalgic chord in you. This is your mother's parenting style."

She laughed. "That isn't true. You're just seeing what you want to see. The book talks extensively about setting boundaries and having rules, which we both know my childhood lacked. This is more about not telling them what to think."

"Someone's going to. Do you want television and their friends to tell them what to think? They aren't old enough to decipher the bullshit. And the section on adolescent boys—Jesus Christ. The author has no clue. All this touchy-feely crap." He snorted in disgust. "That's not how you raise a man."

"You're impossible."

"Am I?" He took the magazine from her hands and tossed it to the floor. "Am I impossible?" He pushed her back against the mattress. "Do you wish I was more delicate?" He pinned her body beneath his, one of his legs moving between hers. "I don't think my sensitive side is what attracted you to me,' he growled against her ear. "Is it?" He pushed his lower body into hers. "Do you want me to talk more, baby?" He began to grind his hips into hers, his breath warm against her ear. "Share my feelings—cry a little maybe?"

"Shut up," she whispered.

"That's what I thought."

— ~

"This book was Mom's," Katie said, holding up a book on palmistry. "It says her name inside the front cover." After lunch at Alice's favorite vegan restaurant, they'd gone back to her house for the afternoon.

"Oh, your mother dabbled in everything back in the day." Alice continued flipping through a beginner's book on astrology.

Katie's eyes widened when she saw a witchcraft book entitled *The Book of Spells*. She pulled it off the shelf. "Do they really work?"

She carefully ran her fingers over the raised letters of the title. She couldn't imagine they did, but what if she was wrong? What if she could actually—

"It all depends on what you believe. Your aunts had a lot of fun with that if memory serves me correctly. Maybe even your mom."

"What made Mom stop believing in this stuff?"

"Joining the Catholic Church." Her grandma held out the astrology book. "This will be a good one to start with. See if it speaks to you."

"You're not Catholic?"

"Oh, heavens no. I don't believe in organized religion." Alice pulled another book off the shelf. "Here's another good one. Read these two and then we'll decide where to go from there."

"How did Mom become a Catholic? Her dad?"

"No, your dad. She joined his church."

"Why?" Katie couldn't imagine willingly going to church.

Alice hesitated, and Katie thought she saw a flicker of sadness in her eyes. "That's a question for your mom to answer."

"Have you done my chart?" Katie asked.

"Of course." Alice tossed her hand towards the opposite wall, which was covered in file cabinets. "Just look under H."

Katie pulled out a folder with her name on it and then noticed one for Phillip Hunter. "You did Dad's?" She looked into his folder, trying to make sense of all the different colored lines and triangles.

"I did your father's within the first week of meeting him. I wanted to see if it was more than sex between them. They were like bunnies."

"Grandma!" Katie pulled back her lip in disgust and put her hands over her ears.

Alice raised her eyebrows. "How do you think you came about?"

"I don't want to think about it."

"Your parents are cosmic soulmates. The only pair I've ever found." Alice laid Phil's and Lina's charts side by side on her desk and began pointing out all the trines and sextiles to Katie. "They're halves of a whole, bound together for all eternity. They couldn't part even if they wanted to. The universe would never allow it. They only feel complete with each other."

"Wow." Katie stared at the charts, her thoughts shifting to Matt as she wondered if he was her cosmic soulmate. "Does everyone have one?"

"Only very advanced souls. Your parents probably lived dozens of lives before they found each other. It's really something to behold." Alice stared down at the charts as if captivated by them anew. "Your father is very powerful, psychically, which makes his disbelief in anything occult related all the more puzzling."

"Does that mean he knows what I'm thinking?" Katie wondered if she could stop thinking in front of him.

"It's possible, but I think it's more centered on your mom. If she needs him, he knows it. No speaking necessary."

"How come I never heard about this before?"

"I don't know. Ask your mom."

"You're not just saying this to get me to talk to her, are you?" Katie asked.

"No, everything I said is true," Alice said.

"What's true?" With curly dark hair falling just past her shoulders and in cut-off shorts and a tight tank top, Shiloh Rayburn was dressed more like a teenager than a thirty-nine-year-old woman, and thanks in part to never having had children, she had the body to do so.

"I was just telling Katie about her parents' connection," Alice said, turning her attention to her youngest daughter. "What are you doing here?"

"Julian is taking me away for the weekend. I came by to drop off the dogs."

"Julian?" Alice shook her head. "I told you last week after I looked at your chart not to make rash decisions. You're in a period of impulsiveness, and you may regret—"

"Hello," Julian said as he stepped into the room, his gaze shifting between Alice and Katie.

"Oh, don't 'hello' me," Alice said, poking him in the chest. "You're as bad as she is! The two of you never learn. You are not compatible! Now get out!"

"Mom! He's my husband!"

"That was your choice, not mine! Out!" She pointed towards the front of the house.

"I started talking to a counselor," Julian said. "I know I was wrong."

"You've run out of chances with me! The last time was too much."

Katie turned her back on them, only half listening as the argument raged on. She hated being around Julian. He was a first-class asshole, and he looked like a weasel with stringy brown hair, a thin face and close-set eyes. Last time he came to their house, he called Shiloh a bitch in front of everyone, and her father banned him from coming over again. They were supposed to be getting a divorce, but she wasn't surprised that they were back together. Shiloh was always leaving Julian and then getting back with him.

Katie opened her backpack and began slipping some books inside.

"What are you doing? You can't take those books home. They are for you to read here."

Katie looked back over her shoulder at her grandmother, surprised to find Julian no longer in the room. "I won't lose them."

"Your parents won't allow those books in their house. You know that. And after the tirade I received from your dad last week over the T-shirt I let you buy, I don't think we should push our luck." She held out her hand. "Come on."

Katie pulled the two astrology books from her pack and handed them to her grandmother.

"Is that it?"

"Yeah," Katie said, closing the bag before her grandma could see the book of spells.

Lina normally avoided the street where she grew up, but she was already late, so she took the most direct route to Alice's, and when her childhood home came into view, she tried not to look. But her eyes were drawn to the brick colonial, and a flood of anxiety gripped her chest. She should have taken the long way.

A few turns later she was at the house Alice had bought two weeks prior to Lina's seventeenth birthday. At the time, Alice said she chose the closing date as a birthday present for Lina so she could be home for her birthday, but Lina never moved into the house, never made it her home, instead choosing to remain with Phil and his family.

Her heart dropped when she saw Julian's black Jeep in Alice's driveway. "What's going on?" she asked Shiloh, who was smoking a cigarette on Alice's front porch.

"What do you mean?"

"Are you back with him?"

"Yes." She avoided Lina's eyes.

"He threw all of your things on your front lawn," Lina said. "You called us crying at one a.m."

"He was drinking. He feels awful about it."

"He always feels awful about it. You were doing so well. Why would you go back?"

"Because I love him, and I wasn't doing well. You just saw what you wanted to believe. I missed him. Every day without him was awful."

"He makes you miserable, Shi."

"I'm more miserable without him, and he's my husband, so I would appreciate if you would keep your negative opinions to yourself."

"Hey." Julian nodded at Lina as he stepped out onto the porch. "You ready, babe?" He slapped Shiloh's butt. "We should get on the road before traffic gets bad."

"Megan's graduating tomorrow," Lina reminded Shiloh. "Aren't you coming?"

"Sorry, I completely forgot," Shiloh answered, slipping her arm around Julian's waist as they left the porch. "We're going to the beach for the weekend. Tell her congratulations for us."

— ⁓ —

"Did you get Gatorade?" Logan was on his feet as soon as Lina and Katie entered the kitchen, relieving Lina of a couple of grocery bags.

"In the back of the car. Would you bring in the rest of the groceries?" As soon as he was out of the house Lina turned to

Katie. "Your grandparents are going to be here within the hour. Would you make sure your room is presentable?"

"I don't want them in my room."

"Well just the same, I'd like to make sure it's picked up."

"Dr. Drayton said it's my sanctuary—that you're not supposed to comment on it."

"Fine," Lina sighed. "Just make sure the door's closed." With Phil's parents' impending arrival, the graduation the following day and learning Shiloh was back with Julian, Lina couldn't handle the stress of an argument with Katie, which, as Dr. Drayton predicted, was now a daily occurrence.

"Need me to do anything else?" Logan asked after bringing in the rest of the groceries.

"Just make sure your room is clean."

Lina was on her second glass of white wine when Phil's parents arrived. Bruce and Susan Hunter were what Lina's mother referred to as "country club" people, but to Lina they were family and had been since they took her into their home when she was sixteen and treated her like the daughter they never had. Ultraconservative, wealthy by most standards, Phil's father was a retired judge, and his mother had served on the boards of numerous charitable foundations until they retired three years earlier to Palm Beach.

"You look stunning," Mrs. Hunter said after releasing Lina from a warm embrace. "Doesn't she look stunning, Bruce? Are you having skin treatments or is your skin naturally keeping that porcelain look?"

"Just the monthly facial," Lina answered before turning to greet her father-in-law.

"Where are my beautiful grandchildren?" Mrs. Hunter asked. "I can't believe I've gone six months without seeing them."

They'd visited over Christmas, but Phil had been too busy to travel down to Florida over spring break as originally planned.

"Megan is at graduation rehearsal…" Lina trailed off as Logan appeared from the front of the house and was enthusiastically greeted by his grandparents, who both were convinced he'd grown six inches since they last saw him. "Why don't you help your grandpa with the bags?" Lina suggested.

"And where is Katie?" Mrs. Hunter whispered. Lina tried to speak to her mother-in-law weekly, so Mrs. Hunter was well versed on Katie's progress.

"Upstairs—her room's a mess, but it's the type of battle I'm not supposed to fight."

Mrs. Hunter squeezed her hand. "I'm just so thankful our prayers have been answered and she's doing better. I'll run up and say hello."

Phil arrived moments later. "I told you not to worry about cooking."

"I didn't want to make your parents go out. I'm sure they're tired after traveling."

"They wouldn't have minded." He took a swallow from her wine glass. "Where is every…" He trailed off when they heard the door from the garage opening, and then Adele was entering the kitchen.

"Why aren't either of you answering your cell phones?" Adele kissed Phil's cheek and then Lina's. Barely five foot three, Adele made up for her lack of height with enough energy to light up a small village. "Luckily I was showing a house down the street," she continued. "Have you talked to Mom or Shiloh today?" Her gaze settled on Lina.

"Yes." Lina averted her eyes.

"What's going on?" Phil asked.

"She's back with Julian," Adele said.

"Fuck." Phil ploughed his fingers back through his hair and gripped the back of his neck. "You knew?" he asked Lina.

"I was going to tell you after graduation."

"Are you okay?"

"I'm fine," she said.

"Let's go outside," Phil said. "The kids don't need to overhear this."

"At least he doesn't physically abuse her. We all know it could be worse," Adele said as soon as the door was closed, alluding to Shiloh's first husband, who had knocked her down a flight of stairs.

Lina crossed to the edge of the deck, staring mindlessly at the pool, aware of their low voices behind her but not attempting to listen to their conversation as tears filled her eyes. She had no solutions, no idea what to do to help Shiloh. She heard footsteps and then felt Phil's strong arms wrapping around her from behind. "She has to see it herself," he said against her ear. "We can't keep her away from him."

"I know. I just hate thinking of her with him."

"Me too." He tightened his hold on her. "I love you."

"I'm okay," she said, knowing he was worried about her. He always worried about her when an issue with Shiloh arose. "Do you want to stay for dinner?" Lina asked Adele as she turned back to the house.

"I would, but I have a date, and if I don't leave now I'll be late."

"Already?"

"Of course already." Adele reached for the door. "I'm not getting any younger."

"Wait—Dan's gone?" Phil asked. "I liked that guy. What in the hell is wrong with you?"

"I'm sorry?" Adele looked back at him over her shoulder. "Did you expect me to keep fucking him because you like him?"

"No. I expected you to keep fucking him because he was a good guy and he was in love with you."

"Well, I wasn't in love with him."

— ⁓

"What time do we have to be there tomorrow?" Phil asked. He was sitting on the side of the bed, looking at the alarm on his cell phone.

"The baccalaureate ceremony starts at ten."

"I'll get up at seven so I can work out in the morning." He set the phone on his nightstand before disappearing into the bathroom.

Phil's phone began to vibrate as Lina turned off her bedside lamp. Her heart dropped when she saw the name "Kim" on the display. Why was Kim calling him at eleven thirty at night? She didn't normally answer his phone but decided to make an exception. "Yes?"

"May I speak to Phil?"

"In reference to what?"

"I'm sorry. This is Kim Ryan. I work with him."

Lina looked up as Phil emerged from the bathroom. "Kim." She held out the phone.

"I think you've lost track of the time. I'm sure whatever you have to say can wait until tomorrow." He ran his hand over the back of his head as he turned away from Lina. "No…No…I'll call you tomorrow and you can tell me whatever you need then…No, it's late and it can wait." He hung up.

Lina watched him. "What was that?"

"She's one of the associates. She's working late and not considering the time or the urgency of what she needs." He set his phone on the nightstand before stretching out on the mattress beside her.

"Do I know her?"

"You may have met her at the holiday party. I don't know." He kissed her briefly on the lips. "Good night."

Long after Phil's breathing deepened in sleep, Lina continued to stare up at the ceiling, her mind swirling between thoughts of Shiloh and Julian and the woman on the other end of the call.

6

The weather couldn't have been better for an outside graduation, with temperatures in the upper sixties and just enough puffy clouds in the otherwise clear sky to offer an occasional reprieve from the June sun. As Lina left the baccalaureate ceremony with Phil, Alice and his parents, she was surprised by how emotional she felt. Halfway through the ceremony, the realization that her baby was graduating from high school had become almost overwhelming as visions of Megan throughout the years played in her mind like a video: the day she was born, her first birthday, her smile without her front teeth, her first soccer game. The video went on and, until Phil slipped a handkerchief into her hand, she was unaware she was crying.

"How are you?" Phil took her hand, lacing his fingers through hers, as they walked along the paved path leading to the seating area for the graduation ceremony.

"I'm a mess. I had no idea it was going to hit me like this. And I forgot my sunglasses."

"Do you want mine?" He brought her hand up to his mouth, pressing his lips against the inside of her wrist.

"No." She leaned into him, and he wrapped his arm around her shoulders as they continued to walk. Her oldest child was graduating from high school. She could barely believe it. Where had the time gone?

She felt a degree better as they reached their seats, and then she was greeting Adele and Phil's older brother, Mike, and his wife, Jeanie. Shiloh was of course absent, which Lina decided was a good thing because she didn't want anything distracting from Megan's day.

"Here." Phil held out a handkerchief. "A fresh one for the new ceremony."

"You brought two?"

"Of course." He leaned in, kissing her softly on the cheek. "I knew you would cry."

"You could have warned me."

Moments later when she glanced back over her shoulder, hoping to catch a glimpse of Megan as the graduates began assembling beneath some trees to their right, Lina found herself instead looking at Dr. Drayton. He was a few rows back, smiling in response to something a woman beside him was whispering in his ear. It felt strange seeing him outside of the office, and she was struck by how handsome he looked in a tan suit, his shirt open at the collar.

His attention shifted in her direction, and their eyes met, and then for the briefest moment his gaze dropped to her body. When his eyes again met hers, she saw unmasked male appreciation. She returned her attention forward, her pulse beating rapidly. He was attracted to her. Or maybe he just found her attractive. Either way, it was unsettling and strangely exhilarating.

As Lina's eyes followed her firstborn child walking towards the stage in a white sundress, carrying a dozen red roses, Lina caught her breath. Megan was all grown up and a female version of Phil with her thick brown hair, wide-set eyes and flawless skin. Her straight nose was a smaller version of his, as were her lips and even the small cleft in her chin. Lina wondered if she contained any of her DNA or if Phil's had somehow permeated her egg and pushed all of Lina's out.

Megan delivered the keynote address flawlessly, exhibiting the same poise and confidence that always came naturally to Phil. And then she was returning to stage again and again to receive one accolade after another. As the headmaster prepared to give the final award to the student perceived by the faculty to be the most outstanding member of the class, he mentioned that this year's recipient had received more votes than any student in the history of the school, and Lina knew before the end of the announcement that it would be Megan.

As she stood with the rest of the audience to give her daughter a standing ovation, she stole a glance at Katie, who was sitting between Alice and Logan, and as Lina feared, she remained seated.

"Tell her to get up," Phil whispered in Lina's ear.

Lina leaned over Logan to tap Katie's shoulder. "Stand," she mouthed.

Katie looked like she might argue or ignore the request, but one stern "now" from her father had her begrudgingly coming to her feet, and to Lina's relief Phil turned his attention back to the stage, ignoring Katie who, although standing, continued to tap away on her phone.

When the last graduate's name was announced, the families assembled at a reception outside the headmaster's house a few hundred yards away, and as Lina and Phil were stepping away from the punch bowl they came face-to-face with Dr. Drayton.

"Oh, hi!" Lina's first thought was that he had the greenest eyes she'd ever seen, and the second, and right on the heels of the first, was that Phil was standing directly beside her. "This is—"

"Phil Hunter," Phil said, holding out his hand.

"Nick Drayton." He returned his handshake.

"Drayton?" Phil repeated, his brows pulled together in confusion. "As in doctor?"

"That's right. Is there a problem?"

"No, not at all. I just..." Phil glanced briefly at Lina before returning his attention to Dr. Drayton. "I wasn't expecting you. Do you have a child graduating?"

"A nephew."

"You're local?"

"Yes. Congratulations on your daughter's accomplishments. I'm sure you're very proud."

"Thank you. We both are." Phil ran his hand over Lina's lower back. "We should get back to our group. It was, uh, good to finally meet you."

"Why in the hell did I picture him as a seventy-year-old with a pipe?" Phil whispered into Lina's ear after they walked away.

"I don't know."

"You've been seeing him every week for months and never thought to mention he was good-looking?"

"Maybe I didn't notice," she teased.

He tightened his arm around her and brushed his lips against her cheek. "Push the handsome doctor from your mind, Lina. This is Megan's day."

Lina was stretched out on her bed halfway through a planned two-hour nap when Katie, wearing cut-off shorts and a black T-shirt that said, "I Think Religion is Bad and Drugs are Good," came into her room and announced she needed a ride to Emma's house.

"The graduation party starts in three hours," Lina said, her voice deep with sleep. "You'd just have to turn around and come back."

"I'm not going to the graduation party. I want to see Ryan's band. They're playing tonight."

"You can't miss Megan's graduation party. And please lose the T-shirt before your dad or grandparents see it."

"No one cares if I'm at the party."

"I care. Your father cares."

"You only care because you're afraid it will make you look bad if I'm not. You can't make me go."

"You're right. I can't make you go, but I am asking you as a member of this family and as a favor to me, to go."

"No." Katie crossed her arms over her chest. "Megan represents everything that's wrong with this society, and I refuse to celebrate her."

Lina had no idea what she was talking about and was too tired to engage her. "I'm sorry you feel that way."

"Now will you take me to Emma's?"

"No. I'm not taking you to Emma's. Invite Emma to come here. There's going to be plenty of food and music."

"Emma doesn't want to celebrate Megan either! Why are you being so unreasonable? Dr. Drayton would never make me go."

"You don't have to attend, but you're not leaving this house, Katie."

7

ina tossed the magazine onto the side table for the third time in as many minutes and then, seconds later, picked it up again and began flipping through it. She was nervous and she hated it. All day she'd been recalling the flash of attraction she saw in Dr. Drayton's eyes at Megan's graduation, and as a result she'd spent a little more time on her appearance, carefully choosing the sleeveless crème linen dress she was wearing. It wasn't that she liked him in any inappropriate way, but knowing he appreciated the way she looked was a welcome stroke to her ego, and she feared the knowledge might make her less comfortable around him.

The apprehension dissolved as soon as he stepped out into the waiting room beside Katie, replaced by a rush of warmth and the realization that she'd missed talking to him. He'd been away for two weeks—on a vacation, she assumed. based on his tan—so they'd gone an extra week between appointments.

"Have you been lounging on a beach?" Lina asked as she walked towards the couch in his office.

"Close. I was sailing."

"That sounds relaxing. You own a boat?"

"We rented a fifty footer in St. Croix and sailed to different islands." He lowered himself into the chair across from her position on the couch. "It was fantastic."

"Wow, I bet. Did you rent a crew too?"

"No, but you certainly can. Do you like boats?"

"I do." She smiled. "But only as a passenger. You must be experienced if you didn't need a crew."

"I grew up sailing." He leaned back in the chair and casually crossed one leg over the other.

She realized how little she actually knew about him, which felt strange considering how much he knew about her. "Was the nephew graduating from your side or your wife's?"

"I don't have a wife."

"Oh, I'm sorry. I just assumed."

"That's okay."

"I just thought—didn't I hear you mention a son to Katie?"

"You did. You don't have to be married to have children."

"I know." She blushed.

"I'm teasing you, Lina." He smiled. "I'm divorced."

The use of her first name made the exchange feel more personal, and she knew the dynamics of their relationship had changed over the past two weeks. "It's not nice to tease me. I blush too easily."

"I'm sorry."

"No you're not." She returned his smile.

"You're right. I'm not." He continued to look into her eyes, and then he was pushing one of his hands back through his hair.

"Katie," he said as if reminding himself why they were meeting. He opened the folder on his lap. "Any concerns?" His demeanor changed from light and flirtatious to serious.

"No." Lina shook her head. Even if she had concerns, she wasn't sure if she'd remember them. She'd been flirting with Dr. Drayton, and she felt a stab of guilt at the realization.

Katie gnawed on her thumbnail as she sat on a chair beside the desk in her bedroom, watching Emma, who was lying on her bed reading a section in the magic book Katie had snuck from her grandma's house. "Well?"

Emma raised her eyes. "You have to do it," she said. "Can you imagine if it works?"

Katie felt a tingling of excitement in her chest. "I have a feeling it will, but how am I going to get a piece of his hair?" The spell called for a few strands of Matt's hair. "Everything else is easy. One of us can just ask him his birthday." She'd seen him twice since the night they met, and although they hadn't really spent any time alone, she had talked to him enough to feel okay about asking him his birthday.

Emma's eyes returned to the book. "So we just need his hair and your hair and a Bible. Maybe you could pretend to want to brush his hair or something."

"I can't imagine him letting me touch his hair." He looked like someone who spent a lot of time perfecting his spiky look. "Does he ever spend the night at your house and do his hair?"

"He does spend the night," Emma said. "So he must do his hair. Next time he spends the night, you should spend the night too."

"I wish," Katie sighed. "You know I'm not allowed to do sleepovers."

"Oh right. When is your dad going to lighten up? You don't even drink."

"I should have gone to Megan's stupid graduation party. I think he's still annoyed I stayed in my room the whole time." Katie thought he wouldn't notice, but instead he tried to force her to come out of her room. Then her mom had said something to him and he didn't bother her for the rest of the night.

"So how long will it take for him to fall in love with you?" Emma asked. "I mean once the spell starts."

"I don't know," Katie said. "My grandma said it depends on how much I believe. The stronger my belief, the faster the universe will respond."

Phil was off with Logan at an early lacrosse game the following morning, and Lina was enjoying a few extra minutes of sleep when Katie entered her bedroom demanding a Bible.

"A Bible?" Lina repeated, surprised, especially considering Katie's latest arguments with Phil revolved around her desire to stop attending church. "Why?"

"I want to borrow it." Katie crossed her arms over her chest.

"Is Emma still here?"

"Yeah, we're going to her house."

"You want to take the Bible to Emma's?" The Bible was Phil's, and Lina knew he wouldn't want it leaving the house.

"No," Katie sighed. "I just want to borrow it."

"Are you going out without showering? Your hair looks—"

"No! Where should I look for the Bible?"

Moments later, Lina was handing Katie Phil's King James Bible. "Thanks." Katie walked off towards the door.

"Katie?"

"What?"

"Why the sudden interest in the Bible?"

Katie shrugged. "Why not?"

"Are you starting to like going to church?"

"No!" She scowled. "Why do you have to analyze everything I do? Why can't you just let me look at a Bible without reading into it? It's annoying," she said before Lina could say more.

— —

"Do you want to go to an Orioles game?" Logan called out after bounding out of Phil's car later that day. "Dad says yes if you do."

Lina, who had been on her hands and knees weeding a flower bed, came to her feet. "You two can go." She wasn't in the mood for a baseball game.

"He said he'd only go if you came too." Logan stopped beside her. "Please." He stuck out his lower lip like he did when he was a little boy and wanted something.

"Logan—"

"They're playing the Yankees. Please." He put his hands together like he was praying.

Lina looked away from the action on the field to watch Phil who, as he'd been doing almost since they arrived, was tapping on his cell phone. "Still work?"

He darkened the display, slipping the phone into the pocket of his shorts as he brought his gaze back to the field. "Work." The side of his jaw was clenched.

"Dad? Could I have some money? We want to get ice cream," Logan said.

Phil handed him some cash, and for the third time since arriving an hour and a half earlier, Logan and his friends went off to get food while Phil again took out his cell phone.

Lina laughed. "Why did you make me come if all you're going to do is text work?"

"Sorry." When Phil looked up from his phone, something in his eyes had Lina's heart rate increasing.

"What's wrong?"

"Nothing."

"What's going on at five thirty on a Saturday that is so urgent?" He rarely worked on Saturdays unless he was in the midst of an important trial.

He lifted her hand and kissed the back of it. "I'm done working. I promise."

True to his word, Phil didn't take out his phone again. Lina settled into the game, actually having a nice time as she drank a couple of beers, ate a soft pretzel and a hotdog and watched the Orioles destroy the Yankees, 10-0.

It was close to 8:30 p.m. when Phil pulled into the garage after dropping Logan's friends at their prospective houses. As Lina followed Logan into the house, she hesitated when Phil called her name. He was still sitting in the car.

"What are you doing?" she asked.

"I have to go out for a little while. Someone screwed up at work, and I need to deal with it."

"Was it Kim?"

A flash of surprise crossed his face. "I shouldn't be longer than an hour or so."

"Answer my question, Phil."

"I have to go."

Lina watched in stunned silence as he backed out of the garage and drove away. This wasn't happening. Her husband wasn't disappearing with barely an explanation on a Saturday night. She quickly called his cell phone.

"Lina," he answered, "please just let me deal with this."

"What's going on? Are you on your way to the office?"

There was a long pause. "I need you to just let me handle it."

"Is it work related?" she thought to ask. "Just tell me that."

"I'm not prepared to answer any questions right now."

"Not prepared?" she repeated, suddenly angry at his vague response. "I'm your wife."

"You're going to have to trust me."

"Trust you to what?" She gripped her forehead as she struggled to maintain control. "Do I have to call Wayne to find out what's going on?"

"Don't do this, Lina. I'm about at my limit right now."

"Oh, you're at *your* limit? At least you know what's going on." She looked at her phone. He'd hung up on her.

***

Katie's chest swelled with emotion at the sound of the soulful male vocalist, knowing before she and Emma reached the barn that it was Matt. He was standing at the center of the stage, his hand gripping the mic, his eyes closed as his haunting voice filled the air.

The band practiced for over an hour, stopping occasionally to discuss an arrangement, but Matt was mostly quiet, strumming his guitar, or scribbling notes on a pad, never once looking in Katie's direction. As soon as they began putting away their equipment, Katie made her way to Matt, offering him a big cup of water.

"Thanks." He tilted the cup back, the muscles of his throat constricting as he swallowed it down.

"You're amazing," Katie said, not caring if she sounded corny, because it was true, and she wanted him to know it.

"Yeah?" He met her eyes.

"I'm not just saying it to say it. I really mean it. You remind me of Dylan or Lennon or one of those guys."

"Thanks." He smiled, and she couldn't tell if it was a pleased or amused smile. "I need some air." He walked past her, taking a few steps before turning back. "You coming?"

"Yeah." She followed him out of the barn and over to a bench, dropping down beside him.

"What's your story, Hunter? Ryan said your parents grounded you for a year for doing drugs. That true?"

Katie didn't want to lie to him, but she was afraid if she was honest he would think she was a freak, so she settled for half the truth. "Six months, but I kind of refused to leave my room because I hated them, and then it made me kind of depressed, and then I didn't want to," she said.

"So you didn't leave your room at all?"

"I went to school and church, and I had to eat meals with my family, but besides that, no." She could feel him looking at her but stared forward, afraid she'd see pity in his eyes.

"What did you do in your room?"

"Read a little, listened to music, but mostly nothing. The first couple months I didn't have a phone or Internet, and by the time they gave them back to me, I didn't care."

"What made you start caring again?"

Katie looked at him then and was surprised to see only interest in his eyes. "They made me go to a psychiatrist, and he…" She wasn't sure what Dr. Drayton had done exactly. "He listened to me, I guess. I sound like I'm crazy or something and I'm not."

"I don't think you're crazy. Things better now?"

"Yeah. This is probably going to sound weird, but when I talk about it, I feel like I'm describing someone else. At the time I just didn't feel like I belonged anywhere."

"I get that. After my mom died I had to live with my dad for a while. It sucked. He has a wife and little kids and this whole life that has nothing to do with me. I felt like I was in this alternate universe where my mom had never existed. I only lasted three weeks. I stayed with a friend until I finished the school year and then found my grandma."

"What did your dad do?"

"Nothing. He knew it wasn't working. I hadn't even seen him for ten years when she died. I barely remembered him. He was like a stranger."

"That sucks."

He shrugged. "I don't give a fuck about him."

The conversation turned lighter then as Matt talked about the job he'd recently gotten at a lumberyard, which would hopefully turn full-time after the summer hires went back to school. "I could make some pretty decent money," he said.

"You're not going to college?" Katie thought everyone went to college.

"I just want to make music. College isn't going to help me do that."

Katie was thinking about how to respond when she saw the blonde from the first night she'd met Matt approaching. He was going to leave, and she'd completely forgotten to get his birth date or a few strands of his hair. "There's something in your hair," she thought to say.

"What?"

"I don't know—just something." Katie reached out and gripped several pieces of his hair before yanking hard.

"Ow." His hand immediately went to his head, his eyebrows pulled together in a frown.

"Sorry." She could feel the hair in her fingers.

"Did you get it?"

"What?"

"Whatever was in my hair." He continued to frown at her.

"Oh, yeah. It's gone."

8

Lina was greeted with a pounding headache and an empty bed the following morning. She peeked at the alarm clock, horrified to discover it was after 11:00 a.m. She couldn't remember the last time she'd slept so late. A note beside the clock caught her eye, and she picked it up, squinting to read it.

"L - Took the kids to church. Didn't want to wake you. I love you, P."

A bottle of Extra Strength Tylenol and a glass of water sat on the nightstand.

The events of the previous night were fuzzy, but she knew why her head was pounding. She'd consumed too much wine. She had a vague memory of Phil slipping pills into her mouth and holding a glass of ice water against her lips. She couldn't recall whether they talked or what time it was when he came home, but he'd carried her upstairs, and he must have taken off her clothes because she was naked. Where had he been? If he told her she had no recollection, but the more she thought about it, the more she was convinced there was someone else. She closed her eyes as a wave of nausea swept through her.

"This was a pleasant surprise," Diane said as she joined Lina at a busy Italian restaurant not far from her house. "Although, why you chose this noisy place—"

"I don't want to be overheard," Lina interrupted. "I think something's going on with Phil." She quickly recounted the events of the previous evening.

"That's it?" Diane raised her eyebrows. "Really, Lina, are you looking for reasons to be upset? Do you know how many times Wayne gets work calls on the weekend?"

"Phil has never received a call on a Saturday night and disappeared for who knows how many hours."

"Now he has. He's not cheating on you, Lina. And don't you dare accuse him of it. He has enough pressure on him at work. Why would you even want to put those thoughts in his head?"

Lina felt relief as she listened to Diane. "I was so sure when he—"

"Honey." Diane gripped her hand. "I don't know what's going on in that beautiful head of yours, but it's all in your imagination. You should see the way he looks at you. Men don't look at their wives the way Phil looks at you when they're cheating."

It was close to 4:00 p.m. when Lina saw Phil for the first time that day. He was in his study at the front of the house, engrossed in something on his computer screen when she paused outside the door.

He removed his reading glasses and leaned back in his chair, his eyes meeting hers. There were light shadows under his eyes, and she wondered how much sleep he'd gotten the previous night.

"Where are the kids?" she asked.

"Out." He pushed back his chair.

"You can keep working, I—"

"I sent them away so we could talk."

Lina took a few steps backwards into the foyer. "It's okay. You were right last night—it's your business to handle. I shouldn't have said anything." She began to walk towards the staircase, intending to go up to their room, but he was behind her, taking her arm and slowly turning her to face him.

"Lina, if there were a way I could avoid having this conversation with you, I would." His eyes were full of sadness.

Her heart began to pound, all of the relief she felt at Diane's reassurances gone. She shook her head, her eyes filling with tears. "Phil, I know you had an affair," she said, her voice breaking. She wanted him to deny it, to shake his head and tell her it wasn't true, to validate the little ounce of doubt she had kept with her and cherished over the past month. But of course he didn't, because it was true. A small part of her died at the realization.

"I don't want to have this conversation standing in the hallway."

"Why not?" Lina whispered, meeting his eyes. "Is there a better place to break my heart?"

"This is going to get a lot worse. We need to be sitting." He led her towards the front of the house and then hesitated. "Is the kitchen okay?"

"Yes," she answered, barely recognizing her own voice.

Lina watched him, her beautiful husband, sitting with his legs apart, his elbows on his knees, staring down at his hands, seemingly struggling with how to begin.

"Are you in love with her?" she thought to ask.

Phil's head snapped up. "No, God no!"

She felt her body exhale. "So you aren't leaving me?"

He reached out and took one of her hands, his fingers sliding over her palm, his eyes meeting hers. "I will never leave you of my own volition."

"Then I don't understand."

"Let me just—let me get through this." He squeezed her hand. "Okay?" When she nodded, he took a deep breath. "This is hard." He shook his head and glanced down at their clasped hands before raising his eyes back to hers. "About five months ago, when I was in New York, I uh, I started sleeping with one of the associates at the firm."

"Kim." Her voice was flat, defeated.

"Yes—"

Lina pulled her hand from his and crossed her arms over her chest. He'd had sex with another woman. Her Phil had taken off his clothes and made love to another woman. It was no longer just a suspicion she could rationalize away. It was a fact. "Is she beautiful?"

"You're the only woman I find beautiful."

"Oh, right, I'm sure you were picturing my face when you were fucking her." She wiped at the tears falling from her eyes.

"Baby, I'm—"

"Don't call me that. Don't you dare call me that. You fucked another woman, Phil. You have lost your right to call me that."

He watched her in silence, his expression grim.

"Why are you telling me this? Why couldn't you have just let me pretend you were the man I wanted you to be?" His only reaction was a clenching of his jaw. "I hate you," she whispered. "I hate you for this." She stood up.

"I'm not done. Please sit down."

"I don't need to hear any more." She began to walk away.

He was out of his chair and behind her, grasping her shoulders. "You have to let me finish."

"Why?" she whispered. "Why can't you just let me be alone with this?" Her voice broke as her head fell forward, her shoulders shaking as tears streamed from her eyes. She didn't stop him when he turned her to face him, her cheek crushed against his chest as he engulfed her in his arms. She took comfort in his familiar woodsy smell, her arms moving around him as she sought comfort from the very person who was causing the pain. She cried for minutes as he whispered reassurances in her ear, and then suddenly the tears stopped, and she began kissing his warm neck, her hands drifting down his back to his butt, gripping him as she tried to get closer.

"Lina?"

"Make love to me."

"I don't think that's a good idea," he said, pulling back slightly.

"Please," she pleaded, her eyes meeting his. "I need you to make this pain go away...Please."

"Lina—"

"We'll talk after." She gripped him through his shorts. "I need to feel you inside me." As demented as it was, she felt an overwhelming desire to know he was still hers.

He caught his breath, and suddenly his mouth was opening over hers, his hands clasping her hips as he pulled her against his growing erection. He led her to the family room and then pushed her back on the couch, quickly removing her panties and then dropping to his knees before her.

"No," she whispered when he began to run his lips along the inside of her thigh. "I need to feel you inside me. Please." She needed to feel their connection.

He stood, removing his shorts and briefs in one fluid movement, and then he was lowering himself onto the couch and between her thighs. He slipped his hand between them, touching her.

"Please," she whispered.

"You're not ready."

"I don't care." She fisted his shirt, pulling him towards her.

"Wait," he pleaded, continuing to touch her. "I don't want to hurt you."

"I need you," she cried. "Please, please."

"Look at me, Lina. Open your eyes and look at me." As soon as she opened her eyes he slowly thrust into her. "Do you know what we're doing?" he asked as he rocked his hips forward, burying himself still deeper. "Tell me." He pulled completely out. "Tell me, Lina." He drove into her again.

"Making love," she whispered, tears in her eyes.

"That's right," he said before kissing her deeply. "Lina," he said when he lifted his head. "Look at me." She lifted her eyes back to his. "You are the only woman I have ever made love to in my life." He continued to move in and out of her, the pace of his thrusts increasing. "I may have been with someone else, but you are the woman I make love to. You are the only woman I will ever love."

They were sitting side by side on the couch, fully clothed. "What kind of woman responds to the news of her husband's infidelity by begging him to make love to her?"

"I don't think there's a protocol here."

"You really cheated on me, didn't you?" She was numb.

"Yes."

"Was this the first time?"

"Yes."

"Why her?"

He hesitated for a long moment. "I'm not sure this is a good idea. I was unfaithful—the details don't seem important."

"They're important to me."

He got up from the couch and pushed his hands into his pockets, staring down at her. "You want me to tell you what led to me being with someone else?"

"Yes, that's exactly what I want."

"Jesus Christ." He shook his head. "It's a cliché. I was away from home and I called you. We had a fight. I went down to the bar. She was there. I talked. She listened. We fucked. That's it. I need a drink. Do you want a drink?" he asked over his shoulder as he walked towards the wet bar.

"No." She slowly followed, crossing her arms over her chest and hugging herself as she watched him pour himself a glass of scotch. "How did it continue for four months? What you just described was a one-night stand."

"And then it became something more," he admitted. "She wanted me. You didn't seem to, and it just happened."

"I didn't seem to?" she repeated. "What does that mean?"

"Lina, we were dealing with Katie, and you were mad at me most of the time."

"So now this is my fault?" she cried.

"No." He shook his head. "This is my fault. This is one hundred percent my fault. I'm just trying to give you a window into what I was thinking and feeling. Lina, I'm sorry."

"Somehow those words just don't seem to cover it." She suddenly felt tired. "It'll never be the same, you know. I will never be able to look at you the same again."

"Lina," he began as he set his drink on the table. "There's something else I have to tell you." He took both her hands in his.

"What else?" Her anger was replaced by an overwhelming sadness.

Phil watched her, his eyes cloudy with regret. "You don't deserve this. God, I would do anything to save you this pain." He squeezed her hands. "Lina, she's pregnant."

9

"Pregnant? I don't under—" Her eyes opened wider at the realization of what he was saying. "By you? She's pregnant with your child?" She took a step back from him, pulling her hands free.

"Yes."

"Oh my God!" She covered her mouth. "She can't have your baby." Her wild eyes flew to his. "Do you want her to have your baby?"

"Of course not." When he stepped towards her, she held up her hands.

"Don't touch me," she whispered as tears continued to fall from her eyes. "Is she...Is she having it?"

"Yes."

"I can't—I can't take any more right now." She headed for the stairs. "Don't follow me," she said when she heard him behind her. "Please don't follow me."

Lina sat on the floor of the shower, her eyes closed, her arms cradling her legs as she slowly rocked, the water splashing over her body, enveloping her in its warmth. She craved showers when she was upset, had since she was a young girl, gaining comfort in the wet solitude. Her husband was having a baby with another woman. How could he possibly be a father to a child who wasn't hers? Why hadn't she thrown him out? Isn't that what most women would do in these circumstances? Well, she'd already proved she wasn't like most women. No, she needed him too much. She shook her head in disgust, trying to clear a vision of him collapsing against her as an orgasm shook his body, his sperm filling her at the same time his baby grew inside another woman. She reached up and turned the hot water knob to the left, forcing herself to endure the spray of ice-cold water. Her skin was bright red when she stepped out of the shower.

She tried to call Adele, but the phone went straight to voicemail, and then she began to call Diane but changed her mind. She didn't want to talk to Diane. Diane was on Phil's side. Diane had been defending him for weeks. She would call Alice.

When Alice didn't answer, Lina dropped down on her bed and stared at her phone. She needed to talk to someone. Suddenly an image of Dr. Drayton flashed in her mind. Before she could change her mind, she dialed his office number. Her body slumped when someone from his answering service picked up. She almost hung up, but instead found herself leaving a message the woman promised would be conveyed to the doctor. It was Sunday, Lina remembered. Of course he wasn't working on a Sunday.

Several minutes later, the ring of her cell phone startled her. "Hello?" she said hesitantly, not recognizing the unfamiliar number.

"This is Dr. Drayton."

His voice sounded different on the phone. Cooler, more professional. "I'm sorry. I shouldn't have called you," Lina rushed out.

"Is Katie—"

"Katie's fine," she managed before she started to cry.

"Lina?" His voice gentled.

"I'm sorry," she whispered, struggling to gain control of her emotions. "I just found something out about my husband. I shouldn't have bothered you. This has nothing to do with Katie."

"What can I do to help?"

She closed her eyes and lay back on the bed. "Nothing. I just wanted to talk." She tried to picture him in the chair in his office.

There was a brief pause. "Would you like to meet?"

Twenty minutes later, Lina pulled her Mercedes into the empty lot in front of Dr. Drayton's office building. She'd left the house without alerting Phil, and he'd called twice during her short drive over. She looked at the display on her phone and discovered he'd also sent a text.

I'm just worried. Please let me know you're okay. I love you. She considered replying but instead slipped the phone back into her purse, deciding she didn't care if he was worried.

Ten minutes passed before a black Porsche convertible turned into the parking lot. She slowly emerged from her car, having a hard time reconciling the person stepping out of the Porsche with Katie's doctor. Gone were the pressed slacks and jacket, and in their place were brushed cotton khaki shorts and a white button-up shirt with the sleeves rolled up on the forearms. He really was handsome.

"Hi." He smiled, and the two Draytons merged in her mind. The clothes may have been different, but the smile and green eyes belonged to the Dr. Drayton she knew. "I hope you don't mind the casual look. I didn't have time to go home and change."

"I prefer it." Suits reminded her of Phil.

"In that case..." He reached into his car and lifted a pizza box from the passenger seat. "I assume you won't mind if I eat."

She smiled. "Not at all."

He hesitated, looking to the right of the building. "There's an outside patio and garden area in the back. If you're okay not going up to my office, we could sit back there."

"This is nice," Lina said a few minutes later as she sat down in the chair he held out for her.

"My first time here," he admitted before sitting down across from her. He'd finished one slice of mushroom and pepperoni pizza on their walk over and was pulling out another. "I can see it from my office window." They were on a stone patio flanked on one side by small trees and on the other by a small koi pond.

"Thanks for meeting me." She looked down at her clasped hands. "I know I'm not your patient and had no right to leave a message with your service, but the truth is I find you easy to talk to, and I needed to talk."

He set down his slice of pizza and wiped his mouth with a napkin. "I'm not going to pretend this is normal, because it isn't, but I wouldn't be here if I didn't want to be. Why don't—" He was interrupted by the ring of her cell phone. "Do you need to get that?"

"My husband," Lina said, looking at the display. "I left without telling him. He's worried."

"Do you want him to worry?"

She shrugged. "Not really, but I don't want to talk to him."

"You could text him," he pointed out.

She nodded, composing a short text that simply said, *I'm fine. Give me a little space.*

"Tell me why you called," he said as soon as she slipped her phone back into her purse. "You sounded upset."

"Remember how I told you I suspected he had an affair?"

"Of course."

"He got her pregnant."

"Jesus!" He sat back, his eyes opening wider.

"Not my best day," Lina said.

"No." He stared at her for seconds. "He told you?"

"Yes." As she relayed the events of the past twenty-four hours, she saw an array of emotions travel over his normally controlled features. The warmth and concern she recognized, but the look of disgust that flittered over his face occasionally was new.

"There is something wrong with me, isn't there?" Lina whispered, a few tears slipping from her eyes.

"No. Why would you say that?" He slid a napkin across the table towards her. "You are dealing with something very difficult."

"Shouldn't I hate him right now?"

"You can hate his actions without hating him."

"My husband had sex with another woman. I think hating him would have been a healthier response than having sex with him." She wiped at her tears. "And I'm sure you do too. You just think I need to come to that conclusion on my own."

"Do you think there is a *right way* to handle the situation you've found yourself in?"

"No, but I think there's a wrong way. And rewarding your husband with sex when you find out he was cheating on you seems like the wrong way for any self-respecting woman."

"Rewarding him?" He raised an eyebrow. "Was that your intention?"

"No." She shook her head. "I wanted the pain to stop. I wanted to stop thinking. And I wanted to feel closer to him."

"So you were trying to comfort yourself. There's nothing wrong with that."

"I feel like I was trying to comfort both of us—like something is happening to *us*. Like he's a victim too." She pressed the tissue against her eyes, tears once again threatening. "My rational mind wants me to be angry at him, but then I look at him and it's Phil. Loving him is part of who I am."

Dr. Drayton curved his hand around the back of his neck, his fingers kneading his muscles, the pizza seemingly forgotten as he listened to her pledge her love to the man who had cheated on her and impregnated another woman. He drew in a deep breath. "Under what scenario could he possibly be a victim? Someone must have chosen not to wear a condom, if I'm recalling sex education correctly."

Bile rose in her throat at the thought of Phil ejaculating into another woman. He hated wearing condoms. He said it ruined his pleasure. It was why Megan was conceived on their honeymoon. Lina had forgotten to pack her pills, and Phil decided his pleasure was worth the risk. "I know he isn't a victim. I was just telling you what I was thinking." She rubbed her fingers over her forehead. "I can't believe this is happening. I feel like this is someone else's life or a bad dream."

"You're in shock. It's a lot to take in."

"How do we get past it?"

"Time."

"There's going to be a child—his child. Am I going to get past that?" Just saying it aloud felt surreal.

"That's not a question I can answer."

"Could you get past it? If you were married and your wife got impregnated by another man?"

He looked surprised by the question, but quickly composed his features. "What I could or couldn't do is irrelevant."

"I want to know."

"I don't know. I know you're looking for something more concrete, but I can't give it to you. Your situation, your relationship is unique to you. Whether or not you can get past it is a question only you can answer. Is it possible? Yes. It's definitely possible."

10

"She's thirty," Lina told Diane the next day over lunch. She'd broken down and told her of Phil's infidelity on the phone the night before. "Which means she has a thirty-year-old body." She shook her head to clear the image.

"Don't give her a second of your attention. She's nothing to him."

"Except the woman who's carrying his child." Just saying the words had Lina's stomach clenching. She pushed her uneaten salad towards the center of the table. She hadn't been able to eat since finding out on Sunday.

"Wayne said she's planning to leave. I think she's interviewing in DC."

"He knew, didn't he? About the affair. That's why he was acting distant to Phil that night."

"Yes. He said she pursued Phil relentlessly from the day she started last fall. He's very upset about the whole thing."

"Does everyone know?" She hated the thought of his coworkers' looks of pity.

"No. Wayne said Phil was very discreet."

"How nice of him," Lina bit out sarcastically.

"Honey," Diane began, covering her hand, "he did something awful and selfish, but he loves you."

"That doesn't make me feel any better."

"It was just a fling. He doesn't want her. He wants you."

"Do you know her?"

"I have a vague memory of her from the holiday party. Blonde, I think—she doesn't hold a candle to you. And once she's gone, you can put this behind you, and it will be like it never happened."

"She's having his baby, Diane. This isn't going away."

It was Tuesday night before Lina managed to sleep, and "sleep" was a generous term for the fitful slumber she fell into, filled with disturbing dreams that had her crying out and forcing Phil to wake her.

"It's okay," he'd whisper, pulling her back into the warmth of his body. "You're dreaming. It's okay. I've got you." And so it went all night as the nightmares that normally only plagued Lina when Phil was away came with a vengeance, and the one person who was able to bring her comfort was the same man whose actions had brought them on.

Phil arrived home just before 7:00 the following evening, laden with carryout bags from a local barbeque restaurant. As Lina watched her children eating ribs, French fries and coleslaw, she was struck with how ordinary everything seemed. Megan was dominating the conversation with a description of decoration plans for her dorm room, Logan was eating with the gusto of a person who hadn't eaten in weeks, and Katie was nibbling on a French fry while staring at the cell phone she thought no one could see in her lap. It was all so normal, and yet nothing would ever be normal again because there was a woman pregnant with their half sibling.

It was too much. Sitting there pretending nothing was wrong. "Excuse me," Lina whispered as she pushed back her chair, and then she was fleeing from the table and running out onto the deck.

"Lina?" Phil was behind her, his hand sliding over her stomach.

"Don't." She shook her head as she stepped away from him, crossing to the edge of the deck and looking out over the darkened yard. "I want to be alone."

"Let me make it better."

"Make it better?" She turned to him. "You're why I'm hurting," she cried. "You hurt me. And do you know what the worst part is? You're the only one that had the power to hurt me like this."

"Baby, don't." He touched the side of her face. "Don't cry." He brushed his mouth against hers. "I love you."

"Stop!" she cried, pushing her palms against his chest. "I hate you!"

"No you don't." His arms were around her, pulling her tightly into his chest. "No, you don't."

"Let me go!" she screamed as she tried unsuccessfully to get away from him. "Let me go!"

"Not until you calm down."

"I hate you! I hate you!"

"Mom?" Logan's concerned voice came from behind Phil. "Are you okay?"

"She's fine. Go back inside!" Phil growled.

Logan took a step towards them. "Mom?"

"It's okay," Lina said, no longer struggling. "I'm fine. Go back inside."

"Get out of here, Logan!" Phil roared when Logan still hesitated. "Now!"

As soon as the door closed, Lina fisted Phil's shirt. "Don't you dare take this out on him!"

"They're watching." He loosened his embrace. "All three."

Lina's anger was gone as soon as she saw the worried looks on her children's faces. "I'm calling Adele. I need to call Adele."

"What? Why?"

"I don't want to be here. I need to get away from you."

"Then I'll leave."

"No. I can't be around the kids, either." She wiped at the tears beneath her eyes. "I need some space."

"Lina," he began touching her arm. "Don't do this. Go to our room. I'll stay away. I'll keep the kids away, and I'll sleep in the guest room downstairs. The kids won't know. Please. Stay."

"But I want to talk to Adele."

"Then have her come here. Call her.' He pulled his cell phone from his pocket and held it out to her. "Call her," he repeated. "This is your house. You belong here. The kids need you here."

Lina was curled in the fetal position on the bed when Adele burst into her room. "What's going on? What happened?"

"Phil had an affair," Lina said, knowing if she didn't say it immediately she wouldn't be able to. "And now she's pregnant with his baby."

A speechless Adele stared at Lina for a full minute before responding, her face pale and her large eyes like saucers. "That motherfucker!" She crossed towards the door.

"Adele, no!" Lina cried. "You can't say anything. The kids don't know. Please! Please don't. Please."

"Oh, baby," Adele whispered. "I'm so sorry." She crossed back to the bed. And then they were both crying as Adele cradled Lina in her arms. "Do you know what we need?" Adele asked when the tears finally stopped. "Ice cream."

"I don't think I can eat."

"Yes, you can." Adele sat up on the bed and typed out a quick text. Within a few minutes, there was a knock on the door. "Relax," Adele said when Lina's body stiffened. "It's just the ice cream."

Seconds later Adele was returning to the bed with a half-gallon of cookie dough ice cream and two spoons. "Courtesy of the asshole."

"What?" Lina asked. Then Adele showed her the cell phone and the text she had sent to Phil. *You fucking asshole. Leave some ice cream outside the door and then go fuck yourself.*

Lina laughed through her tears. "I love you."

"I know." She handed Lina a spoon. "Now eat."

"What am I going to do?" Lina asked. They were stretched out, side by side in bed after finishing almost all the ice cream. "How am I going to get through this?"

"Rayburn women are survivors," Adele said. "It's our special talent—surviving." It was true. Alice had been left with three daughters under the age of ten, and she'd survived. Adele had survived two divorces and still maintained her upbeat attitude.

"Maybe I should tell him to leave." Just saying the words aloud brought on a feeling of panic.

"Do you want him to leave?"

"No," Lina admitted. "But I wish I did. I wish I didn't love him. This wouldn't hurt as bad."

"Do you know what you need to do?" Adele sat up. "You need to have an affair. Let the bastard see how it feels."

— —

"It could have been about anything," Megan was saying to Logan when Katie came upstairs. They were in the upstairs family room, sitting beside each other on the couch. "Maybe they were fighting about Katie."

"It wasn't about me," Katie snapped at Megan as she joined them. "Maybe they were fighting about you."

"I've never seen Mom so upset," Logan said, looking from Megan to Katie. "She was yelling that she hated him. What if they get a divorce or something?"

"They aren't getting divorced," Megan said. "Adults argue. It's normal. Maybe they normally do it in their bedroom and we just don't hear them."

Katie planned to walk by them and into her room, but when she saw the tears in Logan's eyes, she found herself dropping down into the chair across from him. He was pretty cool for a younger brother, and she felt bad that he was sad. "Grandma said they are like soulmates, and they have to be together, so I think that means they'll never get divorced."

"How could she possibly know that?" Megan asked.

"Through her astrology stuff."

"Mom and Dad don't believe in that," Megan said.

"It doesn't mean it isn't true," Katie said.

Logan wiped his eyes, and Katie tried but failed to think of something to say to make him feel better.

"They've been together since they were teenagers. They'd never get divorced," Megan said as she rubbed Logan's back.

"Then why did she say she hated him?"

"I've told Mom I hated her before, and I don't really mean it," Katie said. "I mean, at the time I do, but the next day I don't."

"That means you don't really hate Megan either," Logan said, smiling through his tears.

"No, I really hate her," Katie said as she met Megan's eyes and then, for the first time in as long as she could remember, they shared a smile, and then all three of them were laughing.

— —

"Lina? Lina, wake up." Phil's voice broke into her slumber, and she opened her eyes. "We should go upstairs before the kids wake up."

Lina focused on him first and then looked around the basement guest room. "Why am I here?" Her last memory was falling asleep in their bedroom.

"You came down at about two and crawled into bed." He was stretched out beside her, propped on his elbow as he looked down at her.

"I don't understand," she began and then she did. She'd been looking for him. Even though he had completely devastated her, she'd been unable to sleep without him. "I'm pathetic," she whispered, closing her eyes.

"No, you're not." He pushed her hair back from her face. "You love me." He pressed his lips against her forehead. "That's why you came to me."

"I don't know how not to love you."

"That's because it would be unnatural." He kissed her softly on the lips. "We belong together."

"Don't."

"I'm sorry. I'm so sorry." He pulled her into his chest and wrapped his arms around her, holding her as she cried. "I know I don't deserve you, but I swear I'm going to make this up to you."

11

"He's ready for you." Katie flopped down beside Lina in Dr. Drayton's waiting room Friday afternoon before pulling out a copy of *Siddhartha* by Herman Hesse from her bag.

"Your hair's gone," Lina said as soon as she stepped into Dr. Drayton's office.

He swiped his hand over the top of his head, barely ruffling the short hair as he came around his desk. "My girlfriend assured me she could trim it." He smiled. "It didn't go as planned, so a professional salvaged what he could."

Lina wasn't sure why, but the mention of a girlfriend surprised her. "It looks good. It was just a bit of a shock." Without his hair as a distraction, the attractiveness of his face was more pronounced.

"I prefer it longer, but there wasn't much I could do." He stopped before her, and she caught the faint smell of lavender from his aftershave. "Shall we?" He tossed his hand towards the seating area.

"I want to thank you again for Sunday," she said after they were seated. "It was one of the worst days of my life. I don't know what I would have done without you."

"I'm glad I could help." His eyes traveled over her face. "Are you sleeping at all?"

She knew she looked terrible, but having him confirm it made her feel that much worse. "That bad, huh?" She felt a lone tear leak out and wiped it from beneath her eye.

"No, your eyes just aren't as bright as normal." He held out a box of tissues.

"Thank you. I slept more last night. Every night seems a little better." She dabbed at her eyes with the tissue. "The first few nights, the uncertainty brought on these dreams that I've had since I was a teenager when I'm apart from Phil. I think I was trying to convince myself I didn't need him—that I could live without him. And that made me feel unsafe."

"You don't believe you could live without him?"

"I don't want to," she admitted. "I kicked him out of my room and lasted all of three hours. I realized that by trying to punish him, I was also punishing myself. It hurts enough as it is. I don't want to add to it by pretending I can live without him."

He shifted in his chair and crossed one leg over the other. "You could live without him."

"No." She shook her head. "I couldn't. I mean, if something happened to him and I was forced to, yes, but knowing he was out there with a separate life, living apart from me, no."

He looked like he wanted to say more, but instead he was opening the folder in his lap. "Let's talk about Katie."

"What did I say? Why are you suddenly annoyed at me?"

"I'm not annoyed at you." He met her eyes. "My specialty is adolescents, so I am the wrong person to be counseling you, but dependency of any type—and that's what you're describing to me when you talk about your husband—is unhealthy. Two independent adults coming together—that's the foundation for a healthy relationship."

"You don't understand."

"I think I do, but I'm Katie's psychiatrist. I need to keep these sessions focused on Katie. If you would like the name of—"

"No!" Her face heated. "I don't want a counselor. I'm sorry. This is my fault. I started to think of you as a friend. Let's talk about Katie."

"It's not your fault. It's mine. I'm the professional. I let us take a slight detour, and now we'll get things back on track, okay?" He raised his eyebrows.

She hated the coolness he was suddenly projecting but knew he was right. She was starting to treat him like her therapist. "Yes."

"We are at the point in Katie's therapy where I believe it would be beneficial for me to meet with her father."

"Why?" Her mind was swimming. If Phil found out he knew about the—

"Lina." He waited until she looked at him before continuing. "I need to talk to him about Katie, nothing more."

Even with Dr. Drayton's assurances they would only discuss Katie, Lina still felt nervous as she awaited Phil's return from his appointment the following Wednesday evening.

Two and a half hours after his scheduled appointment, the sound of the garage door opening signaled Phil's arrival.

"You didn't really meet with him for two hours, did you?" Lina asked.

"Yes, I really did." He set his briefcase on the floor beside the kitchen island before meeting her lips for a brief kiss.

"Your dinner is ready. Do you want to eat in the kitchen or outside?"

"Outside." He pulled a beer from the refrigerator. "I don't want the kids overhearing us."

"Are you going to tell me how it went?" Lina asked as she watched Phil dig into the shrimp scampi on his plate.

"It was—" he hesitated with his fork at his lips "—interesting. Interesting and enlightening." He put a shrimp in his mouth, watching her while he chewed.

"Did you like him?" She was confused by his response. He seemed almost amused.

"You mean Nicholas?"

"Nicholas? Did he tell you to call him that?"

"No, but I thought he may have told you to."

"No. I call him Dr. Drayton." She watched him continue to eat. "Are you going to tell me what you think of him?"

He tore off a piece of garlic bread and hesitated with it in front of his mouth. "I think Dr. Drayton has a very unprofessional interest in one of his patients' mothers," he said before tossing the bread in his mouth.

"That's not even funny." She could feel her cheeks heat up.

"I agree it's not funny. The man has completely fallen for you. His entire demeanor changed when he talked about you. And he talked about you *a lot*."

Lina laughed aloud. "That's the craziest thing you've ever said." She could feel herself begin to perspire. "Didn't you talk to him about Katie?"

"Yes. That was fine with the exception of the part where I'm a hundred percent to blame for all her problems."

"That's not true, Phil. He's been giving me parenting advice for months. We're both a part of this. Is that what's wrong with you? You think he thinks I'm a better parent than you?"

"No. I know he thinks you're a better parent than I am, but frankly I don't have a problem with that." He trailed his index finger through the condensation on the outside of his beer bottle, his eyes watching the movement. "What I do have a problem with is my daughter's psychiatrist lusting after my wife, especially when he sees her once a week." He lifted his eyes to hers. "That, I have a problem with."

"He isn't lusting after me. He has a girlfriend."

"Does he?" He lifted his eyebrows. "And how would you know that?"

Lina's blush deepened, and she was thankful for the dim lighting on the deck. "He just mentioned her in passing."

"I bet he did. Has he asked you about us?"

She forced herself to maintain his gaze. "Our relationship impacts Katie."

"I'll take that as a yes."

"You are blowing things way out of proportion."

"He asked me if I considered us happily married, if I was satisfied with our relationship."

"And?"

"And what?"

"What did you say?"

"What did *you* say when he asked you?"

"He didn't ask me," Lina bit out. "How did you respond, Phil?"

"I told him you were taken. I told him we had been *satisfying* each other for over twenty-five years and that wasn't going to change."

Lina closed her eyes, knowing Phil had meant sexually and having no doubt it was conveyed that way to Dr. Drayton. "You're serious, aren't you?"

"Yes."

"Oh my God. Why would you say that to him?"

"Because it's true. And I wanted him to know in no uncertain terms that you were mine."

"I can't believe you. That man brought Katie back to us."

"And what? He plans to take you as payment?" Phil was leaned back in his chair, the ankle of his right leg propped on the thigh of his left, his beer dangling from one hand. "I have spent my career reading people. My comment was not out of line. He is out of line."

"Is that how your session ended, with that remark?"

"No, he assured me that his interest in our relationship was purely professional. I told him he was full of shit. And then I reminded him I'm a lawyer. Do you want to know what the son of a bitch said? He said you weren't his patient."

"What does that have to do with anything?"

"He was implying that lusting after you is okay."

"And then you left?"

"I told him to fuck himself first."

12

"Does he?" Adele asked.

"Does he what?" Lina was sitting beside Adele at their pedicure appointment and had just finished telling her about Phil's appointment with Dr. Drayton the evening before.

"Does he have a thing for you?" Adele's eyes grew wider when Lina blushed. "Oh my God! How come you didn't tell me?"

"There's nothing to tell," Lina insisted, but she could feel her blush deepen.

"You talk about him constantly, but you never thought to mention he has the hots for you?"

"Don't be Phil," Lina said. "He's Katie's psychiatrist. That's it."

"I won't be Phil if you don't treat me like Phil. Your face is bright red. Tell me what's going on."

"It doesn't matter. Phil is taking Katie to her appointments from here on out. I'll probably never see him again." Lina looked away from Adele's prying eyes.

"Wait. What's going on? You're actually upset, aren't you?"

"Of course I'm upset. I've been talking to him every week for months, and suddenly it's done. I'm sad."

Adele's eyes narrowed. "You have feelings for him?"

"Not like you mean," Lina insisted. "I liked talking to him, and now I can't."

"Phil's suspicions aren't unfounded, are they?"

"I don't know. I think he may be attracted to me, but he's never said anything inappropriate. He seems to generally care."

"You should fuck him," Adele said.

"Adele!" Lina looked around, but besides the Vietnamese women working on their feet, there was no one in the shop. "Are you out of your mind?"

"No, I'm totally serious. You said he was good-looking."

"That doesn't mean I want to have sex with him."

— ◆ —

When Lina arrived home, Alice was alone in the Hunter house sautéing spinach. "One of the ladies from yoga was giving it out today, so I took some for you," she said. "I'm cooking it all up so you can freeze it."

"Should I make coffee?"

"Not on my account. I've given up caffeine. I want my body to find its natural circadian rhythm. How are you doing? Have you gotten over the affair?"

"Gotten over it? It's been two weeks!" Her mother never ceased to amaze her. "I doubt I'll ever be over it!"

"I was afraid of this when you told me, but you were so upset, I knew there was no point in saying anything."

"Afraid of what?"

"That you would make this bigger than it is."

"I don't think I could make it bigger than it is."

"Another woman is having his baby, so what? He isn't leaving you. He's still your husband. He's still going to be your children's father. No one's dying."

"You are the only person on earth who would downplay something like this."

"It's only bad if you say it is."

"Well, I say it is," Lina said, crossing her arms over her chest. "And I'm sure ninety-nine percent of the women in this country would agree with me."

"Maybe that's why we have such a high divorce rate—all these ridiculous expectations we hold people to."

"I don't think expecting my husband not to impregnate another woman is a ridiculous expectation," Lina fumed. "I can't believe I'm even arguing with you about this. Your thinking is completely warped."

"Why, because it doesn't line up with yours? Phil is a man, and a very virile man at that. I'm sure women are constantly offering themselves to him. He was bound to give in eventually. And let's face it—monogamy is not natural. Why we hold ourselves to such a ridiculous standard is beyond me."

"Maybe because we're not animals."

"Oh, nonsense." Alice waved her hand forward. "We have so many rules and ideals. You can't breathe without offending someone."

"I happen to agree with some of the rules."

"You were always so conservative," Alice said. "When you played with Barbies, you were the one who always had to make sure Ken and Barbie were married before you would take their clothes off. You must have got that from your father."

"How you can still bring that man up after all these years is beyond me. He abandoned us!"

"He didn't abandon us. He moved to Chicago."

"Without us. He left you with three young children. He barely saw us."

"He supported us, and he's still your father. Do you believe that's just chance? He's part of who you are. His DNA runs through your veins. He just wasn't cut out for the whole family thing. He's a brilliant man, your father. He was offered a tenured teaching position before he was thirty.'

"Can we change the subject? Logan's going to be home soon."

"You and Phil have chosen this path. Don't forget that. What's going on right now is an opportunity for the two of you to really grow as a couple."

"Got it," Lina said.

"I'm just saying if the two of you don't learn the lesson in this lifetime, you'll just come back in the next and do it all again."

— —

Lina slipped on a short, black silk nightgown before getting into bed. They hadn't made love since the day Phil told her about the affair a little over two weeks earlier. There were only five times in their twenty-five-year relationship when they'd gone longer—during the time when he'd been having the affair, after the birth of each of their children and a nine-month period when she was seventeen. She remembered how patient he'd been all those years ago. How he'd held her in his arms, whispering reassurances in her ear, never pressuring her even though his young body, so used to having regular sex, must have been screaming out for it. She knew now, like then, he was waiting for her to tell him she was ready, and he would wait as long as it took.

It was after midnight before he came into their bedroom. Lina was lying in bed reading a novel, the soft glow from her bedside lamp the only source of light in the room. "I was wondering if you were ever coming up. I was about to come looking for you."

He crossed to the bed, the mattress shifting as he sat down beside her. "Is this new?" he asked, fingering the slim strap of her nightgown.

"Yes." She breathed in as he brushed the back of his hand over the top of her breasts.

"You're beautiful," he whispered, lowering his head, his lips following the same path as his hand.

"I miss you." She combed her fingers through his thick hair.

He released a deep breath. "I missed you too."

13

"So now you want me to stop paying taxes?" Phil was asking Katie after their appointment with Dr. Drayton when Lina and Logan joined them at an Italian restaurant.

It had been a little over a month since Phil had begun taking Katie to her weekly appointments, and although Lina was still miffed she wasn't permitted to go and missed speaking to Dr. Drayton more than she wanted to admit, she couldn't deny the improvement the change seemed to bring to Phil and Katie's relationship. Just the time spent in the car traveling to and from the appointments was forcing them to interact more and, as a result, Katie seemed to be loosening up around her father.

Phil stood and met Lina's lips before pulling out her chair. "I ordered Chardonnay for you," he said, nodding towards a glass of wine on the table.

"You said you don't agree with everything our government does," Katie said to Phil, continuing their conversation. "By paying taxes you're condoning it."

"What do you think happens when you don't pay taxes?"

"Thoreau didn't pay taxes. He went to jail because he refused."

"She just finished reading *Civil Disobedience*," Phil told Lina before returning his attention to Katie. "Thoreau didn't have a family to support. He could afford to go to jail. And if I recall correctly, he was only there for one night before one of his relatives *paid* his taxes for him. Do you realize our taxes pay for the infrastructure in this country? If everyone thought like Thoreau, we would probably still be living like it was the 1800s."

"That could be cool," Logan said. "We could shoot our own food."

"And people weren't so materialistic," Katie said.

"Ah, the dreaded materialism again," Phil said, his eyes moving between his children. "The two of you could practice not being materialistic if you're concerned."

"I'm not concerned," Logan said. "That's all Katie."

"That smartphone you're hiding under the table," Phil began as he turned back to Katie. "Do you really believe it's necessary? What do you think Thoreau would think of a cell phone that was probably assembled by someone in China who makes so little money he has to work eighty hours a week just to afford to live? Owning that phone," he said, pausing as he tapped the table in front of her, "is saying you approve of those conditions."

"I didn't pay for it," Katie said, lifting her chin. "You did."

"He's lowered her Prozac again," Phil told Lina as they prepared for bed later that evening. "He's also switching her appointments to bi-weekly."

"Bi-weekly? Is she ready?"

"She's probably been ready for weeks. You were the lure for weekly meetings."

"That's not true."

"Isn't it? Why hasn't he ever asked to meet with me after Katie's session? He used to meet with you, didn't he, by yourself?"

"He had things to tell me."

"Like the fact he's lowering her meds or changing her appointment schedule? He gave Katie a note to pass to me. Not once in the four times I've sat in that waiting room have I heard him call back a parent. He was using Katie as an excuse to be close to you."

"Will you please let it go?" As the words left her mouth, Lina tried without success to recall whether she witnessed Dr. Drayton call another parent back to his office.

— ◆ —

The following Saturday, Lina drove Logan to a sports complex in Baltimore where he'd been invited to try out for an All-Star lacrosse team that would be comprised of the best high school–aged players in the state.

"Just let me out here," Logan said. "I'm going to be late, and I still need to check in."

"Relax, you have fifteen minutes." She touched his arm. "You'll do great."

"Bye." He let himself out of the car.

Lina watched him cross towards the field and felt a tug at her heart. She couldn't remember ever seeing him so nervous. He really seemed to want to make this team. She hoped it was for himself and not his father.

After locating a parking spot, she went back to the fields. It took a full five minutes to locate Logan, but when she did, he seemed fine as he tossed a lacrosse ball back and forth with a boy she recognized from his club team.

She greeted the few parents she recognized and was beginning to walk away from the fields when she noticed Dr. Drayton less than twenty yards away, speaking to another father. It had been over a month and a half since their last meeting, and although Lina had no idea whether he'd even be happy to see her after Phil's words, she couldn't look away. She felt like she was seeing a long-lost friend.

As if he felt her stare, he turned his head. His eyes were concealed beneath aviator sunglasses, and his face showed no reaction, but for an instant his entire body stilled, and she knew he was as affected by her unexpected presence as she was by his. She stood rooted in her spot while he wrapped up his conversation. As he walked towards her, she noticed how graceful he was—not feminine, but lithe like a panther. His strength was subtle, his muscles lean beneath his black T-shirt and faded denim jeans, but there was no mistaking his power.

As if by an unspoken agreement, they slowly walked away from the other parents. "Are you on your own?" he asked as they stopped under a large oak tree.

"Yes. Your son is trying out?"

"Yes. How've you been? It looks like you're sleeping."

"I am." She wanted to apologize for Phil's accusations but didn't know how without highlighting the fact that her husband had accused him of having inappropriate feelings for her.

"Lina, I wanted to apologize for how harsh I was to you the last time you brought Katie in. You were upset, and I wasn't sensitive."

"No. You were right. I got confused. It became about me and not Katie."

"No. I questioned you. I wanted to know how you were coping, and my reactions to some of your responses were unprofessional. It hasn't sit well with me for weeks. Please," he said as he inclined his head. "Accept my apology."

She smiled. "Okay."

He glanced down at his watch. "We have a little over two hours. I was planning to go to lunch. Would you join me?"

"Oh." His invitation surprised her, and she looked down at her compression shorts and tank top. "I was going to run. I don't know if this is restaurant appropriate."

"It is for the place I have in mind. It's right down the street. Outside patio and excellent margaritas."

Lina hesitated, her gaze shifting to the fields, knowing she should politely decline. She was too aware of him, and if Phil found out she even considered having lunch with him, he'd be upset. But she'd missed him, and she didn't want to say no. "Are you sure?" She wasn't referring to her clothes, and she decided he was perceptive enough to realize it.

He inclined his head. "Yes."

Less than fifteen minutes later, they were seated across from each other at a black, wrought iron table with two margaritas, a basket of tortilla chips, salsa and guacamole dip between them. After the decision to join him was made, all Lina's reservations left her, and they had once again fallen into the easy rapport she'd experienced with him from their first meeting.

"I recommend the fajitas." Dr. Drayton was leaned back in his chair, watching her as she looked over the menu.

"The food smells delicious, but I had a late breakfast. I think I'll stick to the chips."

"You'll have to try mine," he said after the waiter left with his order. "They're the best in the city."

"Do you live close by?" He'd taken off his sunglasses, and she was again struck by the brilliance of his eyes in the sunlight.

"I do. Less than a mile away. I assume your son is a serious lacrosse player?"

"I don't think he has much of a choice. Phil won the Tewaaraton Award two years in a row at Maryland."

"No kidding. I had no idea he played Division I lacrosse."

"It was all a bit wasted on me. I'm not a big sports person."

"No?"

"I still don't understand the rules," she admitted. "And I don't like watching. I was always worried Phil was going to hurt someone, and now I worry someone that plays like Phil is going to hurt Logan. It's just too physical."

"I take it Logan isn't a physical player?"

"To Phil's great disappointment, no, not naturally. Phil thinks he can learn to be, but I'm not sure it's something that can be taught. It was innate in Phil to be that aggressive. Logan takes after me, I'm afraid, and he puts so much pressure on himself—trying to measure up. That's why I'm here with him today. He didn't want his father watching."

"I can imagine those would be very large shoes to fill. My son has no such worries. I was never a competitive athlete. I was more of a nerd in high school."

"You weren't a nerd. You may not have been an athlete, but you were definitely not a nerd."

The corners of his lips turned up. "How could you possibly know that?"

"There is nothing nerdish about you."

He ran his arm along the top of the chair next to his, his eyes continuing to meet hers. "I'm not a nerd now."

No, he definitely wasn't a nerd. And as she looked into his eyes, she became very aware that he was much more than a doctor. Nicholas Drayton was most definitely a man.

She lifted her drink and took a swallow, trying to calm her beating heart. "What about your son? Is he a nerd or...?"

"Hardly." He laughed. "He's probably the type of player you don't want your son to play against. His life revolves around lacrosse. It's all a bit wasted on me too. I'm not a fan of competitive sports. I find them pointless. As Rumi said in the thirteenth century, 'Take someone who doesn't keep score, who's not looking to be richer, or afraid of losing. That man is free.' I'm paraphrasing a bit."

"Rumi?" Lina smiled. "I haven't thought of him in years. I used to read his poetry in high school. I loved him."

"Why did you stop?"

"I don't know. Life, I suppose. Different interests." *Phil*, she thought but didn't voice aloud.

"You should pick him up again."

"You're the reason Katie is suddenly reading poetry and philosophy?"

"No. Katie was interested in philosophy before she stepped in my office."

"I had no idea." Lina hated how little she knew of her own daughter.

"Katie's quite introspective for someone so young, the complete opposite of my son, who is only interested in sports and girls, in that order. Oh, and food. He consumes more food in a day than I do in a week."

Lina smiled. "The food part is definitely Logan. He never stops eating." She took another sip from her drink. "If you don't like competition, why do you let your son play?"

"Let him? You should know my parenting philosophy by now. He walks to the beat of his own drum. My role is to guide him, not direct him. He loves the competition. I try not to judge."

"My mother would love you."

"Most mothers do." He winked, and her heart jumped. "Tell me about her. Katie seems quite fond of her."

"No." Lina shook her head from side to side. "You know enough about me. I want to know about you."

"That's not how it works. I'm the doctor, remember?" He finished his own drink and then motioned to a passing waiter for two more.

"You're not *my* doctor," Lina reminded him. "And this certainly doesn't look like your office."

"True, but I am your daughter's doctor."

"We're drinking margaritas and sharing guacamole dip. Right now we're parents of boys trying out for a lacrosse team."

He leaned back in his chair, his hands resting on the table. "In that case, you're going to need to call me Nick."

"Nick," she repeated, and as she met his eyes, a wave of attraction passed between them.

She averted her gaze as the waiter arrived with new drinks and Nick's fajitas. While she took a couple of sips of her margarita and tried to calm her nerves, he proceeded to pile some shrimp, sautéed vegetables, onions, cheese and a dab of sour cream onto a soft tortilla. He placed the plate in front of her. "Tell me that isn't the best fajita you've ever had."

"Thank you." She shifted her legs, and her knee bumped his under the table. She pulled her leg back, her body tingling with awareness.

"What would you like to know about me?" He began to build his own fajita.

"I don't know. A little of everything, I suppose."

She learned that on paper, he was similar to Phil: the younger of two boys, the son of a surgeon, raised in a conservative Catholic home. But whereas Phil embraced his parents' belief system, Nick rejected his. "There's a reason I understand Katie so well," he said. "My mother used to say she thought she was a good parent until I came along. I thought my parents were ignorant and stopped communicating with them, refused to go to church, family vacations. It was hard for them. They didn't know what to make of me. All I wanted to do was read philosophy and sail."

"It doesn't really surprise me," Lina said. "There's something untamed about you."

"Untamed?" He looked amused.

"That's probably not the right word, but when I met you, I knew you didn't fit into a mold. You were different."

He looked down into his drink for a moment and then was lifting his gaze back to hers. "Funny, I thought the same thing about you."

14

Lina knew by the smile on Logan's face as he slipped into the car the tryout had gone well. "So?"

"It was good! I need to call Dad."

She listened as he excitedly told Phil how well he thought he had done. "I was brought on to the top field halfway through the tryout, and I stayed there the rest of the time. I scored six times...No, I played middie mostly...Yeah, I scored a lot, and I wasn't playing forward. Oh, and I met a few guys who will be going to Gilman in the fall. One was that kid we saw at the tournament last month...The one with the blond hair that scored half his team's goals! No one could stop him. He's awesome, and he's totally cool. We're going to get together before school starts. His name is Brian Drayton."

"You saw him, didn't you?" Phil asked later that evening after joining Lina on the back deck.

"Yes." She'd expected the question earlier, but when they'd returned home from the tryout, Logan had been so excited he'd spent most of the evening monopolizing Phil's time, not even letting Megan get in a word as he recounted every detail of the tryout.

"Did you talk to him?"

"Yes."

"How long?"

"Hmm?"

"Lina? What are you feeling so guilty about?"

"I'm not," she lied. She'd been feeling guilty all evening.

"Then why won't you look at me? And why have you been avoiding me all evening?"

She turned her head and met his eyes. "He's Katie's doctor. I'm not going to ignore him."

"Not for much longer, he's not."

"What is that supposed to mean? Because I happen to run into him at a lacrosse field, he's not allowed to be Katie's doctor? That's ridiculous."

"Do you think it's acceptable for Katie to tell him personal details of our life and then have us see him at lacrosse games and school functions?"

Her heart dropped. She hadn't even considered the conflict. "But he's gotten her to open up. Have you seen them interact? She genuinely likes him. That doesn't just happen."

"We don't have a choice. And when he finds out our sons will be going to the same school, he'll be saying the same thing."

— —

The ringing of Phil's cell phone awoke Lina just after 1:00 a.m., and her thoughts immediately went to Kim. "Phil?" She shook his arm. "That's your cell phone."

"It's Shiloh," he said as he squinted at the display. "Shi? Calm down...I can't understand you...Shi, you need to calm down."

Lina sat up and turned on the light, anxiety gripping her. "Is she okay?"

Phil held up a silencing hand as he continued to focus on the phone call. "Look around. There has to be a landmark...Yes... Do you see an address?" He was sitting up and reaching into the bedside stand for a notepad and pen. "Good." He began to write. "Sit tight. I'll be there in fifteen minutes."

"What happened?" Lina asked as he got out of bed.

"Julian left her at a party."

"Oh my God. Is she okay?"

"I think so. She's just very upset."

"I'll come with you."

"No. Stay in bed. One of the kids could wake up."

Lina opened the front door as Shiloh and Phil stepped onto the front porch, her stomach clenching at the pitiful sight of her sister sobbing against Phil's side. "Oh, Shi," Lina whispered, her own voice cracking.

"She's okay," Phil said as they came into the house. "Just upset."

"Come on, Shi." Lina tried to pull her from Phil, but Shiloh wouldn't release her hold on him.

"He was so mean," she whispered. "He said I was stupid in front of everyone at the party and then he just left. I was so embarrassed. Why would he do that? Why does he always hurt me?"

"I don't know." Phil ran his hand up and down her back in a soothing motion. "But you're okay now."

"I'm never going back to him. I know you don't believe me, but I'm not."

"It's late. No decisions have to be made right now. Just get some sleep. You can decide what you want to do in the morning," Phil said.

"I don't want to sleep alone," Shiloh whispered. "I don't want to be alone."

"You can sleep with me," Lina said as she slipped her arm around her. "Don't worry. Everything will be okay."

"Maybe we should help her find a place," Lina said to Phil the next afternoon when he came home from cycling.

"No."

"I think she's serious," Lina went on. "She's calm and—"

"Let's not push her into anything," Phil said. "We have to let her come to the conclusion on her own." He looked past her to Shiloh, who came into to the kitchen from the family room wearing a pair of Lina's shorts and a T-shirt, her face makeup free and her hair pulled back in a ponytail. "How are you feeling, Shi?"

She shrugged. "Sad."

"You can stay here as long as you like. You know that."

She offered a pitiful attempt at a smile. "Thanks."

He touched Lina's arm. "I'm going to shower."

"Do you want something to eat?" Lina asked Shiloh. "I could make you a sandwich or a salad."

"I'm not really hungry." Shiloh looked down at her phone. "He hasn't even called."

"What if by not telling her to leave him, she thinks we want her to stay and goes back to him?" Lina asked.

Phil had finished his shower and was getting dressed. "That's not why she'll go back to him."

"You think she's going to go back to him? He left her at a party to fend for herself."

"I hope she doesn't."

"But you think she will." Lina glared at him. "Why would you think that?"

He sighed. "Because that's what she does. I know it's not what you want to hear, but—"

"You don't know that. Just because she has in the past doesn't mean she will this time. He left her in front of all his friends. Do you know how humiliating that was? What if—"

"Hey," he interrupted, taking her hands in his. "I'm not the enemy. I'm being honest. Don't take this out on me."

"I'm not," Lina said, stepping back from him and pulling her hands free, "but you shouldn't act like you know."

A hard knock on the door preceded Logan's voice. "Dad?"

"Come in."

"Julian's here," Logan said, his breathing elevated. "Aunt Shiloh doesn't want me to let him in. What should I say to him?"

"I'll take care of it." Phil shrugged into his shirt as he walked past Logan and out the door. "Stay upstairs," he said to Logan, who was on his heels. "And tell your sisters the same. This has nothing to do with you."

"I just want to go to the pool."

"Your room, Logan. And don't argue with me," Phil said shortly.

Moments later he was pulling the front door open. "What?"

Julian took a step back as he pushed his hands into the pockets of his jeans, clearly intimidated by the anger emanating from the six-foot-three man before him. "Is Shiloh in there?"

Phil stepped out onto the porch, turning back when Lina began to follow him. "Stay inside," he said, his face stern.

"What are—"

"Lina," he warned.

"Okay." She went back into the house, but left the door partially open and felt Shiloh come up behind her.

"Get off my property," Phil said after turning back to Julian.

"I don't have an issue with you," Julian said, shuffling backwards a few more paces. "I just want to know if my wife is in there."

"When you leave your wife on her own in the middle of the night, you lose the right to ask about her."

"With all due respect, this isn't your business, Phil. I just want to talk to Shiloh."

"When she called me at one a.m. it became my business. Now get off my property. I'm not telling you again."

"Wait!" Shiloh cried.

"Shi, don't." Lina gripped her hand when she began to push past her. "He doesn't deserve you."

"I'm just going to talk to him." Shiloh freed herself from Lina and flew out the door.

"Shiloh," Lina called out, watching helplessly as her sister went to Julian.

"Come on." Phil slipped his arm around Lina's shoulders.

Lina covered her eyes as he led her through the foyer. "She's going back with him, isn't she?"

"I'm sorry." He wrapped his arms around her.

— ⁓

When Katie came out of her bathroom, Megan and Logan were huddled in front of one of her windows. "What are you doing in my room?"

"Julian's here. I thought Dad was going to beat him up," Logan said.

Katie crossed to the window to see her aunt and uncle standing beside Julian's Jeep. "I wish he would."

"She's crying," Megan said. "Dad picked her up in the middle of the night. They must have had a fight or something."

"He left her at some party," Katie said. "I heard them talking. He's such a dick."

"Gross." Logan groaned, pulling his eyes from the window when they started to kiss.

"What does she see in him?" Megan asked. "It's not like he's rich or something, and he's ugly."

"So it would be okay if he was rich and good-looking?" Katie asked.

"No! I'm just saying he doesn't have any redeeming qualities."

"The way you look is just luck, and I don't think being rich is a redeeming quality. That's shallow."

"Then ninety-nine percent of the population is shallow," Megan said.

"If a guy treated either of you like that, I'd beat him up," Logan said.

"You wouldn't have to," Katie said as she turned from the window, unable to stomach another second of their public display of affection. "I'd beat him up myself."

Logan laughed. "You couldn't even beat up a fourth grader."

"Ha. Ha," Katie said dryly. "Just because everyone else in this family is freakishly tall doesn't mean there's something wrong with me. I'm stronger than I look. I could probably beat you up."

"You think?" Logan asked.

"Don't." Katie gave him her most stern expression as he approached. "Logan, I'm serious," she said, but it was too late.

"You're like a baby doll," he announced right before he pounced on her.

"Logan, stop!" Katie cried, trying to sound serious, but unable to keep from laughing as he lifted her in the air. "Logan!" She pounded his back with her fists as he hoisted her over his shoulder, carrying her around her room like a sack of rice.

"Say 'Logan is king', and I'll put you down."

"Logan's the king of dicks!" she yelled. "Stop!" she cried when he began to tickle her.

The door slammed open, and their parents rushed in the room. "What in the hell—" Phil stopped midsentence as his eyes took in the scene. "Put her down."

"Not until she calls me king," Logan said.

"Logan," Phil warned as he reached for Katie. "You could drop her or knock her into something." He effortlessly lifted Katie off Logan's shoulder and set her on her feet.

"I could have gotten away," Katie insisted, looking up at her dad.

"Yeah, I could see that," Phil said dryly.

15

s soon as Lina emerged from her car after attending an evening yoga class, she heard the low timbre of Phil's voice coming from somewhere in the back yard. She frowned as she left the garage and made her way around the side of the yard. He was on the back patio near the pool, and as she approached, she knew Kim was on the other end of the call. There was no other reason he would have traveled all the way to the back patio.

"Calm down," he was saying when she came close enough to hear. "Calm down...I'm sorry. I really am, but there is an easy solution to this...Kim—Kim, listen to me...I understand, but the reality is I already have a family. I have a wife and three kids. They are my priority...No—no. Did I ever tell you I was going to leave my wife? That's not true...No, it doesn't. It doesn't change anything."

Lina leaned back against the house, out of sight of Phil, continuing to listen to one side of the conversation. "You're

on your own if you go forward with this. That's what I'm trying to tell you...Think about the child, Kim. Do you really
want to bring a child into this world that isn't going to have
a father?" There was a long pause before he spoke again. "I
will meet my legal responsibilities and nothing more. Nothing
more! Jesus Christ, why are you being so obstinate? It's not
too late to undo this. If you love me, why are you trying to destroy my life? What? Jesus Christ! I thought you got pregnant
in May...Unbelievable...How could you not have known? This
isn't about Lina...If she left me tomorrow—which she isn't going to do, by the way—I wouldn't marry you. I will never marry
you. Never!"

Lina walked slowly back to the house, pondering the fact her
husband was on their patio talking to a woman who was pregnant
with his child.

"How often do you talk to her?" Lina asked when Phil entered
the bedroom an hour later.

If he was surprised Lina knew about the phone call, his facial
expression didn't reveal it. "More than I'd like, but not often."

"What did she want? I mean besides you?" Lina roughly
tugged back the comforter. "And why is she calling you in the
evening when she knows you're with your family? One of the kids
could have overheard you."

He dragged his hand down the lower part of his face. "She's
going to be at the wedding."

"The wedding?" They were attending the wedding of one of
his associates the following weekend.

"You don't have to go."

"Not go? You expect me to let you go without me?"

He sighed. "What do you think I'm going to do, Lina? I'm just trying to protect you. I know you're going to feel uncomfortable, I—"

"Of course I'm going to feel uncomfortable, but you're not going alone. How far along is she?"

"Over five months."

"Five months!" Her gaze swung to him. "That means she got pregnant in the first month you were with her." And it probably meant he knew the sex of the baby, but she couldn't bring herself to ask. She didn't want to know. It would make it all too real.

— ~

"What did he say?" Katie asked as she pulled Emma's phone from her hands. "He's coming?" Her eyes scanned the text Ryan sent Emma. She'd told Emma to invite Ryan and the band to come to her house for a swim after they finished practice. "Wait, Ryan says he's coming. How do we know Matt's coming?"

"He'll come," Emma said. "Mondays are his day off."

Katie hoped Emma was right. She thought of the Bible in the freezer in the basement and wondered if the spell would be stronger if he was at her house. It had been a little over a month, and so far nothing had happened. Sure, he'd been nice and she knew he liked her, at least as a friend, and sometimes she could feel him staring at her, but he hadn't made any attempt to see her away from Emma's house, and she knew he was still dating the blonde.

"Wear your black bathing suit," Emma said, referring to her most revealing suit. "You look really hot in it."

— ~

Lina's perception of herself as open-minded was being put to the test as she watched the group in the pool. Well, not exactly the group, but the boy-man Katie seemed glued to all afternoon. When the four males arrived, Lina had made an attempt to go out and meet them, but Katie intercepted her at the door and with just one look made it clear she didn't want her mother anywhere near the party or pool. Lina reluctantly didn't push it, afraid she'd discourage Katie from inviting friends over and further alienate her, but that didn't stop her from spying on them off and on all afternoon from the kitchen window. When had she become so judgmental? As a teenager she wouldn't have thought twice about a boy with tattoos, but here she was thinking poorly of someone simply because he had tattoos on his body.

"What are you looking at?"

Lina jumped and spun around at the sound of Logan's voice. "You scared me," she breathed, her hand on her chest. "How was the camp?" He was attending a half-day lacrosse camp at a local school.

"Good. Who do all the cars belong to?"

"Katie has some friends over. They're at the pool." Lina watched him look out the window.

"I'm going to see if they want to play water volleyball," he said, seemingly unfazed that the group looked different than the kids he normally associated with.

"Who's in our pool?" Megan asked when she arrived home an hour later.

"Katie's friends," Lina said.

"Oh my God!" Megan practically gasped. "Katie's sitting next to a guy with a full-sleeve tattoo! Gross."

"Megan!" Lina frowned at her. "You don't even know him. Don't judge a book by its cover."

"What? I'm not allowed to have an opinion? How does she even know him? He looks older than me."

"I think he's friends with Emma's brother."

"Well, so much for hanging out at the pool," Megan said before crossing to the refrigerator. "I'm not going anywhere near them."

***

"Your brother is fourteen, and he's taller than me," Matt said. "What happened to you?" He was submerged up to his chest in water as he lounged on the underwater steps leading into the pool while Katie stood a couple of feet in front of him. The rest of the group, which now included Logan, was playing water volleyball at the other end of the pool.

Katie looked back at Logan, who was laughing at something Ryan was saying. "I take after my mom's family. He's like my dad."

"What does your dad do?"

"He's a lawyer," Katie said.

"He must be good at it." Matt's gaze traveled around the elaborate stone patio.

Katie shrugged. "I guess." Her father was the last person she wanted to discuss. "He's an asshole."

Matt's eyes returned to Katie. "You shouldn't say that."

"Why not? It's true."

"Does he hit you?"

"Of course not." Katie frowned.

"You said he was an asshole."

"He put me on restriction for six months," she reminded him, feeling defensive. "And now I can barely breathe without his permission."

"At least he gives a fuck about you."

"You don't know that." She didn't want to argue with him, but she didn't want him to believe her father was some saint.

"That's what it sounds like to me."

"You're wrong, he—" She stopped midsentence and began to sputter when he splashed water in her face.

"Just cooling you off, Hunter."

"You asshole." She began to splash him back as she backed away to avoid the onslaught of water, and then he was launching himself at her and grabbing her around the waist as he dunked her backwards into the water.

Katie gripped his shoulders, pulling him under with her and wrapping her legs around his waist so he couldn't get away. *He's all muscle* was her first thought, followed quickly by the realization she was skin to skin with him. When they came up for air, they were both laughing and then he was looking into her eyes, their faces just inches apart, and she never wanted the moment to end. His black eyelashes, glistening with droplets of water, were the thickest she'd ever seen, and, as she returned his gaze, her heart began to beat harder. She felt a burning deep in her stomach she'd never felt before.

Matt's gaze shifted to something behind Katie, and she felt his body stiffen. "I think your dad's coming."

Katie scrambled away from Matt, her eyes swinging past the far side of the pool to the stone path leading up to the driveway, where her father was making his way down towards them. "That's him." Of all the days he chose to come home early, why did it have to be this day?

Her father stopped briefly to greet the group on the far side of the pool before making his way to them. "What are you doing home?" Katie asked as she looked up at her dad, who was standing two feet from them, still wearing his suit pants and dress shirt. He looked bigger and more imposing than usual, due in part to the fact they were standing in a pool three feet below him.

"And you are?" he asked Matt, ignoring Katie's question.

"Matt."

"Do you have a last name, *Matt*?"

"Hudson."

"How old are you?"

"Eighteen," Matt answered, and Katie could tell he was nervous. His face was flushed, and one of his hands was gripping the side of his bathing suit. She stepped closer to him, not wanting him to feel intimidated by her father.

"How do you know my daughter?"

"He's my friend," Katie answered.

"I'm not talking to you." His gaze didn't leave Matt's. "When did you graduate?"

"In May."

"And what are your plans now that you've graduated?"

"It's none of your business!" Katie frowned up at her father. "You didn't drill those guys." She nodded towards the boys on the other side of the pool.

"Well, you weren't wrapped around one of them when I came down here," he said.

Katie blushed. "We were just playing around."

"Oh, is that what that was?"

"Yes."

"Well I like to know who my daughter is *playing around* with. Is that okay?"

"I'm just working on my music," Matt answered his original question. "I'm in a band, and I have a job at a lumberyard."

"No college?"

"No."

"And your parents are okay with that?"

"I'm eighteen," Matt said, pushing his jaw out as he stood to his full five-foot-eleven height. "It's what I decide."

Her father's eyes remained locked with Matt's for a long moment. "Katie's sixteen, so it's what I decide."

"I told you he was an asshole," Katie muttered, watching her father's departing form as he walked towards the house.

Matt shrugged. "I probably wouldn't have liked me either, if I was him."

Katie lifted her eyes, but Matt had already turned and was getting out of the pool. "Hey, I'm out of here," he called out to the rest of the group.

"Matt, wait!" Katie caught up to him as he stopped beside a chair and began to gather his clothes. "Where are you going?" She didn't want him to leave.

"Why? You going to come with me?" He smiled as he looked up at her house. "I don't think Daddy's going to let that happen."

At that moment she hated her dad. "Are you going to be at Emma's tomorrow?"

"No. I'll see you around, Hunter."

—◆—

Lina looked up as Phil entered the kitchen from the deck. "I didn't hear your car. What are you doing home so early?"

"Megan texted me about Katie's party. How long has it been going on?" He gestured with his thumb back over his shoulder towards the pool.

"She texted you?" Lina frowned. "Why would she text you?"

"Probably because she knew you wouldn't. She sent me this picture."

Lina looked down at the picture of Katie and the boy with the tattoo standing within inches of each other, his tattooed arm on full display. "I can't believe she took that, or sent it to you for that matter."

"You don't think I have a right to know?"

"A right to know what? She invited some friends over. It all happened today. I would have told you when you got home."

"Did you see that boy? I don't want to see him around here again. In fact, I don't want Katie around him at all." He took a beer from the refrigerator.

"Why? Because he has tattoos? He's probably nice."

"He probably does drugs," Phil said. "And he's already out of school with no plans to go to college. He's the last type of influence she needs."

Lina looked out the window. "What did you do?" She searched the group for the boy with the tattoos, but he seemed to be gone, and Katie was sitting on a chair with her arms wrapped around her knees and her head down.

"I didn't do anything." He took a long drag from his beer. "They were all over each other when I walked up, though."

"You met him?"

"Of course I met him. He's in my backyard." He frowned. "You didn't meet him? Jesus, Lina, they've been here all day and you never bothered to meet them?"

"She's never here, Phil. I thought if I gave them some privacy, she'd start spending more time at home instead of going to Emma's all the time. You probably just guaranteed that won't happen."

"Are you talking about the guy with the tattoo?" Megan asked as she came into the kitchen.

"None of your business," Lina said, glaring at her. "And I don't appreciate you going behind my back and sending pictures to your father."

"What? I just sent him a picture."

"You interrupted him at work. Katie's friends are none of your concern."

"I was just worried about her."

"Well then you should have talked to me," Lina said.

"I tried to. You didn't care."

"I didn't care?" Lina spit out. "I cared. I just wasn't concerned. And you—"

"Lina, calm down." Phil stroked his hand down her arm.

"No, I'm not going to calm down. I'm mad. She isn't Katie's parent. She has no right to an opinion."

"Leave us," Phil said, looking past Lina to Megan.

"I didn't do anything wrong," Megan insisted. "I just sent you—"

"You decided I couldn't parent your sister! You—"

"Go. Now!" Phil pointed to the door. As soon as Megan left, he was turning back to Lina. "Don't take this out on her."

"Take what out on her? The fact that she sent you a picture? Who am I supposed to take it out on? It was wrong. And you shouldn't be encouraging her. She's an eighteen-year-old tattletale."

He chuckled. "Lina—"

"It's not funny." She crossed her arms over her chest.

"I'm sorry." His hands drifted down her arms. "You're right. It's none of Megan's business, and I'll talk to her. But first I'd like to talk about him. I don't like him."

"Your basing everything on the way he looked," Lina said and wished she had met him herself. "Darcy certainly never raised any red flags with you." Darcy was a friend of Katie's who had spent hours at their house and, unbeknownst to them, introduced her to drugs.

"I spoke to him. He had an edge to him."

"I just want her to be happy," Lina said. "And she seems happy."

"Yeah, well, I'm thinking about her long-term happiness."

16

After some prodding from Diane, Lina spent much of the next few days primping for the wedding. "I'm going to help you find a dress that highlights that amazing figure of yours, and when you walk in on Phil's arm you'll be the most beautiful woman in the room."

"I'm forty years old. Those days are over."

"Oh, no they're not. You'll even outshine the bride. I've made us an appointment at Andre's spa all day Thursday. You're going to feel like a twenty-five-year-old when he's done with you."

Lina didn't quite feel as young as twenty-five, but after having her hair freshly trimmed and highlighted, a facial, pedicure and manicure, a waxing and a full body massage, she did feel refreshed and more beautiful than she'd felt in a very long time. She was almost looking forward to the wedding.

"See, there's nothing a little spending can't solve," Diane teased as they enjoyed glasses of Chardonnay and waited for their nail polish to dry.

"Oh, I could definitely get used to this. That massage was…" She paused at the sound of her cell phone. "I don't recognize the number. Let me just make sure it isn't about one of the kids. Hello?"

"Lina, it's Nick Drayton."

The room was suddenly too warm. "Oh, hi." It had been five days since their lunch, and she'd thought of him more often than she should have, considering she was married.

"Is this a good time?"

"Um…" She hesitated as she looked at Diane, who was watching her curiously. "Yes, I'm just—yes."

"Were you aware that our boys befriended each other at the tryout and have been communicating all week?" His voice sounded more professional than friendly, which she was thankful for, given the beating of her heart.

"I knew they met, but I had no idea they were talking."

"My son is attending Gilman in the fall."

"I know," she said softly, knowing the significance of what he was saying. He could no longer be Katie's doctor.

"We can talk about the repercussions of that later. I have a patient waiting. I called because Brian wants to invite Logan to my place at the beach for the weekend. We leave tomorrow and return Monday. I wanted to make sure it was okay with you before Brian extended the invitation."

"I'm sure he'd like that." She knew Phil wouldn't, but she'd handle him.

"I should probably mention my girlfriend is coming. We'll be sharing a bedroom. Hopefully that isn't a problem for you. I know some parents are sensitive about these things."

"That's fine." She felt a strange pang in her chest at the thought of him with another woman.

"Great. I'll text about the logistics later, but I'd rather not drive out to your house until I have a chance to talk to Katie next week."

"I understand."

"I'm calling from my cell, so you have my number now. I'll talk to you soon."

"Everything okay?" Diane asked as soon as Lina finished her call.

"Yes, it was Katie's psychiatrist, but he was calling about Logan." She gave her a quick version of the boys meeting at the tryout and then, because she'd had two glasses of wine and her tongue was loose, confessed to having lunch with him.

"I find it strange that this doctor would take a patient's mother out for drinks."

"It wasn't like that." Lina's eyes dropped to her wine glass. "I consider him a friend."

"He can't be your friend. He's Katie's psychiatrist. That's a conflict of interest. I'm sure even having a drink with you is breaking some type of ethical rules. I'm going to have to agree with Phil. He obviously has inappropriate feelings for you."

"So what if he does? Are you forgetting there's a woman out there pregnant with Phil's baby? A little flirting hardly compares."

"Flirting now?" Diane's eyes opened wider. "What are you doing, Lina? Looking to even the score?"

"No! Of course not. I'm just saying that you're being awfully judgmental about something innocent and very forgiving for what Phil did. You're supposed to be *my* friend."

"I am your friend. I'm very upset with Phil, but I've known the two of you for years. You're my favorite couple, and I don't like the look that comes into your eyes when you talk about this doctor."

"What?" Lina blushed. "That isn't true."

"It is. You have a bit of a crush on him." Diane held up her hand. "I've been listening to you talk about him for months. How wonderful he is with Katie. I know it's innocent, but things start innocently."

— ～

"I only have a minute because I need to finish packing," Lina told Alice over the phone the following morning, "but I'm going to need you to drop Logan with one of his friends sometime between two and four today. I'll leave the address on the counter in the kitchen. He's going to the beach for the weekend."

"Oh, that's unfortunate. Your father was looking forward to spending time with him."

"My father?" Lina paused with a pair of Phil's socks in her hand. "What are you talking about?"

"I thought I told you he was coming with me."

"Coming with you?" Lina sat down on the edge of her bed. "Coming with you to my house?"

"Yes. He's visiting for the weekend. He got in last night."

"He's staying with you?" Lina asked incredulously, having a hard time comprehending what she was hearing. "Drew is staying at your house with you?"

"Yes, Lina. We have three children together. I think it's acceptable for him to spend the night."

"Does his wife know he's staying with you?"

"He's divorced. I thought you knew that."

"No, I didn't know that." Lina looked towards the door as Phil entered the room. "Mom, I have to go. We can talk when I get back."

"I thought I'd have a barbeque Sunday night. He'd love to see you and Phil."

"I don't know. I have a lot going on right now."

"Lina, he's your father."

"I'm not getting into this with you right now. I will talk to you when I get back."

"I need to talk to you about a beginner's astrology class Katie is interested in taking."

"Mom, no. You know how we feel about that. I'm going to be late. I'll talk to you when I get back."

"It's something she's very interested in," Alice insisted.

"I'm not sure how that's possible, considering you aren't supposed to be showing her any of that stuff, but I'm not getting into it right now. Phil is home, and I need to finish getting ready. Thanks again for taking care of the kids," Lina said before ending the call.

"You're not ready?" Phil asked. He looked pointedly at her open suitcase as he walked towards his wardrobe. "You said on the phone you were ready."

"I'll be ready before you finish changing," she answered. "That was my mom. My father is going to be staying here with her this weekend. I think they're a couple."

Phil turned back to her. "We don't even know him. I don't want him staying in my house."

"What do you think he's going to do?"

"I have no idea," he said shortly. "You don't have a problem with him being around the kids?"

Lina considered the question. "No. Maybe it will be interesting for them." She turned back to the suitcase on the bed. "He is their grandfather."

"Your mom knows to stay in the guest room, right? I don't want him in this room."

"He's a professor, Phil. Not a thief. But yes, my mom always stays in the guest room."

"The man abandoned his family and isn't fit to step in this house. If he's still here when we get back, I'll tell him that personally."

— ~

The wedding was being held at the Inn at Little Washington in Washington, Virginia, a two-hour drive from Lina and Phil's home in Maryland. Like Wayne and Diane, they decided to go up a day early to enjoy dinner at the Inn's five-star restaurant and hopefully some quality time together away from children, computers and cell phones.

"The two of you seem normal, happy," Diane commented when the men went out onto the balcony to enjoy cigars. They were in Lina and Phil's private cottage where they'd come after dining together in the Main Inn.

"If I don't think about her we are. I'm not sure how I'll be tomorrow. I just can't believe she's coming, knowing I'll be here."

"It's very nervy," Diane agreed. "Just remember that it's over, and he's yours."

"And therein lies the problem," Lina said as she stared into her wine glass. "He is mine, and he was when she decided to sleep with him. I'm not sure if I'm capable of spending an entire evening around her without confronting her."

17

Lina pressed her lips together in an attempt to blend her lipstick as she stepped back from the mirror. She looked about as good as she could, she decided. Her makeup brought out her large eyes and high cheekbones, and her thick, dark hair fell in soft waves around her bare shoulders. She wore a sleeveless gold-and-beige Mandalay dress which hugged her slim figure and accentuated her curves. It was a perfect balance of sexy and sophisticated.

"Is everything okay in there?" Phil's voice preceded the sound of his knuckles tapping the door lightly. "I have a gin and tonic out here for you."

Lina opened the door. "I need you to zip me up."

"Wow," he said, his eyes traveling over her. "You're stunning."

"It cost you two thousand, seven hundred dollars." It was four times more than she had ever spent on a dress, but after seeing her reflection in the dressing room mirror and hearing Diane's urging, she decided to splurge.

"It was worth it," he said.

She took the glass from his hand and took a sip as he zipped her dress. "I want you to point her out to me."

"Lina—"

"I don't want to be caught unaware." She took another swallow from her glass.

"Please don't get drunk."

"You gave me the drink." She felt strangely calm, the nervousness from the prior days gone.

"I realize that, but you're gulping it down." He watched her finish it.

"Thank you." She held out her glass.

"I'm having a hard time gauging your mood. What's going on in your head?"

"Nothing. You look handsome." Lina ran her hand over the lapel of his jacket. In a custom-cut black tux, white shirt and black tie, his looks could rival a movie star's.

"You're making me nervous. Did you take something?" He tilted his head slightly as he looked into her eyes.

"No, I didn't take something. What would I have taken?"

"Promise me you aren't going to seek her out."

She met his eyes. "I promise."

He squeezed her hands. "Lina, I'm a partner. Half the guests probably work for me. You need to behave."

"I promised. And what do you think I'm going to do?"

"I have no idea, but you seem off."

"I'm not off. If anything, I'm on."

"What does that mean?"

"Remember the girl you met all those years ago? The one we lost that night?"

He drew in a breath, squeezing her hands. "We didn't lose her. She's standing right in front of me."

"But we lost part of her—the tough part, the part that was never afraid. Do you remember her?"

"Yes." His voice was hesitant, unsure.

"I don't think she was lost. I think she was just buried."

About two hundred white wooden chairs faced a simple white arbor covered in green ivy with dozens of candles to the left and right. Lina and Phil were seated on the bride's side midway down and towards the center aisle, beside Wayne and Diane. Despite a light breeze, Lina knew the men were warm in their tuxedo jackets. It was a black tie affair, and she let her eyes wander over the guests, amused at how it was acceptable for the men to dress exactly the same, while women were expected to wear unique dresses.

They were surrounded by familiar faces. All Phil's partners and their significant others were in attendance, as well as at least two dozen associates. The bride had come to the firm after graduating from law school five years earlier and was popular among her colleagues.

"She's two rows up and three seats to the right of yours," Phil whispered, not long after they took their seats, his warm breath tickling her ear.

Lina followed his direction, her heart pumping a little harder as she focused on the back of a blonde head. And then the head was turning, and she watched as Kim's eyes zeroed in on Phil. Kim openly stared at him for seconds before her gaze slid to Lina.

Their eyes met and held. Lina unconsciously lifted her chin, not looking away as the other woman blatantly looked her over, and then Kim's eyes returned to Phil momentarily before she turned back around. Lina released her breath. Kim looked sophisticated and cultured in a classic black strapless dress, no evidence yet of her pregnancy, a string of pearls her only jewelry, her shoulder-length hair cut in long layers. She didn't look like the type of woman who would settle for the mistress role. She was beautiful.

"Lina?" Phil whispered, and she realized everyone was standing. She came to her feet and turned to watch the bride and her father making their way down the aisle. She felt the warmth of Phil's palm as he rubbed his hand over the bare skin of her upper back. "I love you," he said against her ear. "Only you."

A cocktail party in an outdoor garden followed the ceremony, and Lina sipped her wine as she searched the gathering for Kim. "Forget about her, Lina," Phil whispered against her ear. "Pretend she isn't here." They were part of a large group, which seemed to consist entirely of the senior members of the firm and their dates.

"Where is she?"

"I have no idea." He kissed her cheek as he stroked his hand down her arm. "And I don't care."

A question directed at Phil moments later had the conversation turning to lacrosse, and Lina used it as an excuse to separate Diane from the group. "Did you see her staring at me during the ceremony? As if I was the one intruding? There is no way I can go this entire evening without saying something to her."

"Let her stare. You're clearly the one he wants. This is the longest he's gone without touching you since the ceremony began, and that's only because his arms aren't long enough. The man can't keep his hands off you. That dress was worth every penny."

Lina's gaze shifted to Phil, who was in the midst of telling a story that had the attention of the group around him. Diane was right. She was the one he wanted, but that didn't make Kim's presence any more palatable. He said something that elicited shouts of laughter from the group around him, and then he was excusing himself and crossing to her and Diane. "Everything okay?" He ran his hand along the small of Lina's back to her hip.

"We're fine," Diane assured him. "Just a little girl talk."

"Do you need the ladies' room?" His eyes were on Lina.

"No."

"Why don't you walk with me?"

"No thanks," Lina said, and when he hesitated, she laid her hand on the lapel of his jacket and leaned into him, brushing her lips over his cheek. "I'll behave. I promise."

He caught her lips in a slow kiss. "I'll be right back." He kissed her again before walking off.

"That was perfect," Diane said.

"What?" Lina didn't take her eyes from Phil, watching him wind his way through the crowd, patting a few backs before exiting the room and disappearing from sight.

"She was watching when he kissed you."

Lina slid her half-eaten plate towards Phil, knowing he would finish the remaining food. The band was surprisingly good, the venue was beautiful, and if it weren't for the presence of his ex-mistress, Lina probably would have been enjoying herself. But with Kim Ryan two tables over, Lina felt a rising anger that seemed to increase with each glass of wine.

"No, thank you." Phil covered Lina's glass when a waiter attempted to pour her more wine.

"What are you doing?" Lina frowned at him.

"You've had enough."

"What I've had enough of is her staring at you," Lina whispered. "And she had the nerve to smile at me twice.

"Stop looking over there."

Lina couldn't seem to stop herself. And in addition to looking at her, she was imagining her having sex with Phil. She took a deep breath and reached for her wine glass, but then remembered it was empty. "I want another glass."

"No." He curved his arm around her shoulders and lowered his mouth to her ear. "She's trying to get to you. Don't give her what she wants."

Lina met his eyes. "I hate her."

"I know. I'm sorry."

"When I promised not to seek her out, I didn't know she'd be goading me all night."

"Why don't we dance?" He nodded towards the dance floor, which was beginning to fill up. "Come on." He came to his feet. "I promise to try to keep up," he teased.

Lina swayed slightly as she came to her feet, and Phil clasped both her arms. "I'm fine," she assured him when she saw the concern in his eyes. "I just got up too fast." She was tipsy, not drunk, and she knew she'd be fine on the dance floor.

They danced for forty minutes, only taking short breaks for Phil to remove his jacket and then tie, moving together effortlessly across the dance floor. For the first time all evening, Lina stopped thinking about Kim.

She bumped hard into someone to her left. "Excuse me," she said breathlessly, and found herself face-to-face with Kim, standing in the center of the dance floor with bodies jostling them from all directions. "Get away from me, you whore," Lina hissed.

Kim's eyes widened in surprise, but she quickly regained her composure, and a smile came to her lips as her eyes flicked dismissively over Lina. "Your husband couldn't get enough of me."

Lina swung back her hand and then, for the first time in her life, struck another human being, slapping Kim hard across the face.

18

"Slow down or let go of my hand," Lina said as Phil practically dragged her down the cobblestoned path towards their cottage. "I can't walk this fast in heels."

Phil slowed his stride, but the hold on her hand remained firm. He didn't say a word until the front door closed behind them. "What in the hell, Lina?" he exploded, turning to face her. "You can't just hit people."

"Obviously, I can," Lina said as she stepped around him. "I just did."

"I know you did," he said, following. "Everyone in that room is going to know about the affair now." He tossed his jacket on a chair and then roughly ploughed his fingers back through his hair. "Jesus Christ!"

"I'd do it again." She removed one sandal and then the other. "Did you hear what she said to me?"

"You called her a whore. That's what I heard."

"It's the truth. She is a whore. And she was baiting me all night."

"You assaulted her in front of two dozen witnesses. She could have you arrested."

"It would be worth it."

"I'm going to go check on her—make sure she doesn't call the police."

"No!" Lina followed him towards the door. "If you go to her, I'm leaving." There was no way she was going to sit in the cottage by herself while he comforted that woman.

He turned back to her. "Lina, I know you're upset, but I need to do this. It's for your protection."

"No! She wants to hear from you. She wants to know you care, and if you care about her, you don't care about me. You need to choose."

"There's no choice. There was never a choice, and you know it."

"Then there's nothing else to say."

"Lina—"

"Do you know how hard that was? Having to see her tonight? How do you think you would have felt if there was a man in there I—"

"Okay, okay." He took her hands. "I'm sorry. Don't get upset. I'm not going anywhere." He wrapped his arms around her. "I'm sorry."

Katie pushed through the crowd of bodies as she made her way to the back of the house. It was after 11:00 p.m., but with her parents away she didn't feel pressured to make her curfew. Her father told her to stay in for the weekend, but he neglected to tell her grandma, so when Emma texted her about a party she and Ryan were going to, she decided to tag along, figuring her father would be too busy at the wedding to check on her. She'd even risked having her first beer since coming off restriction, knowing her grandma wouldn't scrutinize her like her dad did when she got home.

She had no idea where Emma was, but she needed air, so she stepped out onto the back deck. That was when she saw Matt. He was leaning back against the deck rail, talking to a girl who was standing too close to just be a friend. Not the blonde she usually saw him with, but one who looked equally sleazy with short shorts and a tight T-shirt.

Katie hesitated, not sure if she should interrupt him, but then Matt noticed her, and she knew it would be odd if she walked by without acknowledging him. "Hey."

"Hey." His eyes flicked over her and then his attention returned to the girl before him, effectively dismissing Katie.

When the other girl slipped her hands up his chest, Katie quickly looked away and rushed back into the house, bumping into a boy who was coming out. "Sorry," she mumbled as she stepped around him. She made her way to the other side of the kitchen where a drinking game was in full swing. "Can I play?"

Katie was drunk. Not so drunk she didn't know what she was doing, but drunk enough to not care about the repercussions. "Again?" She looked across the table at the boy who slid a shot glass to her. "I just drank."

"I picked you," he said. "So you have to drink again."

Her mind was fuzzy, so she wasn't sure about the rules or even the game they were playing. "That's not fair. Make someone else."

"I get to pick whoever I want, and I pick you."

"Are you trying to get me drunk?"

"Maybe." He smiled.

She shook her head. "Give me a truth or dare instead."

"That's not what we're playing. Drink it or give up your seat," another boy demanded.

"No, it's okay," the original boy said. "I dare you to kiss me."

Katie squinted her eyes as she looked at him. He was cute, and he wasn't choosing the sleazy girl on the deck over her. "I can't reach you."

"Come here." He pushed back his chair.

Katie stood, and the room spun momentarily, but as soon as she got her bearings she stumbled around the table and dropped down into his lap. "Hi." Up close he was even cuter. "What kinda kiss do you want?"

"A long one."

As soon as Katie lowered her lips to his, he took over, his fingers sliding into her hair as he deepened the kiss, eliciting cheers from the rest of the kids at the table. Katie kissed him back, her mind conjuring up images of Matt as her tongue swirled against his. "Wasn't that better than a shot?" she asked when she broke the kiss, her forehead resting against his.

"Hell yeah."

"Let's go, Hunter," Matt said.

Katie pulled her head back from the boy, frowning up at Matt who was standing beside the table. "I'm in the middle of a game."

"The game's over. I'm taking you home."

"Who is this guy?" the boy asked.

"The guy she's leaving with. You have a problem with that?"

"No, no problem, bro," the boy said, holding up his hands. "We were just playing a game."

Katie's eyes shifted to the girl beside Matt, the same one she'd seen on the deck. "I'm not going with her," Katie said.

Matt turned to the girl. "I have to take her home."

"Why?" the girl asked. "Who is she?"

"Don't worry about it. I'll text you later." He gave her a quick kiss.

Katie glared at the girl until she was out of sight.

"Let's go," Matt said, holding out his hand.

Instead of getting off the boy's lap, Katie lowered her head and kissed him again. "Bye," she whispered before taking Matt's hand. When she wobbled slightly, he clasped his arm around her waist, dragging her against his side.

"What's wrong with you, Hunter?" Matt asked as soon as they were outside. "You want to be on restriction for another six months?"

"Was she your new *girlfriend*? She dresses like a slut."

"You're drunk."

"What do you care?" Katie glared at him as she stepped away from him and into the street. "You don't care about me."

"Yeah, and that's why I'm taking you home. Come on." He took her hand and continued towards his car.

"I was having fun," she grumbled.

He remained silent until they reached the car. "You're not going to get sick, are you?"

Katie shook her head and dropped down into the car. "I can do it," she said, taking the seat belt from him when he leaned over her.

"You okay?" he asked a few minutes into the drive.

"Is she your girlfriend?"

"We just hang out sometimes."

"I don't like her."

"Yeah, well, I don't think she liked you either."

Katie turned in her seat, leaning back against the door so she could see him. "Why were you a dick to me when I saw you earlier? You ignored me."

He shrugged. "I was busy."

Her eyes traveled over his face. He was beautiful. "Why haven't I seen you around lately?"

"I've been working."

"I miss talking to you. Did you miss me at all?"

He reached out and turned on the stereo. "Let me drive."

"You can let me off in front of the house. My parents aren't home," Katie said when Matt slowed the car as he approached her driveway.

"You shouldn't drink so much," he said when she swayed a bit after getting out of the car. "I won't always be there to save you."

"I didn't need your saving. I would have been fine." She leaned against the brick in front of her house as she rooted around in her purse for her key. "I'm a lil' dizzy."

"Here." He took her purse and seconds later was opening the front door. "No one's home?"

"My grandparents are sleeping in the basement." She leaned against the wall.

"You okay?"

"No, I feel—" She covered her mouth before sprinting up the stairs, making it to her bathroom and dropping to her knees without a second to spare, vomiting until there was nothing left in her stomach. She lay down on the cool tile of her bathroom.

She heard steps and opened one eye to see Matt entering her bathroom. "I think I'm dying," she whispered.

"No, you're not." He filled a glass of water and helped her sit up so she could rinse out her mouth. "You think you're done throwing up?"

"Yes."

"Here." He helped her to her feet and led her out of the bathroom and into her bedroom.

"Thank you," she whispered as she lay back in her bed.

He removed her shoes and then sat down beside her on the mattress. "How do you feel?"

"Better." She closed her eyes. "Why are you being so nice to me?"

"Because I'm not a dick."

"Sorry. I didn't mean that." She was still drunk, but she knew she was going to be embarrassed in the morning.

"I'm going to take off. I'll leave your key under the front mat so I can lock the door."

"I don't want you to go." She reached for his hand, lacing her fingers through his. "Would you sing to me?"

"Hunter—"

"Please, just one song. Then you can go."

"What do you want me to sing?"

19

"What did he say?" Lina asked when Phil finished a call with Wayne the following day. They had just started the drive home, and she felt exhausted, the emotional stress from the evening before sapping all her reserves.

"The same thing Diane told you. There were only a handful of direct witnesses, but everyone knew what happened within thirty minutes. Apparently you were the excitement of the wedding. Besides the bride and groom, of course." He rubbed the back of his neck.

"It was harder than I expected," Lina said as she looked out the window. "Seeing her, I mean."

"Don't think about her."

"That's a little easier said than done."

As soon as Lina saw Adele's and Shiloh's cars in front of their house, she remembered the barbeque Alice had planned and felt her whole body tense up. She wasn't up for a family party.

"We have everything under control," Alice said as soon as Lina and Phil stepped out of the mudroom into the kitchen. "Your father and Adele have agreed to handle the grill, and I'm taking care of everything else."

"How was the weekend?" Lina asked.

"Fine, fine." She turned her back to them as she continued to cut vegetables. "Hello, Phillip."

"Alice," he replied.

"You're back," Shiloh said as she came in from the deck. "How was the wedding?"

"Good," Lina lied.

"Is it okay if Julian comes over?"

"No," Phil said shortly. "He isn't allowed in this house."

"He's my husband."

"I'm sorry, Shi. My children aren't going to be subjected to him."

"He apologized and—"

"No," Phil repeated. "I know you've forgiven him, and that's your prerogative, but I don't have to. He isn't welcome here. I'm taking these upstairs," he told Lina, lifting the bags slightly before leaving the room.

"So that's it?" Shiloh asked as soon as Phil was out of earshot. "He's never allowed here again? What about Christmas?"

"I'm sorry," Lina said. "He's not going to change his mind."

"How can he not forgive him? He of all people should know about mistakes. At least Julian didn't get another woman pregnant."

"Shiloh!" Lina gasped.

"He has no right to judge Julian," Shiloh said. "Not when he's—"

"Shiloh, please—the kids don't know," Lina whispered, her cheeks turning red. "Please don't talk about it."

"He's being unreasonable. You need to talk to him, because if Julian isn't welcome that means I'm not welcome."

Lina wiped her hand over her forehead as she watched Shiloh go back outside. "Why did you tell her?"

"I didn't know it was a secret," Alice said. "I never kept things from you girls when you were growing up."

"It's not something we can just blurt out. It's going to be traumatic for the kids."

"Only because of the rigid belief system you're instilling in them."

Lina dropped her face into her hands and silently counted to ten. There was no point in arguing with her. "I thought this barbeque was happening at your house." She stepped to the window and looked out at the group around the pool. Adele was stretched out on a lounge chair and an older man, who Lina assumed was her father, was energetically describing something, his hands moving as his captivated audience, which included Megan and Katie, hung on his every word.

"I thought it would be easier for you and Phil if it was here."

"You mean you knew it would be impossible for us not to attend."

"Relax. You don't have to do a thing."

"I'm going for a run," Phil said when he entered the kitchen several minutes later.

"Right now?" Lina frowned. "We are eating soon."

"Let him," Alice said as she turned from the sink. "I could feel his heavy energy as soon as he walked in the door. The run will do him good."

"Really?" Phil raised his eyebrows. "Do you think a house full of unexpected guests may have contributed to that?"

"I think your life would be much less stressful if you lived in a state of acceptance instead of trying to control everything."

"No, my life would be much less stressful if you understood boundaries. This is *my* house, Alice."

"Mom, please leave him alone," Lina said.

"I didn't know you were back," Adele said as she entered through from the deck. "Love the new haircut." She gave Lina a quick hug before her gaze moved to Phil and her smile faded. "Oh, hello, asshole."

"Adele." Lina sighed. "Don't."

"What? I'm just saying hello to my favorite brother-in-law."

"He's in a bad mood," Alice whispered loud enough for everyone to hear.

"I'm out of here," Phil said to Lina, ignoring Adele completely.

"You don't deserve her," Adele called after him.

"Don't encourage her," Alice said to Adele. "She needs to get over this. It's been months."

The group was ten minutes into dinner when Phil, freshly showered after an hour-long run, dropped down at the table beside Lina, acknowledging Alice's introduction of Drew Rayburn with only a nod of his head. "Where's Logan?"

Lina closed her eyes as soon as Phil spoke. It was amazing how much trepidation two words could evoke. She hadn't told him, and he was going to be furious.

"He's at the beach," Alice said. "He returns tomorrow, right?" She looked to Lina for confirmation.

"Yes."

"Who did he go to the beach with?" Phil asked.

"That delightful Dr. Drayton and his son," Alice said.

"How come you didn't tell me Logan was friends with his son?" Katie asked.

Lina could feel Phil's eyes on her as she focused her attention on Katie. "I was going to. I just hadn't gotten a chance."

"I can see why you go on about him. Such positive energy, and his aura was so clear," Alice said. "Your father was impressed with him too."

"Oh, most definitely, I—"

"I'm sorry," Phil interrupted. "Who are you?"

Drew Rayburn sat up a little straighter in his chair. "I'm Drew—"

"I know your Goddamn name! But who are you to give an opinion? Do you think any of us care about your opinion?"

"I do," Katie said.

"Dad!" Megan gasped.

"Phil," Lina whispered. "Stop it." She gripped his arm and could feel the tension coursing through his body. "Please."

He continued to stare across the table at her father, a look of pure distaste clouding his features, and then he took a deep breath and reached for his beer. "I don't care to hear your opinion at my table," Phil said in a much calmer voice, "or any table for that matter."

"Have sex with him tonight," Alice said as she hugged Lina good-bye later that evening.

"Mom!" Lina pulled back and looked pointedly towards Drew who was seated in the passenger seat and able to hear their conversation.

"Relax. I'm sure he knows you have sex. Phil is wound as tight as a drum. You need to release that tension. Go upstairs, put on something sexy and—"

"It had nothing to do with that." Lina took several steps back from the car, pulling Alice with her. "He blames him."

"Blames who for what?" Alice frowned.

"Drew. Phil blames him for what happened to me and Shiloh. He always has."

"What?" Alice made a scoffing noise. "How could he blame him? He didn't live anywhere near us."

"Exactly."

Katie sat alone at the kitchen table, staring down at her cell phone when Lina came back into the house. "How was your weekend?" Lina asked.

Katie shrugged. "Fine."

"Do you feel okay? You look pale."

"I'm fine."

"So, did you like Drew?"

"We call him Grandpa," Katie answered, looking up from her phone. Hearing Katie refer to Drew as "Grandpa" seemed absurd, and Lina wanted to laugh, but then she realized there was nothing funny about it to Katie. Her grandma had given him her stamp of approval, and that was enough for Katie. It clearly didn't matter what her parents thought. "He's really smart."

"Yes." Lina nodded. "I remember that about him." She sat down at the table across from Katie. "Is he still a professor at the University of Chicago?"

"I guess. Grandma really likes him. She said they might get married."

Phil was right. Her mother was crazy. "She used that word, 'married'?"

"Yes. They slept in the same room. Why was Dad such an asshole to him?"

"He just doesn't approve of the type of father he was, or grandfather for that matter."

Katie frowned at her. "I think he could be a good grandfather. Do you hate him too? Is that why you barely talked to him tonight?"

Lina was surprised Katie even noticed she hadn't talked to Drew. "I don't hate him," she finally said. "He's basically a stranger to me. Do you think you'll see more of him?"

"If Grandma marries him I will." Katie looked down at her phone.

"Would you like that?"

"I guess." Katie began typing on her phone. "Can you stop talking now?"

20

ina was heading into her yoga class the following morning, hoping it would help to shake the feeling of malaise
she'd been experiencing since seeing Kim, when she received a text from Nick.

*Thoroughly enjoyed Logan. Does he ever not smile? We should be back in town
by 3 p.m., so he can be picked up any time after.*

The right thing to do would be to have Phil pick him up, considering he worked minutes from Nick's home, but Lina didn't
want to do the right thing. She wanted to see Nick. Talking to
him would make her feel better. It always did.

Logan was born happy. I'll see you this afternoon.

As Lina sat in her car taking in Nick's three-story brick row
house, which looked similar to the other homes lining both sides
of the street in the tony section of Federal Hill, where restaurants
and the theatre were within a short walk, she pondered what it

would feel like to live in a city. It was so different than her sub-urban lifestyle, with their single-family homes and backyards.

"Come in." Nick stepped back from his door. "The boys ran down to the sub shop around the corner. They should be back momentarily."

Lina passed within inches of him and felt a response in every part of her body. "This is nice." Her eyes took in dark hardwood floors, crème-colored walls and contemporary art as she walked farther into the house, trying to get her nerves under control.

"Thank you."

A baby grand piano dominated the living room to her left, and she crossed to it. "Do you play?" She trailed her fingers over the keys.

"Occasionally." He was leaned up against the doorsill, watching her. "Do you?"

"No." Lina bent down to study a black-and-white photograph on a side table of a teenage Nick and an older man on a sailboat. "Your father?"

"Yes."

"You look like him." She straightened and turned back to him, her heart rate accelerating as she took in his casual stance, his shoulder leaned against the doorsill, one hand pushed into the pocket of his shorts. He seemed to grow more handsome every time she saw him.

"Would you like something to drink? Water, Coke, wine?" He pushed off the wall, leading her into his large kitchen, which encompassed the back of the house.

"Water would be nice. Oh, I love it." Lina stepped to the window, relieved to find her nerves finally settling as she looked out at a private patio overflowing with flowers and plants. "May I take a closer look?"

"Please."

The patio, which was the width of the back of the house, was surrounded on three sides by seemingly every type of flower that bloomed in the Mid-Atlantic.

"It's beautiful," she told Nick when he joined her.

"It's all the previous owners' doing. I just try not to kill them. Do you have a garden?" He was standing so close she could feel the heat emanating from his body and had an urge to lean back into him.

"I do. Several. It's kind of my passion or therapy." She followed him to a small round table. "I spend hours tending to them. The time just disappears."

"I'm sure they're beautiful." His eyes traveled over her face. "What's going on here?" He trailed his finger over the skin below her eye. She caught her breath at the unexpected jolt of attraction.

"I saw her. She was at the wedding we attended. I can't stop picturing them together. I've barely slept in two days."

"I'm sorry."

"How can I love him and hate him at the same time?"

"Life isn't that simple. It's not all black-and-white."

"I wish I hadn't seen her. I shouldn't have gone."

"Would you rather live in denial? I know it's not easy, but it is the reality."

"Have you ever had an affair?"

"No." He met her eyes.

"Would you?"

"Sleep with a married woman?"

"No. Cheat on your wife."

He reached out and pushed a few tendrils of her hair back behind her ear. "I would never have cheated on you, Lina." He let his fingers trail down the side of her face, his eyes never leaving hers. "He must have been temporarily insane."

She caught her breath. "Don't."

"Don't what? Tell you what an idiot I think your husband is?"

"Don't say that."

"Lina, I—" Before he could finish, the patio door was opening, and Nick sat back as the boys joined them.

— —

"Dad's already home," Logan said when Lina pulled into the garage beside his BMW. Logan scrambled out of the car as soon as it was in park.

Phil stepped out into the garage and returned Logan's hug, but he was looking at Lina, his expression grim.

She felt a stirring of anxiety and took a deep breath before opening the door. She shouldn't have gone. What was she thinking? It was wrong.

"We played lacrosse on the beach every night after the lifeguards left," Logan was telling Phil. "Brian tweeted where we were, and random guys showed up. It was really cool."

"Good," Phil said. "Why don't you go inside and let me talk to Mom?"

"He's going to the same overnight camp as me, only a different week," Logan continued. "We're going to see if one of us can switch."

"Okay." Phil patted his back. "Let me talk to your mom now."

"You should see their beach house. It's huge, and it's right—"

"Logan! Enough! I told you two times I needed to talk to your mother. You need to listen. Now go inside."

Logan's smile disappeared, and his shoulders dropped before he wordlessly went into the house.

"He was just excited—"

"No. We're not talking about Logan. Where were you?" He'd rounded his car and was standing in front of her.

"I was picking up our son." Lina lifted her chin.

"At Drayton's house? Doesn't he live in Baltimore?"

"Yes."

"You drove forty minutes when he probably lives within ten of my office? Why?" He tilted his head, trying to meet her eyes. "Why would you do that?"

"Because he needed to be picked up."

"Why didn't you call me?"

"Because I didn't." She moved to walk around him, but he stepped with her. "I want to go inside."

"Do you want to talk in front of the kids? Because we're finishing this conversation."

"You're the one who cheated! Why am I being treated like I can't be trusted?"

Phil took her hand, leading her out of the garage and far enough down the driveway not to be overheard. "I see two possibilities here. You're punishing me, or you actually have feelings for him. Which one is it?"

"Neither! He's a doctor who did more for our daughter than either of us could, and now he is the father of one of Logan's friends. You don't have a right to tell me who I can and can't talk to. I haven't done anything wrong, and I like talking to him." Lina knew as soon as the words left her mouth that she'd said too much.

"You like talking to him?"

"I didn't mean that."

"You told him," he guessed, his eyes narrowing. "He knows about Kim."

Lina blushed. She wanted to deny it, but it was too late. Her face had given her away. She looked helplessly into his eyes. "I was upset at one of Katie's appointments, and it just came out."

"Jesus Christ, Lina!" He pushed his hands back through his hair and squeezed his head. "What in the fuck were you thinking?"

"I wasn't. I was hurt."

"Of all the Goddamn people you could have told, it had to be him! We're done with him. Professionally and personally." He turned on his heel and headed back towards the house.

"What does that mean?" Lina asked, running to catch up to him.

"It means Katie isn't going to see him again. It means Logan isn't going to see him again. That's what it means."

"Phil, stop!" Lina gripped his arm.

"The moment you let him into our personal relationship, his interactions with our children ceased."

"We can't just rip Katie away from him. We're going to transition to the new doctor, but she still needs to—"

"No," he interrupted. "It's done. Either you cancel Friday's appointment or I will, but it's going to be canceled."

"Think about Katie."

"I'm thinking about this family," he bit out. "And he isn't good for this family."

— ~

Logan was standing in front of the open refrigerator when Lina came in from gardening the following morning. "You look like you've grown an inch."

"You always say that when I go away for a couple days." He pulled out a carton of milk.

"That's because it's true. Where did you put your bag? I'm about to do some laundry."

"Emily washed all my stuff yesterday morning. She said she doesn't like to unpack dirty clothes." He dropped down at the kitchen table and poured some milk over his cereal.

"Emily?"

"Brian's dad's girlfriend."

"That's impressive. What was she like? Is she pretty?" Lina tried to keep her voice nonchalant.

"She's cool, and she was totally hot. Like a model or something."

"How old was she?"

"I don't know."

"Well his dad is my age. Was she my age?"

"No, she's young. Not like young, young, but not old like you." As soon as the words left his mouth it was obvious he regretted them. "I didn't mean it like that. You're not old, but—"

"It's fine." Lina turned away from him to fill her coffee cup. "I am old." She was surprised by her level of disappointment at the image of Nick with a hot, young girlfriend.

"Brian thinks she's hot too, and she could end up being his stepmom. That would be weird."

"I doubt she'll be his stepmom."

"She could be," Logan insisted. "Brian thinks she might move in with his dad. That's the first step, right?"

Lina felt a swell of jealousy at his words. "No, it's not the first step," she snapped. "If someone wants to truly commit, they get married. Your father and I would be very disappointed if you lived with someone before you got married."

"What did I do? Why are you mad at me?"

"I'm not," Lina said as she turned back around. "I'm just a little old-fashioned, I guess. I don't want you to think it's okay to live with someone you're not married to, and Dad wouldn't either."

Laughter floated up from the pool hours later as Lina walked out on the deck. Phil, along with Logan, Megan and a couple of the neighborhood kids, were playing their own version of water polo. Logan's body was wrapped around Phil from behind as he tried to get a ball away from him, and Phil was laughing as he struggled to get out of his grasp. She remembered when Logan was much younger and Phil only pretended to struggle because he wasn't big enough to prevent him from effortlessly making it across the pool with him on his back. Her thoughts unexpectedly shifted to Kim, and she found herself wondering if she would have a boy or a girl. There was going to be a child with no relation to her that would call Phil Daddy. What would the child call her?

"Dad, stop!" Megan's laughter brought Lina's mind to the present, and she watched as Phil effortlessly tossed her in the air. She came up from beneath the water sputtering and then she launched herself at him, and, with the help of all the kids, managed to pull his legs from beneath him and give him a sound dunking.

Phil was breathing deeply when he dropped down onto the chair beside Lina's twenty minutes later. "Did you see them trying to drown me? Five against one." He pushed his wet hair back from his forehead, taking a deep breath. "That was a workout." He reached for Lina's wine glass. "I can't stand this humidity. We're definitely not retiring to Florida."

She felt a stab of annoyance as she watched him take a swallow from her glass. He was happy. She was sitting here feeling miserable, and he was acting as if everything were normal. And then she had another thought. They wouldn't be free from children in eight years when Logan graduated from college. Their plan to take off for three months each year to travel the world while they were still relatively young and fit was gone. Phil was going to be the father of an eight-year-old when Logan graduated from college, and regardless of what he said or thought now, she knew he would never abandon one of his children.

"Everything okay?" he asked.

"Fine," she said, her chair scraping against the deck as she pushed it back from the table. "Just thinking about what you said."

21

Lina's heart leapt when she saw a text from Nick on her phone the following morning, assuming he might finish whatever he started to say on his patio. But when she opened it, the text was about Katie.

I apologize for the short notice—can your husband and Katie be at my Hopkins office tonight at 5 p.m.? I have a colleague I believe will be a perfect fit, and tonight is the only time that works for both of us in the next month. I need a reply by 3 p.m. or I'll assume this doesn't work. Thanks, Nick.

Part of her wanted to take Katie and let Phil find out after the fact, but she'd already done that once this week, and she didn't want to create more conflict. Katie was going. That much she knew, and if Phil wouldn't take her, she would, but she was going to give him the choice. She called Phil's office.

Fifteen minutes later, she ended the call with Phil. He had given her instructions to drop Katie at his office at 4:30 p.m. He wasn't happy, and even raised his voice more than once during the interchange because he didn't want to take Katie anywhere near Nick Drayton. But he wanted Lina to be anywhere near him even less, so when he realized she wasn't going to back down and that Katie was going regardless of what he said, he begrudgingly agreed to take her.

It occurred to Lina that she should let Nick know that Phil found out he knew about the affair, so she included the information in her text.

Thank you for making this work. Phil and Katie will be at the appointment at 5. I slipped up on Monday night and now he knows that you know about his affair. He was angry. I thought I should tell you. I'm so sorry for dragging you into this. You've only been wonderful to us. Lina.

His reply came an hour later. *No worries, Lina. I'm happy to hear they can make it.*

— —

"When is it going to start mattering what I want?" Katie asked. She was standing just inside her father's office, waiting for him to finish an email so he could take her to her appointment with the new psychiatrist. It had been an all-around shitty day. First, she'd run into Matt at Emma's, and he'd treated her like a kid sister instead of a potential girlfriend, lecturing her about overdrinking and making out with guys she didn't know at parties, and then her mom told her she had to change psychiatrists.

"What you want matters," her father said absently, continuing to tap away on his keyboard.

"No, it doesn't. You're going to make me go whether I want to or not." She put her hands on her hips. "What you and Mom want is all that matters. It's all that ever matters." She'd been furious with her mom the entire drive into Baltimore, and now she was furious with him.

"We want what's best for you."

"That's not true!" He was the most annoying person alive. "You only want what's best for you! I'm not a little kid. I'm sixteen! What gives you the right to decide what's best for me?"

He lifted his eyes from his computer display. "Lower your voice. This is an office, and people are working. I'm your father. That's what gives me the right. Now get yourself a drink or something. I'll only be a few minutes. We can discuss this in the car." His attention returned to his computer.

"Being my father is just biology. I have my own brain. You don't even know me."

"Well, if that's how you feel, we'll have to start spending more time together, because for some reason God decided I should be your father, so you're stuck with me."

"I'm not spending a second more with you than I have to," she fumed before stomping across the office to the large window overlooking Baltimore's Inner Harbor. The sound of his fingers tapping lightly on his keyboard grated her nerves. She could barely think, she was so frustrated, but he had no problem continuing to write his stupid email. "And I don't even believe in God." The office was suddenly quiet, and she could feel his eyes, but she continued to stare out the window.

"What did you just say?" His voice was low, and she knew he was unhappy, but it was the truth, and she had a right to believe whatever she wanted.

"I'm an atheist."

"Since when?"

"Since I realized I could actually think for myself."

"Is Matt an atheist?"

"No." She'd gone too far. She needed to change the subject. "I'm not going to talk to anyone besides Dr. Drayton. You can make me meet with the new doctor, but you can't make me talk."

"I need to finish this email. We'll continue this discussion in the car."

Katie opened a small refrigerator and reached for a soda but changed her mind and took water instead when she remembered her grandma telling her the previous week how bad sodas were for you. She sipped from the water bottle as she wandered around his office, stopping before his bookshelves and looking at a framed picture of Megan. Figured he'd have a picture of his precious Megan. She meandered to his desk and, as she stopped behind him, noticed a candid picture of herself when she was three or four. She didn't recall seeing it before. She was in his lap, leaned back against him, with her cheek resting on his chest, and he was kissing the top of her forehead. She felt her throat constrict and turned away.

"While you're on medication you have to be under the care of a doctor," Dr. Drayton said. "When you're med free, you can take this up with Dr. Jones. Don't discount him before you've met him. He's a good friend of mine. I think you're going to like him."

"Whatever." Katie looked past him to the window.

"I'm as disappointed as you we can't continue our sessions, Katie, but it's out of both our hands. Our energy should be reserved for those circumstances in our lives where we have control. This isn't one of them."

"You sound like my grandma."

"Wise lady." He winked at her and then, at the sound of a knock on his office door, came to his feet. "There's Dr. Jones."

"Well?" Dr. Drayton asked after Dr. Jones left the office.

Dr. Jones was cooler than Katie had expected, but he wasn't Dr. Drayton, and it hit her then that she might never seem him again. "Why can't my parents be like you?" She stared down at her hands as a knot formed in her throat. Besides her grandma, he was the only adult who got her, and now she couldn't talk to him anymore.

"As hard as it may be for you to believe, your mom and dad both love you very much. Being a parent isn't always easy. None of us is perfect. There are times my son wishes he could exchange me for a different father."

He was lying. His son never wanted to exchange him. He was just saying it to make her feel better. She continued to stare at her hands.

"I'm going to miss you too. Who is going to educate me on the hippest new bands?" He slowly came to his feet. "Come on. I have something for you."

Katie wiped a stray tear from beneath her eye before following him to his desk and taking the book he held out. "My favorite poet," he told her. "I discovered him when I was about your age. I think you'll like him."

The Essentials of Rumi, she read, and then she was opening the front cover and reading Dr. Drayton's inscription:

"To Katie (My favorite 16-year-old)—I hope this book will come to mean as much to you as it has to me. All my best, Nick Drayton"

Katie didn't want to cry, but as with every other area of her life, she apparently had no say in the matter, because the tears came anyway. She covered her eyes with her free hand and then she lost it. Hiccupping sobs gripped her entire body.

"You're going to be fine," Dr. Drayton said as he slipped his arms around her. She gripped his shirt as she cried against his chest. This was what it felt like to lose someone. It would be no different than if he'd died. She was never going to see him again. She cried harder. He ran his hand over the back of her head. "You're going to be fine," he said the words over and over.

Katie felt embarrassed when she was finally able to step away from him, and then, without a word, she opened his office door and stepped out into the waiting room. Her father looked up from his cell phone, and she saw his eyes narrow in concern.

"What's wrong?"

"Nothing," she said, avoiding his gaze. "Can we go?"

"Are you okay?" He touched her arm, looking down into her face.

"Yes. God." She stepped away from him. "I just want to go home."

"I need to have a word with Dr. Drayton first. I'll just be a minute."

22

Lina picked up her cell phone with the intention of calling Phil to see if the appointment with Katie was over but was immediately distracted by a screen full of unread text messages. They were all from the same number, which she didn't recognize.

She sat down on the edge of her bed and opened the first text, her eyebrows pulled together in confusion as she realized they weren't actual texts but pictures of a text conversation. She saw the name Phil Hunter on the top of the screen. They were conversations between Phil and whomever had sent her the messages. Her throat constricted at the realization it was a conversation between Phil and Kim. She read the first message, which was dated March eighteenth. Phil's text appeared gray, and Kim's followed in blue:

> Phil: *On my way. We'll spend the night at your place and leave for New York on the 8 a.m.*

Kim: *I might be in the shower. If I am, join me...*
Lina opened the next text:
March 22, 4:30 p.m.
Phil: *Can you meet me in the apt at 5 p.m.? I have an hour.*
Kim: *Of course*

March 23, 11:00 a.m.
Phil: *Lunch?*
Kim: *Yes, where?*
Phil: *Apt at noon*

March 24, 10:30 a.m.
Phil: *I can come by at noon for a couple of hours. Good?*
Kim: *You can have me for lunch*

April 5, 8:52 p.m.
Phil: *I'll be at your place at 7:30 tomorrow morning. First meeting isn't until 10 a.m.*
Kim: *I'll be in bed. Let yourself in and wake me up with your tongue.*

The texts blurred together as Lina read about one clandestine meeting after another, sometimes two on the same day. There were twenty-four texts in all, and in each one Phil was the pursuer. Tears began to fall from her eyes. She didn't know how long she lay in her bed, but when Phil came into the room some time later, she was no longer crying.

"What are you doing in bed?" His shoes clicked against the hardwood floor as he walked towards his wardrobe. "Are you sick?"

Lina rolled onto her side, curling into the fetal position before closing her eyes and turning her face into her pillow. She heard him cross to the bed, and then the mattress was shifting as he sat down beside her. "Are you okay?" He ran his hand over her back.

"No, I'm not okay." Her voice was muffled by the pillow.

"What's wrong? Lina?" He gripped her shoulder, attempting to turn her over, but she shrugged off his hand.

"Don't touch me!"

He came to his feet, looking around the room before crossing to her dresser and picking up her purse. "Tell me what she did." He began to riffle through her purse. "Tell me!"

"Look at my phone," she said. "Just look at my phone."

She heard the sound of her cell phone sliding over the wood of the dresser and then silence. After several seconds she turned over and watched as he flicked his thumb over her phone display, his lips pulled into a thin line, the side of his jaw clenching and unclenching. His eyes shifted back and forth over the display as he read the texts. When he finished, he clicked the side of the phone, darkening the display.

"You pretended to leave for New York on Sunday nights so you could spend the night with her. You were sleeping in another woman's bed thirty minutes away while I was alone in this one."

"What's the difference, Lina? Whether I was with her here or in New York?"

"There's a difference. You know I can't sleep alone! I'm suffering, and you're down the road *fucking* someone"

"I'm sorry."

"I didn't know you left the house early so you could go to her apartment before work." She pushed herself up on her elbows as she glared at him. "Where are you going with my phone?" she cried out. "Give me my phone back."

"I'll give it back after I delete the messages," he said over his shoulder.

"You're not deleting them. They're my messages." She followed him into his wardrobe and held her hand out. "Give me my phone."

He took off his suit jacket and hung it up before reaching for the knot of his tie. "She's just trying to hurt you. You shouldn't have read them."

"Well, I did read them, and now I want to read them again."

"Why?" He began to unbutton his shirt. Their bodies were less than a foot and a half apart. "Haven't you been hurt enough?"

"More than enough, but reading those texts made me hate you, and I want to keep hating you."

"Tough." He shrugged out of his shirt.

"Give me my phone." She tried to slip her hand into his pants pocket, but he gripped her wrist, taking the phone from his pocket with his free hand, turning his back on her and blocking her with his body as he began tapping on her display.

"What are you doing?" she screamed. She pulled on his arm. "It's my phone. You have no—"

"Here." He turned around, gripped the back of her hand and placed her phone against her palm.

Lina stepped out of the closet and looked down at the phone as she quickly opened the texting icon. "You deleted them! You had no right to delete them."

"You're letting her win," he said. "This is what she wants. This is exactly what she wants."

"This is your fault," she whispered as she turned from him. "This is all your fault."

She crossed back to the bed and pulled back the comforter before lying back down. She listened to drawers opening and closing as he changed clothes and then to the sound of the bathroom door closing. She knew Kim sent the messages to create conflict between them, but knowing it didn't stop the feeling of deep betrayal gnawing at her from the inside.

—⁓

"Honey, it's just more details about an affair you already knew about," Diane said over the phone the next morning.

"I know, but when I think of those texts, I feel like I don't know him. It's like the man I thought he was doesn't exist. I don't know the Phil who would write those texts."

"That's not true. You've been with him for twenty-four years, and you want to redefine who he is because of a four-month lapse in judgment. You have to stop fueling it with your thoughts. He's a good man who made a mistake. You need to forgive him."

Adele wasn't as forgiving. "He's such a selfish bastard. He shouldn't just get away with this. You need to fuck someone else. I'm serious."

Lina laughed through her tears. "You're insane."

"No. Everyone else is. Phil needs to know what this feels like. That's the best way to ensure this never happens again."

—⁓

Dorm-supply shopping with Megan provided an effective distraction for much of the day, but as soon as they returned home and Megan ran off to see friends, Lina once again found her mind returning to the text messages. Phil may have deleted them from her phone, but he hadn't deleted them from her memory.

A Rumi book sat on the kitchen island, and she flipped it open, her eyes traveling over the inscription inside the cover. "To Katie (My favorite 16-year-old)—I hope this book will come to mean as much to you as it has to me. All my best, Nick Drayton." Lina covered her mouth as tears clouded her eyes. He'd given Katie Rumi to read. She recalled the words he spoke to her on Monday. *I would never have cheated on you, Lina.* And he would never have sent another woman those texts.

Is it possible to be with someone for twenty-four years and not really know them? she texted him.

When her cell phone rang at a few minutes past 4:00 p.m. her first thought was Nick, but instead it was Phil. "How are you?" he asked.

"I haven't received any surprises via my phone, if that's what you're wondering." Her voice was cool.

"I'm sorry. I would give anything to undo this."

"Well, you can't. Why are you calling?"

"To tell you not to hold dinner. It's going to be a late night."

"Okay."

"I'll see you tonight—no later than 10 p.m."

"Bye."

"Lina?"

She slipped into a chair and sighed deeply into the phone. "What, Phil?"

"I love you. Please don't lose sight of that."

She tilted her head back and stared up at the ceiling. "It's hard to remember when all I can see are the words you texted her. Goodbye." She ended the call, and it immediately began ringing again. "Leave me alone, Phil," she bit out. "I don't want to hear your voice right now."

"Fortunately for me, I'm not Phil."

Lina closed her eyes when she realized it was Nick on the other end of the line. "I'm sorry, I thought—"

"That I was Phil. I caught that."

She blushed. "I'm not usually like that, it's just—"

"You don't have to explain. I have some things I need to say, but I don't want to do it over the phone. Are you free?"

An hour and forty-five minutes later, Lina stepped into the entrance of the Wine Bar, a cozy restaurant about fifteen minutes from her house. She'd changed into a skirt, wedge heels and a sleeveless black silk V-neck top, her loose hair falling around her shoulders, her only jewelry a silver chain with a diamond pendant at her neck and her wedding ring on her left hand.

She saw Nick as soon as she stepped into the dimly lit bar, and he came to his feet as she approached. She felt the now-familiar surge of awareness as she met his eyes, and then he was pulling out her chair. As she took her seat, she could smell a hint of soap and the lavender of his aftershave.

"Thank you," Lina said after a waitress set a glass of Chardonnay before her moments later.

"So, how are you?" Nick's eyes roamed over her face.

"I've been better," she said before taking a sip of wine. "How are you?"

"I'm going to be blunt."

"Okay." She set down her glass and sat up straighter in her chair.

"I don't like your husband," he began, his eyes meeting hers, "which undermines my ability to be unbiased when I'm talking to you."

She was surprised by his candor. "Oh."

"This is why I was hesitant to respond to your text earlier. You shouldn't trust any advice I give you in regard to him."

Something happened. The air of tranquility normally surrounding him was absent. "He said something to you," she guessed. Of course he'd said something to him. Phil saw him as a threat to their family.

"This isn't because of what he said to me yesterday, although his manner of communication certainly doesn't advance my opinion of him. I felt like I was transported back to high school or a B movie—cool jock warning me with the threat of bodily harm to stay away from his girlfriend."

Lina's cheeks heated. "He didn't!"

He shrugged. "The warning was about his wife, not girlfriend, but yes, he did."

"I'm so sorry."

"Your husband doesn't intimidate me, Lina. I'm here talking to you, aren't I?"

"Did he threaten you?"

"He did, and while I have no doubt he would probably like to leave me in a hospital eating out of a straw, I don't believe it's ever going to come to that. He was upset and resorted to adolescent posturing."

"I'm sorry," she said again because she didn't know what else to say.

"Please don't apologize for him. You aren't responsible for his actions, but I think it's important you understand when you text or talk to me about him, I'm going to say what *I* think as a man, and I suspect you're looking for the response of a therapist."

"I want your opinion. I value your opinion."

"Lina," he began, smiling slightly as he dropped his eyes to his drink. "You shouldn't value my opinion where he's concerned. My judgment is a bit impaired, and it's more complicated than just not liking him."

"I don't understand."

He met her eyes. "I'm attracted to you."

<h1 style="text-align:center">23</h1>

“**I**’m so sorry,” Lina said as waiters swarmed their table to clean up her spilt wine. "The glass just slipped out of my hand.”

"I’ll get you another wine,” Nick said.

She let her eyes drift over him as he stepped to the bar, taking in the play of muscles in his upper back, visible through his shirt, and then her eyes dipped lower, lingering on his butt. She quickly looked away when she realized she was thinking about how nicely it filled out his jeans. It was as if his declaration had given her permission to look at him in a different way.

"Are you okay?" Nick asked when he rejoined her, placing a fresh glass of wine on the table

"Yes, I just…have I been…did I do something?"

"You didn’t do anything wrong, Lina. You were being authentic. It’s all on me. I let my professional wall slip.”

She felt a million different emotions running through her. "I’m not sure what I’m supposed to say.”

"I'm not looking for a response."

They both looked up as a waitress appeared beside the table. "We need another five," Nick told her before returning his attention to Lina. "Do you have time for dinner?"

She knew she should say no. Phil would be furious if he knew she even spoke to him, but the pull she felt towards the man across the table at that moment trumped all else. "Yes, I'm on my own tonight."

As they looked over their menus a band began playing a James Taylor song, and Lina felt herself begin to relax. "I feel comfortable around you," she admitted. "I have since the first day."

He didn't comment as he continued to scan his menu.

"Do you feel like you've known me longer than eight months?" Lina asked.

"I don't really think in terms of time."

"What does that mean?"

"Lina." He set down his menu. "There's no need to analyze this. I told you so you would know I'm not a safe confidant for you. That's the only reason. I know you're still in love with your husband."

She let her gaze stray to the band. "What does this mean for us?"

"It should mean I sever all communication with you." He shook his glass, his eyes tracking the swirling liquid. "But frankly I don't want to."

"So we can be friends?"

"Yes, we can be friends."

After the waiter left with their order, Lina told him about the text messages she received from Kim. "Seeing his words written to another woman—knowing he was sending her texts while he was in the house with me. It was powerful in a very bad way. I hated him."

He began tapping the fingers of one of his hands against the table as he watched her, his eyes unreadable.

"What are you thinking?"

"I'm thinking he doesn't deserve you."

"You are?" Tears came to her eyes. Maybe he was right. Maybe she didn't want to hear what he had to say. "You're wrong, though," she whispered. "You don't know him."

"I know enough. At a time when your family was in crisis and you needed him most, he was seeking comfort with another woman."

Lina blushed. "He made a mistake."

"He doesn't deserve you."

"That isn't true." Anger bubbled in her chest. "And your judgment is impaired. You told me I can't value your opinion, remember?"

"Oh, I remember. But it's true."

"I like you better when you're talking like a therapist."

"Maybe you don't want to be my friend after all."

"Maybe I don't," she agreed. She knew she should get up and walk out of the restaurant. He'd crossed the line, and it was disloyal to Phil to stay, but as she met his eyes she knew she'd regret leaving. She didn't understand exactly why, but she wasn't ready to walk away from him. "You don't understand."

"You're right. I don't."

"He saved me," she whispered. "Without him, I don't know what would have happened to me."

He brought his eyebrows together. "What do you mean, 'saved' you? Saved you from what?"

She could feel her palms begin to sweat. "Something happened to me when I was sixteen—to me and my younger sister,

Shiloh. It's not important what, but Phil saved us. And then his family took me in because Phil refused to leave me. He was only seventeen years old, but he sacrificed everything for me. He had a scholarship to Duke, but he gave it up and went to Maryland instead because he didn't want to leave me."

Nick watched her in silence for several seconds before speaking. "Without more details, I'm operating with one arm tied behind my back. Would you give me a little more?"

"It's not important. Just know that he saved me."

"Tell me this. Did you at least receive counseling after this trauma? I'm assuming it was a trauma."

"I tried. I went a few times. It didn't help. Only Phil could help. I only feel safe with him."

"Feel or felt?"

She considered his words. "I don't know. He's with me."

"Lina." He reached across the table and covered her hand with his. Although the look in his eyes was only one of concern, she still felt a tingling of awareness all the way up her arm. "You are a strong woman, not a traumatized sixteen-year-old. You don't *need* anyone. When we are with someone because we think we need them, the dynamics of the relationship change. It isn't healthy for either of you. I'm not faulting you for what you did over twenty years ago, and frankly I don't have enough facts to give a true assessment, but if that event serves as the foundation of your relationship, I'm concerned."

"It doesn't," she said quickly, maybe too quickly, because the truth was she didn't know whether it did or not. "I loved him before it ever happened."

"You were a child."

"I loved him from the moment I saw him."

He pulled back his hand as the waiter arrived with their food. "Maybe we should talk about something else."

Lina found her appetite as Nick steered the conversation away from Phil. She learned he was a lifelong democrat, loved classical music and, in addition to his love of sailing, was also an avid hiker.

"Like serious hiking with tents and no facilities?"

"I prefer modern accommodations." He set his fork and knife on his almost-empty plate and pushed it towards the edge of the table. "I'm fond of air conditioning, showers and soft beds." He sat back as the waitress picked up their plates. "Would you like coffee?" he asked.

"Please."

"We'll have the sampler and two coffees, please," he told the waitress.

"Where have you hiked?"

"All over the US, Canada and most of Europe. I try to hike a new area each year." He told her of his trip the previous year to Austria, where he'd hiked over one hundred miles and stayed in a different town each night. "We had someone else transport our luggage, which was probably cheating, but worth it."

"It sounds wonderful. I would love to take a trip like that."

"Why don't you? Your husband looks like someone who enjoys exercise."

"Not that type," she admitted. "He's more about the competition. I can't imagine him hiking without a purpose."

Nick was leaned back in his chair with one leg casually crossed over the other, one of his hands lying flat on the table while the other rested on his thigh. "The purpose could be taking his wife on a vacation she would enjoy."

"I suppose," she said absently, wondering if Phil would agree to that type of vacation. "Did you take Brian?"

"No." He chuckled. "Brian isn't a hiker. I took Emily."

"Your girlfriend." Her heart dropped at the thought of him with another woman. "Logan said she's very beautiful and very young."

The corners of his lips turned up. "Yes to both. She's thirty-one."

"Wow." She dropped her eyes. "That's the same age as Phil's... whatever. Must be nice for men."

"Lina?"

"Just ignore me. I'm happy you're happy." Her eyes drifted to the band.

"What are you thinking?"

"It doesn't matter."

"Tell me."

She knew telling him was wrong because she was married, but she spoke the words anyway. "I was thinking how lucky she is."

"Because she's thirty-one?"

"Because she's with you."

"Lina?"

She slowly brought her gaze back to the table, and her chest filled with heat at the desire so clear in his eyes. "Don't look at me like that," she whispered.

"I can't help it."

"I should leave. This is wrong."

"You haven't done anything." He continued to watch her as the waiter delivered their coffee and dessert.

"What I said was wrong. What I'm feeling is wrong. The way you're looking at me." She turned and picked up her purse.

"Please stay. Please."

"I can't."

24

ina blinked a few times in confusion, trying to get her bearings. She was lying on her bed, wrapped in Phil's thick white robe. "Phil?" she croaked. She couldn't see him, but she sensed him. "Phil?"

"I'm here, baby." He came into view with a look of concern etching his features. "How do you feel?"

"My head hurts and I'm thirsty." She held her hand up to shade her eyes from the bedside lamp, and Phil quickly turned it off. "You're all wet." She noted he was still in his work clothes but was missing his jacket, and the fronts of his dress shirt and slacks were visibly damp. "What happened to you?"

"Here's the Gatorade." Megan's anxious voice preceded her appearance.

"Open it for me," Phil said to Megan as he sat down on the mattress beside Lina. He lifted her head slightly, slipping an extra pillow beneath it to prop her up before taking the bottle from Megan and holding it to Lina's lips. "I need you to drink all of this."

The cool liquid soothed her dry throat. As instructed, she didn't stop until she drank the entire bottle. "Thank you." Her voice was still husky but not quite as raspy.

Identical looks of concern were stamped across Phil's and Megan's brows as they watched her. "I found you in the hot tub," Phil said. "You must have fallen asleep. The temperature was a hundred and two. I was very close to calling 911, but you were responsive, so I just carried you up here. I have no idea how long you were in there. Megan had been home for an hour, but—"

"It wasn't my fault," Megan interrupted. There were tears in her eyes. "All the lights were off down there. I assumed you were in your room."

"Of course it isn't your fault." Lina squeezed her hand. "I'm fine. Just a little tired. I don't remember..." She trailed off as the events of earlier in the evening came flooding back. "Oh my God," she whispered. "Oh God." Her eyes filled with tears, and she rolled over onto her side, turning her face into the pillow.

"Leave us, Megan," Phil said.

"Why is she crying?"

"Just leave." His attention was focused solely on Lina. He stripped off his wet shirt before stretching out behind her. "I'm sorry," he whispered into her hair. "I'm going to make this better."

She realized he thought she was distraught over the text messages, which she was, but at that moment she was consumed by an overwhelming sadness at the awareness she would no longer be able to have Nick in her life, not if she stayed with Phil. She thought of Phil's infidelity and her shoulders shook harder, and then she was just crying. Minutes passed before the tears abated, and then she became aware of Phil's warm body behind her, the hard muscles of his thighs pressing against the back of her legs and the feel of his chest sure and strong against her back.

"You saved me," she whispered. "If you hadn't come home and—"

"Shh. That would never happen. I'll always keep you safe, Lina."

"How did you know where I was?"

He pressed his lips against the back of her head. "I just did."

She turned in his arms and looked into his eyes. "I need you, don't I?" she whispered, trailing her fingers down his cheek.

"Yes," he said deeply. "We need each other."

Her eyes drifted over his face, his full lips, his strong jaw, the scar in his eyebrow from the impact of a lacrosse stick at seventeen and the laugh lines that had begun appearing around his eyes a few years earlier. A lump formed in her throat, and a lone tear ran down her cheek. "You hurt me," she whispered.

"Oh, baby." He brushed his lips gently over hers. "I love you more than anything in this world."

"You broke my heart."

"I know." He kissed her again. "But I'm going to fix it."

"How?"

"By loving you," he began, kissing her softly on the lips, "and cherishing you." He kissed her again. "And putting your needs before everyone else's." He kissed her again. "For the rest of my life." He kissed her deeply, his tongue stroking against hers as he pushed her back against the mattress and moved his body over hers.

Lina kissed him back, desperately seeking the security she craved. They kissed for minutes as he seemed intent on communicating his love through just one kiss, and then his hand reached for the knot of her robe.

— ~

Normally, awaking to bright sunshine filled Lina with energy and optimism, but when her head was pounding and details of the previous day were already in the forefront of her mind, she just wanted to keep sleeping.

Phil had woken her twice during the night, once to get her to drink another bottle of Gatorade and a second time because he couldn't tell whether she was breathing. She was, of course, but it took her thirty minutes to fall back to sleep.

"Mom?"

Lina opened her eyes, squinting up at Logan, who was standing beside the bed, his shoulders slumped and his usual smile missing. "What's wrong?" she asked.

"Dad said I can't be friends with Brian. I invited him over, and Dad said I have to uninvite him."

She closed her eyes. "I'll talk to him."

"He's never even met him. Why—"

Lina held up her hand. "Don't worry. I'll take care of it. Has he left for work yet?"

"He isn't going to work today."

When Lina gingerly walked into the kitchen, Alice was at the stove flipping a pancake, Phil was at the table reading the newspaper, and Katie was sitting across from him reading from her Rumi book.

"I was out of milk, so I came here for breakfast," Alice said. "What possessed you to fall asleep in a hot tub? Were you drinking?"

"No. It wasn't intentional."

"What are you doing up?" Phil was out of his chair and beside her.

"I'm fine. You shouldn't have stayed home." She touched his chest.

"I'm going to have to look at your chart and see what kind of aspects you're under. That was dangerous," Alice said.

At the mention of charts, her mother's prediction of infidelity flashed in Lina's mind. She gripped Phil's arm. It was Nick. The prediction was about Nick. How hadn't she seen it?

"Are you okay?" Phil asked.

"I just need coffee. My head is pounding."

"You shouldn't drink coffee," he said. "You're probably dehydrated. I'll get you some more Gatorade."

"I just want coffee. Please." She let him lead her to a chair.

"Give her what she's craving," Alice said. "The body knows better than anyone what it needs."

"I'm sure alcoholics would love that philosophy," Phil said dryly. "And drug addicts and—"

"Always ready to argue," Alice interrupted. "But in fact, I read recently that people use drugs and alcohol to self-medicate. There's an imbalance they're trying to correct."

"So now you're condoning drug and alcohol abuse?" Phil asked.

"No, I'm just explaining why their bodies may crave it initially."

"Please stop," Lina moaned. "My head hurts."

"Would you really have died if Dad didn't find you?" Katie asked.

"It would have taken a long time." She looked up at Phil as he set a mug of coffee and a bottle of Gatorade in front of her. "Thank you."

"Did he find you because you're cosmic soulmates?"

"Alice, really?" Phil looked back over his shoulder at her. "Why are you filling her head with that crap?"

"Denying it doesn't make it less true," Alice said.

"Don't believe anything she says," he told Katie.

"How did you know to go to the pool?" Katie asked Phil. "Megan said you went there first."

"Yes, how did you know to go to the pool, Phillip?" Alice turned from the stove.

"Lucky guess."

"Ha!" Alice laughed. "And when Lina's water broke three weeks early with Logan and you told the judge you needed a recess because your wife needed you, was that a lucky guess too?"

"That never happened."

"Lina?" Alice prompted.

"I'm staying out of it." Lina took a sip of her coffee, remembering how surprised she was when Phil, who was supposed to be in court all day, called within seconds of her water breaking.

"I think it's kind of cool." Katie was watching Phil with something other than distaste in her eyes.

"Mom, is that an engagement ring on your finger?" Lina's eyes centered in on the classic-cut solitaire diamond on Alice's left ring finger, and she had to concentrate to keep her mouth from falling open.

"Oh, yes." Alice looked down at it as if she'd forgotten it was there. "Your father and I are engaged. I thought I told you."

"No." Lina shook her head and then grimaced when it began to pound. "I would have remembered that."

— —

"You can't keep him from being friends with Brian Drayton," Lina told Phil as soon as they were alone.

"The hell I can't. I don't want Drayton in our life. I don't want you driving to his house to drop off Logan or him coming to ours. It's going to be bad enough running into him at Gilman."

Lina still had a dull headache, and she didn't want to discuss Nick with him, but Logan was counting on her. "Brian lives with his mother. How about if we only let him go there? Logan genuinely likes him, Phil, and I think you would too."

"This isn't about Brian Drayton," Phil said. "It's about his father. I don't like him. In fact, I dislike him, and I sure as hell don't trust him."

"Do you trust me?" she asked and then immediately felt a pang of anxiety in her chest, knowing she'd already been dishonest with him.

"Of course I do," he said, making her guilt jump up a notch, "but I hurt you, and I don't want some smooth-talking psychiatrist to take advantage of the situation."

They went back and forth for minutes with neither backing down from their position, and then Lina remembered she had the trump card. "Logan said Brian's the best lacrosse player his age in the state. Don't you think that being around him would be good for Logan's lacrosse game?" And with that one statement, a crack formed in Phil's resolve.

"Maybe it wouldn't hurt to let him come over once, since they took Logan to the beach."

25

"Do you want to listen to the band jam?" Emma asked Katie. They were in Emma's basement watching television, but the faint sound of music could be heard through the window.

"Not really." Katie stared stubbornly at the television. She was still mad at Matt for lecturing her in front of the band two days earlier.

"Seriously? In a couple of weeks they'll be away at college, and we won't be able to listen to them anymore."

"Matt's not going to college."

"Yeah, but there will be no one around to play with. He's not going to keep coming here after Ryan leaves."

Katie was having a self-imposed pity party as she lay in the hammock listening to the band. The spell hadn't worked, and in a couple of weeks Matt would be out of her life. She was losing both Dr. Drayton and Matt. She wiped the back of her hand at the tears slipping from her eyes. She had been so sure it would work. She became aware the band was no longer playing a moment before she heard Matt's voice.

"What's wrong?"

"Nothing."

The hammock shifted as he dropped down beside her. "Tell me."

She turned her head and found her face just inches from his. "Why do you care?" Her heart skipped as she looked into his eyes.

"Because I do."

She shifted her gaze to the darkened sky. "I had to switch psychiatrists. I don't want to start all over with a new one. I just want to stop." It was at least half true.

"Why do you still have to go?"

She shrugged. "Because they're making me."

"You still mad at me for the other day?"

"I don't know." She couldn't think of much beyond the feel of his body pressed against the side of hers.

"I don't want you getting in trouble and disappearing for another six months." The warmth of his breath tickled the side of her face.

"My parents weren't even around."

"Come on." He climbed out of the hammock and held out his hand. "I need water."

They joined a group on the big patio behind the house, and, for the next hour, Katie was in a state of heaven as she sat beside Matt, her body leaning into the side of his. He didn't have his arm around her and wasn't holding her hand, but there was at least a foot between him and the dude sitting on the other side of him, so the fact he was pressed against her side had to be a good sign.

At some point one of the kids lit up a joint and began passing it around the group. When it reached Katie, she thought about passing it along, but then figured if her clothes smelled, she could change into something of Emma's before going home. She brought it to her lips and inhaled deeply. She held it out to Matt, but the boy on the other side of him intercepted it.

"Matt doesn't smoke," he said.

"Put that shit away!" Ryan yelled as he strode towards them. "What the fuck, man? You can't have that here. My parents could come outside."

Katie glanced at Matt, who was coming to his feet. "Where are you going?" she asked.

"Home. I'll see you around."

"He just left," Katie told Emma moments later. "He didn't even ask if I wanted a ride. He was acting different tonight, like he might like me, and then after Ryan yelled at Dustin about the joint, he split."

"Matt's kind of anti-drug. I thought you knew that. He doesn't like being around it."

In the days after the hot tub incident, Lina resolved to concentrate on her marriage and family, but she hadn't counted on Brian Drayton practically moving in and serving as a constant reminder of his father. From his deep-set eyes to the cleft in his chin and the way his lips turned up in the corners as if he were always smiling, Brian was Nick's clone. Even the timbre of his voice was familiar, and on more than one occasion, Lina caught herself watching him and thinking of Nick with an ache in her heart. He and Logan became inseparable, and all of their time was spent at the Hunter house, probably due to the large expanse of grass Phil had turned into a practice lacrosse field a few years earlier and the teenage girls they lounged around the pool with when they weren't practicing.

"Don't you think she's a little old for him?" Lina asked Phil late one afternoon when he joined her on the deck after work. Logan and Brian were at the pool with two girls from the neighborhood, and the one closest to Logan looked more like a fully developed woman than a teenager.

"He isn't your baby anymore," Phil said as he watched Logan wrap his arms around the girl.

Lina pulled her gaze from the pool. "Have you talked to him about...you know?"

"Sex?" He raised his eyebrows.

"Yes," she sighed.

"I have. You're really having a hard time with this, aren't you?"

"He's fourteen. That's too young."

"For sex, yes, I agree, but not to flirt."

The sound of high-pitched screams and giggles floated up from the pool. "Their laughter sounds so forced," Lina said. "I hope Katie and Megan don't do that."

He smiled. "You're not going to be one of those mothers who thinks no one is good enough for their son, are you?"

"No one is good enough for my son." She turned to go back inside.

"Hey." He gripped her hand when she began to walk past him. "Where are you going?"

"To start dinner." She tilted her head back as he pulled her into his arms. "You want to eat, don't you?"

"I want my wife to kiss me." He brushed his lips over hers. "One day when Logan throws you over for another woman, I'll be here to pick up the pieces."

"Ha. Ha," Lina said.

"I love you."

— ⁓

Two and a half weeks after her dinner with Nick, Lina was tending to one of her front-yard flower beds when she heard and then saw a familiar Porsche coming down her driveway. She came to her feet, her heart rate accelerating as images of their last moments together flashed through her mind. She considered pretending she didn't see him, but as she watched Nick emerge from his car less than twenty-five yards away, she knew it wasn't a viable option. He was looking right at her.

She pulled off her gardening gloves as she made her way across the grass, stealing a glance towards the garage, nervous Phil would appear at any moment. "Good morning." She smiled at Brian, who was stepping back from the trunk with a duffel bag slung over his shoulder.

"Hey, Mrs. Hunter." Brian offered her a lopsided smile before jogging off towards the house.

"He looks so much like you," Lina said, bringing her gaze to Nick.

"So I've heard." His eyes were concealed behind sunglasses, and there was no discernible expression on his face. "Nice place."

"Thank you."

"I should go," he said, but made no move to do so. Although she couldn't see his eyes, Lina knew they were traveling over her.

She felt heat in her already-warm cheeks. She wasn't wearing a speck of makeup. Her hair was pulled back in a high ponytail. But her attire was more alluring. She was wearing short, cut-off jean shorts that were frayed and full of holes and a tight cotton tank top. "I wasn't expecting visitors," she said softly.

"You're gorgeous. I need to leave." He turned without another word. Moments later his car roared to life and he was disappearing down her drive.

Lina stood in the center of the driveway staring after him, her heart rate slowly returning to normal. She turned to go into the house and came face-to-face with Phil.

"Drayton was here?"

"Yes, he dropped Brian off."

"What did he say to you?" He was frowning.

"Nothing." She stepped around him. "Less than a paragraph."

Unable to think about anything but her one-minute encounter with Nick, Lina knew she was a poor shopping companion for Adele, but she wasn't sure how to pull herself out of her funk. Seeing Nick had hit her harder than she expected.

"What's with you today?" Adele asked when they took a break from shopping to share a pastry. "Are you missing Megan?"

Lina laughed. Her eldest daughter had been away at college for one week. Instead of thinking of her like she should have been, she was depressed over the loss of a man she should never have developed feelings for in the first place. "I wish."

"What's going on?"

"I have feelings for Nick," she admitted aloud for the first time.

"Nick?" Adele's eyes seemed to grow to twice their normal size. "Who in the hell is Nick?"

"Dr. Drayton."

"Holy shit!" Adele sat back in her chair. "I told you to fuck him, not fall in love with him."

"I'm not in love with him. I'm confused about him."

"Did you have sex with him?"

"No! Adele, you know I wouldn't do that. I'm married."

"Well, so is Phil, and he had sex with someone else."

"Can you just get the revenge stuff out of your head? You're not helping. I know I'm supposed to be with Phil—if there was any question, the whole hot tub incident confirmed it. And since that night things have gotten better with us. It feels almost normal."

"Except there's a woman out there carrying his child." Adele said.

"I said *almost*."

"So what's the problem?"

"I keep thinking about Nick. I mean, not all the time, but a lot. And then today he dropped off Brian. It was the first time I saw him in a couple of weeks, and I felt drawn to him. When I watched him drive away I wanted to cry, and now I just feel sad." She took a deep breath. "I don't know what it means."

"I assume you're attracted to him?"

"Yes." She shook her head. "I can't believe it. It's so wrong. I'm married. I love Phil."

"You're married, not dead. Are you saying in all these years you've never been the teeniest bit attracted to another man?"

"Never."

"Wow."

"What am I supposed to do? I hate thinking about him."

"If you don't see him, it will pass. Just give it time."

"You think?" Lina asked.

"Definitely. And just push him from your mind whenever he comes into it."

"Okay." It would work. It had to work.

"There's something else we could do that would probably permanently cure you of this crush you're carrying," Adele said.

"What?"

"Introduce me to him." Adele smiled. "I'll fuck him."

26

"Is it true if someone keeps popping into your mind, it's because they're thinking about you?" Katie asked over breakfast one Saturday in early October. "That's what Grandma says." She hadn't seen or heard from Matt since Ryan went away to college over five weeks earlier, but she still thought about him all the time.

"Maybe," Lina said before taking a sip of her coffee.

"I believe it," Logan said. "Girls are always popping into my mind."

"Yeah, right." Katie rolled her eyes.

"What?" He smiled. "It's true."

"To be safe, you should just assume everything your grandma says is false," Phil said, not looking up from the article he was reading in the newspaper.

"Ignore him," Lina said.

"I think it's true," Katie said.

"I hope it's not the kid with the tattoos," her father said. "The one that keeps popping into your head."

Katie looked down at her cereal. "I wasn't talking about me." She hated the way he could read her mind. Grandma was right, he was definitely psychic. She could feel his eyes on her but refused to look at him.

"If you say so," he said, sounding less than convinced.

"If they pop into your head while you're showering, does it mean they're thinking of you naked?" Logan asked.

"Gross." Katie scrunched up her face in distaste.

"What is wrong with you?" Phil slapped Logan with his newspaper. "You don't say things like that in front of females."

"You shouldn't say things like that at all," Lina added.

"Sorry." Logan dropped his eyes, but the smile remained.

"Think before you talk," Phil said.

"Okay, sorry." He stole a glance at Katie. They both started laughing.

"Don't encourage him," Phil said to Katie.

"It was funny."

"It was crude."

"It was a serious question," Logan insisted.

"Hey, look at me," Phil said and waited for Logan to meet his eyes. "Enough."

"I'm going to start going to an astrology class with Grandma on Saturday mornings," Katie announced, hoping telling them instead of asking would make them agree.

"No you're not," Phil said. "Absolutely one hundred percent, no."

"Why not?" She frowned across the table at him.

"It's against our religion."

"*Your* religion, you mean," Katie fumed. "I should be able to explore other ideas. I don't need you to think for me."

"When you're an adult, you can explore whatever ideas you'd like. Until then, the answer is unequivocally no." His attention shifted to Lina. "Do you want to talk to your mom or do you want me to?"

"I will."

"You can't imprison my thoughts," Katie said.

"I can certainly try," he said before returning his eyes to the newspaper.

"It's supposed to be eighty today. Can Brian come over to swim?" Logan asked.

Lina was in the garage removing grocery bags from the back of her SUV when she heard the closing of a car door, and then Brian walked in, a backpack slung over his shoulder and a lacrosse stick in his hand.

"I told Logan to call me if you were coming. I drove right by your neighborhood. I could have picked you up."

"I came from my dad's," he said, surprising her.

"Oh." She set down her bags before stepping out onto the driveway, her eyes centering on the Land Rover that was in the process of doing a three-point turn.

"I forgot my cell phone." Brian dropped his things, running past her towards his father's SUV, which had completed its turn and was headed down the drive. "Dad, wait!" he yelled.

The brake lights of the vehicle lit up, and then the door was opening and Nick was stepping out of the SUV. Lina's heart rate quickened as she focused on the man she hadn't seen or heard from in six weeks. She missed him, and as she watched him open the back door of his vehicle so Brian could retrieve his cell phone, she felt a nostalgic pull that made her walk farther out onto the driveway.

When his head turned in her direction, she raised her hand in greeting. He returned her wave before ducking back into the car, and she felt a lump forming in her throat at the realization he was leaving without speaking to her, but then he was emerging once again. Moments later, he and Brian were walking towards her. His hair was longer, and he wasn't quite as tan, but it was him, and her heart leapt in her chest.

"You have the same gait," she called out as they approached.

"Gait?" Brian looked quizzically at Nick.

"We walk the same." He patted Brian on the back as they came to a stop before Lina. "Be good."

"You can let yourself into the house," Lina told Brian. "I think Logan's already down at the pool." She watched him until he disappeared into the garage, and then she was turning back to Nick.

"How are you?" They spoke in unison and then both smiled.

"It's really good to see you," she said.

"Is it?"

"You know it is," she said lightly, her eyes traveling over his face. "I hate not talking to you. I feel like there's a void in my life." As her eyes met his, she felt a connection pass between them.

"I should go. Emily's waiting in the car."

"Emily," Lina repeated, her eyes moving past him to the Land Rover twenty yards away. "How long have you been together?"

"Lina—"

"I'm sorry." She released her breath. "It's none of my business."

"How's Katie?"

"She's good. I mean, still argumentative, but nothing too extreme."

"And everything is working out with Dr. Jones?"

"We see him every three weeks now, and if everything continues to improve, we'll scale back to monthly after the holidays."

"Excellent. How is she doing in school?"

Before she could respond, he was standing up straighter, the warmth gone from his eyes as he looked past her towards the house. Without looking back, Lina knew Phil was approaching. She'd thought he was out cycling, but clearly she'd been wrong.

"Drayton." Phil's voice broke the silence, and then Lina felt his hands gripping her hips as he pulled her back against the hard length of his body, one of his hands sliding over her stomach in a blatant show of possessiveness.

"Good afternoon," Nick said coolly. "Thanks for hosting my son."

"Anytime. He's a good kid."

"Phil?" All eyes turned at the sound of the female voice. A petite blonde, who Lina assumed was Emily, was walking towards them from the Land Rover. "Oh my God, I thought that was you."

Lina felt Phil stiffen behind her. "Hi."

"What are you doing here?"

"I live here," he said.

The confusion on Emily's face was obvious. "You live here? Are you Logan's father?"

"Yes. This is my house. This is my wife." Lina heard the warning behind his words.

"Wow." She shook her head. "I had no idea. I thought you and..." She trailed off, dropping her eyes as she seemed to grasp the situation.

Lina gripped Phil's hands and pried them from around her waist. "How do you know my husband?"

"Lina?" Phil touched her arm.

"Don't touch me," she whispered before taking a step closer to Nick. "How do you know him?" she repeated, her eyes on Emily.

"I'm so sorry," Emily said. "I'm sure I just misunderstood. I..." She paused as her eyes briefly shifted to Phil. "He was in my running group."

"The Saturday-morning running group in Baltimore?"

"Yes." Emily nodded.

"With Kim?"

"Stop it, Lina. You already know the answer," Phil said before shifting his attention to Nick. "Why don't you leave?"

"I'd like my son," Nick said. "I'd be happy to take Logan as well. The two of you need privacy."

"Don't tell me what I fucking need!" Phil exploded, stepping around Lina and directly in front of Nick. "This is none of your fucking business."

"Stop it!" Lina moved between them, her hands on Phil's chest. "You will not take this out on him!" It took a few seconds, but then Phil was taking a deep breath and letting Lina push him back a few steps. "You don't have to take Brian." She turned back to Nick but left her hand on Phil's arm so she would know where he was. "I'm fine. It will be fine. It's a beautiful day. Let's not ruin it for them. They'll spend the entire day in the pool." When she saw the indecision in his eyes, she continued, "Nick, please, I promise it will be fine."

Nick nodded. "Okay." His gaze shifted to Emily, and he motioned with his head towards the car. "Ready?"

"Does she know?" Phil asked. His eyes shifted to Emily and then back to Nick.

"Excuse me?" Nick's eyes narrowed in confusion.

"That you have a thing for my wife. Have you told her?"

Lina flushed with embarrassment. "Phil!" she hissed, turning to face him. "Stop it!"

"It's true," Phil continued. "Isn't that right, Drayton?"

Lina clasped Phil's upper arm, turning him away from the other couple and towards the house. "Stop it," she whispered, glaring up at him. "This is not their fault." She steered him towards the garage, wanting to say something to Nick but afraid of setting Phil off further. She stole a glance in their direction before following Phil into the garage and was relieved to see them walking towards Nick's car. She'd been half-afraid he would change his mind and take Brian.

"That was outrageous," she whispered as soon as they entered the kitchen. "What could possibly compel you to say that to her?" She crossed to the windows and looked out at the pool to make sure the boys were outside and they were alone in the house.

"Nick?" Phil snarled, gripping the back of one of the high-backed bar chairs as he glared at her. "When did he become Nick to you?"

"You are unbelievable! Do you really think that's what we're going to talk about?"

"You've been talking to him, haven't you?" he continued. "That son of a bitch." He turned and was out the door before she could react.

27

As she ran out of the garage, she was relieved to find the Land Rover nowhere in sight. Phil was staring down the drive with his hands on his hips. She slowly closed the distance between them. "You are the one who had the affair," she whispered, poking him in the back with her finger. "And you *dare* to make this about me using the first name of a man I've never had an inappropriate relationship with? You're the lying cheat, Phil, not me."

"Nothing has changed, Lina," Phil said, following her into the house. "I had an affair—you knew that. You've been punishing me for it for four months."

"Punishing you?" she spit out, turning to him. "Punishing you? The only person being punished is me! Every time I think of those texts or the fact there is another woman walking around with your baby inside her!" She looked him up and down. "I don't even know you."

"You don't know me?" he repeated, his hands clenched at his sides. "I'm the same man that made love to you this morning," he snarled. "Tell me what I've done in the last four hours?"

"You've become a stranger to me," she said. "Because the man I thought you were wouldn't have stopped running with his daughter every Saturday so he could see the woman he was already screwing Monday through Friday. You weren't just cheating on me. You were cheating on your children."

"Fuck!" He slammed his hands down on the counter. "So what, now we're back to ground zero? You have to get over it all over again?"

"I don't know." She stared at him, imagining him showing up with Kim as a couple to a running group every week. "Maybe I won't be able to get over it at all."

"What does that mean?" All the anger seemed to evaporate from his body. "What are you saying, Lina?"

"I'm saying what I feel."

He curved one of his hands around the back of his neck. "I made a mistake. One huge fucking mistake. Why can't you just forgive me?"

When Lina drove away from her house, leaving Phil with the boys, she didn't consciously think she had a destination in mind, but when she found herself sitting on the patio of Nick's Mexican restaurant, sipping a margarita and eating from a basket of tortilla chips, she knew she had planned to come to him all along.

The only problem was he wasn't responding to her texts. Over the course of two margaritas, she'd sent him three.

I'm sorry.

I hope everything is okay with Emily.

I wish you would text me back.

She ordered a third margarita and fajitas. When her phone dinged her heart skipped, but it was Phil, not Nick. *I'm sorry. I love you, baby. Come home.*

I need space, she texted back.

Where are you?

Drinking. Leave me alone.

A few minutes later her phone rang, and she glanced at the display expecting to see Phil, but instead Adele was the caller. "Phil's worried about you."

"He should be," she said and then spent the next ten minutes telling her about the altercation in front of her house. "I'm in Baltimore," she admitted when Adele asked her for the third time. "I'm drinking margaritas and texting Nick, but he's ignoring me."

"Tell me exactly where you are."

Sizzling fajitas were set before Lina at the same moment her cell phone dinged with a new text message. This time it was Nick. *I was apart from my phone. Are you okay?*

Are you home?

Close by.

She felt a pang of jealousy at the thought of him and Emily. *Are you with her?*

A few minutes passed before he responded. *Why?*

I want to see you.

I don't think that's a good idea.

I'm at our Mexican restaurant. Please.

"What are you doing here?" Nick asked after lowering himself down into the chair across from Lina fifteen minutes later. His chest was rising and falling with his breathing, and it was obvious he had exerted energy to get there.

"I came to see you." Her eyes traveled over his face. She didn't like the coolness in his eyes. "Don't be mad."

"Why did you come to see me?"

"I miss you." Her voice was barely a whisper.

His eyes dropped to her almost-empty glass. "How much have you had to drink?"

"I'm not drunk, if that's what you're implying."

"I'm not implying anything. I was asking."

"Leave if you're going to be cold to me," she said.

"Lina—"

"I'm serious. I don't want this memory, and I'll just pretend you never came." She finished the remainder of her drink and intentionally turned her chair slightly so she wasn't facing him.

"I'm trying to maintain an air of professionalism with you, but you're making it impossible."

"I don't want you to be professional with me." She turned her chair so she was once again facing him. "I don't think of you as a doctor."

"That's good, because I don't think like a doctor when I'm with you." He paused to order a scotch as a waiter stopped beside the table.

"Are things okay with Emily?"

"I don't want to talk about Emily. This isn't about Emily."

"Do you love her?"

"Lina, what are you doing?"

"Trying to be your friend."

He laughed aloud. "We're not friends. I shouldn't even be here. You have a husband."

"I don't know how to be without him. He's all I know."

"Then you should be home with him, instead of sitting across from me."

"Right now I hate him, but I know it isn't going to last. My mind can't hold on to the anger. I think I can, and then something happens that reminds me how much I need him."

He blew out a stream of air. "I can't do this."

"Do what?"

"Listen to you talk about how much you need him." He met her eyes. "You don't need anyone, especially not him. He betrayed your trust. He had a romantic relationship with another woman while married to you. He isn't the man you seem to want to believe he is."

"You don't understand," she said.

"So you keep telling me." He paused as the waiter set a scotch before him. "But the truth is I do, which doesn't speak very highly of my judgment when it comes to you, because I do know better." He lifted his glass to his lips and took a generous swallow.

"What does that mean?"

"It means I'm incapable of thinking clearly when it comes to you. Instead of staying with a woman who loves me and dealing with the aftermath of the storm your husband's words unleashed, I've left her, upset and confused, so I could come to you."

Lina's heart leapt at his words. "Nick—"

"Hello!" Adele stopped beside their table.

"What are you doing here?" Lina frowned at her.

"I didn't like the thought of you sitting here alone." Her eyes were on Nick as he came to his feet. "I'm assuming you're the famous Dr. Drayton. I'm Adele, Lina's *unmarried* and very available sister."

"Ignore her," Lina said.

Nick nodded at Adele. "I hate to run. There's somewhere I need to be."

Adele touched her chest. "I seriously want you to stay. I've been hearing about you for months, and now I have you in the flesh."

"Another time." He took out his wallet and threw several bills onto the table before shifting his attention to Lina. "Bye."

"Nick! Wait!" Lina was up and following him onto the sidewalk beside the patio. "Please."

"Lina." He stopped, looking down at her. "I need to leave."

"But we weren't done talking."

"Yes, we were."

She didn't like the look of finality in his eyes. "No." She closed the distance between them and hugged him hard. "Don't be upset with me," she whispered into his neck, running her lips along his warm skin.

"I'm not upset with you."

"Then hug me back," she whispered. "Just once."

"You're killing me," he said, but then, as if he had no will-power of his own, he engulfed her in his arms, squeezing her almost too tightly. "I love you," he whispered against her ear. "If you leave him, come find me."

28

"Happy birthday, baby."

Lina opened her eyes and looked into Phil's. He was leaned over her, one hand on each side of the mattress. "Good morning." She stretched her arms above her head. "What time is it?"

"After nine." He met her lips for a soft kiss. "Relax," he whispered against her lips when she moved to sit up. "I turned off your alarm so you could sleep in. Everyone's gone."

"Logan—"

"I dropped him at his stop on my way to the bakery." He straightened and picked up a bag with the emblem from a local bakery from her nightstand.

"You bought me a chocolate croissant?" It was her favorite pastry.

"Of course. And a coffee." He lifted the coffee and then set it back down on her nightstand. "I wanted your day to start right."

"Aren't you going to be late for work?"

"Not if I leave now. We have reservations at Fogo de Chao at seven thirty. I should be home by six." He kissed her again before leaving.

Lina propped herself on her pillows and brought the coffee to her lips, taking a swallow of the warm liquid. Before she could bite into the croissant, her phone was ringing. Over the course of the next half hour she received calls from her mother-in-law, Megan, Diane and finally Adele.

"Happy forty-first! I hope that asshole husband of yours served you breakfast in bed."

"He surprised me with a chocolate croissant."

"Ah, he's pulling out the big guns! Have you groped any handsome doctors in the past three weeks?"

Lina groaned, the memory of her last interaction with Nick still eliciting a myriad of emotions, including guilt, embarrassment and, most distressing, longing. "Please stop reminding me."

"Like you could forget. Still nothing from him?"

"I'm not going to hear from him."

Lina returned home from her annual birthday lunch with Alice to find a dozen red roses and a FedEx envelope on the front porch beside the door. She smelled the roses as she walked towards the kitchen, knowing without opening the card that they were from Phil. He gave her a dozen red roses every birthday.

She set down the vase and opened the FedEx envelope. Inside was a smaller purple envelope, which contained a store-bought card that read "Happy Birthday" across the front in colorful letters. As soon as she opened it, the color drained from her face, and the card, along with the several pictures it contained, slid to

the floor. She fell to her knees, gathering them up, her eyes looking from image to image. She covered her mouth as she struggled
to her feet, barely making it to the bathroom before losing her entire birthday lunch. She kneeled in front of the toilet for minutes,
tears clouding her eyes as she vomited again and again, until there
was no possibility of anything being left in her stomach.

Shakily coming to her feet, she rinsed her mouth out before
making her way to the kitchen. She picked up the pictures and
card from the floor and went up to her bedroom, closing the
door behind her. She crossed to her bed and sat down, spreading
the four photos and the sonogram image on top of the comforter.

Two of the pictures were of Phil sleeping. The first must have
been taken in Kim's apartment. He was in an unfamiliar bedroom that looked feminine, with floral sheets and white rustic
furniture. He was lying on his stomach, completely naked with
his arms slightly above his head, his face obstructed by the pillow, but there was no doubt it was him. It was one of his sleep
poses. She'd seen him in it a thousand times over the years.

The second was the one that made her lose her lunch. It was
taken in their bedroom at their vacation home in Steamboat,
Colorado. He was on his back, one arm flung over his head and
the other on his stomach, the sheet barely covering his lower
body. The picture had been taken from the other side of the bed,
and a framed photograph of Lina and Phil on top of a ski trail
was visible on the nightstand beside Phil's sleeping form. He'd
had sex in their bed with his mistress while her picture was displayed on the nightstand. She felt the bile again coming up in
her throat. She covered her mouth and closed her eyes, waiting
for the wave of nausea to pass.

The third and fourth pictures were of them together. The first
was in a bar she didn't recognize. Kim was sitting on a barstool

wearing jeans and a low-cut black top, her generous cleavage visible, and her blonde hair falling around her shoulders. Phil too was in jeans and a black collared shirt. He was standing beside her, talking to a man she didn't recognize, his left hand resting on Kim's upper thigh, his fingers practically touching the juncture between her legs. Lina's eyes focused on his wedding band, and she wondered if people thought Kim was his wife.

The last picture was the worst to her. Like the others, it was candid, but in this picture he was looking at Kim. They were on a dance floor, and Kim's back was to the camera, her arms wound around Phil's neck. Phil had one hand midway down her back, and the other was gripping her butt as he smiled down at her, dimples creasing his cheeks. The look in his eyes was what Lina couldn't see past. He was looking at Kim with a look she thought was reserved for her. He was looking at her like she was the only woman in the world.

She lifted the final item in the card—a sonogram picture of what she knew was Phil's baby, with an arrow showing it was a boy. He was having a son. She stared at it for close to a minute, her mind almost in a fog, as she tried to come to terms with the fact she was staring at his son with another woman. She set down the slip of paper and focused again on the photo of Phil sleeping in their Steamboat condo. She took a picture of the image with her cell phone before crumbling it in her fist and squeezing it into a small ball. She did the same with the other three pictures before gathering the card, sonogram image and crumbled pictures and carrying them into the bathroom. She stuffed everything into the right pocket of Phil's white terry-cloth robe.

Twenty minutes later, Lina entered the kitchen with a small suitcase in her hand. She set down the case as her eyes focused on the roses. She reached into the vase, lifted out the flowers and carried them out of the kitchen and toward the front of the house, unconcerned with the water dripping on the floor. Seconds later, she was stuffing them in the toilet in the master bathroom.

When she returned to the kitchen, Katie was coming through the mudroom door.

"Happy birthday," Katie said.

"Thanks. How was school?" Lina's words sounded forced to her ears, but Katie didn't seem to notice.

"Good." Katie's eyes fell to the suitcase beside the table. "Are you going somewhere?"

"To the beach with Diane for the weekend."

Katie frowned. "On your birthday? Dad said I couldn't make plans because we were taking you out to dinner."

"No." Lina shook her head. "He forgot I planned this weekend. I didn't realize it was my birthday."

"So you're leaving us with him? I don't want to be alone with Dad all weekend."

"You'll be fine."

As soon as Lina got in her car, she was calling Adele. "Please don't say anything and just listen. I'm kicking Phil out."

"What?" Adele exclaimed.

"I'm telling him to be gone by Sunday afternoon." She drew in a shaky breath. "Please stop by tomorrow and make sure the kids are okay."

"What in the hell is going on? Is he back with her?"

"No—I can't talk right now. Will you stop by?"

"Of course, but where are you going to be?"

"I have to go." She ended the call and then pulled up Phil's name. Moments later she was drafting a text.

You ruined our life. I want you out by Sunday afternoon. I just left and will return after you're gone. She covered her mouth as a small cry escaped, and then she was sending the message.

She pushed her fingertips against her eyes. "You will not cry for him," she said aloud. "You will not cry." She took a deep breath before tapping on her phone display and bringing it to her ear.

The small smidgen of strength Lina had remaining dissolved when Nick opened his front door. "It's over."

He engulfed her in his arms. "Shh," he whispered softly into her hair as she began to cry. "Shh." He ran his hand over the back of her head.

"I'm ruining your jacket," she hiccupped against his chest.

"Ruin it. I don't care."

She released a shaky sigh. "I don't want to cry for him anymore."

"Do whatever makes you feel better."

"Just hold me," she whispered, taking comfort in the feel of his arms around her. "That makes me feel better."

Several minutes passed before he led her to his family room and sat beside her on his sofa, his arm stretched out behind her, his body turned in her direction. "Do you want to talk about it?"

"You must think I'm such a baby," she whispered, wiping at her eyes. "I never used to cry."

"I think you're upset."

"She sent me pictures of the two of them."

"Kim?"

"Yes," she breathed before describing the images now burned in her brain. "He cancelled our spring break this year, claiming he was too busy with work, but it was because of her. He had time to vacation with her but not his family." Just voicing the words had her stomach clenching. "Steamboat was my favorite place. My kids learned to ski there, and I imagined taking my grandchildren there. And now I can never go back."

"I'm sorry."

"I never wanted to be divorced. I never wanted to do that to my children."

"This isn't your fault, Lina."

"Does it matter whose fault it is? They're hurt just the same, aren't they?"

"I'm sorry." He curved his hand around the back of her neck. "I wish there was something I could do."

"Just being near you helps. I feel calmer around you. I always have."

"Good. Will you be okay for a minute? I'd like to change out of my work clothes."

It took thirty seconds for her unease to settle back in, and by the time he returned she was in the corner of the couch, hugging her knees to her chest, trying not to cry. "Lina?" He crossed to her, sitting down on the edge of the couch beside her, his hand gripping her knee. "What's going on?"

"I don't know how I'm going to do this. I don't even know how to be alone. I'm never alone."

"What are you afraid of?"

She gripped his hand, resisting the urge to crawl into his lap. "I don't know. I don't want to think about it. Just don't disappear for long stretches."

"Okay. We'll leave it for now."

"You're being a doctor. I thought you didn't think like a doctor around me."

"Statements like the one you made scream to the doctor in me."

"I'm pitiful, aren't I? A forty-one-year-old that's afraid to be alone."

"'Pitiful' is not a word I would ever use to describe you. Have you had anything to eat today? I could make you something."

"I don't think I can." She thought of the nice lunch she shared with her mother, which ended up in the toilet. "Maybe just a glass of wine for now?"

"Alcohol is a depressant. I'm not sure if that's the best—"

"I'm not planning to get drunk. I just want a glass."

"Okay." He patted her knee, and then he was coming to his feet. "Come on," he said, holding out his hand. "You can keep me company."

She sipped from a glass of wine as she watched him prepare a plate of appetizers, his hands deftly wielding a knife as he sliced cheese, a couple of apples and what looked like fresh pepperoni. She couldn't recall ever seeing Phil slice anything. "You cook." It was more a statement than a question, but he answered.

"I do," he agreed, fishing some olives out of a jar. "I'll make something for you tonight if you'll let me."

"What am I keeping you from? It's a Friday night. You must have had plans."

"I'm exactly where I want to be." He lifted the platter, picked up his wine glass and headed back to the family room. "How about a fire?"

She watched him crouch down in front of his fireplace, arranging several logs on the black grate, and found herself comparing his body to Phil's. There was no question he wasn't as big or broad, but he was clearly fit, and the image of a panther again came to mind.

"My first fire of the season," he said after rejoining her, the orange glow from the fireplace instantly making the room cozier.

"It's beautiful."

She took the cracker he offered, taking a small bite as she watched him take one for himself, the muscles of his jaw clenching and unclenching as he chewed. "So, no Emily tonight?"

"We've gone our separate ways."

"Oh." She dropped her eyes to her wine glass. "Sorry."

"Are you?" He scooped up some almonds, holding his hand between them like a bowl. "Are you sorry?"

"No." She took a few nuts and slowly ate them, adjusting her legs beneath her as she turned to face him, her shoulder sinking into the cushions of the couch.

"What's your plan?" Nick asked.

"What do you mean?"

"You told me you kicked him out, but you seem to be the one who left."

"Oh." She pushed her hair back from her forehead as her gaze shifted to the fire. "I gave him until Sunday to pack his things."

"Have you discussed how you're going to tell your children? This is going to be traumatic for them. Their world is coming unhinged."

"I know," she whispered, shaking her head. "Do we really have to talk about this right now?"

"No, but at some point I think we need to. It's not something—" He stopped mid-sentence at the sound of banging coming from the front of the house.

"What's that?" Lina grabbed his hand.

"Someone's at the door."

29

"It's Phil," Lina said, the color leaving her face.

"There's only one way to find out."

"Wait." Lina caught up to Nick, clasping his arm as he walked towards the front of the house. "You can't let him in. He'll hurt you."

"He isn't going to hurt me, Lina. Trust me."

"You don't know him. He hates you," she cried. "Please—let's just ignore him."

"He isn't going anywhere," he said as the pounding continued. "He probably tracked your phone here."

"Oh my God." She pressed her hand to her mouth. Why hadn't she thought of her phone?

"We're all adults. It's going to be fine." He continued to the foyer and, after a brief look through the peephole, opened the door.

As soon as she saw Phil, standing on the porch in the same dark blue suit he'd left the house in that morning, his hair tousled and his jaw firm, the fear from moments earlier was re-placed by rage as she remembered the pictures. "You bastard!" She squeezed past Nick and launched herself at Phil. "How could you?" she cried as she began pummeling him with her fists. "How could you?"

"What the hell? Lina!" Phil easily restrained her by wrap-ping his arms around her and holding her against his chest. "What happened? What did she do?"

"You took her to Steamboat. You had sex with her in our bed!" she cried.

"Lina," he began, loosening his hold, "I—"

She managed to slap him across the face before he was again holding her hard against his chest. "Let me go!"

"Let her go," Nick said.

"You stay the fuck out of this!" Phil exploded, glaring over Lina's head at Nick. "She is *my* wife."

"Let me go, Phil." She pushed against his chest. "I can't breathe."

He loosened his hold, and she took a step back from him.

"I have nothing to say to you," she said.

"After twenty-five years, I think you do, and I'm not leaving here until you tell me what the fuck is going on."

"Go look in your robe pocket," she said. "Go see what she sent me for my birthday." She turned and began to walk around Nick, but Phil was beside her, gripping her arm.

"She's trying to hurt you. She's trying to get you to leave me."

"Then she wins. She can have you because it's over. I don't know you. You're not the man I thought you were."

"Lina," he whispered, pain evident in his eyes. "Don't do this. I'm begging you."

"I wish I had never met you."

"No." He shook his head. "You don't mean that."

"Yes, I do. Now let go of my arm." She struggled to free herself from his grip. "You've lost your right to touch me."

"You're not going into his house." He yanked her back towards him. "You're still *my* wife."

"Let her go," Nick said.

Phil pushed Lina back behind him before launching himself at Nick.

"No!" Lina cried, but before she could intervene, Phil was throwing a fist towards Nick's face.

It was all a blur in Lina's mind. Nick either ducked or shifted his head to the side, and Phil's fist connected with the brick front of the house. Then Nick dug his fingers into the back of Phil's neck and twisted one of his arms behind his back as he pushed him into the brick he'd just punched.

"This is what's going to happen," Nick said, his voice low and controlled as he held Phil against the wall, his lower body pushed up against the length of Phil's. "You're going to get in your car and leave. And you and Lina are going to take tonight to cool off and start thinking about your children. You can talk tomorrow when you're both calmer. Lina?"

"Yes." Her voice was barely a whisper.

"If you're choosing to stay here, you should go inside now."

She entered his house, stopping just inside the door, continuing to listen as Nick once again began speaking to Phil. "Just so we're clear, I'm not sleeping with your wife. She's an emotional wreck, and I'm not about to take advantage of that. She is here because she needs a friend. I'm a friend. And I suggest you think twice before coming at me again. I am a fifth-degree black belt in karate, and you could get seriously hurt. I'm going to let you go now. Don't do anything stupid."

Hours later, Lina set down the philosophy book she'd found in Nick's guest room, unable to concentrate as thoughts of Phil swirled in her mind. She could feel him. He was upset or hurt or both. She checked her cell phone for the first time since leaving her house and saw over a dozen voicemails, but the two from Phil were from before he came to Nick's. He hadn't attempted to call or text since he left. She was imagining things.

It was 1:45 a.m. She'd avoided thinking about him most of the evening, enjoying Nick's food and company as they shared a bottle and a half of wine and light conversation, but as soon as he left her, as soon as she was alone with her thoughts, she became consumed by Phil. Her mind was her enemy, trying to convince her something was wrong so she would reach out to him. She pulled up the pictures of him and Kim on her cell phone, flipping through them until all desire to reach out to Phil disappeared.

The door to the master suite was closed but unlocked. When she stepped into the room, she could tell from the heaviness of his breathing that Nick was asleep. After quietly crossing to the bed, she lifted the comforter and slid beneath. His deep breathing stopped as soon as she lay back on the pillow.

"Lina?"

"I don't want to be alone," she whispered. "Please—just let me sleep here."

"Just a second." He was off the bed and crossing to his closet.

Lina caught her breath as she realized he was completely naked, the moon coming through the window illuminating his muscled back, butt and legs. His body reminded her of the dancers' she saw when she attended *The Nutcracker* the Christmas before. He disappeared into the closet and moments later reappeared in black cotton leisure pants, his hairless chest bare. An image of Phil's hair-covered chest flashed through her mind.

"Talk to me," he said after stretching out beside her and propping himself up on his elbow.

"I just can't sleep," she whispered. "I don't want to be alone." She slid her body closer to his. "Would you just hold me?"

"Lina, I don't—"

"Please." She turned onto her side, backing her body into the length of his. "Hold me."

He whispered something that sounded to her like "God, help me," and then he was pulling her back into his warmth, his arms wrapped around her body, his chin resting on top of her shoulder

"Thank you." She settled back against him, her hand resting on the back of one his as it lay splayed over her ribcage.

Unable to see his eyes, she found that only his smell was familiar, and even that wasn't familiar in the dark, because it wasn't Phil's mixture of soap, woodsy aftershave and the unique smell that was him. Nick's smell, like the rest of him, had a refined quality. He smelled of a mixture of soap, mint and lavender. His body too felt different. He was harder than Phil and not as comfortable, or maybe he was just different. As she pondered the subtle differences between the feel of their bodies, she found herself relaxing, becoming aware of the strong beat of his heart, which felt exactly like Phil's, and the feel of his chest as it rose and fell with his breath. A feeling of warmth and safety enveloped her, and she fell into a dreamless sleep.

Lina awoke the following morning alone in bed. As the events of the previous day came flooding back, she pulled the comforter over her head, only to be assailed by Nick's aroma. She was in another man's bed. Guilt consumed her as she recalled the feeling of his body wrapped around the back of hers, and she sunk deeper into the covers. She may not have committed adultery, but sleeping in the arms of a man who wasn't her husband had to be close.

She couldn't bring herself to take a shower in his bathroom. It felt too personal. So after brushing her teeth, she slipped on a pair of yoga pants and a loose top and went in search of Nick.

He was sitting at his kitchen table, reading from his iPad, a cup of coffee and an empty plate before him. "Good morning." She gave him a small smile, feeling shy after the intimacy of the night.

He came to his feet. He was still wearing the black lounge pants he'd slept in and had added a long-sleeved black T-shirt. His face was unshaven, but his scruff was light, so his shadow didn't look as heavy as Phil's. Everything about the scene felt intimate, as if he, instead of Phil, were her husband "Sleep okay?" He touched her arm.

"Yes, I'm sorry for that."

"I'm not." He attempted to meet her eyes. "Talk to me. What's going on in your head?"

"I feel like I cheated on Phil," she admitted. "I know it's stupid because I'm not even with him, but I'm Catholic and that's how I feel."

"You didn't do anything wrong."

She lifted her eyes to his. "I slept with you."

"Nothing happened. Believe me, I'd remember." When she blushed he took her hand and squeezed it. "I'm sorry, I shouldn't tease you. Please have a seat. Would you like coffee?"

"Yes."

"We're friends, Lina," he said after she was sitting at the table with a mug of steaming coffee. "You have nothing to feel guilty about, okay?"

She looked into his eyes and felt a fluttering in her stomach. "I'm not sure if that's how I feel about you."

"I'm talking to you as a therapist right now. The only relationship you should be focused on is the one with your husband. You're not emotionally available for more than a friendship with me."

"You told me to find you if I left him."

"I know." He touched the side of her face. "And I meant what I said to you that night."

"Then what are you saying?"

"I'm saying that until you're divorced or on your way to being divorced, we shouldn't take this further. And that's me speaking as a doctor, not a man."

She knew he was right, but the thought of being alone caused a suffocating anxiety in her chest. "Does that mean I can't call you?"

"You can call me as much as you like. This is going to be a difficult time for you and your children. I'll be here as much as you need me, but I want you to know you don't need a man, even if that realization ultimately results in the conclusion you don't want me."

30

s Lina pulled into her garage, she felt like the time with Nick was almost a dream, and she was now waking up to her real life. It was almost 11:00 a.m., and when she entered the kitchen it looked untouched, like the house was still sleeping.

She set down her bag and opened all the blinds before making her way upstairs. When she entered the master bedroom, she heard the sound of water running in the bathroom. The room was in a state of upheaval, with bags open and partially packed. She felt tears in her eyes as she realized what it meant. She approached the bathroom and saw Phil in the shower, his back to her as he stood under the spray of water, a plastic bag wrapped around his right arm.

"What's that?" she asked.

He turned at the sound of her voice. Even through the water-spattered glass she could see the circles under his eyes. "Did you fuck him?"

"No!" She crossed her arms over her chest.

He turned his back to her. "I'll be out by tonight."

"Phil—"

"The kids will be back this afternoon. Mike and Jeanie had them overnight. We can tell them then."

"Why didn't you call Adele?"

"Because I called my brother."

Lina was sitting on the unmade bed when Phil emerged from the bathroom naked, his right hand and lower arm encased in gauze and some type of temporary brace. He ignored her as he stopped before one of the open suitcases and pulled out a pair of boxer briefs, awkwardly stepping into them as he tried to maneuver with one hand.

"How bad is your hand?"

"I'm no longer your concern. You made your feelings perfectly clear last night." He walked towards his wardrobe.

"Did you see the pictures, Phil?" she asked, following. "Did you see my nice birthday gift?"

"I did."

"That's it? That's all you have to say?"

"Yes. That's it." He pulled a pair of jeans from a shelf and turned his back to her.

"You're a bastard!"

He slowly turned, his eyes meeting hers. "Maybe I am, but I never walked into her apartment with her while you were standing on her front porch. I never left you alone with a broken and bloodied hand to drive a manual transmission to the ER. And I sure as hell never made you lie awake all night wondering how many times I was fucking her." He breathed in, and Lina could see tears in his eyes. "Congratulations—you broke my heart." He turned away from her. "Now leave me the fuck alone."

She left the room and leaned back against the wall, covering her mouth to stifle a cry. She felt wracked by guilt at the memory of her night with Nick. She'd shared dinner and a bottle of wine with another man while her husband sat in an emergency room by himself. And then she had curled up against his body and slept like a baby while Phil suffered alone. He didn't deserve her loyalty. He had gotten another woman pregnant, and yet she felt sick at the hurt she saw in his eyes.

She went down to the kitchen and made a pot of coffee before sitting down at the island. Her eyes focused on a bag with a bottle of pills and papers inside. She pulled it towards her and looked through the contents. He had been given a bottle of Percocet for pain. She read through his hospital release papers. His hand was broken in three places and would probably require surgery. She covered her mouth. He wouldn't be able to ride his bike or swim. And he certainly couldn't drive his car. How he managed to drive himself home she couldn't imagine.

"Take my car," she said when he came into the kitchen over an hour later, carrying two bags, one slung over his left shoulder, the other in his hand. "Until your hand is better you should just drive the SUV."

He didn't acknowledge her comment as he continued into the mudroom, but when she stepped out into the garage after he went back upstairs, she saw her trunk door open. He made several trips between the bedroom and the car, and Lina noticed the paleness of his skin and the beads of sweat on his forehead.

"Have you taken any of these?" She lifted the bottle of pain-killers when he stepped out of the mudroom.

"You told me to leave. Stop acting like my wife." He left the room, and for the next couple of hours she saw him sporadically as he did some work in his study, went out to the car a few times and took a soda from the refrigerator.

"I'm telling them about the baby."

Lina turned at the sound of Phil's voice. He was under the arch of the doorway leading into the kitchen from the front of the house. "No." She shook her head. "Not until after he's born." He was having a son. "Did you know? That she was having a boy?"

"I'm telling them," he said, ignoring her question. "I'm not putting them through this twice."

"Are you a hundred percent sure it's yours?"

"She had an in vitro DNA test. He's mine." He disappeared back in the direction of his study.

Lina followed and found him sitting behind his desk. "We can't just tell them. They're going to be devastated enough by you leaving. Why don't we wait?"

"I'm telling them," he said coldly.

"I didn't sleep with him. I didn't kiss him. I didn't do anything wrong."

He looked up from his computer screen. "You chose him."

"No, I didn't," she said, shaking her head. "He's a friend, and I was in pain. Those pictures devastated me." She felt her lower lip begin to tremble. "He's no different than a woman friend."

"Except he's not a woman. He's a man who's in love with you. A man you have insisted on numerous occasions you have no relationship with."

"I don't."

"You went to his house. You ran to him—not your mother, not Adele, not Diane, but Katie's ex-doctor."

"You took her to our vacation home! You fucked her in my bed! You destroyed this family!" Tears gathered in her eyes. "I'm not going to feel guilty for something innocent."

"Then don't. I'm the bastard. I'm the man you wish you'd never met, so why don't you just stay away from me? The kids will be home in half an hour, and then I'll be gone, just like you asked. What do you want from me, Lina?"

"I don't want you to be such an asshole to me," she said, folding her arms across her chest. "You're the one who did this to us."

"You told me you don't want to be my wife. You don't get to dictate how this relationship progresses. I'm not going to be your friend. I plan to have as little contact with you as possible. So get the fuck out of here."

Lina was staring out the kitchen window, wondering if she was in the midst of a nightmare or her husband was really leaving, when Logan and Katie came through the mudroom door.

"What are you doing home?" Logan asked. "I thought you were at the beach."

"Dad made me spend the night at Aunt Jeanie and Uncle Mike's like I'm a baby," Katie complained. "Why can't I choose where I spend the night?"

"Your mother and I need to talk to the two of you," Phil interrupted as he came into the room. "Take a seat at the table."

"What happened to your hand?" Logan asked. He crossed to Phil, his eyes on the brace.

"I broke it."

"How?" He reached out to touch it.

"Just take a seat, Logan. Katie?" he called to her as she began to leave the room. "Please sit down."

"Did you fall off your bike?" Logan asked.

"No. Katie?"

She frowned but followed his instructions, taking the chair beside Logan's. "Did someone die?"

"No." He pulled out a chair opposite theirs. "Lina?" He indicated with a nod of his head that he wanted her to sit, and then he was lowering himself into the chair beside her, staring down at his hands. "Your mother and I love you both very much," he finally said, his eyes moving between Logan and Katie. "Nothing will ever change that. It's important you know that."

"You're getting a divorce?" Katie asked.

"No they're not!" Logan said, the color draining from his face.

"Let me talk," Phil said. "Last February I began a relationship with a woman I worked with—an inappropriate relationship. I had an affair. It ended in May. It's the biggest regret of my life, but I can't undo it. The relationship resulted in a pregnancy."

"You cheated on Mom?" Logan's eyes were full of disbelief as he looked at Phil.

"Is she having your baby?" Katie asked.

"What?" Logan's gaze swung from Katie to his father. "What is she talking about?"

"He just said the relationship resulted in a pregnancy. That means he got her pregnant."

"I did," Phil said. "And yes, she's going to have it. Your mother, understandably, is having a hard time moving past it."

"How could you do that to her?" Logan cried.

A tear slipped from Lina's eye when she saw the devastation on Logan's face. He looked crushed, like he had been told someone died.

"I made a mistake."

Logan shook his head and began to get up. "I don't want to hear any more."

"I'm not done, Logan. I need you to sit," Phil said, his voice remaining calm. "I know this is hard, but I need to finish."

Logan dropped back into his chair, his eyes lowered.

"Your mother and I are separating," he continued. "I've already packed, and I'm leaving as soon as we're done here."

"Are you getting a divorce?" Katie asked, her expression not giving away her feelings.

"For now it's a separation, but regardless of what happens between me and your mother, you're still my children, and you're still the most important things in the world to me. I'm not divorcing you."

"Can I go now?" Logan asked.

"Yes," Phil said, and Logan fled the room.

"Are you going to be like a father to this baby? Is it going to call you Dad?" Katie looked more curious than upset.

"Yes. He's innocent in all of this."

"It's a boy?"

Phil took a deep breath. "He hasn't been born yet, but yes."

"You don't love him anymore?" Katie asked Lina.

"Of course I do," Lina said. "I'm just having a hard time moving past what he did."

Katie's gaze shifted to Phil. "Grandma said men always cheat—that they're not made for monogamy. I thought she was wrong because of you. I guess she was right."

"That's not true," he said, his voice firm. "We're not animals. I know plenty of men who have never cheated."

She shrugged. "Where are you going to live?"

"With Wayne and Diane until I find something more permanent."

He'd called Wayne and Diane. Their best friends knew. Lina felt a knot forming in her throat. This was real. There was no waking up from it.

"I guess we're like everyone else," Katie said before pushing back her chair and leaving the room.

Phil stood and headed towards the mudroom door, and Lina realized he was leaving. "What about Megan?"

He paused but didn't turn to face her. "I'm driving out there tonight. I'll make sure she's okay before leaving her tomorrow."

"You shouldn't be going anywhere with your hand like that. You're supposed to be resting and taking painkillers."

"I'm not telling her over the phone."

"I could go," Lina said, but as the words left her lips she knew it was an empty offer. They both knew Megan would want to hear it from him.

31

The afternoon felt surreal as Lina tried to find normalcy without Phil. She did the things she always did, some gardening and then laundry, but it felt different knowing Phil wouldn't be coming home. As she folded clothes from the dryer, she paused with a pair of his underwear in her hand and realized that she would never again see him wearing them as he stood in the bathroom brushing his teeth or sat on the edge of the bed setting his alarm. It struck her then that life without Phil couldn't feel normal because being his wife was her normal.

She was in the basement in the process of cleaning out her second freezer when Alice joined her. "Did Katie call you?" Lina asked.

"She did." Alice began to take the frozen packages Lina was pulling from the freezer. "How are you?"

"I don't know."

"Do you need a hug?"

"I think so," she whispered before walking into her mother's outstretched arms. "I'm lost, Mom. I have no idea who I am separate from him."

Alice wrapped her in her arms. "That's because you aren't supposed to be separate from him."

"You're not helping. Can't you just be my mom and not an astrologer?"

"The two are the same, and I'm trying to save you unnecessary pain. He's your cosmic soulmate. You can't escape the laws of the universe. You won't be able to find happiness without him."

"Well I can't find happiness with him either, so I guess I just won't be happy." She again began pulling packages from the freezer.

"Is there someone else?"

"What?" Lina spun around. "Of course not! What are you talking about?"

Alice raised her eyebrows. "Adele told me Dr. Drayton has feelings for you, and I've looked at your chart. I told you, you need to be on guard."

"You're unbelievable, and she's unbelievable for breaking my confidence!" She began yanking out packages of frozen meat. "He's the one that cheated. Not—" She stopped midsentence, her eyes focusing on the frost-covered Bible she'd just pulled from the freezer. "What is this doing here?"

"Why did you put that in the freezer?" Alice asked.

"I didn't." Lina removed an envelope from between the pages and, as she unsealed it, remembered Katie borrowing it earlier in the summer. "Oh no," she said as she watched some hair float to the ground. She unfolded a sheet of paper and saw a triangle enclosing the names "Katie" and "Matt." An image of the boy with the tattoos flashed through her mind.

"Oh, she must have done a spell," Alice said as she took the sheet of paper.

"That's exactly what she did," Lina said. "And it's not okay. We don't allow this type of thing in our house."

"She's just having a little fun," Alice said. "You don't actually believe in it, do you?"

"Of course not, but Katie probably does. What are you doing?" she asked as Alice bent down.

"I'm picking up the hair, so we don't ruin her spell."

"This is crazy. I'm not putting the Bible back in the freezer."

"Do *you* really want to be responsible for the spell not working?" Alice asked.

"It's not going to work," Lina said.

"Well, then there's nothing to worry about, is there?" She took the Bible from Lina and put the envelope back in place. "Trust me, Lina, if it doesn't work out with this boy, you don't want her to think it's your fault."

Adele arrived in the late afternoon. As Katie, who appeared outwardly unfazed by her father's departure, assisted Alice with dinner preparations, Lina checked on Logan, who hadn't budged from his gaming console since Phil left. Then she joined her sister for a glass of wine in the family room.

"You need a lawyer," Adele said.

"He's been gone less than six hours."

"The sooner the better. As time goes on he's going to get less generous. You want to keep this house, don't you? And first thing Monday, you need to open a bank account in your name and transfer twenty-five thousand into it. That way—"

"I'm not doing anything," Lina said, her face heating. "He would never hurt me like that."

"Yeah, and he wouldn't take his mistress to your home in Steamboat, would he?"

"He took her to Steamboat?" Logan asked.

"Logan," Lina whispered, looking up at him as he stepped farther into the room.

"I'm sorry, sweetie," Adele said. "I didn't know you were standing there."

"Did he? Take her to Steamboat?"

"You weren't supposed to hear that," Lina said.

"I hate him."

"No, you don't." Lina shook her head. "You don't hate your father."

"Yeah, I do." As he stood before her with his chin tilted up and his jaw clenched, she knew her innocent boy was gone.

— —

It wasn't that Lina was afraid of the dark, but since the horrific night when she was sixteen, she'd never felt as safe when the sun went down. So when she entered her bedroom at a few minutes past 11:30 p.m., she was already mentally prepared for the fear she felt at being alone. What she wasn't prepared for was the ache in her heart when she looked into Phil's wardrobe. About a third of his clothes were gone. She leaned in, intending to close the door, but found herself stepping into his closet and wandering around, running her fingers over his suits, her eyes scanning the half-empty shelves. She could still smell him, his scent permeating the air. She lifted one of his sweatshirts and brought it to her face, breathing him in as tears clouded her vision.

She wanted her Phil back. Not the one who'd had an affair, but the one who would never have betrayed her.

She lowered herself onto her bed and cried into his shirt, releasing the tears she'd been holding all day. Thirty minutes passed before the tears abated, but as soon as she entered the bathroom she was once again overcome when she saw his empty side of the sink. It was as if he had never been there. She wanted to call him and tell him to come home, but visions of him and Kim came into her mind. She didn't feel like she could be with him or without him. Her eyes traveled to the teenage picture of them on her nightstand. She wanted to turn back the clock and bring that boy back.

When the tears finally stopped, she reached for her phone and called his cell. He didn't answer, but moments later she received a text.

I'm with Megan, it read. *I can't talk.*

How is she? she texted back.

Sad.

Could I talk to her? Would you have her call me?

It's midnight, Lina. We're in my suite watching a movie and she's barely awake. I'll have her call you tomorrow.

Okay. Tell her I love her.

Lina was wondering if it was too late to call Nick when her phone chimed with a text from him. *Everything okay?*

She called him, gripping the phone as his voice came over the line. "Hard day," she whispered.

"I know," he said. "I didn't wake you, did I?"

"I wish." She closed her eyes and tried to picture him. "I hate the night. I usually take something to help me sleep when Phil travels, but I don't want to have to take them permanently."

"Taking something temporarily, until you're feeling a little better, is probably a good idea."

"Or you could come over. I'd rather have you than a pill."

He chuckled softly. "I'd love to be your pill, but I think it wouldn't be the wisest decision with Logan and Katie in the house. I assume they're with you?"

"Yes. Logan is so angry at Phil. In an instant, he went from my smiling boy to an angry teenager. I don't know what to do for him."

"Be there. Encourage him to talk. Communication is critical for him right now. How is Katie?"

"Fine—she took it in stride. I'm not even sure she cares."

"She cares. Don't let her fool you."

"Would you stay on the phone with me until I fall asleep?" She knew she sounded needy, but she couldn't bear the thought of being alone with her thoughts. "I'm taking one of my pills, so it shouldn't be too long."

"I'll stay on the phone with you as long as you like. And if you have a dream and you need to talk, you can call me. I'll turn my ringer up and have my phone right next to my bed."

She felt herself relaxing in response to the timbre of his voice. "What would I do without you?"

"That's something you don't have to ponder. I'm here."

32

Lina awoke with her cell phone pressed into the side of her cheek. As her eyes traveled around her room, she felt a dull ache in her chest and briefly closed her eyes. Phil was gone, and he wasn't coming back.

The house was quiet when she went downstairs; both Katie and Logan were still asleep. She looked at the clock, debating whether or not to wake them for church. For Logan's sake, she decided it was a good idea, not wanting to completely turn his life upside down, and an hour and a half later she found herself standing between her children, listening to the priest talk about the importance of forgiveness.

Katie was looking down at her cell phone, and Logan was staring straight ahead at the priest. Without his usual smile, he looked older than fourteen, more like a man than a boy. Lina slipped her arm around his waist and leaned her head against his shoulder in an attempt to assure him everything was going to be okay and was surprised when, instead of pushing her away as she feared, he put his arm around her. As he hugged her to his side she felt choked up for a moment realizing he was trying to comfort her.

— ⁓

Katie read and then reread the text she'd received from Emma. Matt had broken up with his girlfriend. *Are you sure?* she texted back. *I mean how do you know it isn't just a rumor?*

It's not a rumor. He told me himself.

Katie immediately called Emma. "You saw him? Why didn't you tell me you were going to see him?"

"I didn't know. My dad stopped by the lumberyard on the way home from church, and he was there."

"And he just told you? What did you say to him first?"

"I don't know, we were just talking. But he asked about you. I told him about your parents—I hope that's cool. I mean, it's kind of a big deal."

"It's totally cool."

"He seemed into you. Like, asking what you've been up to and stuff. I gave him your number and told him he should call you. But even if he doesn't, Ryan's going to be home for fall break next weekend, and Matt said he'd come by, so you'll definitely see him."

Katie spent most of the day writing a research paper, but her phone was never far from her side. When it rang at a few minutes past 7:00 p.m., throwing her stomach into a nervous flutter, she felt a flash of annoyance when she saw "Dad" on the display. She didn't want to talk to him. He'd been gone all of one day, and it was the second time he'd called.

She begrudgingly answered and, like she'd been the evening before, was asked how she was doing, what she had done that day and what she was currently doing. "I'm working on a paper," she said, hoping it would get him off the phone.

"Anything interesting?"

"Not unless you're into eastern civilization in the fifteenth century. I should probably go now. I have other homework too."

"How's your brother doing?"

"I don't know. Fine, I guess. He's been playing video games for two days straight." She closed her eyes as soon as the words left her mouth, wishing she could recall them. "I mean, not like all the time, but—"

"Put him on the phone."

"What?" She didn't want to give Logan her phone. What if Matt called? "Why don't you just call his cell phone?"

"Because he's not answering."

"I'll tell him to call you."

"Put him on the phone, Katie," he said in what she knew was his serious, don't-argue-with-me voice.

She stomped out of her room and into the rec room, where Logan was sitting in front of the television wearing headphones, his hands clasping a controller, his body jerking from side to side as he stared intently into the television display. "It's Dad," she said, holding out her phone.

Logan lifted his eyes briefly before returning them to the display, continuing the battle raging on the screen. "Wait." Twenty more seconds passed before he removed his headphones and looked up at her. "What?"

"Dad." She again held out her phone.

"I don't want to talk to him," he said before again donning the headphones.

Katie brought her cell phone to her ear. 'He said—"

"Tell him if he doesn't get on the phone, I'm coming over there," he said.

"What?" Logan said into the phone after Katie relayed the message. "Fine...I didn't have any," he said.

Katie dropped down on the couch, no longer worried about a missed text from Matt as she watched Logan's eyes fill with tears and then his bottom lip begin to quiver. "I don't care," he said. "You broke one of the Ten Commandments. You make us go to church, but you don't even follow what they say." His face crumbled, and he began to cry. "I can't," he whispered before tossing the phone to Katie and fleeing to his room.

Katie lifted the phone to her ear. "I think he's too upset to talk," she said, a sick feeling in the pit of her stomach.

"I know," her father said, sounding tired. "I'm going to take the two of you to dinner Tuesday night. Maybe you can tell him that when he's feeling better."

She wanted to ask him if that meant he wouldn't be calling the next night but couldn't bring herself to say the words. He sounded sad, and, for reasons she didn't quite understand, she didn't want to make him sadder. "I will."

"Katie?"

She gripped the phone, knowing what he was going to say. "Yes?"

"I love you."

"Bye, Dad," she whispered.

As she headed back to her room, she paused outside Logan's door, wishing for the first time in two months that Megan was home. Megan would know what to say to make Logan feel better. She knocked softly on his door. "It's me," she said, opening the door. He was lying on his bed, turned on his side and facing the wall.

She had no idea what to say, so she sat down on the side of his bed and said nothing. A few minutes passed, and she was thinking about leaving when Logan rolled over onto his back.

"He's such a fucking liar."

Her eyes widened as she swung her gaze to his. "Logan! You just said 'fucking.'" It was the first time she'd ever heard him curse. "Wow."

He blushed. "Yeah, well, he is. He's always lecturing me about what it means to be a man, and the whole time he…" He paused as if unable to bring himself to say the words. "He was sinning."

"Maybe it's better that he's not perfect. He can't really expect us to be if he's not."

"I still hate him," Logan said.

"I don't think I do, not for this anyway." Katie lay back on his bed beside him. "I think he really regrets it. And Grandma said they're going to get back together by next summer. She looked at their charts."

"Mom won't take him back! He had sex with another woman."

"She probably will. He said it ended in May, and she stayed with him all summer. She still loves him. She told me."

"Maybe she just found out."

"I don't think so. Remember when she was crying on the deck that night and then Adele came over? That's probably when she found out."

Logan considered this for a moment. "I wouldn't take someone back if they cheated on me. I hope she doesn't take him back."

"Do you want her to marry someone else?"

"No!" He turned his lips down.

"Well, I think that's how it works. She's not that old. If they get divorced, she'll probably start dating and stuff. That would be really weird." She couldn't imagine her mom with someone other than her dad.

"I'm never going to cheat," Logan said. "Not even on my girlfriend. It's wrong."

Katie flipped onto her side and stared at his profile. "Do you have a girlfriend?"

He hesitated, which surprised her, because she expected him to say no. "I kind of like Lisa," he said.

She tried to recall a Lisa and then sat up so she could see his face. "Lisa Kendrick? She's my age."

He blushed. "She's nice."

"Oh my God, Logan. You've seen her boobs, haven't you?" She had a huge chest.

"No," he said, but his blush deepened.

Katie laughed. "You are such a liar." She couldn't believe he was hooking up with a girl her age, but then she thought of how Emma seemed to want to talk to him more lately. She always thought of him as so much younger, but maybe you couldn't judge your own brother. And considering he was over six feet tall, he looked older than fourteen. "Have you had sex with her?"

"No!"

This time she did believe him. "Do you want to?"

"I don't want to talk about this with you. It's weird."

"Why is it weird?" She lay back down.

"Because you're my sister."

"It's only weird if you think it is. Emma and Ryan talk about everything."

"I'm not talking to you about sex." He picked up a lacrosse ball off his nightstand and began tossing it up in the air. "What about you? Do you like anyone?"

"Remember Matt?"

He caught the ball and turned his head, meeting her eyes. "You told Mom and Dad you didn't like him."

"I lied."

— ⁓

"Mom?"

"Logan." Lina wiped the tears from her eyes. "Hi."

"Are you okay?" he asked, his eyebrows pulled together in concern.

"I'm fine. I was just—I'm just a little sad." She smiled up at him.

"Do you want me to sit with you or something?"

"No. I was just going to go upstairs and shower. I'm fine. Please don't worry about me."

He stared at her, not looking convinced. "I was going to check that the house is locked up and then set the alarm."

"You don't have to do that. I can—"

"No, I'll do it," he interrupted. "From now on, I'll do it."

"He seems to think he needs to be the man of the house," Lina told Nick an hour later. "He even looks older. And he's trying to comfort me when I'm supposed to be the one comforting him."

"It's all normal," Nick assured her. "He's just trying to find his footing."

"I don't want him to worry about me."

"It's been two days. He's upset. You're upset. If your house seemed normal right now, I'd be more concerned."

She turned out her light, the darkness not scary with his voice in her ear. "Today is the first day since I met Phil that I haven't heard his voice. Over twenty-four years."

"And how does that make you feel?"

"Sad."

"I imagine it would."

"I don't know why I brought him up. I don't want to talk about him. Let's talk about you. What did you do today?"

33

ina awoke with a start in her dark bedroom, unable to catch her breath. "Phil?" She felt the empty mattress beside her. "Phil?" She looked around the room and remembered. He was gone. Her lungs suddenly didn't feel large enough to take in enough air. She grappled on the nightstand for her phone.

"Lina?" Phil's deep voice came over the line. "Lina?"

"I can't breathe," she managed. "I'm suffocating."

"You're not suffocating. Listen to my breaths." He breathed in deeply and then exhaled. "Do that for me. A big breath in, and now let it out."

She followed his instructions, her eyes closed tightly, her hand clenching the phone as she breathed in and out, listening to the flow of encouraging words coming through the phone. It took a dozen or so breaths before she felt the air filling her lungs and her body beginning to relax.

"I tried to sleep without a pill," she said when she could talk without effort. "I woke up and you weren't here. I panicked."

"It's okay." He sounded exhausted. "Are you okay now?"

She knew she should let him go back to sleep but was afraid to hang up the phone. "Do you mind staying on the phone with me for a minute? I'll take a sleeping pill." She was reaching for the bottle on her nightstand.

"Just go back to sleep, baby. I won't hang up until you do."

For the second morning in a row, Lina awoke feeling dizzy with her cell phone pressed into the side of her cheek. She squinted at the clock and groaned when she realized she'd overslept, knowing she wouldn't have time to shower before dropping Logan at his bus stop.

Thankfully, Katie had started to drink coffee, so there was a full pot when she made it down to the kitchen. "What's wrong with your face?" Katie asked, squinting up at her. "Did you sleep on something?"

Lina touched her cheek, feeling the outline of the cell phone. "Yes, my phone."

"Yeah, that's what it is."

Lina gripped the counter as she brought her coffee mug to her lips, taking a long swallow of the warm liquid. "We're getting a dog."

"What?"

"We need a dog."

"Did you say something about a dog?" Logan entered the room looking as tired as Lina felt, his eyes puffier than normal and his hair uncombed.

"Yes." She paused to kiss his cheek. "We're getting a dog. A big dog." One that could sleep at the end of her bed so she didn't have to wake up with a cell phone indentation in her face.

"Cool." He smiled for the first time in two days.

"Why would you call Phil?" Adele asked Lina a couple of hours later as they sat across from each other at a small bakery, sharing a muffin.

"It wasn't a conscious decision, but he's always been the one who could calm me down. After that night with Shiloh...It used to happen to me after that night, and he could always make the suffocating feeling go away."

"But now you're having it because you kicked him out. Do you plan to have him help you get past *him*? How is that going to work exactly?"

"It was one time, and it was the middle of the night. It wasn't planned. And I realized something when I woke up this morning. I have no idea who I am separate from him. I'm completely dependent on him, financially, physically, mentally. I've lost myself."

"That's a profound realization."

"I don't even know how much money we have. He takes care of everything. I've never even looked at our tax returns. I just sign whatever he puts in front of me."

"That's crazy, Lina."

"I know. I took your advice, though. Just before I came here I opened an account in my name and put twenty-five thousand in it—half of what was in our joint account."

Adele gripped her hand. "Good. Now we need to find you a good lawyer."

She went from coffee with Adele to lunch with Diane. "What are you doing, Lina?" Diane said practically before she sat down. "Are you really going to throw your marriage away over a four-month affair? You look terrible, by the way."

"Thanks." Lina looked down at her clasped hands, tears suddenly threatening. After her drug-induced sleep, her emotional state was in upheaval, and the feelings of strength and resolve she'd felt when she awoke and later when she spoke to Adele had been replaced with fear and insecurity. It was as if she were a pendulum swinging from one extreme to another.

"I'm sorry." Diane laid her hand over the back of Lina's. "I know you're hurting, but kicking him out can't possibly be the answer. You look as bad as he does. You should see him. I swear he's already lost five pounds—I couldn't get him to eat a thing last night."

Lina tapped the display on her cell phone and brought up the picture of Phil dancing with Kim, his hand on her butt. "The look on his face," she said as she slid the phone across the table. "I thought that look was only for me."

"Oh, Lina," Diane whispered as she stared down at the picture. "That's a man in lust, not love. Honey, the way he looks at you is different. Why don't you delete this?"

"Because I don't want to forget. There's more. You can flip through them."

"I don't need to." Diane slid the phone back across the table. "I already know he had an affair."

"It's worse when you see the pictures," Lina said.

"Which is exactly why you should stop looking at them. Do you have a plan? What's your plan?"

"I'd like to make it through a night without having to take a pill or call him, and once I can do that, I'll let you know."

⁓ ⁓

"Do you want to tell me why there is twenty-five thousand dollars missing from our checking account?" Phil asked later that evening. She'd been dreading the call all day as she tried to anticipate his reaction, vacillating between feeling completely justified and unsure about her actions. She'd even driven back to the bank to transfer the money back into their joint account but at the last minute changed her mind.

"I just thought I should have money of my own," she said after stepping out onto the deck to give herself privacy.

"Why?" He sounded more confused than annoyed.

"Because I'm forty-one years old, and I've never had a bank account in only my name. I think it's time."

"You realize by putting it into an account in only your name, I've lost access to it. It was my money too."

"I left you half." She dug her fingers into the back of her neck, kneading her muscles.

"You left me half?" he repeated, frustration creeping into his voice. "That account pays all of our expenses—the mortgage, phones, cable, electricity, taxes, school tuitions. I was building it up so there would be enough to pay the tuitions in December."

"I didn't know that. I don't know anything about our finances. You've kept me completely in the dark."

"If you're in the dark it isn't my fault. I haven't hidden a damn thing from you."

"You take care of everything. I never even see our bills."

"Jesus Christ, Lina! Are you listening to yourself? I've been taking care of you for twenty-five years, and suddenly that makes me the bad guy? Have you ever wanted for anything?"

"That isn't the point."

"Then what is the point? Please tell me the fucking point!"

"Don't yell at me."

"I'm sorry, but I don't know what the fuck is going on. You're making no sense."

"You made me completely dependent on you," she rushed out. "I don't want to need you."

"I'm your husband. You're supposed to need me."

"I don't want to."

Seconds passed before he replied. "What are you saying?" All the anger was gone from his voice.

She closed her eyes, a knot twisting in her stomach. "I don't know." Her voice was barely a whisper. "I'm very confused."

"Well, I suppose you'll let me know when you're not confused anymore. In the meantime, I'll start looking for a place to live." When she didn't respond after several seconds, he continued. "Regardless of what someone is whispering in your ear, I would never cut you off financially. Every account we have is in both our names. If you want to understand our finances, just look in the safe. The combination is the month and day we met. The names of our accounts and passcodes are inside. And this is not the first or even second time I've told you this."

He was right. She recalled him telling her before he left with Logan on an overnight lacrosse trip the previous spring. Her guilt over transferring money from their account returned. She should never have listened to Adele. "I'll put the money back tomorrow."

"No," he said. "If that account provides you with some sense of autonomy that you need, I want you to keep it. But please don't move any more money without my knowledge."

34

The plan was to meet in the courtyard outside Nick's building and enjoy the fall weather, but it was raining, so Lina instead went up to his office. "What did you do?" he asked after his last patient left and they were alone in his waiting room. "Buy one of everything?"

She smiled as she came to her feet, two overstuffed bags in her arms. "I couldn't decide, and I knew Logan would finish off anything we don't, so..." She trailed off as he stopped within inches of her, brushing his lips over her cheek.

"It's good to see you." He relieved her of the bags and motioned with his head for her to precede him into his office. "Not as scenic as the courtyard, I'm afraid, but we will remain dry."

The feeling of his warm lips lingered on her cheek as she stepped into his office and watched him set the bags on the coffee table. "I feel like we should be discussing Katie," she said as she sat down on the same leather sofa she'd sat on a hundred times over the past year.

"We can if you'd like." He lowered himself down beside her, his thigh pressing against the length of hers. "How did you sleep?"

"Fine, thanks to the pill. How late did we talk?" She leaned forward and began to empty the contents of the bags onto the coffee table, conscious of the feel and heat of his leg against her own.

"Twelve thirty or one. I didn't look at the clock."

"I'm sorry. I promise this isn't permanent."

"I'm not complaining."

"You're a saint." She handed him a chicken panini.

"Far from a saint, I'm afraid." He removed the foil covering his sandwich and raised his eyes to hers. "Is this a nice coincidence or did you remember?"

"That you had a chicken panini the first time I met you? I remembered."

He breathed in the aroma of the sandwich, a smile lighting his features. "My favorite. Thank you."

"Maybe you'll even get to enjoy it while it's still warm."

"I don't know. I have the same beautiful distraction sitting with me."

She looked down at her own sandwich. "Are you flirting with me?"

"Maybe, although I know you are still very much a married woman, so I probably shouldn't be."

"He moved out. We're separated."

"You told him you loved him last night."

She frowned in confusion. "What do you mean?"

"You were barely conscious and technically you told me, but you thought I was him. It was right after reminding me I had a dental appointment today."

Her face heated. It was true. She'd texted Phil that morning to remind him of his dental appointment. "I'm sorry. I don't know why—"

"Lina, it's fine. You've been separated five days, and you were together a long time. I'm a big boy, and my eyes are wide open. And for now, for that reason and the reasons I gave you at my house last Saturday, we're just friends."

— —

The dog sprinted across the yard, his long legs covering the forty yards Logan had thrown the ball in seconds. "Not so far," Lina said. "He could run away."

It was Friday afternoon, and Lina and Logan had just brought the dog home from a local shelter.

"He isn't going to run away." Logan kneeled down as the dog, a Boxer-Labrador mix, according to the pound, came bounding back to him. "You love us, don't you, boy?" He put the dog in a headlock and began to wrestle with him, rolling him onto his back.

"Be careful," Lina said. "You could hurt him."

"He's fine," Logan laughed as the dog began to lick his face. "Aren't you, Tyson?"

"Tyson?"

"Yeah, because he's part Boxer. Get it?"

"I get it, but his name is Knight," Lina said.

"He's not even black," Logan said.

"No, Knight as in knight in shining armor," Lina said, hoping that's the role he would play for her when she awoke in the night.

"He's funny looking," Katie said as she joined them. "Why is his nose all pushed in?"

"He isn't funny looking," Logan said. "He's half-Boxer."

"Hi." Katie timidly touched his head when he pushed his nose against her leg in greeting. "I thought you were going to get a puppy." She began to pet him with both hands.

"No, I wanted him to be house-trained,' Lina said. "He's about two."

"I guess he's cuter than funny looking," Katie said as she studied him. "What do you think Dad's going to say?"

"Why should he say anything?" Logan snapped, scowling at her. "He doesn't live here. He doesn't have a right to an opinion!"

"Sorry," Katie said. "Calm down."

"Don't get upset with her," Lina said. "She asked an innocent question."

"Well, he doesn't," Logan said before stomping away, the dog on his heels.

"Logan?" Lina called after him, taking a few hesitant steps before deciding to let him cool down on his own. He had been so happy, more like his old self, since picking up the dog two hours earlier, but at the mention of his father he was back to the angry teen he'd been most of the week.

"May I spend the night at Emma's?" Katie asked.

"Katie—"

"What? Am I going to be punished forever? It's been a year and a half."

Lina sighed. She'd known this question was coming. With Phil gone, it was only a matter of time before Katie tried to push her boundaries. "I'll think about it."

"Please." For the first time in at least two years, Katie initiated physical contact, taking Lina's hand. "I won't drink or anything. I swear."

"I just need to think," Lina said.

If it were only up to her, Lina would let Katie spend the night at Emma's, but she knew it wasn't, so she called Phil's cell phone. When it went directly to voicemail, she called his office. "Hi, Anne, it's Lina Hunter," she began as soon as his secretary answered. "Is he in?"

There was a longer than normal pause before his secretary responded. "I'm sorry, but it was my understanding that Mr. Hunter was having his surgery today. He didn't come in."

"Oh, right. I just had a brain freeze. I'm sorry." She hung up her phone and immediately called Diane. "Phil is having surgery?" she asked as soon as Diane answered.

"Not anymore. He had it this morning."

"Why didn't I know? Why didn't you tell me?"

"I never thought about telling you. I guess I assumed you—"

"Where is he?" Lina interrupted.

"His plan was to recover at his brother's over the weekend."

"I can't believe this. I can't believe no one told me my husband was having surgery."

"Don't you mean your estranged husband? Last time we spoke, you sounded like you were on the road to divorce."

"He's still my children's father. I should know if he's having surgery."

"It was his hand, Lina, not his heart. I'm sure he's fine."

"I've got to go." She slammed the phone down. She should have been told. He'd taken the kids to dinner the night before and could easily have come into the house and let her know.

"Did you decide?" Katie asked, coming up behind her.

"Did you know your dad was having surgery on his hand today?"

"Yeah, why?"

"No one told me."

"Oh. Can I spend the night at Emma's?"

"Yes. Get your things. I'll take you now."

"Lina?" Her sister-in-law, Jeanie, stepped back from the door. "I didn't know —."

"How is he?" she interrupted. She hadn't spoken to Jeanie in the week since Phil left, but clearly the other woman knew of the separation.

"I think he's asleep." She twisted her hands together. "Mike just told me everything last night. I'm in shock. I was going to call you tonight."

"It's fine." She liked Jeanie, but they'd never been particularly close, and she had no desire to discuss her marriage with her. "Where is he?"

It had been six days since he left, but the man lying asleep on the bed looked so different he may as well have been a stranger. He had a beard—not a full beard, but he was well on his way, the lower part of his face completely obscured by his dark scruff. And he'd clearly lost weight. His collarbones, visible through the V-neck opening of a white T-shirt, were more prominent than she could ever remember. His right hand, thick with gauze reaching almost to his elbow, was propped up on some pillows. His mouth was open slightly, and his chest was rising and falling with his breathing.

She curled her hands into fists as she resisted the urge to touch him, not wanting to wake him. Her eyes traveled over him, pausing on his left hand, which was lying on his stomach, his wedding band resting close to his knuckle. He was still her husband. She should have been the one waiting for him at the hospital and taking care of him as he recovered. She sat down in a club chair beside the bed, continuing to watch him sleep.

Over an hour passed before his eyes opened, and as soon as they did they were focusing on her. "Lina?"

"How do you feel?" She was out of the chair and beside the bed.

"What are you doing here?"

"I came to see how you were."

"Why?" He shifted slightly, his lips twisting in pain as his injured hand moved.

"Do you need something? When was the last time you took a painkiller?"

He closed his eyes, turning his face away from her. "Go home."

"You'd rather have Jeanie take care of you than me?"

"No. I would rather be home in my own bed, but you kicked me out, remember?" He grimaced.

"Phil, you need to take something."

"No, what I need is for you to leave, unless you're here to tell me you want me back. Is that why you're here?" He opened his eyes and looked at her.

"No, but you're still my husband and—"

"Out." He pointed to the door with his good hand.

"Why are you being like this?"

"You told me you don't want to be my wife."

"You took her to Steamboat."

"Fuck." He gripped his forehead. "I know why. You don't have to remind me. But if you don't want to be my wife, you shouldn't be trying to take care of me."

"I care about you," she whispered, tears coming to her eyes. "I can't just stop."

"Don't." He shook his head. "Don't cry."

"Why won't you let me take care of you?" She touched the side of his face, her fingers running over his beard.

"Stop." He gripped her hand. "This isn't how it works. If you don't want to be dependent on me anymore, you can't expect me to be dependent on you. It's a two-way street, Lina. Either you want to be my wife in every sense of that word or you don't. I don't want the friend side without the lover side, okay?" He squeezed her hand. "Those are my terms, and as long as we're not living under the same roof, our only interaction is going to be in regards to the kids."

"You really want me to leave?" She took a step back, her hands falling limply to her sides.

"Yes."

35

Even with the heat from the fire pit and a borrowed sweat-shirt from Ryan, Katie felt the chill of the late-October evening as she sat in a lawn chair beside Emma, her knees pressed into her chest and her arms cradling her legs as she listened to Ryan strumming his guitar. Several of Ryan's friends were there, but so far there was no sign of Matt, who, despite getting Katie's number from Emma, hadn't called her.

Another thirty minutes passed before Ryan stopped playing his guitar, nodding as he focused on someone behind Katie. "Hey, dude. I was starting to think you weren't going to show."

"I had to get a shower after work."

The chill in the air was forgotten, and butterflies fluttered in Katie's stomach. She stole a look over her shoulder at the boy she hadn't seen since Ryan left for college two months earlier but who continued to consume an inordinate amount of her thoughts. Besides the addition of a black leather jacket, he looked just as she remembered him in worn jeans and a black T-shirt, his dark hair spiked up on top of his head.

"How did the audition go?" one of the other guys asked.

"Good."

"When will you know?"

"I got it."

"Fuck yeah, man!" There was a chorus of equally enthusiastic congratulations as the other guys jumped up to slap Matt's hand or pat him on the back.

"Got what?" Katie asked, too curious to stay quiet.

"Matt auditioned for a legit band in Baltimore that plays some serious venues and shit," Ryan answered.

"Are you going to remember us when you're famous?" Emma asked.

"Yeah, right," Matt said.

"Hey, take my chair," Ryan said. "I'll grab another from the barn."

"Just share with Katie," Emma said. "She's tiny. She barely takes up any space."

Katie looked up at him, her heart skipping. "If you want."

When she began to slide over, he held out his hand, his eyes meeting hers. "You can sit on my lap."

She didn't say a word as he pulled her to her feet and then down into his lap, his hands resting on her jean-clad thighs as she leaned back against him, the heat from his body warming hers.

As Ryan started playing again, Katie began to relax, heat spreading through her chest in response to Matt's closeness. She became conscious of the beating of his heart, the hardness of his chest and the feel of his thighs pressed against the backs of hers. If it had been up to her, the moment would never have ended.

"Do you want to play something?" Ryan asked Matt, pausing after a song.

"No." Matt's thumb was now tracing a circular pattern on her thigh, and if it hadn't been for the others, Katie would have closed her eyes. She wanted everyone else to disappear so she could be alone with him. Every so often she felt his nose tickling the back of her neck as he breathed in. "You smell good, Hunter," he whispered at one point.

The time passed too quickly, and as the guys slowly began to leave, Katie knew it was only a matter of time before the one leaving would be Matt. Although she'd been sitting on his lap for over two hours, they'd barely exchanged a word.

"I'm heading in," Ryan said, coming to his feet. "Are you crashing here?" he asked Matt.

"No, I have to work early. I can give Hunter a ride home."

"She's spending the night," Emma said. "I'm freezing. You guys want to go in?"

"I'm going to stay out here a little longer," Matt said. "I'll put out the fire."

"Me too," Katie said. She made no move to leave his lap even though there were now several empty chairs.

As soon as they were alone, Matt patted her thigh. "Let's go to the barn."

The barn had electricity but no heat, and after turning on a light, Matt led her to an overstuffed couch across from where the band usually practiced, shrugging out of his jacket and draping it over her shoulders. "Put this on."

Too cold to point out that he was only wearing a T-shirt, she slipped her arms into the sleeves, enclosing herself in the smell of him and of leather as she sunk down onto the couch beside him. "Thanks."

"It sucks about your parents."

Katie shrugged. "It's kind of better. I don't think my mom will be as strict as my dad. It's weird though—him calling me at night and stuff. He doesn't live with us, but I talk to him more than when he did."

"When my dad split, I never heard from him again. I guess it wasn't enough time to bond to me or whatever."

"He sounds like a dick," Katie said, hating the faceless father that made Matt feel unwanted.

"Yeah, I guess he is."

"What about your mom? What was she like?"

"She was a drug addict," he said so nonchalantly Katie had to replay his words in her head to make sure she'd heard him right. "She OD'd."

"Fuck," Katie whispered. She'd assumed she died of cancer or something. "I had no idea."

"No one around here does." He leaned forward, his elbows resting on his knees as he looked down at the floor. "I don't know why I'm telling you."

She didn't know what to say, so she stayed silent.

"It was two years ago today," he continued. "I had this job after school working at a hardware store and I got paid that day, so I stopped on the way home and picked up some groceries. Orange juice, eggs, milk—shit like that. She was still warm when I found her. If I hadn't stopped, I don't know—maybe she'd still be alive."

"No," she said, shaking her head. "That's not true."

"I know it's not my fault, but sometimes I wonder whether things would have been different, you know, if I hadn't stopped that day."

"My grandma says that everyone's time is set. That it's already determined. That was her day." She touched him then, running her hand over the muscles of his upper back and shoulders.

"Maybe." He dropped his head forward. "Would you rub my other shoulder too?"

She hesitated, unsure how to reach his other shoulder, and then she was scooting her body behind his to get better leverage, her thighs straddling his hips as she began to massage his upper shoulders and neck. "Like that?"

"Yeah." He tilted his head from one side to the other, groaning when she squeezed a tight muscle. "I still think about her every day. I don't try to. It just happens. Most of the time she was more worried about getting her next fix than what I was doing, but sometimes she was almost like a normal mom, you know, concerned about me and stuff."

Katie wanted to wrap her arms around him, but she was afraid it was too soon, so she contented herself with running her hands over his neck and shoulders and said the words that came to her. "You miss her."

"I used to sing to her. She was always asking me to. That night when I drove you home and you asked me to sing to you, it reminded me of that. She gave me my first guitar."

Minutes passed, her hands sliding over his back and neck and occasionally dipping below the collar of his shirt to the warm skin beneath as she absorbed the enormity of what he'd confided. He'd found his mom dead when he was sixteen, the same age she was now. Tears came to her eyes. She had an overwhelming desire to protect him and keep him from ever being hurt again, to be the one person who would never leave him. In that moment, she knew she couldn't hold back her own truth. He had to know all of her, like she knew all of him.

"Matt?" Her hands began to shake slightly.

"Yeah?"

She'd stopped massaging him and was gripping his shoulders, her forehead pressed against his neck as she prepared to tell him something only her parents, grandma and psychiatrists knew. She closed her eyes. "I cut myself."

36

Matt reached behind him, clasping Katie's wrist and tugging on her until she crawled around to the front of him and was straddling his lap. She dropped her face into the side of his neck, afraid of seeing disgust in his eyes.

"Look at me, Hunter." He curved his hand along her jaw and forced her head back until he could look in her eyes. "Do you still do it?"

"No." She released a shaky breath as she looked into his eyes, which were filled with concern only.

"Why are you crying?"

"Because I'm afraid you aren't going to like me anymore." She began to bite her lower lip.

He leaned in and kissed her, his lips brushing softly over hers. "I still like you," he whispered against her mouth. He kissed her again, this kiss longer and deeper than the first as his tongue dipped into her mouth. Katie wrapped her arms around his neck as she kissed him back, her body melting into his.

After a few minutes he broke the kiss, resting his forehead against hers as he breathed in and out deeply. "Show me."

She closed her eyes and shook her head. She couldn't show him. It was too humiliating.

"Show me," he repeated. He gripped her hips and slid her off his lap and onto the couch beside him.

She shakily came to her feet, undoing her jeans and pushing them down over her butt. Her back was to him as she tugged down the right side of her panties to reveal the five tiny scars approximately a quarter inch in length running down the center of her right butt cheek.

"Why?"

"I don't know. I guess it kind of made me feel better."

One of his hands clasped the side of her hip, his fingers curling around her exposed skin, while the index finger of his other hand traced the scars. "What did you use?"

"A tack."

"When was the last time?"

"I don't know. At least ten months ago."

"Do you ever think about doing it again?"

"Never." She breathed in as his finger continued to caress her skin. "I didn't want to do it. I told my grandma, and that's why I saw the psychiatrist."

He tugged up her panties and then her jeans before pulling her back onto his lap, his arms wrapping around her from behind. "You don't ever have to be embarrassed with me," he said. He cradled her in his arms for minutes, occasionally running his lips over the back of her neck. "I could really fall for you, Hunter, you know that?"

She ran one of her hands over the arms encircling her. "I hope so, because I've already fallen for you."

The arms around her tightened momentarily, and then he was turning her in his lap until she was once again facing him, her thighs on either side of his hips. He framed her face between his hands as he brought his lips to hers. They kissed for minutes. When he finally broke the kiss, dragging his mouth from hers, they were both breathing heavily. "I need you to promise me something," he whispered against her ear, his voice sounding deeper than normal. "No drugs. I can't handle you doing drugs."

— ⌢

The third day after Knight's arrival, Lina made it through the night without the assistance of pills or a middle-of-the-night phone call to Nick or Phil. "We did it," she whispered as she scratched the furry head staring up at her from beside the bed. She'd woken up at 2:00 a.m., sitting up in the bed terrified, but instead of reaching for the phone, she'd forced herself to go to him.

She'd sat down beside his dog bed, trying to catch her breath, running her hand over his coat as she concentrated on her breathing, and telling herself what she knew Phil would if she called him, to breathe in and out deeply, to imagine herself at a beach with seagulls crying overhead as she breathed in the sea air. The first two nights it hadn't worked, and she'd ended up calling Phil and taking a pill, but on the third night, probably because she was starting to care about the dog, his presence calmed her, and ten minutes later she was climbing back into her bed and falling asleep.

"It means I can sleep without someone beside me," Lina explained to Adele when they met later that day. "Do you know how freeing that is?"

"But now you have to be with a dog? How are we going to travel? You can't just bring a dog to a Caribbean resort."

"He didn't calm me down. I mean, he was there, but I calmed myself down. It was always Phil's voice or lately medication, but last night, for the first time, I did it."

"So we can go to the Caribbean without the dog?"

"What are you talking about? I never said anything about going to the Caribbean with you."

"Not now, but this winter. We can go to one of those singles resorts. Oh my God, we'll have so much fun."

"I'm not really in the mood to have fun.'

"What do you mean? I thought you were doing okay without him."

"It's been nine days. I think I'm doing well. I just..." She sighed. "I feel unsettled. I have this underlying anxiety that won't go away."

"That's normal." Adele covered her hand. "Totally normal. You've been with him your whole adult life. Your world has been upended. You just need to give it a little time."

"My whole life revolved around him. Taking care of him was my main focal point, and without him I feel a bit lost. It's like my center is gone. There's this huge void."

"Then come to work for us. You are so good at staging my houses. You may as well make money at it, and it would get you out of the house."

"Dad made you get a job?" Logan slammed down his spoon and roughly pushed his cereal bowl away from himself, causing milk to spill on the table.

"No, honey. He wouldn't make me get a job. I got a job because I wanted one." It was the following morning, and Lina had just told him about her new position.

"Why?" His eyes were narrowed with suspicion.

"Because staging homes is fun, and I'll get to work with Adele. Plus, I'll finally be using my education. You know my degree is in interior design, right?"

"Who's going to drive us around if you're working?"

"It's part-time, and I'll only do it when you're in school. Nothing will change for you. The only reason you'll know I'm working is because I told you."

"What if I'm sick one day?"

"Then I won't work. I would never let it encroach on my time with you guys."

"How much are they going to pay you?" Katie asked, joining them at the table.

"Good question." Lina laughed. "I have no idea. I guess we'll talk about that when I go in."

"No texting at the table," Logan said, looking pointedly at Katie's cell phone.

Katie continued tapping on her phone. "You don't seriously expect me to listen to you, do you?"

"We're not supposed to use our phones at the table," Logan said.

If Logan didn't look so serious, Lina would have laughed. He was sitting at the head of the table, in the chair normally occupied by his father, clearly trying to be the man of the house as he continued to frown at Katie.

"Considering you don't even like him anymore, why are you trying to *be* him? It's weird," Katie said.

"I'm not trying to be him. I'm just trying to keep you from being rude!" he said before stomping from the room.

"Katie." Lina sighed. "Can't you try to be a little nicer? You know he's having a hard time."

"If 'nicer' means letting my little brother tell me what to do, no." She was again tapping away on her phone. "Don't forget, I'm taking my driver's test Thursday."

"I have it on my calendar," Lina assured her before taking a sip of coffee.

"I also need you to make me an appointment at the gynecologist so I can go on the pill."

"The pill?" Lina repeated, staring across the table at her. "Why? Why do you need to go on the pill?"

Katie lifted her eyes from her phone. "So I don't get pregnant."

Lina rubbed her forehead, not mentally prepared to have this conversation with Katie at 6:45 on a Tuesday morning, but at the same time knowing she couldn't put it off. The last thing she needed was Katie pregnant. "I will make you an appointment at the gynecologist, but that doesn't mean I'm telling you it's okay to have sex. In fact, I think it's the opposite of okay. You're only sixteen years old. That's not old enough to—"

"You were fifteen."

Lina felt a rush of heat in her face. "Why would you think that?"

"Grandma told me."

37

"You told my sixteen-year-old daughter I had sex when I was fifteen? What were you thinking?" Lina rushed out as soon as her mother answered her cell phone.

"Oh, relax, Lina. It's not like I made it up. It's true."

"She didn't need to know! Now she probably thinks it's okay to have sex."

"It is okay to have sex. It's natural."

Lina covered her eyes with her hand and mentally counted to ten. Her mother was impossible. "Please don't tell her anything else about my childhood without clearing it with me first."

"She asked me to get her birth control pills, so instead of taking her myself, which I knew you would frown upon, I encouraged her to talk to you. When she claimed you were too conservative, the subject of your own sexuality came up. It was a natural progression. And my advice to you is not to fight this. If a teenager decides they want to have sex, there is no stopping them."

"How could you possible know that? You never tried to stop us."

"That's because I knew it would be a wasted effort. Just take her to the gynecologist and let nature takes its course."

Lina combed her free hand back through her hair. This was insane. "Who is she planning to have sex with? She doesn't even have a boyfriend."

"Oh, I'm not so sure that's true," Alice said. "She asked me what to do with the components used in a spell once the spell had worked."

"Worked," Lina repeated. She dropped down into a chair. It was the boy with the tattoos.

"Don't judge him without knowing him," Nick told her later that night. "Tattoos and a lack of college ambitions aren't enough to discourage a relationship. Katie is a smart girl."

"But sixteen seems too young to have sex."

"I agree, and I'm certainly not condoning a sexual relationship, but as long as she's happy and you don't see signs of increased anxiety or depression, you should let the relationship go forward. Show her you trust her judgment, and before long she'll be confiding in you instead of your mother."

"How come you always know what to say? I was upset all day, and in the matter of a minute, you made everything so clear."

"I'd love to take credit, but I think given time, you would have come to the same conclusion."

"I don't know if that's true."

"Start trusting your own instincts. You may surprise yourself."

Lina was halfway through the drive home from Logan's bus stop the following day when she realized he hadn't spoken since his mumbled greeting after getting in the car. "How was school?"

"Fine." He was sunk low in his seat and staring out the window.

"Sweetie, is something wrong?"

He shrugged. "I didn't make the all-star team."

"The all-star team?" she began in confusion and then realized what he was talking about. He hadn't made the team he had tried out for over the summer. "That's okay. You'll make it next year."

"That's the best I've ever played. I'm just not good enough," he said in a voice so downtrodden it broke Lina's heart.

"You did your best. That's all you can do. Coaches aren't perfect. They're not always right." She patted his thigh. "I know you're disappointed and it seems like a huge deal right now, but I promise you, it isn't."

"I'm never going to be as good as he was, am I?"

Her heart sunk. "Oh, Logan, you're not your father and you're not supposed to be."

"That means no."

"It means you shouldn't be comparing yourself to him. You're your own unique person. You're kind and honest and—"

"I don't care about that stuff. I wanted to make the team. He would have. At my age, he would have made the team."

"It was one tryout. You can't let it define you. If you really want to be on that team, you can work hard and make it next year."

"Maybe his new son will be as good as him."

She took her eyes off the road momentarily and looked at his profile. "Don't say things like that."

"Why not? It's true. I know I'm a disappointment to him."

"That's not true! Your father is very proud of you."

"It doesn't matter." He turned his body towards the window, effectively putting his back to her. "I don't want to be his son anyway."

"You don't mean that."

"Yes I do."

Lina waited until she was getting into bed to call Phil. "I've never seen him so down. I don't know what to say to him."

"I'm taking them out to dinner tomorrow night. I'll try to get him to talk then."

"Don't make him feel bad about not making the team. He's upset enough."

"Do you really think you need to tell me that? Are you redefining me completely? Am I an insensitive father now too?"

"I didn't say that, but you've always been too hard on him about lacrosse."

"I push him to meet his potential—that's what I'm supposed to do. It's what my father did to me, and that's what he'll do to his son one day."

"He feels like you're disappointed in him."

"That's not true. He's feeling sorry for himself. You baby him too much."

"I'm his mother. That's what *I'm supposed to do.*"

"Have you ever heard the expression 'mama's boy'? Is that what you want him to be?"

"No, but I don't want him to be sad."

"He's had a tough couple of weeks," Nick said when Lina took advantage of the fact that Logan and Katie were dining with Phil and joined him for dinner in Baltimore. "I didn't realize he didn't make the team. I'm sorry to hear that."

"Brian made it?"

"Yes."

"Well, at least one of them is happy. It's hard seeing him so down. I rarely see his smile anymore."

"I know I'm beginning to sound like a broken record, but continue to encourage him to talk about his feelings. Katie too. That's critical right now."

"You're going to have to let me pay for dinner. You seem to have to be in psychiatrist mode all the time with me lately."

"Not true. I'm myself with you." He leaned back in his chair as a waiter delivered their drinks. "So, this Knight of yours seems to be working out."

Lina smiled. "He's a Godsend. Last night I didn't wake up once. I had a dream-free night without medication for the first time since Phil left."

"These dreams—they're flashbacks to whatever happened to you at sixteen, aren't they?"

"Yes, or variations of it anyway." She reached for her water glass. "And no, I don't want to talk about it."

"You're going to eventually trust me enough to tell me what happened to you, aren't you?"

"It's not a matter of trust. I trust you. I just don't see the point in talking about it. It was twenty-some years ago. Why rehash it?"

"It's still affecting your sleep."

"No, that's not what was affecting it. It was awful and trau-matic, but I'm over it. I've been over it for a very long time. But somehow in the process of getting over it, I decided I needed

Phil. That's what I need help with—getting over him—not something that happened over two decades ago."

It was 9:30 p.m. when Lina turned into her driveway, an hour later than she'd planned to be out. She was surprised to see the SUV Phil was driving parked in the garage. Katie, lounging on the family room couch watching television, was the lone occupant of the lower level of the house.

"Where's your father?"

"Upstairs with Logan."

"Is everything okay?"

She shrugged, not looking away from the television. "Logan was crying."

38

Lina heard the low timbre of Phil's voice as she reached the rec room outside Logan's bedroom, and she hesitated at his door, debating whether to interrupt. "No," Phil was saying, "you don't have a right to judge me. You are fourteen years old. When you are forty-two and have lived a life mistake free, you can say whatever you'd like to me."

"I'll never do what you did," Logan said.

"I hope that's true."

"It is," he said firmly. "Are you going to move in with her, the woman who is pregnant?"

"No. I'm never going to live with her. I don't love her. I love your mom."

"Then why did you have sex with her?"

"I was weak and not thinking. I was wrong, Logan, but I can't undo it. There's no redo. Every action we take has consequences. I'm paying for what I did, and I may have lost your mother, but

I'm not going to lose you. I'm your father and there is no undoing that. God decided that a long time ago."

"You're going to be that baby's father."

"Yes."

"Are you going to see him? Like he's your son?"

"He is going to be my son. Do you think God would want me to turn my back on him?"

"I don't know," Logan said so softly Lina had to step closer to the door to hear him. "I don't want him to be your son."

"Look at me," Phil said. "Logan, look at me. Now, I want you to listen to me very carefully, okay? Are you listening?"

"Yes," Logan croaked, and Lina covered her mouth when she realized he was crying.

"The first time I looked into your eyes was one of the most powerful moments of my life. I was in the delivery room, and you were less than a few minutes old when one of the nurses handed you to me. They say babies can't really see, but I swear you could see me. You looked into my eyes and just stared up at me. You recognized me. You already knew I was your father. No one will ever replace you or take up a bigger part of my heart. You will always be my firstborn son. Do you understand me?"

Lina felt a lump forming in her throat as she went back downstairs, her thoughts instantly transported back in time.

> *"It's a boy," the doctor announced.*
>
> *Lina closed her eyes, the words barely penetrating her consciousness after a grueling eighteen-hour labor. When she opened her eyes again, she saw Phil cradling their son in his arms, tears filling his eyes, and then he was beside her, leaning down and meeting her lips for a soft kiss.*

"Thank you, baby," he whispered before kissing her again. "He's perfect. You're perfect. Our family is perfect." He leaned his forehead against hers. "You make me so happy."

The following morning, she was nursing Logan when Phil arrived, two-year-old Katie clinging to his side, her little arms around his neck, while Megan walked beside them, holding her father's hand. "There they are. I told you Mommy was okay," he said to Katie before kissing the top of her head.

"I want to see him! I want to see him!" Megan said, jumping up and down.

"Okay, but no touching," Phil said as he lifted her with his free arm and settled her against his hip. "Your hands aren't clean."

"Baby," Katie said, pointing at Logan, her eyes wide.

"It's Logan," Megan said. "His name is Logan, Katie."

"Baby," Katie repeated.

"Logan," Megan said. "Say 'Logan,' Katie."

"Baby," Katie said again.

"Katie—"

"It's okay, Megan," Lina said. "She can call him baby for a while."

"But his name is Logan."

Lina met Phil's eyes and smiled up at him. As exhausted as she was, Phil's obvious pleasure was contagious. He'd told her he didn't care what the sex of the baby was, he just wanted it to be healthy, but as she watched the joy come to his eyes as they traveled to Logan, she knew it wasn't true. Of course he would have loved the baby regardless of the sex, but he wanted a son, and she was happy she could give him one.

Lina was at the kitchen island sipping a glass of wine and absently stroking Knight's head when Phil appeared from the front of the house a short time later. "How is he?" She came to her feet.

"He's angry at me, but less so than before we talked."

"Good." She met his eyes, which looked bluer in contrast to his dark beard.

"I'm taking him to the Ravens game on Sunday. I'll talk to him more then."

"How's your hand?"

He looked down had his bandaged hand. "It's fine."

"It doesn't hurt?"

"Don't." He shook his head. "I told you Friday. If you don't want to be my wife, don't act like you are."

"So I can't even ask you how you're feeling?"

"No." His gaze traveled to Katie as she entered the kitchen from the family room.

"Don't forget I'm getting my license tomorrow," she said to Lina.

"You have to pass the test first."

"Grandma said if you want something, you should talk as if you already have it—that makes the universe bring it to you."

"Practicing helps too," Phil said dryly.

"Will you take me to get a car on Saturday?" Katie had taken out the orange juice and was pouring herself a glass.

"If you pass, yes, but early."

"I thought she was going to drive Megan's old car," Lina said.

"No, she changed my mind." He stepped over to Katie and kissed the top of her head. To Lina's amazement, she had no negative reaction. "I'll see you Saturday."

"Bye, Dad." Katie headed back towards the family room with her orange juice.

He turned to leave and bumped into Knight. "Sorry, boy." He swiped his hand over his head and Knight's entire body wiggled with excitement.

"I know you never liked the idea of a dog in the house, but he's a nice distraction for the kids."

He frowned. "I always wanted a dog."

"No, you didn't. You always said no when the kids asked you."

"That was because you didn't want one. Remember the Lab puppies the secretary at work was giving away? You said no."

He was right. How had she forgotten? The kids were all still young and he had wanted to bring one of the puppies home, but she had said no because she thought it would be too much work. "You never asked me again."

"That's because I figured you'd tell me if you changed your mind."

— —

Lina assumed Nick would be alone, so when she approached the fifty-foot sailboat moored on the end of the dock at a marina in Annapolis, she was surprised to see several people mingling about near the helm, drinking what looked to be mimosas and otherwise enjoying the mild late-fall temperatures. He had texted her early that morning asking if she wanted to join him on his sailboat, and with Katie off car shopping with Phil and Logan at a friend's, she'd said yes.

Her steps slowed as she advanced, not recognizing Nick among the group and wondering if it was the right boat. She had come to a complete stop when she saw him emerge from the cabin below, looking every bit the boatman with windblown hair and a light jacket. A smile creased his features when he saw her, and then he nimbly maneuvered around the others and off the boat.

"Any problems?"

"No. Your directions were perfect."

"I'm glad you could make it." He brushed his lips over her cheek. "Come meet everyone."

"Everyone" turned out to be three of his classmates from medical school and their significant others, plus an exceptionally attractive woman named Dana who was the sister of one of the other women. Although Lina's arrival undoubtedly thwarted a setup attempt, the other women were friendly, and after a couple of mimosa, Lina felt herself relaxing and enjoying Nick's friends.

"So, how do you know Nick?" one of the women asked Lina.

"I—"

"Our boys are friends," Nick answered before she had to. "They attend the same school."

The conversation turned to education, and as the group conversed, Lina only half listened, her attention more focused on Nick as he and one of the other men put up the sails. He made it all look so effortless, and she felt her attraction to him growing as she watched his hands gripping and maneuvering various ropes while he skillfully handled his boat. When he was done, he held out his hand to her. "Let me give you a tour."

The tour ended in the cabin, which looked like a small apartment. "You could actually live here," Lina said.

"People do it all the time. I prefer a little more space."

She stopped before a map, which had red tacks in various locations. "Are these all the places you've been?"

"In this boat." He was directly behind her.

"Which one's your favorite?"

"If I had to pick, I'd say the French side of the Virgin Islands." He reached around her and tapped the map, his chest pressing into her back.

Lina closed her eyes. With the alcohol in her system, she had no willpower to resist him. "We shouldn't," she whispered.

"Shouldn't what?" His hand slid down her waist and gripped her hip. "Look at a map?"

"Stand so close." Even as she uttered the words, she was leaning back into him.

"You smell so good," he whispered against her ear.

"I thought we were just friends."

He ran his hand over her stomach, pulling her back still farther. "My mind isn't in control of me right now." He brushed his lips over her earlobe, eliciting goose bumps from half her body.

"Hope I'm not interrupting," came a booming voice as one of Nick's friends entered the cabin.

"You're definitely interrupting," Nick said, stepping back from Lina. "I was showing her my favorite Caribbean destinations."

"Yes, I could see that," he said dryly. "I just came down to make some more mimosas."

"I'm going back up," Lina said, avoiding Nick's eyes as she stepped around him.

Lina joined the rest of the group in the helm area of the boat, sinking down onto a cushioned bench seat as she breathed in the sea air and tried to get a handle on her emotions. Her heart felt like it was beating a hundred miles a minute.

"How long have you and Nick been together?" Dana asked.

"We're not together," Lina said quickly. "We're just friends."

Another woman laughed. "I've known Nick over fifteen years, and he definitely thinks of you as more than a friend."

"He's just coming out of his relationship with Emily, so..." She trailed off when Nick and a fresh pitcher of mimosas arrived.

Lina lost herself in the day, not thinking of her children or Phil as she drank, ate and laughed with Nick and his friends while they enjoyed a beautiful day on the water. Where Phil's conversations with his friends, brothers or colleagues would invariably turn to sports, Nick's exchanges that day jostled from the plight of women in the Middle East, to ideas on battling the increasing addiction to drugs in America, to the upcoming theatre season. The only time the conversation even remotely touched sports was a brief discussion on the rising number of concussions in youth soccer, and while she knew she was a bit outmatched by the breadth of some of their knowledge, Lina still found their discussions a refreshing change.

"Do you see the house with the two chimneys to the right?" Nick asked, pointing towards the shore. "Just steer towards it." He was standing behind her at the wheel of the boat. "That's it. Just keep on that course."

"Are you sure? I don't want to be responsible for turning the boat over."

"I don't want you to be responsible for that either," he teased. One of his hands rested on her hip, a place it had been more often than not over the course of the day.

"I'm serious," she laughed. "I've never steered a boat before."

"You're fine." He began dropping feather-light kisses on the side of her neck. "More than fine."

"Nick," she breathed.

"Yes, Lina?"

"You said we could only be friends for now."

"I changed my mind."

39

$\mathcal{I}$t was almost dark when Lina and Nick walked across the marina parking lot towards her car, the sound of gravel kicking up under their feet piercing the evening air. "This is me," she said, stopping beside Phil's BMW.

"New?"

"No." She tossed her things in the back seat before turning from the car, her heart rate accelerating as she met his eyes.

He took her hand, tugging her towards him. "Thanks for coming."

"Thank you." Lina could hardly think as she looked into his eyes. "You should say good night," she said breathlessly.

"Good night, Lina," he whispered before lowering his mouth over hers.

As soon as his lips touched hers, she was kissing him back with an abandon that could only be the result of weeks of longing. He hooked one arm low around her waist as he hauled her body into his, his other hand framing the side of her face as he deepened the kiss, he too appearing completely overwhelmed.

She circled her arms around his neck, wanting, needing to be closer. It wasn't until the feel of his erection pushing against her stomach penetrated her desire-filled haze that she was able to break the kiss, turning her face into his neck. "We have to stop," she breathed.

"Come back to the boat with me."

"I can't," she said, brushing her lips along his collarbone, her mind and body at odds over what she should do. "I need to get home." Even as she said the words, she was curving her hand around the back of his head, her fingers threading through his hair as she pulled him down for another kiss.

Nick opened his mouth over hers, their tongues tangling together as he deepened the kiss, his hand stroking her lower back and hips as he pressed his lower body into hers.

The sound of approaching voices and laughter served as a splash of cold water, and Lina again broke the kiss, dragging her mouth from his as she dropped her forehead into his chest. "I have to go—my kids."

He wrapped her in his arms, holding her body firmly against his, his chest rising and falling with his breathing. "I'm sorry," he whispered against her head. "I lose all reason with you."

The magnitude of what she'd almost done hit her full force. "I have to go. Please." She pushed her hands against his chest.

"Lina?"

"Let me go."

He loosened his arms, drawing in a breath as she stepped away from him. "Don't get upset with yourself."

"I'm not even legally separated." She yanked open her car door and was immediately besieged by Phil's familiar scent. "Oh my God."

"Lina, nothing happened," Nick said. His grip on the door kept her from pulling it closed. "We kissed."

She pressed her forehead into the steering wheel. "I know."

"Tell me where your mind is."

"I don't know. I'm just confused."

"About what?"

"You," she whispered, tilting her head up so she could see him.

"I'm sorry." His brows were pulled together, a look of concern etched across his features. "I should have exercised more control."

"It's not your fault. I wanted it too. I just feel so guilty."

"Do me a favor and try not to overthink this. We kissed, nothing more."

"I kissed him," Lina said as soon as Adele answered her cell phone.

"Shut up!"

"I did and now I feel so guilty." Lina had pulled the car to the side of the road and called Adele as soon as she left the marina.

"Lina, stop! You have nothing to feel guilty about. Phil —"

"Don't mention him. I don't want to think about him." She rubbed her eyes. "I knew this would happen."

"Stop it! Stop thinking. You like him and you kissed him. You are separated. It's not like you're going home to Phil."

"I know." Lina drew in a breath. "You're right. Why am I feeling like this? Why do I feel like I'm cheating on him?"

"I don't know, but you're not, so get it out of your head. Now tell me about the kiss."

Lina leaned her head back against the headrest and then, as briefly as possible, told Adele about the day, going out on the sailboat, meeting his friends. "They were so well-read and smart. I need to—"

"Okay, get to the good part," Adele interrupted. "Well-read, smart people sound boring."

"They weren't boring. They were interesting and—"

"Can you move forward to the kiss? I don't care about the other people on the boat. If they hadn't been there, we would be talking about more than a kiss right now."

"Fine." Lina told her about their interaction in the cabin, his undivided attention throughout the day and, finally, the kiss.

"You should have gone back to his boat with him. Just one look at him and you can tell he'd be great in bed."

"You can't say that," Lina said, even though she suspected the same thing.

"I think I can," Adele said. "I have a *lot* more data than you."

"I'm not discussing this with you."

"Why not? You're single again. This is the kind of thing single women discuss."

"Not this one."

———   ⁓

A dark Honda sat in the driveway when Lina arrived home, and she assumed someone was visiting until she saw the temporary license plate on the back of the car. "Is that Katie's new car?" she asked Logan, who was stretched out on the couch with Knight, watching a college football game, a passion he and Phil shared each fall.

"Yes."

"It's used."

"It's what she wanted. It has top safety ratings. She printed a bunch of stuff out to show Dad. She found it online."

"Good." Lina was impressed by both Katie's tenacity and Phil's willingness to not force a car on her that she didn't want. "Did you see your dad?"

"He was here when I got home," Logan said, continuing to stare at the television.

"Did you talk to him?"

He shrugged. "He watched the first half of the game with me."

"That would explain this," she said as she picked up an empty beer bottle from the coffee table. "Unless there's something you want to tell me."

He looked at her then. "Are you trying to be funny?"

"Yes. I want you to smile. I miss your smile."

He gave her a fake smile before turning his attention back to the television.

"Logan—"

"I just want to watch the game."

The moment Lina stepped into her master bedroom she knew Phil had been in the room. It wasn't that anything was out of place, she could just sense him. She crossed to his wardrobe and stared into the empty space. Every physical trace of him was gone. She pulled the door closed, refusing to let her mind dwell on the finality of it. She opened the drawers to his dresser, and they too were empty. He had expunged himself from the room and yet, as she looked around, her eyes traveling from the bed to the sitting room and everything in between, his presence was palpable. There were too many memories.

"How long was your dad here today?" Lina asked Katie, who was sitting in front of a mirror in her room, applying mascara.

"I don't know. I didn't pay attention. He took a bunch of his clothes. Uncle Mike helped him, and then he came back again I think."

"Did he find somewhere to live?"

"Yeah, a furnished house in Farside," Katie said, referring to a ritzy neighborhood less than a mile away. "The owners are in Europe or something. It's big." She turned from the mirror. "I think he expects me to spend some weekends with him. I shouldn't have to suffer because the two of you are separated. I see him more now than when he lived here, plus he calls me every night. It's ridiculous. I'm sixteen, not six."

"He calls you every night?" This was news to Lina.

"Yes, and there isn't that much to say." Katie returned her attention her eyelashes. "I want to tell him to stop, but he seems sad, and I don't want to hurt his feelings. Would you talk to him?"

"No, it's not my place."

"You're the reason he's sad."

Lina didn't feel it was appropriate to remind Katie that he was the one who had an affair, so she instead changed the subject. "Why are you putting on makeup?"

"I'm going out."

"With who?"

Katie hesitated. "Just friends."

"Katie?"

"What?" Katie opened her eyes wider.

"I need to know where you're going and with who."

Katie rolled her eyes. "Not that's it's any of your business, but I have a date."

"It is my business. And before you go out on a date I need to meet the boy."

"How do you know it's not a girl? Maybe I'm gay."

Lina raised her eyebrows. "What time should I expect him or *her*?"

"At eight. Please don't embarrass me."

"I wasn't planning to." Lina began to leave but paused at the door. "They are welcome to join us for dinner. It'll be ready in a few minutes, but I can hold it half an hour."

"No." Katie spun around. "Do you know how weird that would be?"

"No. I don't think it would be weird at all. They do eat, right?"

"He's not eating with us, and don't ask him any questions. Don't talk to him at all."

"I'm going to ask him questions. I'm not letting you leave this house with a stranger."

"He isn't a stranger to me," Katie fumed. "You're as annoying as Dad. Why are you trying to act like him?"

"I'm acting like a parent," Lina said, realizing as she said the words that, like with the dog issue, she had let Phil voice the unpopular decisions.

When he showed up in jeans, black biker boots, a tight black T-shirt and tattoos covering the visible skin of one of his arms, Lina's first impression, or second, if the day in the pool counted, was that Matt was bad news. But with Nick's words ringing in her ears, she ignored her apprehension and approached him while he was bent on one knee greeting Knight just inside the foyer.

"He likes you," Katie said.

"I love dogs." Matt came to his feet, continuing to scratch Knight's head as his gaze shifted to Lina.

As soon as she met his soulful eyes, her reservations dissolved. His eyes were the same eyes that reflected back at her in the mirror when she was his age. The eyes Shiloh still wore. He had lived through trauma, and his vulnerability pulled at her heart.

"I'm Lina Hunter."

"Matt." The steadiness of his gaze as he returned her handshake surprised her. There was a strength there she hadn't recognized at first. He seemed older than eighteen.

"Are you hungry, Matt? Logan is still eating. There's plenty."

"Mom!" Katie frowned at her.

Matt shifted his attention to Katie. "You don't want me to eat?"

Katie's voice gentled. "Are you hungry?"

"I could eat."

"Okay." Katie took his hand and led him to the kitchen.

Two things became apparent over the next fifteen minutes. Matt had been hungry—he ate two helpings of chicken parmesan—and he adored Katie. His entire demeanor softened whenever he interacted with her. For her part, Katie seemed equally infatuated, moving her chair directly beside his, their thighs pressing against each other as they talked softly while he ate.

He wasn't unfriendly, talking to Logan occasionally and thanking Lina more than once for feeding him, but it was clear his focus was on Katie, and as soon as he finished eating, the two were standing.

"I don't know what your plans are, but you're welcome to hang out here," Lina said. "You can order a movie. We won't bother you."

Matt looked down at Katie. "Up to you."

It was after 1:00 a.m. when Lina followed Knight into her bedroom. She'd spent most of the evening in the family room with Logan, watching a movie and feeling riddled with guilt over her kiss with Nick, while Katie and Matt watched the television in the upstairs rec room. She'd checked on them twice, once when she delivered a bowl of popcorn and a second time when she pretended to be concerned about where Knight ran off to. On the second occasion, it was obvious from Katie's swollen lips and Matt's deep breathing that she had interrupted a make-out session, but to her great relief they were both fully clothed.

⚊ ⚊

Lina rolled over in her bed, burying her face in her pillow. She'd dreamt she was having sex with Phil, and it felt so real her body was still in a heightened state of arousal. It was the first sexual dream she could recall having, and she'd had it the night after kissing Nick for the first time. It had to mean something. She closed her eyes and attempted to go back to sleep but couldn't stop fantasizing about Phil, so she reached for her cell phone and pulled up the images from Kim. As anticipated, her desire for him was extinguished but not her confusion, and it was almost light out before she fell back to sleep.

A low whine and a cold nose ensured that Lina no longer stayed in bed past 9:00 a.m. "Okay, Knight, okay."

She was in the front yard, bundled in one of the few sweatshirts Phil left behind, tossing Knight a ball, when Phil arrived. Anxiety filled her chest at the memory of her kiss with Nick. "What are you doing here? It's barely nine."

"I'm picking them up for church. They didn't tell you?"

"No." She reached out to take the ball from Knight's mouth, but he trotted over to Phil, pushing the ball against his thigh.

To Knight's obvious delight, Phil threw the ball three times farther than Lina could, and Knight charged after it. "You're welcome to join us," he said.

"No."

"Why haven't you looked at me since I arrived? What are you feeling so guilty about?" Phil asked.

"Nothing." She began to perspire despite the chill in the air.

"Dad?" They turned to the door at the sound of Katie's voice. "Can I just go to a later service? I—"

"No."

"Why—"

"Don't argue with me," Phil said. "Get your brother and let's go." As soon as the door was closed, his attention returned to Lina. "I'll have the separation agreement drawn up this week. Try to refrain from seeing him until it's signed."

"I'm not."

"Don't bother lying to me. The truth is all over your face."

40

$\mathcal{L}$ina set a manila folder on the table at the café where she was meeting Adele for lunch and sat down, her mind still reeling from her meeting with the divorce attorney. "A glass of Chardonnay," she said as soon as a waitress appeared.

"I'll have the same," Adele said as she rushed up and pulled out a chair. "Well?" She looked expectantly at Lina. "What did she say?"

"She said in her twenty-five years of experience as a divorce attorney she'd never seen a more generous offer, and he either loves me beyond reason or he's crazy. But regardless of why, that I should sign it immediately before he changes his mind."

"Good," Adele said, nodding. "I'm glad he did what was right."

"He's going to continue to pay the mortgage and take care of the maintenance on the house until Logan graduates from college, and then we'll sell it or I can buy him out. He's also giving me half of all our other assets, paying all school tuition, plus child support and alimony, until Logan graduates from college. She said if I wasn't extravagant and hired the right financial planner, I wouldn't require much additional income and could retire by sixty."

"Wow." Adele sat back in her chair. "I suppose I should stop calling him a bastard, but he's giving you nothing more than what you deserve. He doesn't want the kids to have to move, and that's what would happen if he insisted on splitting the house now."

"True. Thank you," she said to the waitress before bringing her wine glass to her lips. "I'm literally shaking."

"I can see that. Why?"

"I just—going to a lawyer and talking about severing all ties to Phil. It's something I never considered." She took another swallow of wine. "A year ago I wouldn't have believed it possible."

"Oh my God," Adele said. "You're a mess."

"Just a little. He's barely acknowledged me since he accused me of dating Nick, so I was expecting him to not—I don't know—not to be so generous. And that part's a relief, but at the same time I'm sad. He was more than my husband. He was my friend, and that's gone. I've lost my best friend."

"You have me."

"Thank God for that. I couldn't survive without you."

"And Phil will come back around. Once you're divorced and you've moved on with your lives, he'll become civil again."

"It's insane. He got another woman pregnant, and he's upset with me for having a friendship with a man.'

"Friendship?" Adele paused with her wine glass at her lips. "Are you in the habit of tongue kissing all your friends?"

"Is that necessary?"

"Don't bullshit me. He's more than a friend."

"I don't know what he is. I haven't even seen him since the day on the boat, and ever since that day I've been dreaming about Phil."

"Sex dreams?"

"It's like Phil is haunting me. Why am I dreaming of him? Why can't it be Nick?"

"Maybe because you've never had sex with Nick."

"I've never had Phil catch me after falling off the top of a mountain either, but I dreamt that too. And then we had sex on a snow drift. I woke up and my room was freezing because I had left the window open."

"This is one for Mom. I have no clue what that means."

With the separation agreement signed, Lina met Nick at a small French bistro in Baltimore. "This is nice." She looked around the restaurant in an attempt to calm her nerves. "Do you—"

"Lina." His hand covered hers. "What's the matter?"

"I don't know." She shook her head. "I just…" She paused and took a deep breath. "I feel guilty for, you know, last time."

"Nothing happened."

"That's not how it feels to me." She took another sip of her water. "God, I must come across as so unsophisticated."

"No, but maybe loyal to a fault."

"I know it doesn't make sense, but it doesn't change the reality of how I feel. I may as well have had sex with you for all the guilt I'm feeling."

"May as well," he agreed, but when she met his eyes she could tell he was teasing her. "It was too soon. I know better, but my impulse controls seem to disappear when I'm around you. I'm no better than an adolescent boy." He ran his thumb over the back of her hand. "Forgive me."

"It's not like it's just you. I wanted it as much as you did."

"I very much doubt that," he said, treating her to a full, heart-melting smile.

The arrival of the waiter saved her from responding, and she relaxed back into her seat as she listened to him discuss wine choices. "When will the guilt go away?" she asked as soon as the waiter left with his order. "I even feel guilty for being attracted to you."

"It's been less than a month. It will take some time before you're ready, and until then, we'll be friends—just like I originally said. No pressure—just friends.'

41

Thanksgiving was one of Lina's favorite holidays, but as the day approached, the separation from Phil served to temper her normal enthusiasm. It was Phil's family traditions that made the day special. They would start the day with a touch football game at Jeanie and Mike's, followed by a recorded viewing of the Macy's Thanksgiving Day Parade, which would inevitably prompt groans of protest from the males in attendance who, nonetheless, sat down for the supposed torture year after year. Next they would watch football and snack on light appetizers before partaking in a traditional Thanksgiving feast that gave way to watching more football and finally, after the sun went down, a competitive family-against-family game of charades.

Although it broke her heart, Lina made the kids go to her in-laws' without her, politely declining invitations from both Jeanie and her mother-in-law, feeling her attendance would make the day awkward for everyone else. She'd planned to spend the day with Alice and her sisters, which is what she told Logan when he was worried she'd be alone. But when the day arrived she couldn't bring herself to do anything, afraid spending the day away from her children would be hard enough without adding a dose of Julian and Shiloh to the mix. So she feigned a headache, which actually materialized midafternoon, effectively alleviating any guilt, and spent the day in bed cuddling with Knight, watching football and feeling sorry for herself. As the game came to an end, she realized how much she associated watching football with Phil and how much she missed it.

A late-day shower did little to alleviate the sadness that had been consuming her all day, so after slipping into her most comfortable sweats, she poured herself a large glass of wine and curled up in the corner of the couch, hoping she could find something on the television to snap her out of her melancholy.

As she reached for the television remote, her eyes focused on a framed photograph of Phil and the kids taken at least ten years prior. Phil was sitting in the grass, laughing while a four- or five-year-old Logan clung to his neck, and Megan and Katie stood behind them, throwing leaves in the air. It had been taken the day before Thanksgiving. Lina remembered seeing them through the kitchen window as she stirred the filling for a pumpkin pie and grabbing the camera so she could catch the moment. It occurred to her then why people became depressed around the holidays—it was the memories of better times.

The chime from her cell phone pulled her from her reverie, and an instant later she was reading a text from Phil. *Happy Thanksgiving.* And then, before she had a chance to respond, *Katie and Logan are on their way home. Megan wants to spend the night with me. Is that okay?*

Happy Thanksgiving. Of course. She'd barely seen Megan since she arrived the afternoon before, but Lina wasn't going to force her to come home. Lina's eyes drifted back to the photo of Phil and the kids. Her throat constricted, and she hesitated with her fingers over her phone, considering for a moment pulling up the photo of him and Kim, but she couldn't bring herself to, not on Thanksgiving.

Watching *Christmas Vacation* on Thanksgiving night was a relatively new tradition, but one Logan started, so as soon as he and Katie arrived, laden with leftovers from their feast, he demanded they watch it together.

"I can't," Katie said. "Matt is coming over."

"Right now?" Lina looked at the clock. "It's almost nine."

"I haven't seen him in three days, and he hasn't had a real Thanksgiving meal because his grandma had to work." Katie began opening the packages of leftovers.

"He can watch it with us," Logan insisted before heading into the family room.

Matt arrived and, despite Katie's protests, agreed to watch the movie with Logan and Lina. "I want to be part of one of your traditions," Matt told Katie before following Lina into the family room with a plate overflowing with food.

"It's not even a real tradition," Katie grumbled, dropping down beside him on an oversized chair. "He started it like two years ago."

"All traditions have to have a beginning," Logan said. "One day the two of you will be telling your children that Uncle Logan started this one."

"Shut up." Katie tossed a pillow at him. "I would never torture my kids with this movie."

"You mean our kids," Matt said before shoveling a forkful of stuffing into his mouth.

Lina settled back on the couch beside Logan, considerably happier than an hour prior, but her gaze continued to return to the picture, and a mild undercurrent of sadness remained in her chest.

— —

The sound of a leaf blower greeted Lina the following morning, and when she looked out her bedroom window she saw Phil in jeans, a sweatshirt and a dark beanie, blowing leaves into a pile in the front yard.

"Coffee or water?" she asked half an hour later after joining him outside.

"What?" He turned off the leaf blower.

"Coffee or water?" Lina held up an insulated coffee cup in one hand and glass of water in the other.

"Thank you." He took the water first and finished it in several long swallows, and then he was handing her back the glass and taking the coffee.

"When did the cast come off?"

"Wednesday. I'll take my car back today."

His face looked different, and she realized he had shaved his beard. "Are you sure it's okay for you to be doing this? Maybe you should be resting it."

"It's fine. When you go back inside, would you wake up Logan for me and tell him to come out and help?"

"Have you eaten? I could—"

"I've eaten," he interrupted. "Just tell Logan."

"How was yesterday?" Lina asked when he began to turn away.

"Fine."

"Fine? Really?" His coolness annoyed her.

"What do you want me to say?" Phil asked.

"The truth."

"Why? Is that going to change anything? I think you know exactly how yesterday was, and I'm sure Christmas is going to be worse. Megan's already talking about spending Christmas Eve with me and letting Logan and Katie stay with you. I don't want them separated."

"I'm surprised she hasn't asked to move in with you completely."

"She has."

"Wow." She dropped her eyes. "That didn't take long." His words stung.

"Their lives are in an uproar too."

"I know."

"I'm going to get back to work."

"If you're open to it, maybe we should consider a combined Christmas just for this year. You don't have to answer now, but think about it." She hadn't planned to say the words, but as she did, she knew it was what she wanted. Thanksgiving had been too hard.

— —

"Stop right there," Lina called out the following afternoon as she descended the stairs and saw Matt stepping into the foyer with dirty boots. "Go back outside and come in through the basement."

"I'm coming from work," he said, looking down at his shoes.

"I don't care where you're coming from. You're not going to track dirt through the house." She took his arm and led him back outside. "Logan, go open the basement door for him."

"Katie said I could shower here so I don't have to go all the way home. I have practice tonight."

"That's fine. You can use the basement shower. Just go around back and Logan will let you in." She closed the door and practically ran into Megan.

"Who was that?"

"Matt. He's coming from work, and he's covered in sawdust or something."

"Who's Matt?" Megan asked.

Lina hesitated. She'd completely forgotten Megan didn't know about Matt. "Katie's boyfriend."

"Katie has a boyfriend? Since when?"

"At least a month ago," Lina answered. It was odd that someone who had ingrained themselves into her heart and home was yet unknown to her oldest daughter. "He's downstairs showering. You can meet him when he comes up."

Megan scrunched up her face. "Why is he showering at our house? Does he live here?"

"No, of course not. He works ten minutes from us, but thirty from his own house, so he's cleaning up here to save time."

"Who is he? Does he go to McDonogh?"

"Matt's here?" Katie asked, joining them.

"Yes, he's downstairs showering. Katie?" Lina called out when Katie crossed to the door leading to the basement. "Where do you think you're going?"

"To see him."

"I just told you that he's showering. You can wait until he comes up."

Katie rolled her eyes but dropped her hand from the door-knob. "Oh, brother," she mumbled.

"How come you didn't tell me you had a boyfriend?" Megan asked.

"Why would I tell you?" Katie looked at Megan like she had two heads. "We don't talk."

Lina threw together a plate of leftovers and had just set it on the kitchen table when Matt, in jeans and a tight black T-shirt, his sleeve tattoo on full display, emerged from the basement. "Here, eat," she said.

He hesitated. "I don't think I have time."

"You're not leaving without eating," Lina said. "Sit."

He gave her one of his smiles, which until recently had been elusive. "If I lose my spot in the band, it's your fault."

"From what I hear, you're way too talented for that." Lina squeezed his shoulder. "I'll get you some milk." Like Logan, he seemed to drink milk by the gallon.

"I thought we had to leave by five," Katie said as she came into the room.

"You're going with him?" Lina asked.

"Yes."

"To Baltimore? Why is this the first I'm hearing about it?"

"I'll take care of her," Matt said. "She'll be with me the whole time. You don't have to worry."

As Lina met Matt's eyes, her apprehension dissolved. "Okay, but no alcohol."

"He doesn't drink," Katie said.

"No drugs. And if for some reason you forget all that—call me and I'll pick you up, no questions asked."

"I never drink or do drugs," Matt said. "You never have to worry about that with me."

The opening of the mudroom door preceded Logan's appearance. "I want some," he said as he focused on the plate in front of Matt.

"We're having dinner in an hour,' Lina said. "They're leaving, so I fed him early."

"I'm starving," Logan said, continuing to stare at Matt's plate.

"Don't even think about it," Matt said, holding up his fork as if to defend his food.

Lina ran her hand down Logan's back. "Sit down and I'll make you a small plate." Between Logan and Matt, she felt like she was always feeding someone.

Megan came into the room and, after meeting Matt, took Lina's arm and led her into the dining room. "Is that the guy from the pool?" she whispered.

"Please, just stay out of it."

42

Is Matt the boy I met at the pool this summer? Lina read the text as the front door closed, signaling Katie and Matt's departure. "Megan?" She stepped into the family room, where Megan and Logan were watching TV. "You texted your father?"

"He would have wanted to know."

Lina bit her bottom lip. As much as she wanted to chastise Megan, she knew doing so would risk alienating her completely. "I wish you would have discussed it with me first," Lina said in the calmest voice she could muster.

"Why? Were you going to tell me not to tell him?"

"No, I—" She looked down as her cell phone began to ring. "Never mind," she said, turning to leave the room. "Phil—"

"That kid just took a shower in our house?" Phil barked out.

"Calm down," Lina whispered as she headed upstairs.

"Don't tell me to calm down! I told you last summer what I thought about him!"

"If you don't lower your voice, I'm hanging up."

"You don't have a right to make unilateral decisions. I'm still her father!"

Lina ended the call, continuing up the stairs and into her bedroom, her heart pounding in her chest. The phone began ringing again. She waited for four rings before she brought it to her ear. "If you yell, I'm hanging up."

"Lina," he began, his voice intense but low, "don't hang up on me."

"He's a nice boy."

"I met him. He's *not* a nice boy." His voice was clipped but controlled.

"He is. I've spent hours around him."

"Hours? You've spent hours around him, and I'm just hearing about him today?"

"It's not my fault she didn't tell you. How would I know you didn't know?"

There was a long pause. "Did you think I knew?" he asked, his voice losing its intensity. "Really?"

"No," she admitted, her voice resigned. "I mean, I didn't know for sure, but I figured you didn't know."

"She's my daughter too. It should have been you or Katie, not Megan, telling me."

"You're right. I should have told you, but I was afraid you would react just the way you're reacting. You're condemning him based on the way he looks."

"Give me a little more credit than that. I had a conversation with him, remember? I want what's best for her. It's as simple as that. And he isn't it."

"See? You're not even willing to give him a chance."

"He's out of school, Lina. She should be dating boys her own age."

"There's just two years between them."

He didn't reply for so long she looked at the phone to see if the call had disconnected, but then he was speaking again. "I don't want to fight with you about this," he said, and she could hear the fatigue in his voice.

"I don't want to fight with you, either. I just—I want you to give him a chance. I like him."

"Fine."

"Did you just say fine?

"Yes."

"Mom?" Megan entered her bedroom as she ended the call with Phil. "Can we talk?"

"I'm not going to talk about Katie with—"

"No, about you and Dad," she said as she came farther into the room.

"Sure." Lina patted the spot beside her on the mattress.

"Why can't you forgive him?" Megan asked.

"What? Honey, it's complicated. Did he say something to you?"

"No," Megan said. "But I've never seen him so sad. I know what he did was really bad, but he loves you so much. I don't understand why you can't just forgive him."

"It's not that easy," Lina whispered. "I wish it was."

"How can you love someone that long and just stop?"

"I haven't stopped." Lina looked away from Megan as she fought to keep her emotions in check.

"If you love him, it's crazy to stay apart. Think about us, Mom. I don't want to have to go to two different houses every time I come home for break. It's not fair. I don't want to be from a broken family."

In the weeks between Thanksgiving and Christmas, Lina's weekends were normally filled with nonstop shopping and holiday parties, and while the shopping was the same as previous years, with less than a week before Christmas, Lina hadn't attended a single party. Adele claimed it was because Lina wasn't comfortable in her new status as a single woman, and that may have been partially true, but it was more that Lina wasn't in a partying mood. It took enough energy to put on a happy face for her children, and she just wasn't willing to do it for neighbors and casual friends, so she politely declined invitations from other couples in the neighborhood and passed the invitations from Phil's colleagues to him.

"What do you mean you're not coming?" Diane asked when they met at the mall for shopping. "You're my best friend. You have to come to my Christmas party."

"I'm not spending the evening with Phil and everyone from the law firm. I'm not up to it," Lina said. She stopped to look at a black leather jacket.

"Come on. It will be good for you. A couple of glasses of wine and you'll be fine."

"No, I really can't. I'm sorry."

"I'm really starting to worry about you. You don't socialize enough."

"I socialize every day. I'm working, remember?" The truth was between her job, holiday shopping and taking care of the kids, Lina barely had any free time. Even her time with Nick was limited to only a dinner or two a week.

"Who are you shopping for? I can't imagine Logan wearing that. It looks like a biker's jacket."

"I was thinking about Matt." Lina's attention returned to the jacket. "I've noticed his is looking a little worse for the wear."

"So they're still going strong?"

"Oh, yes." Lina found the right size and lifted the jacket from the rack. "You know what the funny thing is? As a direct result of their relationship, my relationship with Katie is improving. Matt likes coming over to the house, so she spends more time at home. She's no longer escaping to Emma's every chance she gets. And she's starting to talk to me again. She still likes to argue, but I think that's just her. I told her the other day she should consider being a lawyer."

"Has Phil met him yet?" Diane asked.

"No, but he's not going to be put off much longer. I think he's agreed to wait until after the holidays. I know Katie's nervous about it, but I think it's going to be fine."

"What did you decide about Christmas? Are you splitting the time or—"

"He's spending it with us," Lina admitted. "He's coming Christmas Eve and staying through Christmas Day."

"Really?" A smile lit up Diane's features.

"Don't make a big deal about it."

"But it is a big deal. He's spending the night?"

"In the basement. It's for the kids."

"I'm sure it is," Diane said, the smile remaining on her face. "I'll stop by tomorrow with some mistletoe."

"Ha. Ha." Lina handed the jacket and her credit card to the cashier. "It was the only solution that made sense. Megan was insisting on spending Christmas Eve with Phil so he wouldn't be alone, and Logan was upset with Megan. It was just the best solution."

43

"Merry Christmas," Nick said as he slid a gift across the table to Lina. It was three days before Christmas and they'd met in Baltimore for dinner.

"Did you wrap this yourself?" It was obviously a book, perfectly wrapped in holiday paper.

"I did."

Lina smiled. "I'm impressed. Whenever Phil tries to wrap something it's uneven and looks..." She trailed off. "Sorry."

"Don't be."

"I have something for you too," she said before handing him the Rumi book she'd bought him. "Hopefully you don't have it yet."

"No, I don't," he said after unwrapping it, his eyes traveling over the cover. "Thank you."

She smiled when she peeled back the paper on her own gift to reveal a book of poetry by Walt Whitman. "Thank you. It looks like we're on the same wavelength."

"Indeed."

"Oh, before I forget." She reached into her bag and pulled out the copy of *Zen and the Art of Motorcycle Maintenance* he'd let her borrow. It was the third book he'd given her in as many weeks. The first she'd studied and somewhat enjoyed. The second was similar to the first, only not as enjoyable because she found herself trying to think of clever things to tell him about it when she finished, which made it feel more like a school assignment. And the third, well, the third was her breaking point.

"I'm impressed," Nick said, taking the book. "I thought it would take you longer."

"Don't be impressed," Lina said. "I didn't make it through the second chapter." And she'd only made it that far because he said it was one of his favorite books and she thought it might get better. "Sorry, it just felt like too much work. I'm starting to think of you as my professor instead of my... my—"

"Friend," he offered, smiling. "That's okay. It's not for everyone."

"I know you like to talk about philosophy, but I'm really not that much of a reader. I mean, I love poetry and commercial fiction, but I'm not really into the philosophy books." She wasn't going to pretend to be an intellectual when she wasn't. "Sorry."

"Philosophy isn't a prerequisite to our friendship," Nick assured her.

"That's a relief."

"I hope everything goes smoothly for you on Christmas," Nick said after walking her to her car.

"Do you think it's odd that I'm letting him spend the night?"

"I don't know." His hands were pushed deep into the pockets of his coat. "Do you?"

"You sound like a psychiatrist."

He rocked back on his heels. "Occupational hazard I suppose."

"It's a little odd, I think." She drew in a breath. "Thanksgiving was awful though, and I just—I don't want to go through that again."

"I understand."

Lina met his eyes. "Well, good night I guess."

"Good night." He leaned in, kissing her softly on the lips, releasing a flutter of butterflies in her tummy. "Merry Christmas."

— ⁓ —

Lina was pulling a baking sheet full of cookies from the oven when Phil stepped out of the mudroom on Christmas Eve. "Smells good," he said.

"Oh!" She brought her hand up to her chest as she spun around. "You scared me. I didn't expect you so early."

"Sorry." He met her eyes.

"It's fine." She turned back to the cookies.

"Logan wanted me to help him put the train together." He was behind her, one hand pressing into the small of her back as he reached around her with the other for a cookie. A tingling of awareness shot up her spine.

"He's in the living room. He's been working on it all day." She tried to sound casual as she stood with her back to him, her pulse racing.

"It's harder than it looks." He bit into the cookie, moaned his approval and then was taking another before leaving the room.

Lina gripped the counter and took a deep breath. Her physical reaction to him shook her. It was the drought of physical contact, she rationalized. As much as her mind knew he had betrayed her and the separation was the right decision, her body clearly operated under a different set of principles.

Despite her shaky start, the day went surprisingly well—almost too well, considering at some points Lina had to remind herself that Phil no longer lived with them. Even Knight behaved like Phil was the rightful alpha of the house, obeying his commands more quickly than he ever responded to Lina or Logan.

After their traditional Christmas Eve dinner of tenderloin, mashed potatoes and asparagus, they attended a 10:00 p.m. church service. As Lina sat between Phil and Logan, her hand drifted to Phil's thigh as it had a hundred other times over the years. It wasn't until she felt the clenching of his thigh muscle that she realized what she had done, and she snatched her hand back.

"I'm starting a new tradition," Logan announced as soon as they arrived home. "Every Christmas Eve, we'll watch *Elf*!"

"It's too late, Logan," Lina said.

"No it's not. I'll find the disc," he said as he jogged towards the family room.

Lina curled her feet up under her as her eyes traveled over the scene in her family room. Katie was stretched out under a blanket on the oversized chair she usually shared with Matt, Megan and Phil sat on the loveseat, and she was beside Logan on the couch. It seemed so normal. This was her family and yet it wasn't, not anymore. Phil no longer lived with them. She took a sip of wine and brought her attention to the television, pushing away her negative thoughts. She wasn't going to go down that road tonight, not on Christmas.

"Refill?" Phil asked thirty minutes later, before taking her almost-empty wine glass. When he returned, instead of resuming his place beside Megan, who was now asleep, he crossed to Katie.

"Dad, no!" Katie whined when he began to lower himself down beside her. "There's no room."

"Sure there is."

"You're so annoying."

He lifted the blanket and resituated it over them before curving his arm around her shoulders. "When you were little, you told me you'd never leave me."

"That was before I really knew you."

He laughed aloud. "It's Christmas. Be nice to me."

Lina openly watched them. Katie was leaning into Phil's side as she once again began watching the movie. They were healed, or well on their way. Six months earlier, Katie would never have stayed in the chair with him, but now she was curled against him.

"I'm not a fan of this movie," Phil called out to Logan. "We should be watching *It's a Wonderful Life* or *A Christmas Story*."

"Boring," Katie said. "This is the first tradition of Logan's I like."

"You have to watch it a few times to appreciate it," Logan said. "Everyone thinks it's dumb the first time."

"It is dumb," Phil said dryly.

"Dad! Shh." Katie elbowed him in his side. "You can't talk through the whole movie!"

It was almost 2:00 a.m. before the kids were in their bedrooms and Lina and Phil were able to bring the gifts up from the basement where they were stowed away.

"You outdid yourself," Phil said as he admired the large assortment of wrapped packages beneath the Christmas tree. "It will take them half the day to open those."

"It's no more than normal. And some are for you."

"I'm teasing you. It's late. I'm going to set the alarm and head downstairs."

"Okay." She touched his hand. "Thanks."

"Good night." He leaned in and brushed his lips over her cheek. "Sleep well."

"Good night." The warmth of his lips lingered on her cheek as she watched him leave the room. She took a final look at the Christmas tree before making her way upstairs.

— —

Lina turned in to Phil's warm body, her hands sliding over his chest as she slipped her leg between his. She was dreaming, and she didn't want to wake up because it felt too good. She began running her lips along his jaw, her tongue darting out to taste him. Never had a dream felt so real. She could even smell him. Her whole body stilled and her eyes opened.

She wasn't dreaming. "What are you doing here?" She scrambled back from him, barely able to make out his features in the darkened room.

"You came to me."

"What?" She sat up, clutching the sheet against her chest as she looked around. She was in the basement. "Oh my God. I can't believe this."

She felt the mattress shift and then Phil's warm hand sliding up her arm. "Look at me."

"No."

"Lina." He clasped her shoulder, pushing her back down on the bed. "Look at me."

She was naked. She'd fallen asleep in a nightgown, but she'd obviously removed it before climbing into his bed. She felt his hand slide over her hip to her stomach. "Don't."

"Shh." He brushed his lips over hers. "Don't think. Just feel." He took the kiss deeper, his warm tongue stroking hers.

There was no way she could resist him. Her body had been craving his since the moment he walked into the kitchen, and she wasn't strong enough to stop, not when he was touching her like a man who knew her body better than she did. She slid her hands up over his muscular shoulders and around his neck, offering her surrender, and he moaned deeply as he settled himself between her thighs.

"Do you know why you came to me?" he asked minutes later as he thrust his body into hers. "Because you're mine, Lina," he said, driving into her again. "You were made for me. You know that's true, don't you?" He paused, his body deep in hers, the muscles of his arms and shoulders straining as he held himself over her. "Tell me."

"No," she whispered, hating the power she knew he had over her.

"Why are you fighting this?"

"Stop talking."

"I know I hurt you, but I promise, if you'll let me I'll spend the rest of my life making it up to you. I love you." He lowered his mouth over hers as his body again began to move.

Lina was almost asleep, her body tangled with Phil's, when he asked the question that had probably been consuming him for two months. "Were you with him?"

"No."
He released a breath.

— ~

"You had sex with him?" Adele whispered within five minutes of arriving the following afternoon.

"Adele," Lina hissed, grabbing her arm and backing her into the empty dining room. "Shh. I have a house full of people."

"I told you this would happen, didn't I? And you said, 'Oh no, I would *never* do that.'"

"He told you?"

"He didn't have to. He has that whole, I got laid for the first time in months look all over him. He's strutting around like a fucking peacock."

"Oh God." Lina dropped her face into her hands. "It wasn't my fault."

"What did he do, get you drunk?"

"No. It wasn't his fault."

"So, what, your bodies just merged on their own?"

"Kind of. It was a temporary lapse, that's all. It was neither of our faults."

"How many times did you have this 'temporary lapse' that was neither of your faults?" Adele asked. "I'm guessing more than once."

"Okay, now you're starting to sound like Mom. Let's drop it."

"You're back with Phil?"

Lina spun around at the sound of her mother's voice. "What?"

"Phil, he seems happy. Did you work things out?"

"No, he got laid last night," Adele said.

"Adele!" Lina glared at her.

"What, you don't think she'd figure it out?"

"Figure what out?" Drew asked as he joined them.

"Nothing," Lina said.

"Lina and Phil had sex last night," Alice said.

"Okay." Lina held up her hands. "No more! And if you don't mind, I'm going to get back to the kitchen." She left the dining room and walked straight into Phil.

"Whoa." His hands clasped her hips.

"Stop smiling," she whispered, fisting his shirt. "My entire family knows we had sex because of you."

"What?" He frowned down at her.

"That's right. Just one look at you and they could tell. So stop smiling."

Whereas Christmas Eve included only the immediate family in the Hunter household, Christmas day was the one time a year both Lina and Phil's families combined for a joint celebration. Like she had on the previous day, Lina felt as if Phil had never left, watching him seamlessly fall back into his role of host as he made drinks, kept the fire going, adjusted the thermostat when the house felt too warm and otherwise acted like the man of the house. She kept expecting to wake up out of a dream and realize Phil had never actually moved out.

Only his mother's behavior kept her rooted in reality, as she was teary-eyed one minute and hugging Lina the next. "I know he broke his vows to you, but he loves you and it breaks my heart to see the two of you apart," Mrs. Hunter said to Lina when she managed to pull her into a quiet corner. "Can't you find it in your heart to forgive him?"

Lina's throat constricted as she met Susan Hunter's tear-filled eyes. "It's complicated," Lina whispered, squeezing Susan's hands.

"I love you like you're one of my own, so I'm going to speak to you like you're one of my own. No marriage is perfect and no person is perfect. Forgiveness is part of being a good Christian. Think about your children."

"Mom." Phil was behind his mother, his hands sliding down her arms. "This isn't the time or the place for whatever you're saying."

"I—"

"Jeanie is looking for you in the kitchen," he said as he gently nudged her away from Lina. "Let me talk to my wife."

"It's fine," Lina assured Phil as soon as his mother walked away.

"No it isn't. It's not her place."

"I don't think that's how it works with parents."

"How come you didn't tell me Drew was coming?"

"Because it was none of your business. You're a guest this year too." When she attempted to step around him, he wrapped his fingers around her upper arm.

"What is that supposed to mean?"

"You don't live here anymore." She yanked her arm from his grasp. "You don't get a say in the guest list."

"What did I do?" He frowned down at her. "Why are you suddenly angry at me?"

"You're acting like you still live here, and you don't."

"How do you want me to act? I'm trying to help you."

Lina drew in a deep breath. She was being completely unreasonable. "I'm sorry. That wasn't fair. I just don't want you to think anything has changed because of last night."

"Why are you trying to convince yourself you don't want this? You came to me in your sleep. Doesn't that tell you something?"

"It was a temporary lapse."

"Oh, is that what it was?" He slid one hand along the side of her jaw, tilting her head back. "That's not what your eyes tell me."

"You're just seeing what you want to see." Her hands pressed against his abdomen.

"I don't think so."

"You're not about to have another lapse right in front of everybody, are you?"

Lina jumped back at the sound of Adele's voice. "We're just talking."

"Yeah that's what it looked like."

"This is none of your business, Adele," Phil said shortly. "No one asked for your opinion."

"Stop." Lina touched his chest. "It's Christmas and we have a house full of people. We'll talk later."

Lina was finishing up the dishes after the last guest departed when she felt a pair of strong hands slide up her back to her shoulders. "Let me stay another night," Phil said against her ear.

"No." She turned off the water and stepped away from the sink, putting distance between them.

"It's still Christmas. I'll leave tomorrow."

"No," she whispered. "We're not having a repeat of last night."

"Why not?"

"Nothing's changed. Last night I wasn't thinking. I didn't let myself think. But I am now, and I'm not going back there."

"You still love me. I can see it in your eyes when you look at me. I could feel it in your body when you were under me—"

"Stop!" she hissed, pressing her fingers over his lips. "They'll hear you."

"I don't care. I'm fighting for them too."

"No." Lina shook her head. "I'm finding myself. I can't do that with you. You swallowed me."

"Swallowed you?" He frowned. "I have no idea what you're talking about."

"I got a job. Did you know I have a job?"

"Yes, I heard."

"You never wanted me to work."

"I never discouraged you from working."

"You never encouraged me to."

"You never showed the slightest interest in working outside our home. If it was something I knew you wanted, I would have been a hundred percent behind it."

"You're my husband. You should have been encouraging me to expand my world. Instead you just let my whole existence revolve around you."

"Are you looking for reasons to hate me?"

"No. I'm just telling you how I feel."

"You were happy, Lina. We were happy. The stress with Katie..." He paused. "We had one bad year. Don't go back now and redefine the last two and a half decades so you can find a way to stay angry with me."

"I'm not."

"I think that's exactly what you're doing. But it's not going to work. You can't delete all those years—all those memories."

As she met his eyes she felt their connection pulsing between them, and she broke their gaze. "It's late. You need to go home."

— ⁓ —

Lina looked guiltily at the cell phone on her bedside stand. She'd turned it on long enough to send Nick a "Merry Christmas" text earlier in the day but knew he would be expecting a phone call, a phone call she couldn't bring herself to make after spending the night in Phil's bed. She linked her hands behind her neck and dropped her chin onto her chest, hating the guilt twisting in her stomach, but knowing it was too late to undo the betrayal she was sure Nick would feel.

It was almost 1:00 a.m. when Lina reached for her cell phone, knowing she wasn't going to be able to quiet her mind enough to fall asleep until she spoke to him. The voice greeting her was deep and sleep filled.

"I'm sorry for waking you."

"Everything okay?" Nick asked.

"I slept with him," she whispered, and then unexpectedly began to cry. "I'm so sorry."

"Lina, no. Don't cry."

"You've been so wonderful to me. I don't know how I would have made it through the past two months without you, and I feel so guilty. I don't know how it happened. I wasn't planning it. I don't know why I went to him."

"Shh—don't do this to yourself. You didn't do anything wrong."

"How can you say that?"

"Because it's true. Listen to me. I told you the morning after you spent the night at my house that you weren't emotionally ready for another relationship, and that's still true. If anyone should feel guilty it's me. I've repeatedly exercised poor judgment with you. I shouldn't be a factor in your decision making. If you want to sleep with your estranged husband, you shouldn't have to worry about what I'm feeling or thinking."

"I don't want to hurt you."

"Oh, Lina," he sighed. "I'll be fine. My eyes are wide open, remember?"

"Does this mean we can't talk?"

"Only if that's what you want it to mean."

44

"We can leave as soon as we finish eating," Katie told Matt as he pulled into the parking lot outside the restaurant where they were meeting her father for dinner. "The whole thing is stupid anyway. I don't care what he says." She hated that Matt was nervous. He'd been quiet since picking her up at her house, and with his freshly shaven face and toned-down hair, it was obvious he'd spent extra care on his appearance.

"It's better if he likes me," Matt said. "I don't want to start sneaking around."

"But we would," she said, her own anxieties kicking in.

Matt turned to her then, his dark eyes meeting hers. "No one is keeping me from you."

Her father stood as they approached his table, obviously coming straight from work in a dark suit, and Katie felt Matt's whole body stiffen.

"Matt, how are you?" He held out his hand.

"Good." Matt returned his handshake.

"We don't have a lot of time," Katie said. "I have homework." She sat on her father's left, directly across from Matt.

"If you're a meat eater, their filet is excellent," he told Matt as they looked at their menus.

"Sounds good." Matt closed his menu.

"So." Phil turned his attention to Matt as soon as the waiter left with their order. "Last time we talked you were playing in a band and working at a lumberyard, I believe. Is that still accurate?"

"You know it is," Katie said. "You asked me that last week."

"And now I'm asking Matt."

"You already know the answer," Katie grumbled.

"Yeah, it's still accurate," Matt answered.

"Still no plans to go to college?"

"He's a musician," Katie answered. "He doesn't need college to do that."

"I think Matt is capable of speaking for himself."

"I'm not going to college," Matt answered. "School isn't really my thing."

"What if the band doesn't work out? Do you—"

"It's going to work out," Katie interrupted. "He's amazing."

"That's good to hear," Phil said, his focus remaining on Matt. "How serious are you about my daughter?"

"Dad!" Katie glared at him. "You wouldn't ask one of Megan's boyfriends that question."

"Sure I would."

"You never even made one come to dinner."

Her father pushed back his chair. "Matt, excuse us for a minute."

"What?" Katie asked as soon as they stopped in a private corner just inside the bar.

"This is going to be easy or difficult," her father said. "It's all up to you. I came here to get to know him, and that's going to require speaking to him."

"You don't have to ask him embarrassing questions." Katie crossed her arms over her chest. "You wouldn't be doing this to Megan."

"This isn't about Megan. This is about you, and your history is a little different than your sister's, and we both know it. So I'm going to take a bit more care with you."

Katie dropped her eyes. "It's so unfair. You treat me like I'm a little kid."

"No, I treat you like you're my daughter. You care about this boy. You're spending a great deal of time with him, so I want to get to know him. What are you afraid of?"

"Nothing."

"Katie?" he prompted.

"I don't want you to hurt him."

"Hurt him?" He frowned in confusion. "What are you talking about?"

She lifted her gaze back to his. "By acting like he isn't good enough for me or something."

He observed her in silence for several seconds. "I'll do my best."

Lina was getting ready for bed when Phil called to let her know how the dinner went. "I knew you would like him if you gave him a chance," she said.

"'Like' is generous. He was tolerable, but considering his tattoos were covered, that may have played in his favor."

"You're not that shallow."

"No, but just the same, I'm not sure what you're seeing. The kid's out of high school. Why can't she date a boy her own age?"

"She'll be seventeen next month. They are a year and a half apart. He's had a rough life by no fault of his own. Why don't you reach into that Catholic heart of yours and try not to be so judgmental?"

"I'm her father. I'm supposed to judge people that come into my children's lives, especially hers. She doesn't exactly have a great track record. He looks like he could do drugs."

"He doesn't do drugs."

"You don't know that."

"I do. He's a hundred percent against drug use." She hesitated, weighing Matt's trust in her against Phil's right to know about the boy Katie was dating. "His mom died of a drug overdose—he was the one who found her."

"Jesus," Phil said, his voice low.

"So you can rest your mind about drug use."

"My God, Lina, I feel for this kid, but he's the last boy she needs to be involved with."

"What is that supposed to mean?"

"You don't survive something like that unscathed, and she isn't exactly emotionally stable. It's like a train wreck. How in the hell did they find each other?"

"I can't believe you. This is not his fault."

"We just spent ten thousand dollars on psychiatrists for her. A year ago she was cutting herself. They have no business together. He's probably in worse shape than she is."

"Don't be so insensitive."

"I'm sorry this happened to him, but my priority is Katie and she is too young and emotionally fragile to deal with whatever's going on inside his head. What do you think his childhood was like?"

"I suppose it's a good thing your parents didn't have your attitude, or we never would have been together."

"There's no comparison."

"You don't think I was emotionally damaged? I guess you should have just turned your back on me."

"We were already together. I loved you and I was stable. I didn't have Katie's history."

"What about Shiloh? Should she have been judged because of something that wasn't her fault?"

"Is that what this is about? Shiloh? You can't save her so you want to save him?"

"Don't be ridiculous," Lina said, trying to keep the frustration from her voice. "And he doesn't need saving. And if you would give him a chance, you would realize it. He isn't broken. He is mature and sensitive, and he adores Katie."

"Why can we never agree about her?" He sighed. "Just once I wish we could be in agreement."

"Well, maybe if you weren't so pig headed."

"Oh, is that what it is?"

Her voice softened. "I think so."

"I don't know why I bother to argue with you. You always win."

"That's not true. I didn't want to put her on restriction for six months."

"And look how that turned out."

"That's not what I was saying. That wasn't your fault."

"No? I think we both know if I hadn't confined her to the house for six month she wouldn't have cut herself, but we can't go back, and I don't know what a better solution would have been."

"It wasn't your fault," Lina insisted. "I never thought that. But I like Matt, Phil. I mean, I really like him. I think he's good for her, and she seems happy with him. Can't you just try and give him a chance?"

"At this point I don't think I have a choice, do I? She seems completely infatuated with him. I don't think she looked at her phone once during dinner. She was too busy looking at him."

"They're young and in love. Don't you remember what that felt like?"

Seconds passed before he answered. "I remember exactly what that felt like." His voice was like a caress.

Lina closed her eyes. "It's late. I should go."

"I know you still love me."

"Has she had the baby?" It had been in the back of Lina's mind for weeks. "Answer me," she said when the other end of the phone stayed silent.

"Yes."

Her heart dropped. "When?"

"Last month."

"Last month?" she repeated. "Before Christmas?"

"December 23rd."

"So when you were with me, you knew?"

"He has nothing to do with my love for you."

"Have you met him?"

"Yes."

He had another son. It was surreal. "How many times?" Lina asked.

"Baby, why—"

"Don't call me that. Does he look like you?"

"I think he looks a little like Logan."

"I hate you," she whispered.

"I don't believe you."

"You have a baby with another woman, Phil. There is no un-doing that."

"You're right, there isn't. And I regret the circumstances surrounding his conception and how much I've hurt you, and I wish to God he was yours, but I am not ashamed of him and I can't regret him. He's my son."

45

Phil's words replayed in her mind for days. *He's my son.* He had another son. Her children had a brother. This was real.

"Did you expect him to deny his own child?" Alice asked when Lina told her of the conversation.

"No, of course not." Lina was pacing back and forth in her mother's kitchen. "But I didn't expect him to say he didn't regret him. That hurt."

"How could he regret his own flesh and blood?" Alice asked. "Regardless of how he came to be, it's his baby. He looks just like him."

Lina stopped pacing. "How would you know that?"

"I saw his pictures."

"You saw his pictures?" Lina frowned at her mother. "When, on Christmas?"

"No, last weekend. He was over here replacing my sliding glass door."

"What? Why?"

"It's been giving me problems for months, so I—"

"I mean why did Phil fix it?"

"He always fixes things for me."

"We're separated. You shouldn't be asking him to do things around your house."

"Why ever not? He's like a son to me. Do you expect that to change because you've decided to throw your life into chaos?"

"Yes." Lina nodded. "That's exactly what I expect. You're my mother. You're supposed to be on my side."

"I am on your side. That's why I keep waiting for you to come to your senses."

"Sometimes I think you live in a completely alternate universe."

"Maybe I do, but it's probably saner than the one everyone else inhabits. I mentioned the beginner astrology course for Katie to Phil. He seemed more receptive."

"He did not." Lina knew her mother was lying.

"He didn't say yes, but he wasn't as short as normal, so I saw that as progress."

"She's not going," Lina said. "It's not just Phil, it's me. I don't want her to go."

"You don't think I know that? But what I'd like to know is why. What are you so afraid of?"

"I'm not afraid of anything, and I don't have to justify my decisions to you. It's bad enough she did a spell in my freezer. I'm not letting her take an astrology class."

"You're still blaming astrology for what happened that night. Evil is what happened that night. It had nothing to do with astrology."

"I know it wasn't astrology's fault, but it reminds me of it, okay? When I see your books and charts and all of the stuff, it brings back that night. And I don't want to bring it back, so the answer is no, regardless of what Phil says. Katie isn't going to a beginner astrology class."

"You're letting them win, even after all these years. You're still giving them power."

"Maybe I am, but I'm not changing my mind."

"Do you remember this?" Alice asked, holding out a book on palmistry. "You used to have fun with this. You were even pretty good."

Lina took the book, her eyes traveling over her name inside the front cover. "I remember."

"You believe in this stuff?" Phil, shirtless and in a pair of exercise shorts, paused at the bookshelf in Lina's bedroom as he pulled out a book on palmistry. It was Saturday morning, and he'd told his parents he was spending the night before at a friend's, which was what he told them most weekends so he could stay with Lina.

Lina stepped up behind him and wrapped her arms around him. "I think so. Why? You don't?"

He shrugged. "Not really."

"Do you want me to read your palm?"

Five minutes later they were sitting cross-legged on the center of her bed, his palm covered in baby powder as Lina stared at the lines, trying to remember everything she could from the crash course she'd been given by one of her mother's friends a couple of months earlier. "Long life," she said as she traced her index finger over his heart line in the center of his palm. "You're going to make lots of money," she said, touching the soft padding below his thumb.

"How about wives and kids?" he asked "Does it show that?"

She turned his hand to the side and looked at the lines below his pinky. "There I am," Lina said, touching a deep horizontal line. "And you see these, the ones that cross through vertically?"

"Yeah."

"Those are our children."

"Three?"

"Yeah," she said as she looked at his hand. "Wait—four," she said, touching a line that wasn't as deep as the others. "I think that's one too."

"I want us to have at least three." Phil lay back on the bed, staring up at his hand.

"Let's give them unique names that no one else has." She snuggled into his side.

"I want to name our first son Logan after my grandfather. Show me where I am on your hand," he said, and a moment later was looking at the lines on Lina's hand. "Maybe everyone has the same lines," he said as he traced them with his finger.

"No, I've looked at other hands."

The sound of the door opening had them both sitting up. "You're supposed to knock," Lina said, frowning at her mother. "You know the lock doesn't work."

"I knew it was safe. The bed stopped creaking twenty minutes ago."

"Mom!"

"There is nothing to be embarrassed about. Everything you do in here is beautiful."

"Please leave." Lina fell back on the mattress and threw her forearm over her eyes.

*"I'm taking breakfast orders," her mother said. "Would you
like French toast or an omelet, Phillip?"*

"Um. Could I have both?"

"Of course."

"Your mom is so cool," he said after the door closed.

"What's wrong?" Alice asked.

Lina pulled her mind back to the present. "Nothing." She
handed the book back to her mother. "I have to go." She headed
towards the door.

"Oh, your father and I are getting married in July," her
mother said as she followed her into the foyer. "Make sure you
talk to me before you plan any trips."

Lina turned with her hand on the doorknob. "You're having
a wedding? Like with guests?"

"Of course, and I would like Katie and Megan to be
bridesmaids."

"Oh my God." Lina left without another word.

- ~

Over the next month, with dozens of new homes scheduled to
go on the market, Lina lost herself in work, running from one
house to another and fitting what easily could have been a full-
time job into about thirty hours a week. Her life became something of a routine. After getting Logan and Katie off to school,
she would walk Knight, attend a yoga class at a nearby studio or
go for a run and then go into work for several hours, usually
picking Logan up at his bus stop on her way home.

On Tuesday and Thursday evenings, while the kids were with
Phil, Lina would either study home décor books or go to dinner

with Adele, Alice or a friend from yoga. She'd seen Nick several times, and while he remained friendly, he was more reserved since her Christmas confession, no longer initiating phone calls or meetings. But his eyes couldn't mask his feelings, and unless Lina was having a particularly hard day, she tried to limit her calls to a couple of times a week, knowing until she was free from Phil, she wasn't being fair to Nick.

Lina's favorite times were the weekend nights when both Logan and Katie would stay in. Matt would come over and sometimes Brian or another of Logan's friends, and the house would be filled with the bustle of activity. Her estrangement from Phil felt more real with each passing week. Although he was a frequent visitor, either to pick up Logan or do one of the myriad of chores that inevitably popped up in the house—a clogged sink one day, an unhinged closet door the next—he'd made no attempt to engage Lina in any discussions of substance since the phone call about his son.

Gradually, Lina had transformed from a married, stay-at-home mom to a single, working mom, and although she didn't make enough money as a stager to support her current lifestyle without Phil's financial assistance, his help was now legally guaranteed, and therefore for all intents and purposes, she'd attained the independence she craved. She was free to do and be whatever she wanted.

"Wow!" Adele said, fanning herself as soon as Katie and Matt left the house. "If I was twenty-five years younger, I would fight her for him. He's swoon worthy. Those eyes and—"

"Calm down," Lina said. "You're starting to creep me out."

"I'm serious," Adele said as she followed Lina towards the kitchen. "He's what I imagine James Dean was like. Sensitive bad boy, but with a voice. Can't you just imagine girls in the audience stripping as soon as he opens his mouth?"

"Seriously." Lina gripped Adele's shoulders. "You spend too much time with Mom. Normal people don't talk like that about their niece's eighteen-year-old boyfriend."

"'Normal people'? You sound like Phil."

"No, I sound like me."

— ⁓

The vibration of the music filled Katie's body as she and Emma stood to the left of the dance floor, just two among the throng of people packed into an eighteen-and-over club in Baltimore listening to Fugitive.

"I have to take a video for Ryan," Emma yelled to be heard over the crowd. "Matt's, like, famous. Look at all these people."

It was overwhelming. When Matt said he could get her and Emma in to listen to him play, Katie pictured a gathering similar to the ones that used to come to hear Ryan's band—fifty or so people—but this was a sold-out venue of at least two hundred, and if the chatter around her was any indication, the majority were there to hear the group's new singer, Matt Hudson.

"He's so hot," a girl beside her was saying. "He's met my eyes like three times. I'm going meet him during the next break. I'll blow him if there's time," she said, eliciting giggles from her friends.

Katie stepped away from their group, only to stumble into another speaking in similar terms. "I need a drink," she said to Emma. "Let's find someone old enough to help us."

Katie was on her second cranberry and vodka when the band took a break, and she was half-surprised when Matt found her. "Hey." He cupped her face in his palms and began to kiss her, only to pull back as soon as his tongue found hers. "You're drinking?"

"You don't own me." She took a long draw on her straw.

"What's wrong?" Matt asked.

She dropped her eyes. "Nothing."

Matt took her hand, dragging her behind him as he walked away from the bar. "What happened?" he asked as soon as he had her in a quiet corner behind the stage.

"I don't like all these girls looking at you," she admitted as she stared down into her drink.

He took the glass from her hand and set it on the stage. "Look at me." He touched the side of her jaw and tilted her head back. "Do you think I give a fuck about any of them?"

Katie shook her head, reading the answer in his eyes. "I still want to scratch their eyes out. I hate it."

"You're the only girl I want," he said as he pressed her back against the wall, his body inches from hers. "I love you."

"You do?" Katie whispered.

"More than anything else in this fucking world." He held the sides of her face, his mouth meeting hers for a deep kiss. "I need you to promise me something, Hunter," Matt said after lifting his head. "I need you to promise me you aren't going to get drunk because you're upset about something. If you're upset about something, you come and talk to me. Drinking doesn't make anything better—if there's something on your mind, deal with it. Don't cover it up."

"Okay." She kissed his chin. "Tell me you love me again."

"I'm serious. I know how dangerous this is and you do too. Didn't that doctor you like so much teach you how to deal with shit you don't like?"

Katie felt stupid. "I'm sorry."

"Don't be sorry—just don't do it again. Your mom trusts me to protect you when we're out. What do you think she's going to do if I bring you home drunk? You think she's still going to trust me?"

"Don't be mad." She gripped the front of his shirt. "I won't do it again. Don't be mad at me."

"I'm not mad at you." He brushed his lips over hers. "But I don't want you to do dangerous shit."

"I won't. Tell me you love me again."

"I love you."

Matt's words were Katie's first thoughts when she awoke the following morning. *Do you still love me?* she texted.

I'll always love you, Hunter. You've bewitched me or something.

As soon as she read his words, Katie called Emma. "It's the spell, isn't it? That's why he feels this way. I tricked him into loving me. I need to tell him the truth."

"Katie, no! He loves you. It's real. His feelings are real. Why would you tell him about the spell?"

"It just seems wrong, you know, making him love me. I wish he had just fallen in love with me on his own without a spell."

"Love is love," Emma said. "And anyway, it's too late. Just forget about it. Matt loves you and you love him—that's all that matters."

46

With an entire Saturday stretched before her and no set plans, Lina decided to ask Nick to lunch. "I'm sorry, I woke you, didn't I?" she asked when she heard the huskiness of his voice.

"I needed to get up, anyway. Everything okay?"

"Yes, I just had a free afternoon and thought of you."

"Would you hold for a second?" he asked, and then she heard the distinct sound of a female voice and his muffled response. "Sorry about that," he said a moment later.

"I'm interrupting something."

"No, it's fine. I'm—it's fine."

"You have company," she said. He was with a woman, probably in bed. "I shouldn't have called so early."

"I always want to hear from you. Never doubt that."

"What do you expect?" Adele asked when she recounted the phone call. "You won't even kiss him, and you barely see him."

"I don't expect anything," Lina insisted. "I'm just telling you it felt weird. He knew what I thought and he didn't correct me."

Adele laughed. "That's because you were right. He was in bed with someone. Maybe he was getting a blowjob."

"No he wasn't! Why do you have to be so crude?"

"Does it bother you? The thought of another woman's mouth—"

"Goodbye, Adele." Lina ended the call, but Adele's question lingered in her mind. Did it bother her knowing he was with another woman? Yes, she decided after a moment, but not nearly as much as it would if it were Phil.

At first it was odd being paid to do something she enjoyed so much, but as winter gave way to spring and the real estate market picked up, running from house to house, sometimes three to four in a day, quickly began to feel like work. Between her job, dog and children, Lina was almost too busy to think, so when Phil asked about spring break, she had no choice but to tell him she couldn't afford the time away, and so for the first time in her life she was completely alone while Logan and Katie enjoyed a Caribbean vacation with their father.

"You've never been alone overnight?" Diane asked over dinner, the day after Phil and the kids left.

"Not until last night. I went from my house to Phil's, and we were married while he was in law school and then had babies before he ever traveled, so no, I was never on my own."

"And how did it feel?"

Lina shrugged. "Fine. To tell you the truth, I was too tired to notice. I was asleep by nine thirty."

Diane laughed. "You've turned into a career woman over-night. You realize this is the first time I've seen you in over a month."

"I know. I'm sorry. It's just been so busy. I haven't seen any-one besides the kids and Adele. Can you believe I hired an as-sistant? I actually have an employee. To think a year ago I wasn't even working and had never really worked, and now I'm some-one's boss. It's surreal."

"It must be agreeing with you. You look good."

"Do I? I feel like I look tired."

"No, there's a healthy glow to you. You're happy."

"Happy," Lina repeated, forcing a smile. "I'm not sure I would say happy, probably 'not sad' would be a more apt descrip-tion. I'm not sad anymore."

The next night, Lina met Adele and a few coworkers for happy hour. What at first was fun—chatting with work friends and nib-bling appetizers—quickly became depressing when Adele invited a couple of men from a nearby table to join them and Lina found herself making small talk with an accountant who was staring at her like she was his next meal.

Her eyes traveled the bar as she absently listened to him complain about his ex-wife. Lina wondered if Phil frequented similar places on the nights he wasn't visiting the kids or ex-ercising. If he did, she had no doubt women approached him, just as Adele had approached the men currently sitting with them.

"I'm going to leave," Lina whispered to Adele.

"What? Excuse us for minute," Adele said to the men before grabbing Lina's arm and leading her to a quiet hallway near the bathroom. "Why would you leave? They're cute."

"I'm tired. I just want to go home."

"No, have another drink. This is good for you. It's a tame introduction back into the singles' world. That guy seems genuinely nice. You don't have to go home with him. Just flirt with him a little. It's good practice."

"Practice for what?"

"Life. Your new reality."

"If I just wanted a boyfriend, I'd pick Nick."

"Then why don't you?" Adele asked. "Why don't you pick Nick?"

"I'm leaving."

"Lina—"

"Sorry, I'm just too tired for this."

An hour later, curled on the couch with a glass of wine and a book, Lina's thoughts were still back at the bar as she pondered Adele's words. Was that really supposed to be her new reality—meeting men from failed relationships with other women? There was no way she was cut out for the singles' scene, and yet she couldn't imagine spending the rest of her life alone. Why wasn't she with Nick? He was handsome, successful, and he clearly wanted her. Sure, he was a bit too cerebral at times, but no one was perfect. The truth was she wasn't over Phil. She couldn't forgive him, but she couldn't move past him.

She pulled a photo album from its place beneath the coffee table and, because she must have been a glutton for punishment, leaned back into the couch and began looking through old photographs of them. She hesitated when she reached a photo of them at the beach, his arm thrown over her shoulders, both of hers wrapped around his middle as they smiled at the camera.

It was senior week. Phil had just graduated, and they were staying at one of his friends' beach houses for the week. "Put your clothes back on, baby," Phil said as he watched Lina skip along the surf, the moonlight reflecting off her skin. "Anyone could come." He was stretched out on a blanket where they'd just made love. "They can probably see you from the house."

"I don't care." She twirled around as she spread her arms out wide. "I feel so free. Come swim with me."

"It's two o'clock in the morning."

"Are you going to make me swim alone?" Lina splashed into the surf and dove under a small wave, swimming several yards before she felt his strong hands gripping her hips and pulling her back against his naked body.

"You're crazy. You know that?" He wrapped his arms around her.

"For you." She turned in his arms and snaked her own up around his neck. "Promise me you'll always swim naked with me, even when we're old and wrinkled."

"I promise."

"I can't believe you're going to leave me in three months."

He shook his head. "I'll never leave you. I'm just going to college so I'll be able to have a career and take care of you forever."

"Maybe I'll have a career. Maybe I'll be the one supporting you."

"Do you want a career?"

"No." Lina wrapped her legs around his waist. "I want to have your babies and live in a big house with a pool in the backyard and a white picket fence. That's all I want."

"Then that's what you'll have."

"I should come with you. You could hide me in your dorm."

> *"Okay." He smiled.*
> *"Seriously, what if you fall in love with some southern girl?"*
> *"Never." He brushed his lips over hers. "I found my girl."*
> *"Why do you love me so much?"*
> *He breathed in, his eyes meeting hers. "Because when I saw you, I knew."*
> *"Knew what?"*
> *"That you were mine."*

Lina wiped a lone tear from her cheek. She had read once that it took twenty-five percent of the length of a relationship to get over it. She had about six years to go.

47

"**Y**ou said your job wasn't going to get in the way of any-thing," Logan said a few weeks after spring break as Lina drove him to his bus stop. "But you haven't come to any of my lacrosse games."

"Doesn't your dad go to most of your games?" Lina asked.

"Yeah, but a lot of moms come too."

"When's the next game?"

A few days later, Lina exited her car and walked towards the Gilman lacrosse field. Logan thought work was the reason she hadn't attended any of his lacrosse games, but the truth was she didn't want to chance being in the vicinity of both Phil and Nick at the same time.

As the field came into view, Lina scanned the crowd, easily locating Phil because of his height. He was standing in the midst of several other fathers. As she watched, an attractive woman approached him, and he smiled in greeting. Giving no more thought to Nick, Lina made a beeline for Phil.

The game still hadn't started, and the woman at his side, who Lina didn't recognize, was monopolizing his attention to the point that he didn't notice Lina until she was practically on top of them. "Hi," Lina said.

They both turned to Lina. "I didn't know you were coming," Phil said.

"He asked me to." Lina looked pointedly at the other woman, who she had noted wasn't wearing a wedding ring. "Hi, I'm Lina Hunter."

"Oh, hi." The other woman returned her handshake.

"Did you remember to call your mom?" Lina asked, turning her back to the other woman as she faced Phil.

He frowned. "Why would I—"

"It's her birthday."

"Did you—"

"Yes, I sent her flowers," Lina answered. "But you should call her." She saw the other woman walk away in her peripheral. "Are you really picking up women at your son's lacrosse game?" she whispered.

"Is that a serious question?"

"Yes." She folded her arms over her chest as she awaited his response.

"No." His attention turned to the field as the game started.

Lina mindlessly watched the game, barely registering when Logan was on the field, too lost in her thoughts. When she and Phil were divorced, she'd have to see him with other women. He'd probably get married again, maybe even have more kids.

"What's wrong? Are you sick?"

"What?" She realized he was speaking to her. "No, I'm just—I was thinking about something."

"It couldn't have been very pleasant."

"No, it wasn't," she admitted as she returned her attention to the game.

"I've got to get back to work," Phil said as soon as the game ended. "Tell Logan good game and I'll call him later." His hand clasped Lina's shoulder as he leaned in to kiss her.

As soon as she felt the brush of his lips on her cheek, Lina turned her head and pressed her lips against his, consumed by an overwhelming need to let any women watching know that Phil wasn't available. It was all the incentive Phil needed. He took her face in both his hands, his tongue dipping into her mouth and stroking over hers.

The kiss ended almost as soon as it began, Phil clearly appreciating that it wasn't the proper venue for a make-out session. "I like this possessive side of you," he whispered in her ear before his long strides took him away.

Lina was pressing her fingertips to her lips, her mind racing with thoughts of what she had done, when she felt a presence beside her. "Nick," she breathed. "I didn't see you. Were you here for the whole game?"

"Half. I would have come by earlier, but I didn't want to interrupt."

Her face reddened, realizing he'd probably witnessed their kiss. "We're not back together."

"No?"

"I just—we..." She paused as she dropped her eyes. "I don't know what to say."

"You don't have to say anything. You were together a long time. The bond is undoubtedly very strong."

"How was your weekend?" she asked, wanting to change the subject. "Did you end up taking your boat out?" He'd told her when she met him for dinner the week before that he'd probably go sailing for the first time that season.

"I did. It was cold, but it was great to be out on the water."

Brian and Logan bounded up, demanding food. "It's only four thirty," Nick said, glancing at his watch.

"I'm starved," Brian insisted. "Can we all go to that new hamburger place on the corner?"

"Please?" Logan asked, looking at Lina.

Nick met Lina's eyes. "What do you say?"

The boys carried most of the conversation over dinner, excitedly discussing the game and an upcoming school dance, but Nick was relaxed, and if he was bothered by the kiss, it wasn't evident in his friendly demeanor.

"Mom?" Logan turned to Lina halfway through the drive home. "Were you and Dad kissing on the sideline? Brian said he saw you."

Lina squeezed the steering wheel, continuing to concentrate on the road as she formulated a response "I kissed him goodbye before he left. Maybe he saw that."

"Maybe," he said, sounding unconvinced. "Are you—do you like him again?"

"I never stopped liking him. I just couldn't get past what he did."

"Do you think you might? Get past what he did?"

"I don't know," she said honestly. "What would you think if I did?"

He shrugged. "It would be okay. It was kind of better when he lived with us, and it was weird going away without you. A lot of women come up to him, and Katie said eventually he'll like one and then he'll get married again."

"Was he with any of them? I mean did he spend time with them?" She tried to keep her voice detached.

"No, he just hung out with us."

— ~

"Hello? Earth to Lina," Adele said the following day as they stood in the foyer of a house about to go on the market. "Where are you today?"

"I don't know. I'm just…" Lina sighed. "I'm not happy." Ever since she'd voiced the words to Diane, it was as if she'd given herself permission to feel the truth behind them.

"Since when? I thought you enjoyed working."

"No, I do. I'm not talking about the job. I'm talking about my life. I'm busy and I love what I'm doing, and I love the kids, but I can't shake this underlying discontent I have."

"I've been meaning to talk to you about that," Adele said. "You should probably get back with him." She picked up a vase. "Should this stay or go?"

"Wait—what?" Lina took the vase from Adele and set it back down. "Just like that? After months of wanting me to hate him, you want me to get back with him?"

"I never wanted you to hate him. You wanted to hate him, and I was supporting that decision, but it's obvious you aren't going to move on, so you may as well go back with him."

"How long have you been feeling this way?"

"I don't know, a couple of months I guess. Don't take this the wrong way, but you're actually too boring to be single. At first I thought you just needed some time to get used to it, but then I realized you were going to continue to act like you were married even though you were technically separated, so what's the point? If you're going to act like you're married, you may as well have a husband. The few times I got you out to happy hour, you just stared at your drink and acted like a dud. You have hands down the hottest doctor I've ever seen panting after you, and you won't even sleep with him. You just want to be his BFF. And I swear you're getting more prudish and conservative without Phil than you ever were with him."

"That's not true!"

"It is, and Phil seems less conservative without you, although I think he may just be acting that way in an attempt to get you back, because there is no way he would have let Katie date Matt if he had been living in the house. The fact that he knew about it and allowed it to continue is a testament to how far he was willing to go to get you back."

"Stop talking," Lina said, squeezing her head. "You're confusing me. I need to think."

"It's been six months. The time for thinking is over. You need to just feel." Adele picked up the vase. "Go or stay?"

— ∼

Lina looked at her cell phone for the third time in as many minutes. After the kiss they'd shared on the side of the field, she expected to hear from Phil, but it had been three days without a word from him. She squeezed the bridge of her nose. She'd been waffling back and forth all evening about sending him a text. She shook her head, let out a deep sigh and typed.

Logan's dance is tomorrow night. Did you want to go to the pre-dance party to take pictures? It starts at 6. She pressed send before she could change her mind.

With you?

She sunk her teeth into her bottom lip. *It's in Baltimore, so if it's more convenient you could just meet us there.*

I'll pick you up at 5:30.

Lina stared at the engagement ring on her finger. Her eyes had focused on it as soon as she opened her jewelry box, and after slipping it on, she couldn't bring herself to take it off. She wasn't going to dwell on what it meant or what message she was sending Phil. He probably wouldn't even notice.

It wasn't until they arrived at the home of the family hosting the pre-dance dinner that Lina considered the possibility Nick could be there, but to her great relief he wasn't. As she mingled with parents she knew and met others, Lina was keenly aware of the attention Phil garnered from the opposite sex. He was handsome and fit, and women's eyes were drawn to him. It had probably always been the case, only she hadn't noticed. He had been hers and she'd never considered the possibility of him being with someone else. Now the situation was different. She experienced the same feelings of possessiveness towards him that gripped her at Logan's lacrosse game, so when she felt the warmth of his hand stroking her lower back or sliding down her arm as they conversed with other couples, instead of distancing herself from him, she found herself leaning into his touch.

"Dinner?" Phil asked as soon as they were in the car.

"Yes."

He took her to a small Italian restaurant in Baltimore. "I have something to say," Phil said after they shared a companionable silence through the first course. "This doesn't require a response. I just want you to ponder my words." He waited for her to meet his eyes before continuing. "Have you ever considered the possibility that a flawed version of me is better for you than a perfect version of anyone else?"

"Phil—"

"No." He covered her hand with his. If there was any doubt as to whether he noticed she was wearing his ring, it ended as his thumb slid over it. "Just think about it. And think about who you want to swim naked with when you're old and wrinkled. Do you remember?"

"Of course," she whispered, her heart aching as she stared into his beautiful eyes. "We were so innocent. I didn't think anything bad could ever happen, and then, less than two weeks later—"

"Don't." He squeezed her hand. "Let's not go there. That wasn't my point. My point is that I believe I'm still the man you're supposed to grow old with."

Lina wanted to turn back the clock, to erase the last two years so she could do them differently. "How did we get here?"

"I betrayed you." He lowered his eyes to their clasped hands, drawing in a deep breath before raising his tear-filled eyes to hers. "And I will regret it every day for the rest of my life. But it doesn't have to be the end for us."

"Phil..." She wanted to comfort him, to say something to take away his pain. "I should have noticed you were unhappy—"

"No," he interrupted, shaking his head, the side of his jaw clenching and unclenching. "This was all me, Lina. I put us here." His fingers tightened around hers. "I am one hundred percent responsible. I broke my vows to you."

Lina lowered her gaze, afraid she would cry if she continued to look into his pain-filled eyes. She began to play with his hand, sliding her fingertips back and forth over his palm. "I didn't lose myself," she said after almost a minute of silence. "I told you that you made me too dependent. That wasn't true."

"No?"

"You were my world," Lina said. "I wanted you to be my world—you and the kids. I didn't want more. I was content."

"And now?" He laced his fingers through hers.

"Now, I don't know," she began, continuing to watch their hands. "I can sleep by myself without having a panic attack. That seems to be the most positive thing that's come out of this."

"You have a job—a career."

"I do," she agreed, knowing that didn't begin to make up for what she'd lost.

"Lina?"

"Do you ever go out with other women or to places to meet other women? Bars or—"

"No." He shook his head. "Never. You're the only one I want."

"Then why did you go forward with the separation agreement?" She had been pondering the questions for months. "You filed that, not me."

"I did it for you. To give you the independence you needed."

"Even if it meant losing me?" she asked.

"There hasn't been a day since we separated that I haven't prayed for you to come back to me. But I promised to take care of you. I will always take care of you. I love you, Lina. Nothing will ever change that."

"Phil," she began, tears swimming in her eyes. "I don't know what I'm supposed to say."

"Nothing. You don't have to say anything. I just want you to consider what I said earlier. Whether you can forgive me enough to take me back."

The waiter chose that moment to deliver their main course. Lina averted her gaze, brushing away a few tears that had fallen to her cheeks. "Thank you," she managed to say as an entrée she knew she couldn't eat was set before her.

They remained mostly silent after the waiter left, each seemingly lost in their own thoughts. "Is something wrong with your food?" Phil asked when after several minutes she set down her fork.

"No. It's delicious. I'm just not very hungry."

"I don't want you to be sad," he said.

"I'm not sad." Her hand drifted over the back of his. "I just—I didn't expect to have this conversation today. My mind is in a million different places."

"Lina—"

"I don't know how we can go back," she whispered. "So much has changed." Her thoughts went to his new son.

"Not back, baby, forward." He leaned towards her, his hand gripping hers. "Forward together."

"But how?"

"You still love me, Lina."

"Of course I love you. You're the father of my—"

"You're *in* love with me," he clarified. "It's in your eyes when you look at me. Even now."

She felt a wave of attraction pass between them. "Don't."

"Don't what? I want you back."

"Just—I need to think." She pulled her hand from beneath his. "I need to think."

"That's all I'm asking," he said.

Phil didn't say more. But when they left the restaurant, stepping out into the cool April evening, his arm was tight around her waist, pressing her into his side. She felt the heat of his body and knew as she leaned into him the walls she'd erected around her heart were crumbling.

As they rounded a corner near the street where they'd parked, they almost ran into couple coming from the opposite direction. Lina felt the tenseness in Phil's body a moment before she saw Nick. "Oh," she said breathlessly. "Hi."

"Good evening," Nick said.

"Lina?" his companion said in surprise.

Lina dragged her gaze from Nick's to look at the person beside him. It was the woman she met on his sailboat. "Dana!"

Dana smiled. "Small world." Her gaze shifted to Phil.

"This is Phil," Lina said. She continued to look at Dana but could feel Nick's eyes looking at her. "He's my...my—"

"Husband," Phil finished.

"Oh." Dana's eyes widened in surprise.

"We're separated," Lina rushed out, knowing even as she uttered the words how ridiculous she sounded. Phil had situated his body behind hers with one arm clasped firmly around her ribcage while his other hand was splayed over her tummy, pressing her body back into his.

"Oh," Dana said again.

Lina's face heated. "Well, it was nice to see you." She couldn't fathom a moment feeling more awkward.

"You too," Dana said.

Phil draped his arm around Lina's shoulders, offering a tight smile to Dana before leading Lina away.

"No," Lina said when Phil turned off the engine after parking in front of the house. "You're not coming in."

Phil laid his hands on the top of the steering wheel. "Lina—"

"I'm confused and I need to think."

"May I kiss you goodnight?" He made no move to touch her as he met her eyes in the dimly lit interior of the car.

"I don't think that's a good idea." Her heart had begun to beat faster.

"Just one kiss. I promise."

Even with her mind telling her to get out of the car, Lina found herself leaning across the center console, her hand sliding over the stubble on Phil's jaw. "I'll kiss you," she said before pressing her lips against his. "Good night," she whispered, successfully fighting the urge to invite him in.

"I love you, baby," he said as he stared into her eyes. "Dream about me."

After a night of very little sleep, Lina called to tell Adele she couldn't meet her for lunch and a manicure. "I need to figure this out."

"I think you already have."

"Maybe after what he did he doesn't deserve me, but I still want him. Am I supposed to punish myself because he betrayed me?"

"No," Adele said. "Take him back."

"I'm so afraid if I continue to push him away he's going to settle for someone else and then for the rest of my life I'm going be the one punished because I'll have to live with the knowledge that I gave him away. I'm so tired of pretending I don't want him. It's exhausting."

"Hello? Are we having a conversation or are you just talking to yourself?"

"Thanks. I know what I need to do," Lira said before ending the call.

48

Nick stood as she approached the table he occupied at the Mexican restaurant Lina thought of as their own. "So, you and Dana," she said after she was seated across from him.

"We're friends."

"I like her."

He looked up as the waiter approached. "I took the liberty of ordering you a drink."

Lina smiled as a margarita was set before her. "Perfect." Lina took a long swallow, trying to gather her thoughts. "This is hard."

"It doesn't have to be. We can just enjoy each other's company and have a nice meal."

"I feel like I owe you an explanation."

"You don't owe me anything. You never have, and this," he began as he reached out and ran his thumb over her engagement ring, "tells me everything I need to know."

Lina's eyes dropped to their hands, watching as Nick continued to run his thumb over the ring Phil had run his thumb over twenty-four hours earlier. "I—" She stopped midsentence as her cell phone began to vibrate. "Let me make sure this isn't one of the kids." She pulled her hand from beneath his and turned over her phone, reading her mother's name on the display.

"Do you need to get that?"

"No, I'll call her back." As soon as the phone stopped vibrating, it began again.

"Are you sure?"

"I'll just be a second." She put her head down as she brought the phone to her ear. "Mom, I'm at a restaurant. Can this wait?"

"No. It's Shiloh. There's been an accident."

— —

Katie stole a glance at her cell phone. It was almost 8:30 p.m. Her father told her they were only going to Mike and Jeanie's for dinner, but dinner had ended thirty minutes earlier, and he continued to talk as if he had nothing better to do than spend the evening sitting around their kitchen table.

Katie was debating how to get his attention without being totally rude to her uncle, who was celebrating his birthday, when her father suddenly pushed back his chair. "We have to go."

"We haven't had the cake," Jeanie said. "Let me—"

"Sorry, no." He looked at Logan and then Katie. "Let's go."

"Why couldn't we have cake?" Logan asked as soon as they were outside and headed towards Phil's car. "I—"

"Have either of you heard from your mother?" he interrupted, staring down at his phone.

"No, why?" Katie frowned.

"My phone is dead. Call her."

Before she could make a call, Katie's cell phone was ringing. "It's Grandma. Should—"

Her father snatched the phone from her hand. "Alice, what's going on?"

— ~

Lina's mind was in a fog as Nick ushered her out of the elevator and into a waiting area at Baltimore Medical Center's Shock and Trauma Center.

"Are you sure this is right?" Lina asked as she looked around the empty room.

"Yes, she's right through those doors." He nodded towards metal swinging doors.

"Where is everyone?"

"We're probably the first to arrive." He led her to a chair and she sat down beside him.

"What did they say?" She knew she had already asked him, but she couldn't remember his answer.

"She's in surgery. There's internal bleeding. Several broken bones. Possible head trauma."

"I feel sick." She leaned forward, hugging herself.

He ran his hand up over the top of her back. "This is one of the top trauma centers in the country. She couldn't be in better hands."

The elevator doors opened and Alice and Adele, followed by Phil, were coming into the room. "Any word?" Alice asked, her face drawn in concern.

Lina's eyes locked with Phil's, the other occupants in the room fading away as she found her way into his arms. "I'm so scared."

"I know," he whispered, his breath warm against the side of her head as he wrapped his arms around her. "I'm here, baby. I'm here."

— ⁓

"I don't think she's going to die," Katie said as she stared into the flames kicking up in the fire pit. "I just don't have that feeling, you know?" She was sharing a lounge chair with Matt on her backyard patio, wedged between his legs as she leaned back against his chest. "I think I'd have a feeling."

"Yeah." His arms tightened around her. "You probably would."

"You know that weird connection my parents have? The one my grandma told me about?"

"That they're soulmates or whatever?"

"It happened tonight. I saw it. We were at my aunt and uncle's, and suddenly my dad just pushed back his chair and said we had to leave. It wasn't from a text or phone call or anything. He just knew that my mom needed him, and then my grandma called and told us about my aunt."

"It seems kind of fucked up that they aren't together then."

"My dad told us that he knew the moment he saw her that he loved her."

"I knew the moment I saw you." he said, his breath tickling the back of her neck. "I felt like I was hit by lightning or something."

"No you didn't," she said, leaning forward enough to look back at him. "You barely looked at me."

"I thought you were too young for me." He trailed his finger down her cheek. "But I couldn't stop thinking about you."

"Why are you lying?"

"I'm not lying. Why do you think I drove you home from Ryan's all those nights? Do I look like a Boy Scout to you?"

"Why didn't you ask me out?"

"I told you, I thought you were too young. I was going to wait until you were older, but then your dad split, and..." He shrugged. "I was tired of waiting."

It wasn't the spell. He'd fallen in love with her without the spell. She crawled up his legs until she was straddling his lap. "I love you," she whispered as she cupped his face.

"Why are you crying?" he asked.

"Because I'm happy."

— —

Lina was vaguely aware of Adele, Nick and Alice occasionally talking and Nick disappearing a couple of times to get the rest of them coffee, water and some type of cookies no one ate. She stayed silent, curled into Phil's side on the lone couch in the waiting room, taking comfort in his familiar strength as she stared at the door leading back into the surgical area, waiting as if in a nightmare to hear whether her sister would live or die.

At some point a distraught Julian showed up, one arm casted and a bandage on his forehead. They'd been on their way home from dinner when they were broadsided by an SUV. He sat beside Alice, crying off and on and promising God and anyone else who was listening that he would treat Shiloh like the princess she was if she survived.

It was almost 2:00 a.m. when an exhausted-looking surgeon appeared. As soon as he said, "She's a very lucky woman," Lina turned into Phil, sagging with relief, hearing "no brain trauma" but not much else, too emotionally drained from the hours of worry to concentrate on the surgeon's words.

After the surgeon left, Lina broke away from Phil to hug her mother and Adele, and then she was turning to Nick. "Thank you," she said, taking his hand.

"You're welcome. I'm going to head home. Let me know how she does."

Lina nodded. "I'll walk you out."

"No. Stay with your husband." The meaning behind his words was clear.

"Thank you," she whispered, embracing him briefly.

"I'll walk you out," Adele said. "I could use some fresh air."

It was an hour later when Lina preceded Phil into Shiloh's hospital room, halting when she saw her sister's bruised and battered face. Lina heard Phil's intake of breath before he gripped her upper arms, pulling her back into his chest.

"Oh my God," she whispered.

"Don't think about it," Phil said, but it was too late. Her mind was already going back.

Shiloh was screaming. Lina scrambled off her bed and ducked down on the floor, her heart racing as she felt the wall shake. Something terrible was happening. She needed to get to a phone and call 911. There was no one else home. Adele and her mother were away at a college visit. Another scream. What was happening?

"Get her fucking legs," a male voice yelled. "Shut the fuck up, girl!" The sound of a slap pierced the air. "Did you check that room?"

Lina slipped under her bed as footsteps approached. They were coming for her. She was never going to see Phil again. She covered her eyes and prayed to a God she didn't even know if she believed in.

"What have we got here?" a voice with a distinct southern accent asked before someone gripped her ankles.

"No!" she cried, kicking at the intruder as she was pulled from beneath the bed. "Phil! Phil, help me! Phil!"

"Shouldn't you be calling for Lucifer, pretty girl?" a boy no older than eighteen said as he pulled her to her feet, his fingers bruising as they dug into her arm. "Ain't that who you worship?"

"Don't hurt me," she whispered. "Please."

"'Please,'" he mimicked. "You scared?"

Lina nodded, hating how weak she felt. "Don't hurt me."

"You gonna make it worth my while not to hurt you?" He roughly squeezed her breast through her nightshirt.

She recoiled from him, pushing his hand away. "No!"

"No?" He grabbed a handful of her hair and yanked her head back. "Don't you fuckin' tell me no." He pushed his hand beneath her shirt and palmed her breast. "You like that, don't you, whore?"

"Let's go," another guy said as he stepped into the room. "There'll be time for that later."

"Hear that, baby?" He pushed his groin against her leg. "You're gonna take care of me later."

Lina let him lead her out of the room and down the hall, her mind so consumed with thoughts of escape, it wasn't until they were halfway down the stairs that she registered the sound of skin slapping against skin, punctuated by deep moaning. "Fuck yeah, man. Give it to her."

Lina slowed her steps, but as soon as the living room came into view and she saw Shiloh, spread out on the floor with a man on top of her, his pants pushed down around his knees, all thoughts fled. "No!" Lina screamed. "No!" She was across the room and on the back of her sister's assailant, pulling his hair and scratching his face.

Strong arms encircled Lina from behind and she was dragged backwards. "No!" Lina continued to scream.

"Shut her up!"

"Lina!" Phil's strong voice pierced through the air.

Lina buried her face in Phil's neck, clinging to him as she had the entire time they were questioned by the police, when a paramedic approached and asked to examine her. "Don't let them touch me," she whispered.

"We just want to examine her—make sure she's okay," the young woman said.

"She's okay," Phil said.

"Son," Mr. Hunter began, "they need to look at her."

"No," Phil said firmly as he enclosed his arms around her. "She's okay."

"We just need to verify that."

"No! No one is touching her!"

"You should take Lina home now," Alice told Phil a short time after she and Adele arrived in Shiloh's hospital room. "She needs to sleep."

Lina stared at Shiloh's battered face. Both eyes were swollen shut, her nose was broken and her lip had been busted. If Lina's *bedroom had been closest to the stairs, it would have been her and not Shiloh lying in the hospital bed. It should have been her. She was older and she hadn't been a virgin. Lina felt something on her face and realized she was crying.*

"Lina." Phil's voice penetrated her reverie. "I'm taking you home."

"No, I..." She paused as she again focused on Shiloh's battered face. "Did someone beat—"

"No, it's from the impact with the airbag," Phil told her before speaking to Adele and Alice, who were beside Shiloh's bed. "I'm taking her home. I'll come back—"

"Don't worry about us," Adele interrupted. "We can take a cab or Uber. Just get her out of here."

Lina sunk into the soft leather seat of Phil's car, pushing her thumb and finger into her eyes as she tried to quiet her thoughts, hating the visions swirling in her head of Shiloh's battered face.

"She's going to be okay," Phil said, curving his hand around the back of her neck.

"Did it make you think of that night?" Lina asked.

"Yes."

"I could never have made it through that without you," Lina whispered on a shaky breath. Her mind once again transported back to the hospital all those years ago.

"Let's go home," Phil said.

Lina was sitting on Phil's lap in Shiloh's hospital room, leaning back against him as he held her in his arms. "You won't leave me?"

"Never."

"I can't go back to my house," Lina said as soon as they were in his car. "Take me to yours."

Mrs. Hunter came from the back of the house when they stepped into the foyer. "Oh, sweetheart," she whispered when she saw Lina. "Are you okay?"

"We're going to bed," Phil said as he led Lina towards the stairs.

"Good idea. The guest room is all made up. If she needs towels—"

"She's sleeping with me," Phil said before following Lina up the stairs.

"They thought we were devil worshippers," Lina told Mrs. Hunter a few days later. "Their dad sent them to get us. They were going to kill us—a sacrifice or something. The police found this whole setup in their barn. It was because of my mom's astrology."

"No, sweetheart," Mrs. Hunter said, covering Lina's hand and giving it a reassuring squeeze. "It was because they were evil people. They were just using that as an excuse to do bad things."

"But if my mom wasn't an astrologer, they wouldn't have come for us." Lina folded her arms across her chest. "Phil said I could start coming to church with you."

Several weeks later, Lina donned a pair of shorts and a T-shirt of Phil's before making her way downstairs. She was approaching the kitchen when she heard his father's voice and paused outside the doorway. "You can't do that. I know you love her and she's been through something no one should ever have to go through, but jeopardizing your future serves no one."

"I'm not jeopardizing my future," Phil said.

"Giving up Duke is jeopardizing your future," Mr. Hunter insisted. "It's everything you've worked for. You can't just walk away. If she loves you, she won't ask you to. Your mother and I have been more than understanding with the two of you over the past month. This is a Catholic home and we're allowing you to sleep in the same bed with—"

"We're not doing anything," Phil said. "She can't sleep without me."

"Well, she needs to. She's welcome to stay here with us when you go away. Your mother will take good care of her."

"I'm not leaving her," Phil said, his voice calm. "I'm going to Maryland. I've already called the coach."

"You're committed to Duke!"

"Not anymore."

"Are you asleep?" Phil asked, bringing Lina out of her recollection.

"No." She took his hand and held it between both of hers. "Let's go home."

— —

"Are you back together?"

Lina opened her eyes, lifting her head from Phil's chest as she adjusted to her surroundings and Logan, his eyes narrowed in confusion, staring at her from the doorway between the kitchen and family room.

"Are you?" he repeated.

"Gives us a minute, Logan," Phil said, his voice husky with sleep. "We've barely slept."

"No church, right?" Katie asked as she appeared, holding a bowl full of cereal.

"Not for us, but you can take your brother," Phil said.

"Why don't you just tell us?" Logan asked.

"That's not fair," Katie complained. "Why should I have to go if you're not? You're the one who likes it."

"You can pray for Shiloh," her father said.

"Grandma said she's going to be fine. I don't need to pray for her. Plus, if I don't believe—"

"Katie, would you just listen to your dad and stop arguing?" Lina asked. "Please?"

"If he's moving back here, you need to make him understand that Matt eats dinner here all the time. That's not going to change."

"Go," Phil said, pointing towards the kitchen, "both of you. I need to talk to your mom."

"How did we fall asleep here?" Lina asked, her head returning to his chest when Katie and Logan retreated to the kitchen.

"We were going to talk, but you fell asleep on me." He began to scrape his fingers over the back of her scalp. "How are you feeling?"

"Tired." She closed her eyes.

"Maybe we should go up to bed."

"Maybe we should."

Phil's hand stilled in her hair. "Together?"

"Don't stop rubbing my scalp. It felt good."

His fingers again began to run over her head. "What do you want to do?"

"I want you to come home, Phil."

Epilogue

"Are you going to need this?" Phil asked, holding out a handkerchief.

Lina turned her head and saw the amusement in his eyes. "No."

"Good, because I might, and I only brought one."

"Behave," she whispered, but couldn't hide her smile.

"This means you're no longer from a broken home. My mom will like that."

"Shh, it's starting." She squeezed his thigh.

Her parents were getting married again. And as her mother had promised they weren't just getting married at the courthouse like a normal sixty-something couple. No, Alice Rayburn, in her typical unconventional style, was having a traditional wedding in front of one hundred and fifty guests with the man who left her and her three daughters more than three decades earlier.

Lina watched Katie, in a strapless teal dress, begin to walk down the aisle. Lina's eyes shifted to Matt, who was temporarily distracted enough by Katie's appearance to stop pulling at the knot of his tie, which he'd insisted earlier was choking him. After Lina made Phil look at it to make sure it wasn't actually choking him, Matt admitted it was the first time he'd ever worn one.

"How can you stand it?" he'd mumbled to Phil.

"You get used to it," Phil assured him. He wouldn't admit it, but Lina knew Matt was starting to grow on him. Phil had stopped complaining that Matt was at the house too much, and if he needed another pair of strong arms for something, Phil would ask for Matt's help if he saw him before Logan.

Megan was next, looking beautiful and older than her nineteen years as she took her place beside Katie.

"Did Alice invite Julian?" Phil asked.

Lina followed his gaze to see Julian sitting beside Shiloh, who miraculously was almost one hundred percent recovered from her injuries. As promised, Julian had stepped up and treated Shiloh like a precious flower during her recovery, but Lina was only cautiously optimistic that the change was permanent. "She's giving him another chance," Lina said.

"We're not."

"I know. Shh, here they come," Lina said as Logan, looking more like a man than a boy in a black tuxedo, began to walk Alice down the aisle. "She's beautiful," Lina whispered as they came to their feet. In a cocktail-length white wedding gown, her hair swept up in a chignon bun, Alice Rayburn shined like a bride.

"She is," Phil agreed.

As Lina's eyes focused on her parents standing before a minister, she thought of her own marriage and the promises she and Phil made to each other all those years ago. Phil broke one of those promises, testing the very strength of the foundation binding their family together—a foundation conceived, built and nurtured by years of shared experiences. And as painful as the past year had been, their foundation was now stronger, not because of the infidelity, but because when they believed their foundation was crumbling, the thousands of memories it was built upon flashed before their eyes, reminding them of what they knew when they saw each other across that dance floor twenty-five years earlier—they belonged together.

"Where are you?" Phil's voice in Lina's ear pulled her from her reflections.

"With you," she answered as she took his hand. "Always with you."

Also by Laura

When I Sa

A Sense of B